Luminous Traitor

ALSO BY MARTIN DUBERMAN

YOUNG ADULT

Lives of Notable Gay Men and Lesbians, editor (1994–1997), 10 vols.

Issues in Lesbian and Gay Life, editor (1994–1997), 4 vols.

DRAMA

Radical Acts: Collected Political Plays (2008)

Mother Earth (1991)

Visions of Kerouac (1977)

Male Armor: Selected Plays, 1968–1974 (1975)

The Memory Bank (1970)

In White America (1964)

The publisher and the University of California Press Foundation gratefully acknowledge the generous support of the Constance and William Withey Endowment Fund in History and Music.

Luminous Traitor

THE JUST AND DARING LIFE OF ROGER
CASEMENT, A BIOGRAPHICAL NOVEL

Martin Duberman

UNIVERSITY OF CALIFORNIA PRESS

3064515371835

University of California Press, one of the most distinguished university presses in the United States, enriches lives around the world by advancing scholarship in the humanities, social sciences, and natural sciences. Its activities are supported by the UC Press Foundation and by philanthropic contributions from individuals and institutions. For more information, visit www.ucpress.edu.

University of California Press
Oakland, California

Library of Congress Cataloging-in-Publication Data

Names: Duberman, Martin B. 1930–, author.
Title: Luminous traitor : the just and daring life of Roger Casement,
    a biographical novel / Martin Duberman.
Description: Oakland, California : University of California Press, [2019] |
    Identifiers: LCCN 2018019776 (print) | LCCN 2018021091 (ebook) |
    ISBN 9780520970854 (Ebook) | ISBN 9780520298880 (cloth : alk. paper)
Subjects: LCSH: Casement, Roger, 1864-1916—Fiction. | Human rights
    workers—Fiction. | Indians of South America—Amazon River
    Valley—History—Fiction. | Congo (Democratic Republic)—History—
    To 1908—Fiction. | Ireland—History—Autonomy and independence
    movements—Fiction. | LCGFT: Biographical fiction.
Classification: LCC PS3554.U25 (ebook) | LCC PS3554.U25 L86 2019 (print) |
    DDC 813/.54—dc23
LC record available at https://lccn.loc.gov/2018019776

28 27 26 25 24 23 22 21 20 19
10 9 8 7 6 5 4 3 2 1

It is impossible to understand the past with certainty, because we cannot divine men's motives and the essence of their minds and so cannot interpret their actions. Our psychological analysis does not suffice even with those who are near us in space and time, unless we can make them the object of years of the closest investigation, and even then it breaks down before the incompleteness of our knowledge and the clumsiness of our synthesis.

Sigmund Freud to Lytton Strachey, *December 25, 1928*

CONTENTS

PART I

The Years of Innocence

IN THE AUTUMN OF 1884—at just the time Otto von Bismarck is opening the watershed conference in Berlin designed to bring order to what has been a fractious European scramble for power in Africa—Roger Casement, a mere lad of twenty, is working beside his close friend Herbert Ward on preparing a survey for a railway designed to run between Matadi and Stanley Pool on the Upper Congo.

The two young men share a close friendship, though you'd hardly know it from their contrasting appearance. Ward prides himself, against the odds, on immaculate grooming, even as Roger takes humorous pleasure in teasing him about his relentless attempts, despite the heat and heavy underbrush, to manage a daily shave. He also likes to bait Ward about the way he picks with distaste at their only source of food, the native *quanda*—a mix of pounded root and coconut milk—which Roger devours with spirited gusto, tossing the leftovers to his beloved bulldogs, Paddy and Biddie. Ward, in turn, cheerfully denounces Roger as a "shameless ruffian—yes, all six foot three of you, a skin and bones scarecrow for all the sustenance that wretched *quanda* provides!" The two take great enjoyment in mocking each other, secure in their affection. Ward even makes fun of his friend to others, and deliberately within Roger's earshot: "Look at him, will you?! Tramping ahead of even the bearers, his beard down to his ankles, his clothes in ribbons, pieces of bark for shoes secured with pieces of string! Her Majesty's representative in full regalia!"

Roger is not yet in fact in government service. He works—and will for a good half dozen years more—for a number of commercial enterprises exploring and surveying the region for possible economic exploitation. Like Ward, Roger sees European expansion on the Africa continent as a "civilizing" mission, bringing the blessings of Christianity and (in his words) "useful and diligent" labor to a native population that is at present "disinclined." Yet, unlike most of his European contemporaries, including Ward, Roger has from the first seen much to admire in native customs and beliefs and wishes to see them preserved; he is still more unlike them in being (as his friend Ward puts it) "so regardless of personal advancement." It's all of a piece, Ward reckons, with Roger's "high-minded, courteous, singular charm"; his disposition, Ward attests, is "the gentlest imaginable ... emotional, tender, always sweet-tempered, ready to help, condemning cruelty and injustice in any form."

Roger's temperament is not the kind that could have sat comfortably with the representatives of fourteen nations who gather around a horseshoe table in the large music room of Bismarck's house on the Wilhelmstrasse. European interest in the African continent has been rapidly intensifying of late, and the job of the assembled delegates is to sort through the unseemly chaos of overlapping claims and bring a proper sense of order to the "advance of civilization." Several of the nations represented have already secured considerable territory and are anxious to keep it intact. Britain has large holdings but fears most for the loss of the "informal" parts of her empire: the Niger region and East Africa (having already lost Togo and Cameroon to the aggressive Germans). France, too, is fearful, and in particular of Bismarck's announced intention to secure the enforcement of free trade. Portugal, finally, is nearing bankruptcy and deeply uneasy about its ability to hold on to Angola and Mozambique in the face of King Leopold of Belgium's obvious ambitions.

The delegates sit from November 1884 to February 1885, and when the conference is finally adjourned, the adroit, self-assured King Leopold, with his flair for flattery and intrigue, has succeeded in playing the other nations against one another—in part by shrewdly (and falsely) stressing his own lofty "philanthropic" aims, including a promise to form through a series of treaties a confederation of Free Negro Republics. The General Act of Berlin that results from the conference places under Leopold's personal supervision some one million square miles of Congolese jungle and bush.

Almost simultaneous with the Conference's adjournment, Herbert Ward decides to leave Africa. Over the next few years he will marry and settle for a time in Paris; when his first son is born, Ward names Roger the godfather (he will name his third son Roger Casement Ward). Roger himself becomes for a time somewhat adrift, serving in a wide variety of short-term positions, ranging from work for the Sanford Exploring Expedition, to map-making treks into the little-known interior, to continued surveying for the pending railway from Matadi to Stanley Pool. When that last project comes under

King Leopold's control in the late 1880s, Roger resigns rather that serve in his employ. He returns on leave to England and Ireland and then, for three months during 1890 and 1891, joins his old friend Herbert Ward on a lecture tour to the United States based on a book Ward has written about his experiences in Africa.

Finally back in Matadi Roger meets by chance the writer Joseph Conrad, seven years his senior and then serving as the captain of a Belgium company steamer in the Congo. "I've made the acquaintance of Mr. Roger Casement," Conrad writes in his diary, "which I should consider a great pleasure under any circumstances and now becomes a positive piece of luck. Thinks, speaks well, most intelligent and very sympathetic." The two share a room together for two weeks, and when Roger decides to leave Matadi for an overland trip to Leopoldville, they part (in Conrad's words) "in a very friendly manner." Arriving in Leopoldville, Roger continues to work on facilitating transport over the challenging cataractous region before again returning on leave to Ireland in the early summer of 1891.

By then Roger has become known as something of an anomaly. In the tangle of ambition and greed that characterizes the "scramble for Africa," he refuses to carry arms ("lest I be tempted to use them"), thinks nothing of walking twenty miles a day, refuses to wear the standard pith helmet (claiming he "doesn't feel the sun"), seems uninterested in gaining personal wealth, and treats all those, European and native alike, with a gentle gallantry perhaps intrinsic—so he himself would claim—to his Irish upbringing. Though part of the colonial mechanism, Roger is, as it were, a soulful conquistador, immune to the avarice that drives most of the white men who come to Africa and from the beginning of his service is wholly opposed to the brutality that accompanies their imperial progress.

Roger's excellent reputation for hard work—not his morality—finally produces in the summer of 1892 an appointment to the staff of West Africa's Niger Coast Protectorate, making him for the first time an official of the British foreign service. He serves directly under Sir Claude MacDonald, Britain's consul general in the Protectorate, and a relationship of mutual respect quickly develops. Sir Claude and his wife, Lady Ethel MacDonald, are much taken with the young Casement and invite him often to join them at tea on the rundown terrace of the local hotel. For Ethel MacDonald, Roger feels admiration bordering on awe. Her first husband, an officer in the Indian Civil Service, died of cholera, along with their children. She somehow survived her grief, married Sir Claude, and audaciously insisted, despite multiple warnings about alarming conditions—Sir Claude's predecessor had died of fever—on accompanying him on his new assignment to West Africa's Niger Coast.

Sir Claude's Sandhurst schooling and devotion to the army make him a bit brisk—especially when administering his formal duties—for Roger's taste. Yet he deeply admires Sir Claude's patient tact; his intricate knowledge of the trade in palm oil; his advocacy of *peaceful* penetration into the interior to cultivate cocoa, coffee, and rubber; and, above all, his uncommon regard for the native Africans he governs. Before assuming his post as consul in 1890, Sir Claude had toured the territories to ask the local peoples what form of government they preferred—excluding self-government of course. To the scoffing Foreign Office that had been considered tantamount to polling the mosquito population as to its preference among brands of netting.

Yet Roger is not an unqualified enthusiast of African folkways. He deplores any number of practices characteristic of certain areas in Africa—burying alive servants of a deceased king, female circumcision, cannibalism, trial by poison (survival equaling innocence)—and he endorses the standard notion of the day that assigns to the white man an obligation to wean the natives from their "superstitious" belief in a spirit world, as well as their "casual attitude towards labor." Yet the more time Roger spends in Africa, the more appreciative he becomes of the indigenous cultures that most European invaders are intent on destroying. Above all he values the intimate connection Africans have to the physical world and to their own bodies—the sanity of their easy acceptance of the body's needs and functions. He feels a strong kinship with the innocent ease of their sensual gratification.

He admires, too, the rapport Africans have with their immediate surroundings—their insistence on protecting, not ravaging, the land and on ceding consequential authority to a universe of mysterious creatures, uncontrollable seasons, and immortal stars. He's partial to the African acceptance of coexistence with nature, rather than the European "civilizers" insistence on mastery of it—on rerouting streams, burning forests, killing off wildlife, and hacking sap from rubber vines.

On this particular late afternoon June day, Roger has been stationed with the Niger Coast Protectorate for a bit more than two years, and as he makes his way to the hotel's terrace for tea with the MacDonalds, he smiles at the realization that they must have sipped together something like a thousand cups of tea since he first arrived. Approaching the terrace, Roger is surprised to spot the outline of another European seated at the MacDonalds' table.

He'd assumed that the party would, as usual, consist of just the three of them. At Old Calabar the social pickings are slim and visitors few, which is fine with Roger. Given his easy charm, people tend to think him gregarious, but he prefers to limit socializing to the company of a few friends, where the premium is on connection rather than surface chatter. He counts Sir Claude and Ethel MacDonald among those few.

As Roger mounts the steps to the terrace, he's surprised to see that the unexpected guest is a white woman. That's a rarity. Oh dear, Roger thinks, she's doubtless from one of the missionary stations, probably that overenergetic Mrs. Kemp from the Methodist mission, making another plea for more European clothing to cover up the natives. Roger sighs, How foolish; how can the velvety softness of African skin and the graceful contours of their bodies be "offensive"? He has to remind himself that despite their restrictive morality, many of the missionaries are well-intentioned, decent people, kind to the local inhabitants and contagiously humble about their own unimportance—that is, except for the Americans, few in number but loudest in their self-admiration. Roger holds out hope that the natives will have more success in Africanizing the missionaries than the missionaries do in Christianizing the natives.

"Roger, this is Mary Kingsley," Sir Claude says, as Roger approaches the table. "This is her second trip to West Africa, and she's, she's terribly . . . well, keen. Miss Kingsley, allow me to present Mr. Roger Casement. He's an old African hand, though still a mere teenager." Claude chuckles at his own drollery.

Roger finds himself staring down at a slender, angular woman, sharp-featured yet handsome, with a no-nonsense air, and dressed in an unfashionably floor-length cotton dress, with muttonchop sleeves buttoned at both wrists. Good grief, Roger thinks, Calabar is a relatively cool spot but she must be roasting alive in that get-up. She looks like the high priestess of prudery, despite that animated face—those eyes above all, her deep-set, restlessly mocking eyes exuding a vitality that contradicts her conventional dress and posture. Here is someone, Roger thinks, both unassuming and passionately alive.

"From a distance," Roger lightly offers, "I took you for a missionary. I must be going blind."

"I'll take that as a compliment, Mr. Casement. Some of my dearest friends are missionaries. Perhaps you know Mary Slessor here in Calabar."

"I do indeed. And admire her greatly." Roger seats himself at the table and nods yes when Ethel MacDonald mutely holds up the teapot.

"Slessor's one of my jujus!" Mary says. "Unlike her Scots-Presbyterian brethren, she cares not a fig about stamping out polygamy—or the liquor trade. I was with her just a few days ago at Ekenge. Do you know she's been living in that thatched mud encampment for nearly twenty years?"

"Gone for bush," Sir Claude vaguely says, addressing no one in particular. "Peculiar, don't you think?"

Mary's eyes sparkle with animation. "Not a bit. Her home is here, not England. She's put the mournful Presbyterians behind her, has relaxed into Africa's cheerful animism. I understand completely." Turning to Roger, she gratuitously adds (her tone a mix of pride and merriment), "I'm not really a Christian. I'm a high and dry Darwinist. I worship the great God of Science."

"Then, unlike Slessor, you *do* regard England as home," Roger says, with a mischievous smile.

"I hope to go back and forth. Prior to my first visit here two years ago, absolutely nothing had happened to me, nothing at all. I took care of my invalid mother. When she died, I kept house for my bachelor brother. Not even a proper education. But our house had a library, and, between chores, I read my way through it. My parents died within two months of each other. My brother began to travel. So I came to Africa. Simple as that! Never been healthier—or happier."

"Never had malaria?"

"Of course! It's the price of admission. But nothing else, give or take a few cuts and bruises. Nothing serious, no *kraw kraw,* guinea worm, yellow—no, not a one of them. . . . Back in England I was always down with something. If it wasn't flu, it was migraines. If it wasn't migraines, it was rheumatism. If not rheumatism—well, you get the picture."

"I know it well," Roger says with a sympathetic twinkle, "England's climate of damp fog."

"Indeed!" Mary laughs appreciatively. Sir Claude frowns, mumbles something about Slessor romanticizing the natives, and Ethel MacDonald, who's been quietly disengaged, suddenly says, "That business with the twins was an awful mess."

"Slessor saved that poor woman!" Mary vehemently responds.

"What happened?" Roger asks. "I don't know anything about a 'mess' or twins."

Mary twists in her chair impatiently but, sensing that Roger is a potential friend, decides to explain. "You know, the Cross River people believe that the birth of twins signifies an evil spirit has slept with the mother, and the only way to get rid of it is to kill both mother and offspring. Africans are as frightened as Europeans at deviations from the norm—and *almost* as quick to condemn them. Slessor intervened and the villagers gave in. They call her 'Mother of All the Peoples.'"

The MacDonalds rise from their chairs, Sir Claude mumbling something about the need to check on repairs for the water tank, and he and Ethel quickly take their leave. "I like them both," Ethel whispers to Sir Claude after they've reached the bottom of the terrace steps. "As do I," he replies, "though Miss Kingsley is a bit too outspoken. I value candor, but it can be unseemly in a woman."

Back on the terrace, as if on cue, Mary is telling Roger that she fears MacDonald isn't handling the Nembe uprising as well as he might.

"But he's negotiated in good faith," Roger replies, "of that I'm sure. King Koko isn't responsive, and his raid on the company's headquarters at Akassa certainly didn't help—the wide destruction and loss of life. Her Majesty's government, I would say, has been rather lenient, if not indulgent."

Mary flares up. "Indulgent?!' They've kicked Koko off his throne, razed Nembe, and killed three hundred of his people! If that's indulgence I'd hate to see what harshness looks like!"

Roger is surprised at her intensity. "Koko did kill his hostages," Roger tentatively offers.

"Of course he did!" Mary indignantly replies. "He warned the British he would, unless concessions were made. The Nembe didn't ask to be included in the Oil Rivers Protectorate, nor to have the Royal Niger Company take over all trade along the kingdom's rivers into its own hands. It was the Nembe who'd been masters of the palm oil and liquor trades. Now the Nembe are starving, literally starving."

"That's true. I've seen it myself," Roger quietly admits. "I understand Sir Claude's been telling the London authorities that the rebellion's due to the *company,* not the natives."

"He has. And for that deserves all credit. But MacDonald can't break the company's monopoly all by himself. And, frankly, I'm not sure he wants to. Sir Claude is, in the end, old-school."

"I'm a bit that way myself," Roger says, his tone mocking. "As an Irishman, I like to think of myself as sensitive to the plight of subject people."

"You need to be *more* sensitive." Mary's tone is surprisingly sharp. "For an 'old hand,' you should have seen more by now than you apparently have." Mary is unsmiling.

"You may be right. I was very young when I first came to Africa," he adds straightforwardly. "I do see more clearly now."

"If you still think *at all* well of the Royal Niger Company, you have quite a ways to go! They started as slavers, you know. Still are, in a sense."

"They do get credit for starting the training school a few years back." Roger can hear the note of defensiveness in his voice, and regrets it.

"How wonderful of them!" They all but wipe out the Igbo in the slave trade and then provide the remnant with *pencils!* You really do need to talk to Mary Slessor. She'll give you an earful about the suffering the British have brought to this region."

"How did you ever find Slessor's place?" Roger asks, trying to shift the subject. "Ekenge is buried rather deep in the forest."

"First by canoe, then by foot."

"Unaccompanied?"

"Good heavens, Mister Casement, I go everywhere unaccompanied. Except, of course, for my tripod and plates, specimen jars for fish samples, medicinal supplies—I've had some training as a nurse—a waterproof tarp for the blankets, skirts and blouses, and, of course, a revolver and a bowie knife."

"You carry all of *that?!*" Roger exclaims.

"No, silly man! I go with four or five Kru boy bearers and make sure that at least one has enough pidgin English to help me translate."

"You're wise to pick the Kru. As a coastal people, they've known Europeans for four hundred years. And survived to tell the tale. . . . What do you do when you get there, wherever 'there' is?"

"I'm a self-taught ethnographer, but when I go into the interior, I'm a trader. Never had a bit of trouble. Oh, the natives are startled when they first see me. Some villages have never seen a white person before, but when I—"

"Certainly not a white *woman!*"

"Yes, quite . . . yet when I bring out the beads and cloth, gin and rum, they're eager to barter. I'm fair-and-square businesslike, and they're quick to see that I'm on the up-and-up, not out to cheat them. There's no humbug about me, I'll say that much for myself. They can spot it. At night they fill me up with fried fish and cassava, manioc, yams, and pour on the palm oil. Then they escort me tenderly to the best hut in the village to sleep in."

Roger shakes his head in admiration. "That's remarkable. . . . But how do they pay you for the beads and cloth? In copper rods?"

"Mostly ivory. Of late, rubber. Valuable stuff, not that I want it. Too heavy to carry around. Besides, though I play the trader, what I'm really after is fetish."

"Fetish?"

Mary is genuinely surprised. "You've never heard the term before?"

"Mind you, I've been around, Miss Kingsley," Roger says teasingly. "Vice-consul here in Calabar, before that surveying for the railway to Stanley Pool, part of Sanford's exploring expedition, and so on, but no, Miss Kingsley," Roger laughs, "no one has ever mentioned 'fetish' to me!"

"It's the only thing that *matters!* It's simple, Mr. Casement. 'Fetish' is the belief system. Customs, rituals, values, laws—it's the African mind I'm after!" Her eyes dance with excitement.

"In my experience, the variations from village to village, and tribe to tribe, are considerable. Isn't that so?"

"Quite so. But certain commonalities bind them together. Like the practice of polygamy. Like the belief in a spirit world. Like the meaning of 'disease.' Like what makes the sun go down and the moon come up. Like the sexual—well, you get the picture."

"What have you learned so far? I'm interested, truly."

"I believe you are. I've learned enough to realize how little I know. I'm after *big* game, Mr. Casement. The *big* questions. I want to know why Africans think they're *here*. What the meaning of life is. How we should treat one another. Little things like that!" Mary laughs in high-spirited self-mockery.

"Maybe Africans are too smart to pose unanswerable questions," Roger says playfully.

"Nobody's that smart!" Mary was having a fine time. "I *must* uncover the essence of African fetish: customs, beliefs!"

"Must?"

"So I can better protect them against European missionaries bent on converting them, and European expansionists bent on wiping them out."

"You just sang Mary Slessor's praises! *She's* a missionary!"

"Slessor's different. There are others like her, missionaries who try to enter African life, not obliterate it. Most of them want to destroy the native culture, substitute their own thin spiritual gruel. Some of the natives fall for it. Or revise Christian tradition to make it fit comfortably into the African story. Most learn to keep secret what they most cherish. Do you know what I find the saddest thing? When African converts come face-to-face with the silence of the white man's god. It's totally alien to them. When the African calls on supernatural forces, he knows they will listen, will pity, will answer. Is it any wonder so many converts return to their old ways? The missionaries treat Africans like children. But there's nothing childlike about the African mind. Most Africans are remarkably astute—more common sense than Gladstone and Salisbury combined."

"You're quite amazing, Miss Kingsley!"

"Nonsense! I'm as ordinary as a corncob, Mr. Casement. I'm a latecomer to Africa."

"*When* you come to Africa isn't as important as what you see once you get here. The Portuguese arrived four hundred years ago. All they've seen is wealth to plunder and natives to enslave. Hearing those sentiments from me may surprise you, after my glib remarks about the Nembe and King Koko."

Mary swivels abruptly in her chair to face Roger directly. "Now look here, I've done all the talking! I know next to nothing about *you!*"

Roger laughs. "I agree with most of what you've said."

"I want to hear about what you don't agree with. What you left out is what I most want to hear."

"Should I start with King Leopold?"

Mary literally jumps in her chair. "King Leopold?! Don't tell me you work for that skunk?"

"*Did* work. Briefly, a number of years ago, for his International African Association."

"I've been to his Congo Free State. 'Free'—ha! Was ever a benighted land less aptly named! I hope never to return."

"During my time there, no one knew any better."

"No white man, you mean. George Washington Williams knew better."

"Who?"

"You've never heard of him?" Mary's raised eyebrows convey alarm. "How about William Sheppard, who's *still* at work in Africa?"

"That name does jog my memory, but I can't quite—"

"Ooh, Mr. Casement, what *do* you know? ... Is it because they're Americans? *Negro* Americans?"

"My prejudice doesn't run along those lines. Remember, I'm Irish. Our bias already has a focus: the English."

"Well then, it's my duty to enlighten you. Or are you dashing off to romance some native girl?"

"I'd much rather talk with you." Roger smiles broadly.

Mary looks reluctant, then yields. "Very well ... sit back and have more tea. ... We'll start with George Washington Williams, alas no longer with us. Amazing man. Something of a rascal, I do admit—I mean, inventing a PhD he didn't have, skipping out on a wife and child. Without chicanery, how else is a Negro in the United States to rise? And rise Williams did. Became a minister, wrote a history of his people, met everybody from President Grover Cleveland to Frederick Douglass. None other than railroad magnate Collis Huntington—who has his own finger in our African pie—sponsored Williams's trip in 1890. And—here's the kicker—your old boss King Leopold granted him an interview."

"Really? That's more than I ever had. I'm told he's personally charming."

"Williams called him 'one of the noblest sovereigns in the world.' Leopold was—*is*—immensely clever in promoting his humanitarian image. Though Williams caught on far sooner than most."

"During my years in the Congo, I've seen terrible misery, not only the Arab slave traders, but tribal cruelties. If we're to civilize the Congo—I can see you don't agree—we need to instill a sense of responsibility in the natives. . . . The African must give off idling and learn to participate in regularized labor."

"Yes, that's the traditional view," Mary laconically says. "Williams needed only a few days in the Congo to realize it was a penal colony." Mary frowns, pulling irritably at her wrist cuff. "You need to read his 'Open Letter to His Serene Majesty Leopold Two.' It was published *five years ago,*" she says with emphasis.

Roger frowns. "I can't think how it escaped me."

"I can get you a copy, though the Open Letter was widely distributed at the time." Mary hears the censorious overtone in her voice and backs off; after all, she tells herself, Roger Casement is clearly a decent sort, an ally to be cultivated, not an enemy.

As if confirming her estimate, Roger quietly says, "Perhaps I was hoodwinked. Though I did resign. Didn't trust the man."

"Few people have ever seen through Leopold's veneer of benevolence. Williams documented every charge he made. He proved that Leopold's claim to the so-called empty land of the Congo is nothing more than the sum of his dirty tricks to dupe tribal chiefs into ceding their lands. But nobody listened. And barbarism goes on—villages burned, the people enslaved, chain gangs, and starvation, punishment with the *chicote*—"

"That I *have* witnessed. Those whips!" Roger flinches at the memory. "Dried hippopotamus skin . . . it cuts deeply into the flesh. I've heard tales of people beaten to death with the *chicote.*"

"The tales are true and easy documented. Mind you, Williams—like you—had some blinders of his own. He held the natives at least partly responsible for their mistreatment. In his view—yours too, I gather—Europeans needed to teach the benighted savage what you call the dignity and reward of regular labor."

Uneasy, Roger makes no reply. Mary lets the silence deepen until Roger unexpectedly asks if he correctly understood her earlier remark that few people believed the Open Letter.

Mary harrumphs with scorn. "Williams' own benefactor, Collis Huntington, defended Leopold as 'beneficence incarnate.'"

"Did Leopold respond to the letter?"

"Of course not," Mary scoffs. "Beneath his dignity. But he made damned sure the Belgian press was flooded with denunciations of the 'unbalanced negro George Washington Williams' and his absurd 'slanders' against his Majesty. A few journalists did call for an inquiry, but in the Belgian parliament there was a groundswell"—Mary's indignation is undiluted by any suggestion of sarcasm—"a patriotic groundswell that swept the chamber with cheers for the gallant, kindhearted Leopold."

"Appalling."

"I think so," a gratified Mary replies.

"And where is Williams today?"

"Williams is dead. Of consumption, at age forty-one. And our 'altruistic' Leopold has a tighter grip on the Congo than ever. It makes my blood boil," she angrily adds.

The two again fall silent. Roger's absorption in Miss Kingsley's tale has blocked out everything else. He's aware, though, of the telltale throbbing in his temples that always precedes a malarial headache, and he's sweating through his shirt. He hears acutely the increasing cacophony of noise that signals the onset of night in West Africa.

"It's something, isn't it?" Mary says softly, as if reading his mind. "I'll never get used to that symphony. I love it. Love *most* of it. I could do without the vocalizing of the frogs and bats. Too dissonant for my taste."

"*Anything* but the sound of mosquitoes!"

"How true!" Mary laughs appreciatively. "But I'll probably miss even that when I go back to England."

"Is that soon?"

"Very soon. I don't like to think about it. But I hope to return before long. That is if my dear brother can bear to part with me as his housekeeper. I'll need to be home for a while—I want to write a book."

"I'm glad to hear it. You have a great deal to say."

"We'll see. My opinions about Africa won't win me many friends. I'll play the humble female, of course. You know, a fragile, weepy thing, tentatively offering her overwrought amateur advice."

Roger laughs. "You won't carry it off. You're about as fragile as a mountain lion."

Mary smiles. "Why, Mr. Casement, I do believe you've paid me a compliment!"

"Better make it two mountain lions!"

"Oh my, you're veering into insult! Time to go!"

Mary rises from her chair, and Roger follows her lead.

"But you've never told me about that other fellow. . . . William Sheppard, wasn't that his name?"

"Oh no, Mr. Casement, not tonight! You've quite worn me out. Perhaps some other time . . ."

Roger persists. "I'm keen to know about him. What you've told me of Williams has been a revelation."

"Keep your eyes open. I suspect you're a keen observer. You'll see everything Williams did, maybe more."

"I've seen some of it already. I just haven't put the pieces together."

"Sheppard will help you. Unlike Williams, he's still very much alive, and very cordial. He lives among the Kuba people, straight up the Kasai River, not so far from here. The Kuba are marvelous craftsmen. It's worth the trip just to see their helmet masks. You can bring home a carved wine cup, maybe even a cosmetic box!" Her eyes twinkle with audacity. Roger pretends not to have heard and adopts a neutral tone.

"I'm deeply indebted to you." He holds out his hand.

"I certainly hope so. I need every ally I can get!" She warmly presses his hand.

.   .   .

Roger's awakening to the wonders of Africa runs parallel to his heightened disgust with the disreputable stir underway to exploit the continent and its people. It's what made him feel immediate sympathy for Mary Kingsley's sassy iconoclasm and what now has set him off on his journey to find William Sheppard. Yet he can't help but wonder, as he pushes his way through the unyielding, and seemingly endless, stretches of underbrush, whether he misunderstood Mary about Sheppard's mission station being "not so far";

perhaps, he somewhat uneasily thinks, her sense of distance is as peculiar as her sense of womanhood. In any case, the journey to Sheppard's station in Luebo is taking far longer and proving more arduous than he expected—and he feels pressed for time. Soon after Kingsley's departure from Calabar, word arrived from the British Foreign Office "immediately" transferring Roger to Lourenco Marques, the principal town in Portuguese East Africa, to serve as Britain's consul there, which is something of a promotion. It's in the nature of a parting gift to himself that he's decided to locate Sheppard before leaving the region.

Roger is an experienced hand in surveying the interior, but to go overland to Luongo is to go deeper into the Congo than he's ever been. Though accompanied by two trusted Kru, the journey is proving uncommonly difficult. The first leg, from Calabar to Boma, the capital of the Congo Free State, was easy enough, and upstream from Boma to Matadi the landscape continued to be familiar: the sharp rise in elevation and sharp decrease in temperature after leaving the coastal plain, the Baptist mission at Tunduwa, the Christian cemetery with its "mounds of triumphant martyrs"—fifty-five victims in the past ten years, most of them in their twenties. ("If you want to go to heaven soon," the quip goes, "become a Congo missionary.")

But from there the route is less familiar. At Matadi the railway construction—it has already cost thousands of African lives in forced labor—is finished only up to Mukimbungu (it won't reach its destination at Stanley Pool until 1898), and living conditions are squalid. Stopping one night in a mud-walled hut at the American Baptist station at Lukunga, Roger spends the major part of it squashing a nest of scorpions he finds buried in a door, and though he's greased his feet with palm oil to ward off the miniature fleas called chigoes, he awakens the next morning to find a number of painful bumps along his thigh.

After trading beads, brass wire, and cowrie shells for supplies (mainly crackers and tea, along with a few eggs), Roger and his two porters are ferried in a hardwood native canoe across the dangerously swift currents of the Mpozo River. They're greeted on the other side by the sight of several ivory caravans making their way to the coast, the natives chained together at the neck and carrying heavy loads weighing nearly as much as they do. The human cost lies all along the road: sun-bleached skeletons of native carriers who, on collapsing from exhaustion or disease, have been unchained and dropped off to die. To complete the scene of horror, Roger watches as a thirty-foot-long python squeezes a donkey into pulp and then swallows it.

Once reaching the juncture of the Congo and Kasai Rivers, the territory becomes wholly unfamiliar to him, though the conditions of travel ease somewhat. Steamers are able to navigate on the Kasai, and Roger hitches a ride over a considerable distance. As the steamer passes villages along the riverbank, more often than not members of the local tribe rush to the water's edge, brandishing spears and bows and arrows and shouting threats—according to his porters' translation—to kill them if they set foot ashore. Agents of King Leopold, it turns out, have often raided these villages to kidnap and enslave a number of their younger men. Roger himself has long known about the so-called Van Kerckhoven Raid, atypical only in its size, that Leopold had sent out in 1890: a group of armed Belgian officers headed by Captain Van Kerckhoven stole a large cache of ivory and burned down villages all along the river.

Finally, after more than a week's journey, Roger's small band arrives at Sheppard's mission station at Luebo, ideally situated near the junction of the Sankuru and Kasai Rivers, entry point to the vast, insulated Kuba Kingdom that lies beyond. Roger has notified Sheppard in advance, and the missionary has laid out a warm welcome for him, including "crocodile cutlets"—a prized delicacy. The two men take to each other easily; one may be white and the other black, one English and the other American, but their personalities are closely aligned: both are emotionally warm, charming, seemingly fearless men, insatiably curious, embracing challenge and welcoming the unfamiliar. Sheppard is somewhat more expansive and outgoing, Roger more grounded in exacting detail and more personally ambiguous. If Sheppard had been a purposeful bear, Roger might have been a more pliable lioness.

They're on a first name basis almost immediately. William delights in showing off the mission compound and in touting the wonders of the locale: fifteen hundred feet above sea level with an average daily temperature of seventy-five degrees year-round, no tsetse flies carrying sleeping sickness, few mosquitoes (known as bothersome but not yet known as the bearers of malaria), vast expanses of grassland and sixty inches of rainfall annually. Duly impressed, Roger wonders aloud if the isolation—800 miles from a doctor, 1,200 from the coast—isn't a problem, to which Sheppard the evangelist predictably replies, "Lo, I am with you always. Jesus's ministry absorbs my every minute: teaching, preaching, and healing." Besides, he adds, "I'm in constant contact with the surrounding villages, keeping busy learning local languages and customs. I go hunting with my native friends or fishing between the sand banks. And I have a wife, you know, though she's currently back in the States on a visit."

William's tone is so amiable that Roger feels able to ask whether he and his wife, as Negroes, "are more readily accepted than us whites are?"

"The natives say there's nobody like 'Mundele Ndom'—the black, white man—that's me," William says, chuckling. 'Mundele,' as you know, means 'a man who wears clothes.' So I'm a black man who wears clothes—all but unheard of, except on the coast, where pidgin English has taken hold."

"Still, with your wife away, you must get lonely," Roger suggests. "I'm told the steamers run irregularly and for only a few months of the year."

"True, quite true. But I don't mind. I have the entire Kuba Kingdom to explore! I must take you. But first perhaps a hippo hunt. The noise of my rifle is usually enough to send the creatures stampeding." Roger's quizzical expression makes William laugh. "Just last week I killed one off with a shot straight to its forehead. We cut the beef off the carcass then and there, cooked it over a slow fire, and had a fine feast. I've seen hippos come up under a canoe and toss it off like so much matchstick."

"I'm not one for hunting, to be frank. I hope you won't hold that against me."

William reaches up—Roger's nearly six feet three—and warmly pats him on the back. "Why, of course not. I understand. The animals are God's creatures too. But God put them in front of us. Didn't want us to starve."

"Have you actually penetrated the Kuba Kingdom?" Roger asks, trying to change the subject.

"Ah, that's a story," William replies. "Wait until dinner when I can do it justice over some palm wine."

Sheppard lives in a comfortable bamboo house built on poles, the roof made of long palm leaves sewn together, the exterior surrounded with plantain trees and small enclosures that house chickens, parrots, and monkeys for future dinners. Sheppard puts out a splendid spread that evening: catfish, python steaks, fried cassava root. When Roger politely passes on the heralded delicacy of fried white ants, an amused William tells him, "It's better to eat them than to have them eat you! Before I learned better, we used to keep the palm oil uncovered. A column of driver ants caught the scent and decided to move in. There must have been a million; they went everywhere, including under my blankets and in my nose. Now we keep the palm oil covered and clean up the slightest spot of grease. Driver ants are serious warriors—they can kill and carry off everything from a mouse to a goat—and fast too!"

Roger shakes his head in wonderment. "You're a resourceful fellow!"

"Have to be. I always wanted to live in Africa. I felt that I'd be happy here, and so I am. The wonder of it all! When tribal musicians come to the village to celebrate the birth of a child, I shout with joy, join in the break-down dancing, jumping and twisting with the rest of them! Which brings me back to the Kubas, the extraordinary Kubas! I thank my precious Lord for the wonder of witnessing their amazing works!"

"You must be the first, the very first, isn't that so?"

"The first Negro missionary in Africa," William proudly answers. "And now the first to gain entrance into the Kuba Kingdom. It's out of a fairy tale."

"How did you manage it? The ivory traders now and then bring out a report. I heard one about the king's edict threatening any Bakuba who showed a stranger the road to the capital in Mushenge with beheading. Yet here you are stuffing me with this splendid feast!"

William laughs. "By a hair—or should I say by the grace of the Lord. There's no other way to explain my good fortune. You see, I set myself to studying the Kuba language soon after I came out here four years ago. And I made a point of befriending Kuba traders who passed through, paid them court, dined them in style, and got them to describe the villages and paths between here and Mushenge."

"A clever strategy."

"I decided to get an expedition ready to go inland in the direction of Mushenge. But no one was willing to go. Everyone knew the danger. To enlist nine men, I had to part with a month's supply of cloth and beads! Anyway, we started off heading northeast, through swampland, across streams, with me mumbling all the while to myself, 'The Lord is the strength of my life, of whom shall I be afraid.'" William laughs. "Yet I was! Only a fool would not be. After an arduous few weeks we came by chance on a group of Kuba ivory traders headed back to Mushenge and managed secretly to follow them to the village of Bishibing. We thought we'd kept ourselves cleverly hidden, but, no, the Kuba traders discovered us."

"They attacked you?"

"Worse. They sent word to King Kot aMbweeky that foreigners were only a few miles from Mushenge. Back came the command that our party, along with the entire village of Bishibing, were to be brought to the capital for beheading!"

"How did you escape?" Roger's eyes are wide with amazement.

"We didn't try. It would have been futile. Instead I spoke Bushonga to the messenger—which astonished him—and explained that the Bishibing chief had begged us to leave and that I alone was guilty of trespass. The messenger reported to the king that this odd stranger—me!—was dressed in outlandish clothes, spoke Bushonga, and had managed to reach the outskirts of the kingdom without a Kuba guide. The king concluded that this mysterious person could only be the reincarnated spirit of Bope Mekabe, an earlier Kuba king. We were escorted straightaway to Mushenge!"

"How did you carry off *that* impersonation?"

"I didn't have to do a thing. The king had decided I was Kuba royalty, and that was that! With a blast of ivory horns, the word went out to prepare a great celebration, the people to appear in their finest cloth to welcome the return of Bope Mekabe. We were shown—and shown off—everywhere. I stayed two months and, to tell you the truth, had trouble dragging myself away. An amazing people! A great civilization!"

"What did you see? What was so amazing?" Roger has become nearly as excited as William.

"It was like entering the lost city of Atlantis. Servants spread leopard skins all along the ground leading up to His Majesty's throne, covered with antelope hides, the backrest superbly carved ivory tusks, the royal feet resting on a lion skin, a crown of eagle feathers on his head. I timidly approached. He rose and stretched out his hands. 'Wyni,' he called out, 'you have come.' I bowed low and replied, 'Ndini, Nyimi'—'I have come, King.'"

Roger slaps his knee with delight. "William, you *are* amazing!"

"It was not my doing. I was merely an instrument. This was just two years ago. Can you imagine, Roger, the prospect of Christianizing so huge a kingdom?!"

"Surely they have some sort of religion of their own?" William catches the shadow of disapproval in Roger's voice but pretends he hasn't.

"They have an all-powerful, mysterious God called Chembe, who shows his displeasure through crop failures and lightening storms. But in general Chembe is elevated too high to take much interest in human affairs. The Bakuba do not pray to him, yet they're a splendidly moral people. They value honesty, have laws against stealing and drunkenness."

"That's all very well," Roger says, his tone ironic, "but have they produced a Rembrandt? A Titian?"

William smiles in acknowledgement of the joke, then turns serious: "They're *magnificent* artisans. Kuba tapa cloth is something to behold! Made from mulberry pulp trees—intricate designs without even the aid of patterns! And everything from household items to musical instruments exquisitely carved."

"Tapa cloth? Good heavens, my man, I am referring to High Art!" Roger's tone remains deliberately arch.

William humors him with a warm smile and pours them both more wine. "Yes, I know the litany," he says. "Primitive people collect slaves and multiple wives. They could never produce the High Art we Europeans create."

"I'm reminded of the Benin bronzes," Roger says, his tone now straightforward. "You've heard of them?"

"Benin? The Edo people?"

"Precisely. A few of the bronzes made their way to England and caused a sensation. The British are mounting an expedition next year. Rumors are flying. Its widely believed that artistic works of such skill and sophistication—such evidences of 'civilization'—could not possibly have been done by the Edo themselves. One theory gaining currency is that a Portuguese sailor shipwrecked off the coast made his way to the Benin Empire in the interior and then, to while away the time, churned out the magnificent bronzes."

William gasps in astonishment. "No—you're making it up!"

"It's true! There's one little problem with the theory: the earliest bronzes go back to the thirteenth century, and the first Portuguese to sail down the west African coast came in the late fifteenth century! But not to worry—the experts will find a way out."

"Anything but to validate the accomplishments of a dark-skinned people."

"Exactly. If you're going to invade and destroy, make sure you dismiss the locals as savages. Calling them 'heathen' helps too."

"Mind you," William somberly responds, "even the Kuba remain very much in need of enlightenment."

"How so?" Roger realizes the question is a mistake; it opens up a discussion that he senses should be avoided—if, that is, he hopes to win Sheppard's full confidence and get him to share whatever evidence he might have to confirm Mary Kingsley's account of Belgian atrocities. "Like you," Roger continues, thinking—mistakenly—that Sheppard will find the comment congenial, "I consider Christ my personal Savior, but isn't it possible that 'Chembe' is simply the native term for Christ?"

"Christ is responsive to prayer. The Kuba do not pray." William's monotone suggests displeasure.

"Or perhaps pray in their own way?" Roger's candor is as obstinate as it is guileless. It's only with difficulty that he ever controls it.

"Surely you know as well as I," Sheppard says stiffly, "that some Kuba practices are deeply abhorrent. They treat their slaves well in life but bury them with their deceased owner. They believe in the supernatural power of witches ('in Europe we call them priests,' Roger wants to say, but doesn't). The characteristic feature of marital relations is polygamy. Need I go on?"

Call it "promiscuity," Roger thinks, and it gets my vote. What he actually says is "Africans don't believe in romantic love."

Expecting Roger to add, "which is deplorable," William's expression softens. "How dreadful for the women to have to share their husbands!"

Roger can't resist: "I know you've met Mary Kingsley. She sent me to you."

"Yes, of course. A remarkable woman."

"She insists African wives *prefer* polygamy."

William's expression is a mix of shock and disgust. "That's absurd!"

"Why would I make up such a thing? Ask her yourself. The way she explained it to me, there are simply too many duties in an African household for one woman to carry out. With several wives the chores can be shared. Plus, African women routinely suckle their babies for two years or more and during that time refuse sexual relations, so it makes perfect sense for their husbands to have alternate wives. Most important, Miss Kingsley says, is that polygamy spares a single woman the ignominious fate of remaining without family—a form of social death. Mind you, those are Mary's—that is, Miss Kingsley's—arguments, not mine," Roger hastily adds.

"I should hope not!" Williams indignantly bellows. "What's got into the woman?! Would she destroy the sacred bond between a husband and wife?"

"Miss Kingsley says that for Africans the strongest bonds are those of blood—between parents and children, between sisters and brothers—not the economic and sexual connections characteristic of the husband-wife relationship."

"This is what comes," William replies with considerable heat, "of a woman traveling alone in Africa. That sort of impropriety clouds the mind. No wonder she's understood so little."

With a brushfire about to turn into a blaze, Roger moves abruptly to douse the flames: "If I may, Sheppard, I'd greatly appreciate your opinion on another matter entirely."

Still in the throes of his indignation, William mumbles something about "Yes, yes . . . I'm here to be of help. . . ."

"The stories are multiplying—surely you've heard them—that King Leopold's representatives are employing forced labor, slavery, wreaking awful reprisals against those who resist. I gather his agents have not yet reached the Kuba Kingdom?"

Still simmering, William responds with a non sequitur: "The slave trade is officially forbidden in the Congo Free State."

"The *Afro-Arab* slave trade—yes, that was agreed to at the Berlin Conference in 1885. Much impressive rhetoric about 'caring for the moral and material well-being of the native tribes.'" High principles! But all of it, apparently, a cloak for Leopold's ambitions. The conference confirmed his *personal ownership* of the Congo! In exchange, of course, the other powers won the guarantee of free trade."

"I've heard." Sheppard's tone is grim. "They've declared all African land not currently being cultivated as 'vacant land.' A nice bit of thievery!"

Roger is relieved. With the conservation's turn to Leopold, he feels that he and Sheppard are back on the same page. Roger raises his wine glass to propose a toast: "Three cheers, for bringing 'Commerce, Christianity, and Civilization' to benighted dark Africa! Hip, hip, hooray!"

"I'll confine my toast to 'Christianity,'" Sheppard says good-naturedly. They clink their glasses together.

Roger repeats his earlier question: "You haven't said—have Leopold's agents infiltrated the Kuba?"

Sheppard hesitates, gloom spreads across his face. "Only recently. It worries me. . . . It's because of the sudden boom in rubber. It's a tidal wave. . . ."

Roger can feel his apprehension mounting—and his impatience. "Yes, yes, I know. The bicycle and all that. . . . Then that damned Scotsman has to go and invent an inflatable tire. . . . The demand is skyrocketing. . . . It's as if the ivory trade no longer matters."

Sheppard's eyes widen with awe. "The rubber vine grows as high as two hundred feet, as thick as a man's body. You make an incision, and boom! The milk-white juice pours out, like liquid gold. The Congo Free State is suddenly the most profitable colony in Africa. No expensive equipment is involved and no skilled labor. Anyone can make an incision, collect and dry the sap, roll it into a ball, and—"

"And force enslaved natives to carry fifty-pound bundles on their backs to the coast, many dying along the way or being killed for 'malingering.' . . ."

"It started here in the Luluabourg area two or three years ago. A group of Zappo Zap warriors appeared. They'd already enslaved many of the Luba, one of—"

"The Luba?"

"One of the tribes the Kuba rule. So far the Kuba Kingdom itself remains sealed off, but I doubt they can hold out. I fear it's only a matter of time before the Zappo Zaps invade. . . ."

"Who are the Zappo Zaps? I've never heard of them. . . ."

"We call them the 'filed-teeth people,'" Sheppard explains. "They're cannibal marauders, a branch of the BaSonga Menos tribe. They tattoo their faces, file their teeth to a sharp point, use steel arrows and guns. They worked for the Arab slavers; now they're mercenaries for Leopold, enforcing state policy. Brutally. They cut off the right hand of slaves who malinger, then cook the hand, dry it on a bamboo stick, and present a bundle of them—sometimes it's ears—to Leopold's agents to prove their ferocity."

"Good God!" Roger nearly shouts. "This is going on *now?!*" I had no idea things were that bad! Why has nothing been done?!

"I blame myself in part. . . ." Sheppard's tone is muted. "Several refugees from a Luba village came to the mission, asked for help. . . . What could I do against the Zappo Zaps? They'd kill me straightaway. None of the missionaries know what to do, other than wring our hands. . . . If we speak out, Leopold will close the missions down, choke off God's work of Christian conversion. . . ."

"William! William! . . ." Roger pushes back his chair and starts to pace the floor, too agitated to monitor his words. "What good is a *dead* convert?! There are two hundred Catholic and two hundred Protestant missionaries in the Congo, and *all* of them have kept silent?!"

"Nearly all," Sheppard quietly replies.

"This cannot go on! You know it cannot. God would not will such barbarism! Christ would not have died for—!"

"I know, I know!" Sheppard shouts, then instantly quiets down to a mere whisper. "You're right, of course. . . ." His husky voice is barely audible. "Yet it's hard to know what to do . . . impossible really. . . ."

Roger makes an effort to quiet down; he doesn't want to alienate Sheppard. "Mary Kingsley," Roger says, "told me that a man named Williams, George Washington Williams, published a pamphlet about all this, about Leopold and the—published it *five years ago!*"

"I knew Williams. Not well, but our paths did cross. A difficult man, but courageous. More than most. Yes, much more than most . . . a pity he died so young. Williams never hesitated in speaking out. . . ."

"Nor should we . . . But first we must find out more, William, as much as we can, in detail. The matter cries out for—for us . . . to *do* something. . . ."

. . .

Already behind schedule in vacating his post at Old Calabar, Roger has to cut short his visit to Sheppard. But before the two men part, they vow to keep in contact and to coordinate efforts to combat the atrocities. . . . No sooner does Roger arrive back in Calabar than he finds a dispatch from the Foreign Office waiting for him, demanding to know why he hasn't already left, as ordered, for his new post at Lourenco Marques in Portuguese East Africa. Hastily resolving consular business, Roger packs up his personal belongings, says good-bye to old friends like Sir Claude and Lady MacDonald, and arrives in Lourenco Marques—widely considered the unhealthiest port in southeast Africa—in midsummer 1895. Suddenly, he's on the other side of the continent, far from the Congo, far from his intended protest on behalf of the indigenous population, and forced instead to address complaints from resident British subjects about various Portuguese injustices that strike Roger as infuriatingly petty in comparison with the suffering he's witnessed in the Congo.

From the first, Roger is intensely unhappy with his post in Lourenco Marques. The consulate building itself is deplorably dilapidated, with the iron ceilings continually raining down filings that stain everything from books to bedcovers. The consulate's affairs are in even greater disarray, and Roger is immediately forced into the full-time tedium of bureaucratic life. His restless temperament works against his finding even minimal satisfaction in routine consulate work; but still seeing himself as a loyal servant of the empire, he applies himself diligently to the tedious minutiae at hand.

In 1895 Roger may be a somewhat shaken believer in Europe's "civilizing" mission, yet a considerable believer he remains. Though he's begun to question the brutality inherent in the scramble to divide up the African continent, he remains firm in his allegiance to the British Crown, though his patriotic ardor never approaches the outright jingoism of a Cecil Rhodes, founder of the De Beers Mining Company, who spoke for many in Britain when he said, "I contend that we are the finest race in the world, and that the more of the world we inhabit, the better it is for the human race." Casement, after all, is an Irishman; his sympathy for the underdog is inbred and his distrust of British intentions instinctive, if currently still dormant.

During his brief tenure in Lourenco Marques, one matter alone engages Roger's genuine attention: the mounting conflict between England and the Boers—the Afrikaner descendants of Dutch settlements made at the southern tip of Africa in the mid-seventeenth century. The conflict has long been brewing. In the mid-nineteenth century, the Boers had migrated inland in an effort to escape British expansion, and in particular its official opposition to slavery, which the Afrikaners employ and defend. Deeply conservative Calvinists, fiercely independent, they're convinced of their divinely ordained racial superiority and remain profoundly resistant to all forms of modernity. Following their trek into the interior, they set up the independent entities of the Transvaal and the Orange Free State and for a time feel secure in their isolated enclaves.

But the discovery of diamonds in the region in 1867, and later of gold, leads to a rush of prospectors, most of whom are British nationals— "Uitlanders" (Outsiders) the Afrikaners call them—and investors and settlers continue to pour into the region. Fearing they'll soon be overwhelmed— and by an immoral nation who, monstrously, hints at extending a limited form of the franchise to black men—the Boers in 1880 rise in armed resistance (the so-called First Boer War). It's an inconclusive struggle that ended with the 1884 London Convention granting the Transvaal limited sovereignty only and thereby guaranteeing that Afrikaner resentment would continue to simmer.

By the time Casement arrives at Lourenco Marques in 1895, the competition among European powers for colonies of strategic or economic value has greatly accelerated—as has British aggression. The new colonial secretary, Joseph Chamberlain, announces that same year that "the time for small kingdoms has passed away. The future is with the great Empires"—and he moves quickly to ensure that Great Britain be preeminent among them. In central and northern Nigeria, the British take possession of a huge area, claiming not only political control but also ownership of the land, a claim the local population bitterly resists and that leads to a series of fiercely fought battles in which the British—using machine guns against spears—defeat a series of indigenous uprisings. In West Africa the British establish "protectorates" over a large stretch of the coast, and in South Africa they close off Afrikaner access to the sea—Lourenco Marques, situated on Delagoa Bay, remains the single open port.

Casement's involvement in the mounting conflict is never more than peripheral. Lord Salisbury, the British foreign secretary as well as prime minister, directs him to "keep watch" over the Boer's accumulating stockpile of arms and, secondarily, to sniff out the extent of Kaiser Wilhelm II's attempt—eager as he is to undermine British hegemony—to form a chummy relationship with the Boers. Meanwhile, Colonial Secretary Chamberlain is working behind the scenes to precipitate a notorious incident that becomes known as the "Jameson Raid."

Cecil Rhodes, from his domain as governor of Cape Town, has watched with growing alarm as the Boers consolidate their power in the Transvaal in possible preparation for another armed struggle against the British. When Chamberlain gives Rhodes clandestine assurances that the British government will support an Uitlander uprising against Boer "tyranny," Rhodes arranges for Leander Starr Jameson, a British colonial, to instigate an uprising in the Transvaal city of Johannesburg, which has a large Uitlander population. It never takes place. The Boers defeat the Jameson forces before they ever reach Johannesburg and cart off the survivors to jail in Pretoria.

A few days after the failed raid, Kaiser Wilhelm sends off an ill-chosen telegram to Transvaal president Paul Kruger, congratulating him on the Boers' success in putting down an attempted coup "without the help of friendly powers." The allusion is to the kaiser's prior decision to maintain German forces at full strength in the neighboring colony of South West Africa to—as he words it in the telegram to Kruger—"have enough troops at our disposal . . . first to put down immediately any revolts stirred up by England, but then so as to have a strong column available to come to the aid of the Afrikaners."

When the "Kruger Telegram," as it comes to be known, is made public, it produces a furious outcry in the British press, while the kaiser, as is his wont, decides that *he* is the aggrieved party. His grandmother, Queen Victoria, disagrees; she sends him a personal rebuke, characterizing his telegram to Kruger as having made a "painful impression." The kaiser replies to "dear Grandmama" that he is merely trying to promote peace. The claim is so transparently false—the queen dismisses it as "lame and illogical"—that she feels tempted to pursue the matter further, but Lord Salisbury's advice to accept the kaiser's lamentable behavior and move on, prevails. Roger credits his own dispatches with having alerted the Foreign Office to a possible attempt by Germany to annex Delagoa Bay, and when the kaiser's designs are checkmated, he takes personal satisfaction in "the failure of the Emperor's little game to be Suzerain of the Transvaal." Some twenty years later, ironically, it will be to Germany that Casement will turn in search of a potential ally for winning Irish independence.

Roger's satisfaction at the outcome of the Jameson Raid doesn't dilute his intense unhappiness at his current post. To escape the bureaucratic tedium, he pleads illness and the need to recuperate from it—alternately citing the effects of malaria, neurasthenia, and "weak circulation"—to secure periodic leaves of absence that culminate in 1898 in a trip back to England, where he all but begs the Foreign Office for reassignment. The Lourenco Marques post, he writes Lord Salisbury, puts "a severe strain on my time and temper . . . forced as I now am to interview anyone, whether black, white or Indian, who calls throughout the long day at this consulate, often upon trifling business or in quest of unimportant details."

Valuing Casement as a keen observer, the Foreign Office agrees to shift him to the consulship at Saint Paul de Loanda in Portuguese West Africa. In doing so, Lord Salisbury instructs him to keep a particular eye on King Leopold's recent imposition of import duties, as well as other possible departures from the 1885 Berlin free-trade accord—though Salisbury makes no mention of Leopold's failure to fulfill his promise to abolish Afro-Arab slavery in the Congo Free State.

Reports have begun to mount that the Belgian king has simply substituted his own brand of enslavement for the Arab one. In 1897 several missionaries in the Congo—including William Sheppard—summon up their courage and publish firsthand accounts describing the parallel escalation of the rubber trade and a shockingly abusive forced-labor system. As one missionary puts it, "the soldiers drive the people into the bush [to collect rubber]. If they will not go, they are shot down, mutilated, their right hands cut off to be given as trophies to the *Commissaire*. . . ." Additional reports begin to pile up of resistant natives being flogged to death. The MP Charles Dilke brings up the evidence of ill-treatment in the House of Commons but is assured that such excesses, even if true, are isolated incidents, the work of renegade low-level employees who've run amuck; the benign intentions of King Leopold himself, Dilke is assured, remain beyond reproach.

Having himself seen considerable evidence of mistreatment, Roger has no trouble believing the worst. But he wants more proof. He uses his new post in Loanda to study trade reports for the Upper Congo, and he discovers that trade goes almost entirely in one direction: boatload after boatload of rubber arrives at the port of Boma bound for Europe, but all that comes back in return are guns and ammunition. The return ships do *not* carry the kind of goods that paid laborers might buy—leaving the strong implication that the laborers are *not* being paid.

Determined to press ahead in investigating conditions on the Upper Congo, Roger is mulling over plans to make such a journey when word comes from the Foreign Office that he is to return at once to Lourenco Marques: tension between the British and the Boers in southern Africa has again reached a boiling point, and Roger is instructed to pay special attention to arms shipments from Germany that may be passing to the Boers through Delagoa Bay. The Jameson Raid has, for the Boers, marked a point of no return; British aggression, however denied officially, has signaled to the Afrikaner leadership that it's only a matter of time before they'll have to resort to open warfare in defense of an independent Transvaal.

A crucial step in that direction comes in May 1897, when Colonial Secretary Joseph Chamberlain appoints Sir Alfred Milner as high commissioner for South Africa. Chamberlain knows his man; whereas the colonial secretary is a somewhat devious expansionist, Milner is a wholly unapologetic imperialist. "It is idle to talk of peace and unity," Milner reports to his boss. "The case for intervention [in the Transvaal] is overwhelming." Though Milner doesn't emphasize the fact, the discovery of rich deposits of gold have transformed the Transvaal into the most prosperous region in Africa. Milford is too clever to base his case on economic greed—or on his own settled belief in the superiority of English folkways. Instead, he evokes as a rationale the "plight" of the Uitlanders under Boer rule: denied citizenship, they obtain the right to vote only after a residency of fourteen years.

The Uitlanders' political grievances are real, but most of the pressure for change in the Transvaal comes from wealthy British mining interests whose chief complaint is the "exorbitant" tax rate the Boers have leveled against them. Milner, who has had nothing to say about the forced labor of Africans, righteously protests the "serfdom" being imposed on the Uitlanders: "thousands of British subjects," he indignantly informs Lord Salisbury, are being "kept permanently in the position of slaves." He makes clear his disinterest in negotiation at a conference called at Bloemfontein to mediate differences with the Boers. Milner offers proposals designed for rejection, and when they are, he decides—without consulting London—to withdraw from the conference, denouncing President Kruger as "immovable."

The basic issue at stake isn't getting the vote for Uitlanders, nor even who is to gain a monopoly of the prospering gold mines—it's Britain's determined drive to become the dominant power in a region of mounting importance. A furious President Kruger understands this well and reacts bitterly: "It is our country you want." In his anger, Kruger puts forward counterdemands considered so extreme—like the withdrawal of all British troops from the region—that Chamberlain, in rejecting them, is able to claim that what the Boers really want is war. In contrast, Chamberlain insists, Britain stands for "morality"—one man, one vote (meaning, given the plurality of British subjects in the region, an immediate British takeover of political control). And so it is that in October 1899, war—a far more bloody affair than anticipated—duly arrives.

Initially Roger's sympathies are uncomplicated: long repulsed by the Boers' harsh treatment of native Africans and still loyal to the empire ("I feel so strongly that England is the rightful and wisest ruler of South Africa"), he feels "in a nutshell . . . [that it] is either Boer or British. It can't be both." There isn't room for divided rule. He feels, too, that "while war lasts it should be thorough and severe—so that it may sooner be over." To the surprise of many, the early skirmishes go to the Boers—they're highly disciplined and motivated, well-armed, and fighting on familiar turf—and the British forces suffer heavy casualties. London is aghast, the world in shock that David is besting Goliath—but only, as it will turn out, temporarily, until British reinforcements can arrive, and their superior numbers overwhelm the opposition.

In the interim Roger comes up with an audacious plan of his own. Self-confident and something of a daredevil (in his private life as well, as will soon become apparent), he suggests to Milner that he, Roger, lead a mission from Cape Town to blow up the railway line recently completed between Pretoria and Delagoa Bay that provides the Boers with their only access to the sea—and to receiving additional arms shipments from Germany. The idea appeals to Milner, and with his approval Roger quickly gathers his forces. He's already set out with part of his expeditionary force when word arrives from headquarters that the mission has been called off. Milner has apparently concluded that the Boers could quickly repair any damage to the rail line; that even if the railroad is somehow wholly disabled, trade could continue by road; and that therefore British soldiers could be more usefully employed elsewhere.

Deflated at having his bold plan annulled, Roger's somewhat consoled when word arrives that the Foreign Office is yet again reassigning him—this time to the Upper Congo, with a mandate to establish a new consulate at Kinshasa. He'll later describe himself at the time of his departure from southern Africa as having been well "on the high road to being a regular imperialist jingo." The subsequent course of the Boer War—which he henceforth has to follow from a distance—will itself do much to turn him around, and in particular the series of concentration camps that the British government establishes. Reports of the shocking conditions in the camps gradually leak out, and by the end of the war in 1902, twenty-eight thousand Boers interned in them—80 percent of them children under sixteen—will have died from poor sanitation, inadequate food, lack of medical care, and tainted water supplies.

Among the war's casualties, in her capacity as a volunteer army nurse, is Mary Kingsley. No friend of imperialism and regretful that the war has shifted focus away from the plight of native Africans, she had decided that it was her duty to do what she could to alleviate wartime suffering. Assigned to take care of wounded Boer prisoners, she'd been appalled at the bayoneting of sixteen-year-old boys, the delirium of grown men calling out for their mothers, the "gangrenous wounds," "unutterable stench," and "groans and racking coughs." Ultimately, she too comes down with high fever, aching joints, acute stomach pain, diarrhea, and, finally, delirium. She dies of typhoid on June 4, 1900, age thirty-seven.

While en route to southern Africa to take up her nursing duties, Kingsley had written a letter to the editor of *New Africa* summarizing her anger at those "stay-at-home statesmen [who] think that Africans are awful savages or silly children." She took pains in the letter to warn Africans against relying on Christian missionaries—urging them instead to see their own beliefs in a positive light: "unless you preserve your institutions, above all your land law, you cannot, no race can, preserve your liberty." It will now be up to others to implement the remarkable testament of a most remarkable woman.

Roger will be in the forefront of those carrying Mary Kingsley's legacy into the future. At the time of her death in 1900, he's still in his midthirties and already moving away from his earlier position as a loyal functionary of the empire. Within two years Britain's dutiful defender will, in fits and starts, emerge as one of its most severe critics.

. . .

In England, on leave before taking up his new post at Kinshasa, Roger receives word from the British ambassador to Belgium that King Leopold, having learned of Roger's appointment to the Upper Congo, wishes to make his acquaintance and to that end has invited him to luncheon at the Royal Palace in Brussels. Roger is startled at the invitation and wonders if the king, known to be charming when he chooses, isn't attempting to neutralize him in advance as a potential critic. Yet he accepts, curious to meet the man who seems to have outfoxed those who would censure and control him.

On October 18, 1900, Roger is ushered into a luxuriously appointed parlor room, and almost at once the king himself appears. An imposing figure almost as tall as Roger, Leopold is dressed in the gilded uniform of the Belgian army. Broad-shouldered and bearded, with an aquiline nose and piercing eyes, his face is fixed in an expression of distant amiability. As he crosses the room toward Roger, Leopold addresses him in English, speaking slowly and authoritatively. "I understand you knew the deceased Miss Kingsley."

"Yes, though not as well as I would have liked." Not knowing if the gesture is appropriate, Roger extends his hand in greeting.

Ignoring the gesture, Leopold explains, "I do not shake hands, Mr. Casement. Germs, you know. I would not have reached my midsixties in such splendid health had I not always taken precautions against contamination." He gestures toward a straight-back chair stitched in needlepoint and takes the one opposite for himself.

"It's wise of you, therefore, to have avoided a visit to the Congo!" Roger says, smiling pleasantly.

"Visiting the Congo is no guarantee of *seeing* the Congo. Miss Kingsley has managed to get nearly everything exactly wrong."

"You've read her book then?"

"I've had its contents summarized for me. There are a great many demands on my time."

"I found it very lively. Perceptive, too."

"Perceptive?" Leopold's voice carries a clear overtone of disdain.

"The many instances of cruelty it relates—of cruelty to the natives."

"*Many?*" Leopold sniffily replies. "I very much doubt Miss Kingsley's accuracy. When I first decided to involve myself in that benighted land, I had as my chief purpose, my obligation as a Christian, to bring at least a modicum of well-being and good government to a people sunk in savage superstition. I have repeatedly impressed that obligation on my officials."

"Quite a number of them, I fear, have ignored your instructions."

"Quite a number? I suspect your descriptive powers, Mr. Casement, are— I'm told you're Irish—how shall I say, 'extravagant.' There will always be a *few* renegades who disobey instructions, just as there will always be natives who refuse to understand that to earn the benefits of civilization, they must devote themselves to regularized labor."

"Instead of forced labor"—Roger passes lightly over his rewording—"why not a simple tax, a just one?"

"*Forced* labor? I don't know what you refer to." Leopold's tone is icily aloof.

"I've seen the photographs, Your Majesty, of severed hands—the punishment meted out to those who fail to turn in their quota of rubber or who resist enslavement."

There's a brief pause, while Leopold works to contain his anger. "As I have said, the extent of such punishment has been grotesquely exaggerated. It is difficult to find men able always to control their temper when faced with the sly guile of the natives."

"The English Foreign Office has opened a Congo Atrocities File. I doubt it would have done so if there were only a very few cases."

"The Foreign Office should concern itself with Germany's schemes for expansion, not with false rumors about the Congo. Belgium is a tiny country that must satisfy itself with a few—only a few—of the crumbs that fall from England's well-stocked table."

"According to some accounts, the profits accruing from the escalating rubber trade are very substantial."

"I have poured several fortunes into the Congo," Leopold replies, his tone one of controlled anger. "Finally, a *small* profit is being achieved, which I devote entirely to the Congo's civilizing mission. Surely you of all people are aware, Mr. Casement, that four years ago—*before* Miss Kingsley published her book—I appointed a Commission for the Protection of the Natives. The press widely, indeed excessively, sang my praises—especially the English press—for showing the determination, quite unbidden, to root out administrative excesses." Leopold has the triumphant look of having caught a tiger by the tail.

"I do indeed know about the commission."

"I appointed to it six of the most prominent missionaries in the Congo—three Belgian Catholics and three foreign Protestants."

"None of them, I believe, are stationed in the rubber-producing areas," Roger calmly replies, "from where most of the atrocity reports come."

"The commissioners are free to travel wherever they wish," Leopold smoothly responds. "Nothing stands in their way."

"Begging pardon, Your Majesty . . . nothing except the money needed for supplies and guides, plus the conviction that their primary mission is to bring Christianity to the heathen."

"I have done nothing to obstruct their inquiry."

("Nor anything to facilitate it," Roger wants to say, but doesn't.) "The Congo covers a thousand miles of difficult, treacherous terrain," he says instead. "One would have to be very well supplied and very determined."

"I cannot solve all problems, Mr. Casement. I cannot rid the Congo of crocodiles, nor can I make the climate more temperate." Leopold smiles at his own cleverness.

"Is it not true, Your Majesty, that the commission has met only twice in four years?"

"Their instruction is to meet as often as they feel necessary. I await their report."

"The commissioners will have great trouble gathering information, even should they wish to. Most of the missionaries serving in the Congo, with a few exceptions, like William Sheppard—" Roger pauses for an instant to see if Leopold will react. He doesn't.

"Unlike William Sheppard, most of the missionaries," Roger continues, "are not known for their candor in describing local conditions. They live in fear that their Godly work of conversion will be suppressed."

"I cannot be responsible," Leopold replies with a hint of impatience, "for the phantom fears of such people. It is enough for me to know that I am doing my duty. You must remember, Mr. Casement, that you cannot recruit the best, the most morally outstanding men, to serve in a region where disease and death lurk in every byway, where the blistering heat loosens every fiber of restraint."

And so it goes, for another hour and a half, neither man acknowledging the arguments of the other, though with Leopold convinced at the end that he's charmed Casement—as he has so many others—into believing his philanthropic declarations, and with Casement more convinced than ever that the king remains obdurately indifferent to the fate of the African people. As they part, Leopold, sounding grandly magnanimous, urges Casement "to write me privately at any time, and to write frankly, should there be anything of interest that you can, unofficially, advise me of." They two men will never meet again—nor ever again playact at cordiality.

. . .

During his extensive leave, Roger takes the opportunity to visit his favorite relative, Gertrude Bannister, daughter of his mother's sister, Grace, and ten years his junior. Roger's immediate family had its roots in northern Ireland's County Antrim, but both his parents had died before he reached the age of twelve. His father, also Roger, was an Ulster Protestant descended from landed gentry but compelled, as a younger son, to make his own way. An extravagant, irascible man, he managed to have a military career of sorts and expressed sympathy for Irish and other independence movements (he was once entrusted with a message from the Hungarian rebel Lajos Kossuth to Lord Palmerston, pleading for intervention). But he was never able to secure a steady income, and the family lived in a series of rooming houses, reliant on occasional assistance from relatives.

Roger's mother, Anne, warm and expansive, gave birth to eleven children, four of whom survived. Nina, the eldest, gained a reputation for being "difficult," yet Roger felt deeply attached to her throughout his life. His two older brothers, Tom and Charlie—both of whom would spend much of their adult lives in, respectively, South Africa and Australia—were considered more convivial than Nina but, like their father, frequently strapped for money. The youngest child, Roger was apparently his mother's favorite—she's remembered as having "adored" her baby boy. Herself a converted Catholic, Anne had her children secretly baptized to avoid a confrontation with her Protestant husband. Roger was only nine when his mother died of liver cirrhosis at age thirty-seven; three years later, in 1877, his father died as well.

A series of relatives raised Roger and his siblings and managed to get him a good secondary-school education at the Ballymena Diocesan School—he was one of only five students who boarded there. His sister, Nina, described him as a happy, healthy child, popular with his teachers as well as the other boys. He would later complain that Ballymena had taught him "nothing about Ireland," but that belated gripe aside, he got a solid grounding in English literature, studied the classics, loved history, learned French, started to write poetry (several of his verses deplored England's conquest of Ireland), and won a number of prizes.

His historical studies fed his incipient Irish nationalism. He made special heroes out of the trio of Manchester Martyrs (William Allen, Michael Larkin, and Michael O'Brien) who'd been hanged for their leadership in the 1867 Fenian uprising, which had dared to proclaim an Irish Republic. He also avidly followed the "land wars" then current and pasted up on his bedroom wall newspaper pictures of Michael Davitt and Charles Stewart

Parnell, leaders of the National Land League, founded in 1879 to put a stop to the widespread eviction of Irish tenant farmers by often-absentee Anglo-Irish landlords; the league aimed at making land cheap enough to allow tenants themselves to become owners of a plot. During the land wars the dispossessed Irish peasantry utilized tactics that included physical coercion to prevent evictions, the setting up of extrajudicial courts, and the withholding of labor at harvest time from recalcitrant landlords. The fierce struggle was at its height in the 1880s and had fueled the youthful Roger's anger at the truculent cruelty of the established order.

"Dispossession" would become an emotional thread running throughout Roger's life. It would range from a childhood of living in rented rooms and losing his mother at an early age, to his adult outrage at King Leopold "repossessing as vacant" all land in the Congo he happened to covet, to mounting bitterness over Ireland's thwarted right to nationhood and its historical dislocation. Most of Roger's relatives regarded his youthful nationalism, along with the romantic poetry he wrote, as mere adolescent extravagance. They felt it necessary to warn the "dashing young fellow"—an unusually handsome lad who had, one of his adult relative's thought, an "undue estimate of himself"—that dreams of an "elevated" career could not be supported on his marginal income and lack of social standing. He might do well, his relatives urged, to become a bank teller or perhaps a clerk in a mercantile house. At any rate, they could not or would not finance an advanced education they considered irrelevant to the limited career options open to him. Lack of funds forced Roger to leave the Ballymena School before his sixteenth birthday, and for the next three years, from ages fifteen to seventeen, he lived with the Bannister family, his mother's relatives, in Liverpool.

Cousin Gertrude's father, Edward Bannister, had himself served for a short time as vice-consul at Boma, the west African port, and he'd been among the first to speak out boldly—to no avail—about the mistreatment of the inhabitants. Throughout the period Roger lived with the family, Bannister was employed by a company involved in the Congo trade, and he'd succeeded in getting Roger a job with Elder Dempster, a prominent shipping concern involved with West African trade. Roger's initial tour of duty had landed him in the Congo in 1884 at age twenty, and that first extended stay of two years had taught him much about the region and had as well led to the formation of a number of friendships with young Englishmen also employed in the area. Among them, Roger had been a popular, admired figure. Herbert Ward in particular would remain a close friend, seeing in Roger a "pure Irishman" with "a captivating voice and a singular charm of manner . . . high-minded and courageous, impulsive and poetical." Over the next five years in the Congo, Roger had been involved in a variety of activities, including exploring expeditions and railway surveys, had traveled over much of the country and (as he put it) "learned to love and pity the natives."

When given home leave, Roger always repaired to the Bannister household in Liverpool. It's on this visit in 1891 that his closeness to his cousin Gertrude ("Gee," as Roger calls her) greatly deepens, and she becomes something of a real confidant. It begins when the two are alone one day, reading on the small porch off the side of the kitchen. Glancing up from her book, Gee notices how tired Roger looks and expresses concern that he's been overworking. Touched at her kindness—most people assume that Roger's restless energy is inexhaustible and automatically dismiss signs to the contrary—Roger admits that he is, at age thirty-six, feeling very much at a crossroads, dissatisfied with the current shape of his life yet uncertain about a future direction.

"Your work on the transport system?" Gee asks tentatively.

"In part that, yes." Roger hesitantly replies. "It's a general sense of malaise, Gee. If . . . if I understood it better, I could describe it to you more clearly. Sometimes I think it's Africa itself rather than the particular role I'm playing there."

"The climate sounds beastly. And it *has* made you ill."

"I'm not as ill as all that! 'Run down,' the doctor says, but the only concrete problem he comes up with—forgive the reference, dear Gee—is hemorrhoids!" Roger laughs. "I hope I haven't offended you."

"Goodness, no! I'm not one of those women who feels bodily parts shouldn't be mentioned in polite society."

"I'm glad to hear it. Let's *not* be polite with each other!" Roger smiles and pulls his chair a bit closer. "The doctor recommends an operation, but I've heard that advice before. The matter usually resolves itself."

"My impression is that you're happier when in Africa than here at home. Am I wrong?"

"I often think that Africa *is* my home. Perhaps that's part of the problem. I love the people, but I don't love what's happening to them. I'm less convinced than ever, Gee, that what we call 'civilization' has been in any way beneficial. Your so-called savage has *life*—your white destroyers have *things*. That's the whole distinction: the savage *is;* the white man *has*. This awful war with the Boers hasn't helped."

"It's enough to make the heart sink. Those terrible camps."

"Sometimes I feel sick *about* Africa. Other times I feel sick *of* Africa. Talk about divided feelings, eh?" Roger smiles but he sounds defeated. "It's not the Earthly Paradise I once thought. . . . Maybe I'm just getting older and want more people like myself around me. . . . Maybe I should try for some comfortable, healthy post. . . ."

"I always thought you felt most at home in Ireland. Do you still read Irish history like you used to?"

"I do, but less so. At the moment Ireland too seems stuck. Since Parnell's death, I have no hero. Nor does Ireland, it seems. No one is interested any more in Home Rule. . . . If we don't want it, why should the English give it?"

Gertrude perks up. "Do you still read William O'Brien's sheet, *United Ireland?* Wasn't it Parnell's favorite?"

Roger frowns. "Never trusted the man. Now O'Brien's criticizing the Boers for 'delirious enthusiasm'—yes, delirious for being penned up in those camps."

"But his Plan of Campaign *has* helped the tenant farmers. You must give him that, Roger. . . ."

"He's unleashed more disorder on the tenant farms than we've seen in years, if that's what you mean."

"I doubt that's true, Roger." Gee's voice is firm. "After all, evictions are less frequent, what with the tenants paying only what they can afford during a downturn."

"Credit for that, Gee, goes to Parliament and the Local Government Act—taking total control away from the big property owners and giving some of it to elected county councils."

"O'Brien calls it 'killing Home Rule with kindness.' I tell you, I don't know what to believe any more. Or who."

"Then you're right where I am, Gee." Roger's smiles impishly. "And here I thought you didn't believe there was an Irish nation at all, no trace of a distinct race except for torpor and decay."

"What I believe is that your average Irishman—like your average anybody—wants coins in his pocket. Wants land. He couldn't care less whether it's Lord Rosebery or dear departed William Gladstone who's heading up the show." Gee's tone is mild but spunky—which delights Roger.

He draws himself up in mock horror. "Which can only mean that you're an Ulster Unionist and a loyal supporter of that blackguard Sir Edward Carson?"

Gee laughs. "Well, he *is* for women's rights!"

"But no rights for poor Oscar Wilde!" Roger is surprised at his own remark and tries to backtrack. "I know, the trial was five years ago, and poor Oscar's dead in Paris at forty-six."

"He should have followed Bernard Shaw's advice: dropped the case and left the country." Gertrude's tone is neutral, with no trace of judgment.

"As many suggested at the time. You remember Oscar's reply? 'Everybody wants me to go abroad. I've just been abroad. One can't keep on going abroad, unless one is a missionary. . . .'"

They both laugh, then Roger quietly says, "I wonder if he'd have been convicted if Carson hadn't been the Marquess of Queensberry's defense lawyer."

"Of course he would have. He did lead many a young man astray."

Startled, Roger is momentarily silent. "You can't believe that, Gee," he says solemnly.

"I'm not saying *I* do. I'm saying that most people feel that way—that he was morally degenerate."

"So said Edward Carson, defender of the faith!"

"I don't care for the old bully either. But . . . but—oh goodness, Roger, now you've got me all confused!"

Roger wants to change the subject too. Badly. He shouldn't have let it go on this long. How did they get on to Wilde in the first place? It's a subject he's always steered away from, certain—rightly—that few will understand. He does want to get closer to Gee—she's already his favorite relative. But he knows this isn't a part of his life he should share with her, not now certainly and probably never. She'd be shocked, would try to understand, out of kindness would feign understanding, but it would be too foreign to her.

He gently pats Gee on the arm. "No more confused than I am, dear Gee. Come, let's take our afternoon stroll by the estuary. I'll buy you some lovely flowers."

· · ·

Roger's sex life is a thing apart, an activity, not a topic of conversation. It's unconnected to love or friendship, though it might briefly brush up against one or both. It has nothing to do with domesticity and a home life. It centers on anonymity and adventure, not cuddling and sweet talk. It's something that happens along the way, usually with pickups, sometimes involving money, always and only with other men. It's closed off, sequestered, set apart.

Periodically, Roger becomes smitten with one of his pickups, sees him half a dozen times, then loses touch either deliberately or because he moves about so much. He has no sustained romantic relationships, though a little later in life he'll meet a young bank clerk named Joseph Millar Gordon who will marginally qualify as an on-again, off-again companion, sexual and otherwise. Roger, handsome, accomplished, and charming, likely has multiple opportunities to form lasting bonds. Yet he never makes himself eligible (though he might claim otherwise). Consciously or not, he avoids anything resembling a sustained commitment, permanence—he never even settles into a home of his own.

He does not affiliate with any of the groups that surround contemporary figures like Oscar Wilde or George Ives; nor adopt any of the outer signs of artifice and aestheticism associated with them; nor frequent any of the network of pubs (like the Café Royale or the Criterion), hotels (the Victoria or the Savoy), and theaters (the St. James or the Empire on Leicester Square) at which they gather. Roger isn't interested in drinking port or exchanging witticisms with his fellow transgressors.

No, he prefers the outdoor cruising spots, the solitary hunt. And in London many such venues exist, ranging from the docks (if working-class partners are the particular object of desire), to public parks (Hyde Park specializes in soldier prostitutes), to West End streets that include the Strand and Marble Arch, to the iron urinals that began to appear (in Paris as well) beginning in the 1860s. The efflorescence after 1900 of scientific debate about the nature of sexual "deviancy" is less pronounced in England than on the continent, but deviant *activity* is at least as prevalent—as well as a concomitant abundance of arrests and prosecutions. Roger takes full advantage of London's many opportunities for casual sex but seems—even after Oscar Wilde's conviction—atypically immune to apprehension about potential consequences.

Periodic, fleeting intensity may be the pattern (or lack of one) best suited to Roger's audacious temperament; he finds highly charged, risky encounters far more congenial than the routine repetitions of coupledom: Roger the adventurer, not Roger the homebody. Or perhaps his meandering ways—he would have liked the bumblebee metaphor: snatching nectar from blossom to blossom—relate more to the shattering childhood loss of his adored mother, followed by a peripatetic childhood designed to build still higher a defensive wall, solid if not quite impenetrable, against making too heavy an investment in any one individual, no matter how compatible. The original loss possibly implanted in him a profound wariness against forming intense attachments ultimately "bound" to disappoint and disappear.

He once—exactly once in his many writings—refers to homosexuality as a "disease," but that's not a view he holds consistently; in fact, the single reference to "disease" may well represent little more than an almost inevitable spasm of self-recrimination at a time and in a culture that overwhelmingly viewed homosexuality as a degenerate illness. Far more typically, Roger records his sexual exploits in his diary with an overtone of blameless bravado; if he ever or often feels guiltily culpable, he doesn't say so—or even imply as much.

Roger's in danger of exposure not simply for his erotic attraction to the wrong gender but for indulging it so often—the literal sailors in every port—and with the wrong kind of déclassé people. Yet the actual incidence of his sexual activity doesn't warrant the accusations that will later be made that he was a "compulsive, sexual addict," not unless he's being judged on the basis of assumptions that "sex is for procreation" or that "sex outside of a committed relationship, or before marriage, is immoral." By those sex-negative standards Roger's behavior can certainly be viewed as "abnormal"—but then, so can the assumptions that condemn it.

When Roger starts to keep his barebones "sexual diary" in 1903, he jots down brief notations—little more—of his encounters. His appetites hardly seem unusual: cruising that results in actual sexual contact ranges roughly from two to four times a month, downright anemic, it might be argued, for a young adult ruled by hormones more than guilt. He also does a good deal of cruising that leads merely to glancing contact or none at all; Roger often jots down sightings of attractive men or semierect penises (easily visible in an era where underwear is uncommon). But such spectator sport is a routine part of city life, and Roger's attentiveness to his environment seems the very definition of a healthy, functioning adult, hardly meriting the term "compulsive."

He's among the subset of homosexual men who have through time refused to abide by what they view as the unnatural demands of a monogamous marital bond—which is one reason for the rage historically leveled against them. For Roger and for those like him, it makes no sense for it to be okay to have multiple orgasms with one's monogamous partner but not okay to have the same number of orgasms with multiple partners. He would want to know who sets up such rules and by what right. Since the rules, he knows, have historically kept changing, the current ones should logically be regarded, he feels, not as a function of universal truths but of socially defined, ever-changing notions of "propriety." He's heard about various explorers and ethnographers—and even read the published accounts of a few—who tell of peoples like the Keraki of New Guinea, who mandate regularized anal intercourse between an older man and a young boy as a necessary ritual to ensure the boy's satisfactory progress to manhood. He was amused to hear of another tribal group on New Guinea, the Anga people, who, alternately, insist on the *oral* ingestion of semen as the essential, magical prescription for virile growth. In both instances, Roger has learned, the boys apparently move unproblematically as adults into heterosexuality.

Nor can the fact that Roger often gives his casual sexual partners money (not that it's often demanded—he is, after all, an exceedingly handsome man) be simplistically dismissed as a "merely commercial" ("disgraceful") transaction. Due to his erotic preference for working-class men who might well be in need, Roger's offer of money can, at least at times, just as reasonably be ascribed to his sensitive nature and kind heart as to some "callous" commercial bargain. Nor are his partners—another common accusation that will later be made against him—ever prepubescent boys, though at the time and to this day, "pedophilia" is mistakenly used as a synonym for "homosexuality." Fairly often Roger's partners are young men in their late teens or early twenties, and their raging hormones probably provide a more valid definition of the appropriate "age of consent" than can any artificial equation that links a precise time line (age fourteen? sixteen? eighteen? twenty-one?) with sexual maturity.

Roger must have realized that should his sexual activities ever be discovered, scandal and punishment will likely follow (especially if it becomes known that his preference is to assume the "passive"—that is, "unmanly"—role in anal sex). In late nineteenth-century England, libidinal constraints are more pronounced than in France or Italy (or perhaps even in Ireland—straitlaced prudery will become a more defining feature of Irish life after the 1922 establishment of the Irish Free State and the ascendency of Catholicism than in the period preceding).

The animus against homosexuality in late nineteenth-century England doesn't prevent sex-starved, upper-class lads at Eton and Harrow from pleasuring one another (*and* their masters); keep soldiers of the Royal Horse Guards from donning full regalia the better to sell their services to perambulating gentlemen in Piccadilly Circus, Charing Cross Road, the Marble Arch, and a dozen other outdoor locales; or, for a time at least, interfere with the notorious male brothel at 19 Cleveland Street, which entertains any number of prominent Englishmen, including Lord Arthur Somerset (son of the Duke of Beaufort), the Earl of Euston (heir of the Duke of Grafton), and, it's rumored, the eldest son of the Prince of Wales. This activity, of course, is confined to a small minority of the population, and its participants never publicly boast—so powerful is the public association of homosexuality with "degeneracy"—about their unique "identity."

One of the great scandals of the late nineteenth century—preceding Oscar Wilde's trials by a decade—is the so-called Dublin Castle Affair of the mid-1880s; it is certainly the one that would have drawn Roger Casement's curiosity, as did all matters relating to Ireland, and that might even (if anything could have) thrown the fear of God, or the law, into him.

The "Castle" is, in the 1880s, the local seat of the English government in Ireland, and uncovering the "iniquities" taking place there is largely the work of two Irish nationalists, Tim Healy, one of Charles Stewart Parnell's leading lieutenants, and William O'Brien, the proprietor of *United Ireland*. At a time when the land wars are still in full swing, Dublin Castle, the seat of English power, is widely and accurately viewed as the chief enforcer of landlord privilege—which gives the charges of homosexuality against some of its leading officials a sharp political edge; from the point of view of Irish nationalists, it's synonymous with an attack on the hated Anglo-Irish landowning class. Both the chief accusers, Healy and O'Brien, are motivated primarily by political not moral considerations. Healy, in the context of the times, is known to be downright indifferent to homosexuality, and O'Brien's concern is focused not on sexuality but on the wretched lives of rural Irish laborers and farmers.

Through an informant, O'Brien learned that James Ellis French, the English head of the Criminal Investigation Department in Dublin Castle, is a "known sodomite," and he promptly publishes the rumor in *United Ireland,* writing that scrutiny of "the life and adventures, and what is known as the 'private character' of various Crown Employees in Ireland" is long overdue. French promptly sues for libel. He also falls ill with "nervous debility, softening of the brain and paralysis," causing the trial to be indefinitely postponed.

Undaunted, O'Brien proceeds to make similar accusations in *United Ireland* against several other Dublin Castle bigwigs, including the Crown solicitor and the chief secretary of the post office. A number of arrests follow, though the charges are generally aborted. Nonetheless, O'Brien has succeeded in his main purpose: to link British rule in the public mind with moral corruption (i.e., homosexuality). Irish nationalists hail his patriotism more fervently than his stance against sodomitical pollution. Roger Casement, a sodomite, looks elsewhere for his patriotic heroes.

Ten years later, Tim Healy tries to intervene with the solicitor general following Oscar Wilde's conviction in an effort to spare him the horrors of the British penal system—but to no avail; the Irish press, moreover, shows a good deal more sympathy for Wilde than does the British (for what one Irish paper calls the "ill and anxious" prisoner). Irish nationalism plays a role in muting or attempting to circumvent Wilde's sexual "crimes," and some of Ireland's leading cultural figures fight actively on his behalf. William Butler Yeats gathers letters of support for Wilde and assigns "the rage and contempt that fill the crowds in the street" to an "over-abundant normal sexual instinct." George Bernard Shaw is also sympathetic, though more ambivalent: Wilde's "perversity," he writes, "does not imply any general depravity or coarseness of character." In general, the English establishment is more relentless and uniformly punitive in regard to lechery than are the Irish or the French, where the influence of Catholicism, with its emphasis on human frailty, the ubiquity of sin, *and* the necessity of forgiveness, is more widely established.

In England, on the other hand, the sodomy laws are rarely thwarted—other than by the periodic flight to the Continent of those wealthy enough to afford exile. Yet aristocratic privilege does provide some protection—Lord Alfred Douglas, the Earl of Euston, and Prince Braganza are among those who escape prosecution without having to flee the realm. In 1898, Parliament adds injury to insult with the passage of the Vagrancy Law Amendment Act, itemizing prison terms for men who "in any public place persistently solicit or importune for immoral purposes." In criminalizing *non*sexual behavior—like "loitering" in a park—the new vagrancy law goes beyond mandating punishment for sodomitical *acts* to include the far murkier areas of nonnormative "comportment" or "presumed intent." An effeminate gesture, a carnation in the lapel—and it's off to the precinct to be charged with "disorderly conduct." Even being clean-shaven becomes grounds for suspicion in an era where beards are considered emblematic of masculine respectability. Not surprisingly, there's a steady increase in arrests and prosecutions in Britain throughout these years. And punishment is sometimes harsh—in at least one instance thirty lashes followed by confinement at hard labor.

PART 2

The Congo

THE IVORY TRADE, long the chief source of wealth extracted from Africa, is by the turn of the century being rapidly overtaken by a sudden growth in the need of rubber. Following the 1890 invention of an inflatable rubber tire, the popularity of bicycle riding soars—seven million bikes are in circulation by 1895—and, soon after, the market for automobile tires also expands rapidly. The double development leads to a huge demand for rubber. In the forests of the Congo, the wild rubber vine, easily tapped, abounds, and as the need—and price—for the product mounts, the region's economy is transformed. Between 1890 and 1904, earnings from rubber increase year after year by leaps and bounds, with profits reaching 700 percent. The "Congo Free State"—Leopold's personal fiefdom, independent of Belgium—becomes the most profitable colony in all of Africa.

To maximize his profits and to keep potential European competitors at bay, King Leopold—a mere six years after signing the 1885 Berlin "free-trade" agreement—takes absolute and exclusive control of a hundred thousand square miles of the Congo's richest rubber-producing region. He issues what becomes a protracted series of secret decrees to his officials in Africa, declaring himself the sole owner of not only the land but also the forests and minerals, and ordering them to see to it that the previously thriving trade between the native people and merchants from European countries be swiftly ended. Henceforth, Leopold declares, the Africans are tenants of the Congo Free State and subject to its authority; they may own *only* the small patches of cultivated land surrounding their huts; all the rest is declared "vacant"— which is to say, the property of Leopold.

In 1888 Leopold establishes the Force Publique, armed native troops chosen to serve in areas distant from those of their birth and under the command of European officers. He also instructs his agents zealously to ensure—at the point of the bayonet if need be—that the "slothful" natives be transformed into a rigorously productive workforce. The harsh regime of the *commissaires* is henceforth to hold sway. As agents of the Congo Free State, they are to work strictly on commission; if they wish to maximize their income, it's up to them to create, by whatever means necessary, a diligent and dutiful army of laborers.

The effect on the native workforce is catastrophic. As the demand for rubber soars, so too does the level of barbarity inflicted on the indigenous population. Several of the braver missionaries—William Sheppard, for one—are among the few to speak out against the endemic cruelty. The most forceful voice is that of the Swedish Baptist missionary E. V. Sjoblom; so vigorous and unyielding are his complaints that the local authorities threaten him with five years imprisonment. Undaunted, Sjoblom takes his case directly to London.

Richard Fox-Bourne, secretary of the Aborigines Protection Society, organizes a public meeting in the spring of 1897, at which Sjoblom speaks: "Within my own knowledge," he tells the crowd, "forty-five towns have been burnt down. Soldiers are stationed in every village—the so-called sentry-system—they live off the people, and drive them into the forest to gather india-rubber. I saw one soldier seize an old man who, to keep from starving, had dared to fish for food in the river; they shot him dead right in front of me. If the natives' quota of rubber is short, I've seen sentries beat them so badly that some die, then they cut off their hands and bring them to the Commissioner as proof they're doing their job. One day, when I crossed the stream, I saw some dead bodies hanging down from the branches in the water. As I turned my face away from the horrible sight, one of the native corporals—Leopold's agents employ natives from distant or hostile tribes—said, 'Oh, that is nothing, a few days ago I brought the white man 160 hands and they were thrown into the river.'"

Sjoblom's revulsion at the endemic cruelty in the Congo is far from typical. The large majority of the missionaries keep mum about the horrors they see around them, fearing that their calling to bring Christianity to Africa might be compromised. Yet a few, like Sjoblom, are conscience-stricken, and by the late 1880s their outspoken accounts have begun to trickle through. One such account reports native women being forced into concubinage, another of women and children being bayoneted and thrown into the river, a third of widespread starvation as the people, dragooned into gathering rubber, are prevented from planting and tending crops. "This rubber traffic is steeped in blood," one missionary writes, "and if the natives were to rise and sweep every white person on the Upper Congo into eternity there would still be left a fearful balance to their credit." In 1900 these are still voices in the wilderness, anguished cries that Leopold's unctuously clever reassurances—abetted by clamorous praise in the press for his wondrous expansion of European commerce and Christianity—easily drown out.

Roger returns to London on sick leave in July 1900. He explains to the Foreign Office that he's suffering from a "general condition of rundownness," compounded by an attack of jaundice. He omits mention of a return bout of piles, as well as his doctor's recommendation for additional surgery for the *fistula-in-ano*—a common side effect of frequent anal intercourse—for which he'd been operated on five years earlier. As his health gradually improves, Roger spends a month traveling in Europe, with his sister Nina accompanying him for part of the trip. In Spain he attends his first bull-fight—and finds the spectacle appalling: "an exhibition of bad butchery carried on in the bloodiest and most revolting manner."

Italy—"my eternal joy and delight"—helps erase the memory of Spain's national "sport" of "blood lust." He adores Naples above all. In a letter to his fellow Englishman Richard Morten—they first met in Africa and then (as with Herbert Ward) became close friends—Roger sends a glowing report replete with sexual innuendo: "It is the most human town in Europe. People there do what they think. . . . It is a last link with the outdoor life of the ancient world, when men were quite natural. Whether it is better to hide our hearts—to muffle up our lives—and to live the truer part of our lives in secret as we do today, the future only knows—for my part I cannot help feeling that the world lost something when discretion became the first of the ten commandments."

Roger returns to Africa at the end of 1900—though not to Kinshasa, as expected. The Foreign Office has changed its mind and decided to locate its new consulate instead at Boma, the coastal administrative center of the Congo Free State. Roger has of course heard the ugly talk about Leopold's policies, and his own recent audience with the king had confirmed his distrust. But what is wanted, Roger feels, is more concrete proof of Leopold's misdeeds, the sort of evidence William Sheppard has been unable to provide. Even before taking up his consular duties at Boma, Roger decides to organize a trip into the Congo interior to see for himself what conditions are actually like. What he finds leaves no doubt in his mind that gross mistreatment of the natives is even more widespread and horrendous than suspected and that Leopold, during their private interview, had simply been lying.

Roger sends off a dispatch to the new British foreign minister, Lord Lansdowne, describing his findings. "By a stroke of the pen," Roger writes, "the Congo has become the private property of one individual, the King of the Belgians." Aware that commercial arguments will have more impact at the Foreign Office than humanitarian ones, Roger stresses in his report that the 1885 Berlin accord that supposedly guaranteed free trade in the region has not been even marginally honored. A month later, after completing another inspection tour to the interior, Roger sends Lansdowne a still more forceful call for action. Leopold's Commission for the Protection of the Natives, Roger reports, has proven worthless, less than a fig leave. The situation has become so grave that Roger urges Lansdowne to intervene directly: "The only hope for the Congo, should it continue to be governed by Belgium, is that its governor should be subject to a European authority responsible to public opinion, and not to the unquestioned rule of an autocrat whose chief preoccupation is that autocracy should be profitable."

Lansdowne rejects Roger's suggestion out of hand. Should the Foreign Office rebuke Leopold, Lansdowne replies, the aggrieved king might seek support from Germany; meddling in the Congo could, in Lansdowne's view, result in swelling the territorial possessions of both Germany and France. He smugly assures Roger that the Foreign Office will keep its Congo Atrocities File updated should the time ever come when intervention seems more appropriate than it does at present. Roger gets the message: the Foreign Office is focused on imperial ambition, not on the welfare of "savages."

Dispirited, Roger is forced to bide his time. Bereft of compelling work or sustained companionship (except for his beloved dogs), he grows lonely and restless. His distress is accompanied by a (temporary) spell of disenchantment with Africa itself, along with a deepening (and permanent) revulsion over the British Empire's lofty arrogance. Africa, he writes Richard Morten, "isn't the Earthly Paradise I once felt it—or rather I'm no longer the bird of that Paradise. I've grown old and grey—and now I want peace and music—and nice people round me. . . . I shall try for some nice healthy post."

As for the empire, the Boer War and the hideous conditions of the concentration camps into which the British had thrown its prisoners had horrified Roger. He is no less appalled at the importation of Chinese laborers to work in the British-owned South African mines, where conditions are deplorable— the men confined in prison-like compounds, cut off from their families and (thanks to Lord Milner's approval of flogging) subjected to harsh punishment. From Roger's perspective, the British government has proved willing to encourage, and collude with, the abysmal greed of the mine owners.

Granted an extended leave of absence in England, Roger returns to Africa in the spring of 1902 with his energy considerably recharged and his outlook somewhat more positive. He decides on another inland expedition to track down concrete evidence of the Congo Free State's inequities, but no sooner are his investigations begun than he comes down with a recurrence of malarial fever, made more miserable still by "bleeding badly aft" from a series of sexual encounters. His doctors insist this time on a sustained period of rest, and the Foreign Office concurs. After several weeks of recuperation in the Canary Islands, Roger's condition improves, yet he's still unsure if his uncertain health will allow him to stay in West Africa long enough to make a difference. It's in this depressed state—with the Foreign Office detached and unresponsive and the rumors of atrocities mounting in tandem with the exponentially expanding rubber trade—that Roger happens upon a set of articles by a young journalist named Edmond "E. D." Morel.

Born in France, Morel is a naturalized Englishman, and his background is strikingly similar to Roger's: both their fathers died penniless, both left school at fifteen, both got their first jobs with the Elder Dempster shipping firm, and both had earlier been somewhat conventional imperialists. Morel has initially discounted reports of atrocities in the Congo put forth by what he then called the "misinformed philanthropists" Charles Dilke, MP, and Richard Fox-Bourne, secretary of the Aborigines Protection Society. Adopting what was then the conventional defense of colonialism, Morel characterizes Dilke's and Fox-Bourne's tales of mutilations and massacres as—even if true—inescapable byproducts of an essentially benign enterprise: no European nation "which has undertaken the heavy responsibility of introducing the blessings and vices of civilization into the Dark Continent," Morel writes, "can claim immunity for its representatives in this respect." Morel, unlike Roger, initially shares the common assumption of the day among Europeans that the black race is inherently inferior (a view, in diluted form, Morel will continue to hold, later denouncing France during World War I for using black troops—for, as he would write, "thrusting her black savages . . . into the heart of Germany," where "primitive African barbarians" would become a "terror and a horror").

Morel's shifting views on the blessings of empire begins not with a direct protest about the exploitation of Africans in the Congo Free State but with

Leopold's interference with the right of free trade mandated under the terms of the 1885 Berlin agreement. It's the same emphasis Roger had earlier placed—for strategic reasons—when appealing to the Foreign Office for action, knowing that commercial rights would be of far more concern to the powers-that-be than native rights. But once Morel, like Roger before him, begins to study trade reports from the Congo Free State, he's led, like Roger, to the inescapable conclusion that native laborers are unwilling slaves, not salaried employees—that forced labor is systemic in the Congo, the foundational stone for the huge profits of the rubber trade.

Morel writes up his findings from the trade reports in a series of articles that catch the eye of those longtime reformers, Dilke and Fox-Bourne. The three men organize a protest meeting at the Mansion House on May 15, 1902. The turnout is small, but it marks the beginning of an attempt to rouse public opinion against the man Morel calls the "royal megalomaniac." A number of other British journalists take up the cry, and articles against Leopold's rule start to appear in publications as diverse as the *Morning Post* and the *Manchester Guardian*. The Foreign Office, however, continues to shrink from any involvement; when Dilke appeals to Lord Lansdowne for action (just as Roger had earlier), the foreign secretary makes it clear that in his view any reopening of the Pandora's box of the 1885 Berlin agreement could be tantamount to risking a reconsideration of the partition of Africa that has turned out so splendidly for Great Britain.

Morel persists. In May 1903, working through his humanitarian allies, and Dilke in particular, he gets a Congo resolution through the House of Commons, calling for the signatories to the Berlin act "to abate the evils prevalent in the Congo State." The sponsors acknowledge, however, that before a paper resolution can be converted into action, much more eyewitness evidence of widespread mistreatment is needed. Though they aren't aware of it, Roger has already set the wheels in motion for achieving precisely that end. His plan hinges on the fact that Leopold's agents have been hiring black West Indians, themselves British subjects, to serve as overseers in the Congo, and word of their discontent has reached Roger's ears.

Here is the entering wedge he's been waiting for. Roger personally arranges for the repatriation of several West Indians who'd been illegally jailed in the Congo—and reports this "abuse of British subjects" to the Foreign Office. The tactic works. Lord Lansdowne denounces the "terrible story" and authorizes the Colonial Office to warn West Indians against signing up to work in the Congo. Capitalizing on this success, Roger cables for permission to mount another expedition into the Congo interior to gather additional information. By return cable the Foreign Office authorizes him to proceed whenever he feels ready.

As Roger is making final preparations for the trip, news arrives that Sir Hector Macdonald, an army major general who's served for thirty years in India and South Africa, has committed suicide. It turns out that Macdonald decided to take his own life on his way to face court-martial proceedings in Ceylon on charges of homosexuality. Roger records his dismay in an emotional entry in his newly inaugurated diary, characterizing the news—though he's never met Macdonald—as "pitiably sad! The most distressing case this surely of its kind and one that may awake the national mind to saner methods of curing a terrible disease than by criminal legislation."

It's here, in relation to Macdonald's suicide, that Roger uses for the first and only time the word "disease" (or anything comparably pejorative) to describe same-gender sexual relations. Perhaps the shock of Macdonald's death set off in him a level of self-scrutiny—and self-doubt—he ordinarily skirts; perhaps too the incident shakes his confident sense of invulnerability, causing him briefly to employ the derogatory terminology then current and only beginning to be challenged by the new "science" of sexology being pioneered in Germany by Magnus Hirschfeld and in England by Havelock Ellis and Edward Carpenter.

Roger makes the prudential decision to employ a severely truncated shorthand—a kind of crabbed, telegraphic code—for any diary entry he makes that relates to his sexual activities:

[CAPE VERDE]: "Enormous, stiff and music"

[LIVERPOOL]: "Walk. Medium—but *mu nua ami monene monene beh! beh!* [in the Kikongo language: "in my mouth very big"]

[MADEIRA]: "Augustinho—kissed many times. 4 dollars."

[DUBLIN]: "Enormous. Came, handled and also came."

[LONDON]: "Walked. Dusky—depredator—Huge. Saw 7 in all. Two beauties."

And so on . . . "Saw 7 in all"—that comment will serve as grounds for particular disgust once hostile eyes later read his diary. Yet the meaning of the phrase isn't transparent: "saw" doesn't necessarily equate to "had." Nor can the transient nature of most of Roger's encounters be automatically equated with anonymity; the particular musculature of an arm, the bulge of a thigh, the way the hair is parted on the head—any physical property of a total stranger—can instantaneously trigger an emotional memory or cue an attraction (or revulsion) based on some earlier event barely recalled, if at all, more often than can any polite verbal exchange. It's possible, of course, that Roger did actually have seven orgasms that evening, which could be regarded, depending on one's value set, either as "depravity" or as an enviably prodigious sexual energy.

Roger also starts to keep, intermittently, a second, much fuller diary that, unlike his shorthand erotic journals, expounds expansively and often in great detail on aspects of his public life. This unusual disjunction between two kinds of diary keeping represents not—as sometimes claimed, then and now—a "soul divided" or a schizoid personality but rather a sensible decision, mandated by social convention, to make *some* effort at concealing those aspects of his behavior regarded at the time as transgressive (at best) or "degenerate" (at worst). Of course, Roger need not have kept a sexual diary at all: the surest way to keep his "offensive" behavior secret would be to never write about it, never to run the risk that other, disapproving, eyes might see it.

But the daredevil in Roger overrides his cautionary side. The rebel who defies authority and courts danger is a distinctive element in his private as well as public life. The temperament that allows Roger to challenge public arrangements of power also expresses itself in his challenge to current norms of personal behavior—and all but guarantees that in any contest between defiance and discretion, he will almost certainly choose defiance. The mindset is reminiscent of Gwendolen Fairfax in Oscar Wilde's *The Importance of Being Earnest,* when she brazenly announces, "I never travel without my diary. One should always have something sensational to read in the train."

Roger is finally able to set out for the interior with a file of porters—and his beloved bulldog John—on June 5, 1903. Having briefly been in the Congo interior sixteen years before while serving a youthful apprenticeship, Roger has a personal frame of reference against which he can measure recent changes in local conditions. The changes are profound—beyond anything he anticipated, though he thought himself prepared for the worst.

He reaches the upper Congo by early July and spends the next two and a half months investigating conditions there. Early on, one missionary confides to him that (as Roger writes in his diary) "the rule of the State has swept off the population wholesale." Roger confirms the statement with his own eyes when he arrives at Chumbiri on July 6. It's a village he'd visited on his trip in

1887, when "the settlement contained from 4,000 to 6,000 people." What he finds in 1903—as he'll later describe the scene in his 1904 Congo Report to the Foreign Office—is that most of the villages "are entirely deserted, the forest having grown over the abandoned sites, and the entire community at the present date cannot number more than 500 souls." Sleeping sickness, he discovers, has been a factor in decimating the population; another is flight—to another village, into the forest, or across the border—all to escape the onerous hand of the state.

Carefully interviewing survivors, Roger concludes that those who haven't taken flight have been forced to labor long hours—primarily in hunting for rubber but also in cutting wood to supply government steamers, keeping the undergrowth clear for the government's telegraph line, preparing *kwanga* (cassava root), and carrying the food a considerable distance to the government post. The villagers complain bitterly to Roger about having received no payment—the recognized currency is in brass rods—for a year, or payment only in short rods that undervalue what is owed. Their forced labor, they tell him, has become so exhausting and time consuming that they're unable to plant and weed their own plots of land. If they complain, they're beaten—or killed.

Moving farther north into the interior, Roger stops next at Bolobo. He knows the place from his earlier visit as the thriving center of the Bobangi tribe, remarkable for their skill as traders and hunters. The town's population back in 1887 had been around forty thousand; it's now "not more than 7,000 or 8,000 souls." Where numerous large canoes once plied the river, Roger can locate almost none. The surviving inhabitants, Roger gradually comes to understand, are on call at all times to answer the needs, or whimsies, of state officials. Should the order come to cut wood, hoe and weed, or prepare and serve food, they must comply on the instant or face beatings, imprisonment, or death. One long-standing project that began when Roger earlier visited is still underway: the construction of a wooden pier to enable visitors to disembark. Roger estimates that the Bobangi have already been forced "as a public duty" to cut down some two thousand trees and saplings and carry them a considerable distance to the pier site—for which they have been rewarded with neither food nor pay.

By the third week in July, moving still farther into the interior, Roger arrives at two large villages of the Batende tribe. He discovers that fully half the population are Basengili refugees, skilled blacksmiths and brass workers, who've sought asylum with their friends, the Batende. "Life had become intolerable," Roger writes in his report, "nothing had remained for them at home but to be killed for failure to bring in a certain amount of rubber or to die from starvation or exposure in their attempts to satisfy the demands made upon them." He makes a point of checking on the accuracy of these accounts and all his sources, including a local Baptist missionary, confirm it.

At the town of Mpoko he visits a Basengili blacksmith's shed; the five men in the shed stop working and, with the help of an interpreter, talk to Roger at some length. He asks them why they decided to leave their own villages. One of the men replies, "I am Moyo. These other two beside me are Wankaki and Nkwabali. . . . Each village had to take twenty loads of rubber. These loads were big: they were as big as this." He produces an empty basket that comes up nearly to the handle of Roger's walking stick. "That was the first size. We had to fill that up, but as rubber got scarcer the white man reduced the amount. We had to take these loads in four times a month."

ROGER: "How much pay did you get for this?"

ALL FIVE MEN: "We got no pay! We got nothing!"

MOYO: "Our village got cloth and a little salt, but not the people who did the work. Our chiefs eat up the cloth, the workers get nothing. . . . It used to take ten days to get the twenty baskets of rubber. We were always in the forest, and then when we were late, we were killed. We had to go farther and farther into the forest to find the rubber vines, to go without food, and our women had to give up cultivating the fields and gardens. Then we starved. Wild beasts—the leopards—killed some of us when we were working in the forest, and others got lost or died from exposure and starvation, and we begged the white man to leave us alone, saying we could get no more rubber, but the white men and their soldiers said, 'Go! You are only beasts yourselves, you are *nyama* (meat).' We tried, always going farther into the forest, and when we failed and our rubber was short, the soldiers came to our towns and killed us. Many were shot, some had their ears cut off; others were tied up with ropes around their necks and bodies and taken away. . . . Some white men were good. . . . These ones told us to stay in our homes . . . but after what we had suffered we did not trust more any one's word, and we fled. "

ROGER: "How do you know it was the white men themselves who ordered these cruel things to be done to you? These things may have been done without the white man's knowledge by the black soldiers."

NKWABALI: "The white men mocked the soldiers: 'You kill only women; you cannot kill men. You must prove that you kill men.' So then the soldiers, when they killed us"—here Nkwabali stops and points to the genitals of Roger's bulldog John, asleep at his feet—"then they cut off those things and took them to the white men, who said, 'It is true, you have killed men.'"

ROGER: "You mean to tell me that white men ordered your bodies to be mutilated like that, and those parts of you carried to him?"

ALL THE MEN, SHOUTING: "Yes! Many white men!"

ROGER: "You say this is true? Were many of you so treated after being shot?"

ALL, SHOUTING: *"Nkoto! Nkoto!* (Very many! Very many!)"

Writing up his account that night, Roger concludes that "there was no doubt that these people were not inventing. Their vehemence, their flashing eyes, their excitement, was not simulated. Doubtless they exaggerated the numbers, but they were clearly telling what they knew and loathed."

Roger adds a kind of coda: "Poor frail, self seeking vexed mortality—dust to dust—ashes to ashes—where then are the kindly heart, the pitying thought—together vanished." He elaborates his anguish further in a letter to cousin Gee: "I know not where to turn to, or to whom to make appeal on behalf of these unhappy people whose sufferings I have witnessed and whose wrongs have burnt into my heart. How can they, poor, panic-stricken fugitives, in their own forest homes, turn for justice to their oppressors? The one dreadful, dreary cry that has been ringing in my ears for the last six weeks has been, 'Protect us from our protectors.'"

As Roger proceeds further in his investigation, he does find reason now and then—a missionary's kindness, a black soldier's sympathy—to feel a modicum of restored faith in human nature, but the bulk of the evidence he continues to gather clusters heavily on the side of dismay. The tales are often so horrific that Roger fears Europeans might discount them out of hand as yet another instance of the "childlike exaggerations" typical of the "savage" imagination. When it later comes time to draw up his formal report, Roger will append a number of signed and witnessed affidavits, making sure to include some by "reliable" (i.e., white) missionaries.

He also makes sure to implicate Africans whenever he finds them collaborating with the authorities in enforcing ruthless punishment. Near Lake Mantumba, he comes across a training camp at which eight hundred native troops are being drilled by a European staff to join the notorious Force

Publique—Leopold's personal army, the largest in Central Africa, equipped with rifles, bayonets, and machine guns. All the officers are white, and most of the soldiers black. Ill-paid and ill-fed, flogged for minor infractions, they sometimes resist and run away (one large-scale uprising lasts for three years). But the white officers shrewdly play off existing intertribal hostilities and post black sentries in villages inhabited by their traditional enemies, where—like their white masters—they too sometimes engage in rape and other atrocities, including use of the *chicote,* the whip made of hippo hide that cuts deeply into the flesh.

One such episode involving Africans—it becomes widely known as the "Epondo Case"—involves a young boy of fourteen or fifteen, answering to the name Epondo. Roger comes across him in the Bonginda area; the boy's left arm is wrapped in a dirty rag, and when Roger removes it, he finds the arm has a bullet wound and has been hacked off at the wrist. When Epondo tells him that a sentry has done it, Roger succeeds in finding the man and in front of the chief and headmen of the town, accuses him of the crime:

ROGER (TO EPONDO): "Who cut off your hand?"

EPONDO: "The sentry Kelengo there."
 (Roger calls several of the headmen, and they testify to the same effect. Nearly everyone present, numbering some forty people, shout out that Kelengo is guilty of cutting off Epondo's hand. Roger now calls Kelengo himself to testify.)

ROGER (TO KELENGO): "*Did* you cut off this boy's hand?"

KELENGO: "Kelengo is not my name. I am Mbilu."

ROGER: "Answer the question."

KELENGO: "The people of this place have done bad things to me."

ROGER: "Please confine your answer to the question I asked. We can talk later of other matters. Your refusal to reply 'yes' or 'no' to a direct and simple question leaves me convinced that you cannot deny the charge."

KELENGO: "I know nothing about Epondo's hand being cut off. Perhaps it was the first sentry here before I came, who was a very bad man and cut people's hands off."

ROGER: "How long have you been in this town?"

KELENGO: "Five months."

ROGER: "You are quite sure?"

KELENGO: "Five months."

ROGER: "Do you then know this boy Epondo? Have you seen him before?"

KELENGO: "I do not know him at all."
(The crowd roars with laughter. Several people shout out their mocking praise of Kelengo for his skill in lying.)

KELENGO: "It is finished. I have told you all. I know nothing of it."

Roger finally accepts no for an answer, but he subsequently files a report with the governor general of the Congo Free State, insisting on an investigation. There is no reply. Epondo then recants his testimony, now claiming that a wild animal had bitten off his hand. Roger isn't persuaded. He points out that Epondo also has a gunshot wound; did that too come from a wild animal?

In his notes Roger focuses his indictment not on Kelengo the individual but on the system that spawned him. In the course of his further inquiries he learns of many more cases, besides that of Epondo, of dismemberment—including one youth who had both hands beaten off by a rifle butt against a tree trunk and another who after losing a hand stayed absolutely still on the ground for fear that the soldiers would kill him if they realized he was still alive.

Later, when Roger comes to write up his final report—amply documented with photographs he's taken—one Belgian newspaper will insist that unfortunates like Epondo suffer from cancer of the hands. Another will maintain—declaring it inconceivable that any European would participate in such practices—that severing limbs has long been a customary punishment among African tribes and that Epondo and the others are victims of fellow Africans.

The writer Joseph Conrad will be among those who deride such complacency. More than a dozen years earlier, he'd met and admired Roger when their paths crossed at Matadi; Conrad had then described him in his diary as "most intelligent and very sympathetic." When in 1903 Roger tries to solicit Conrad's public support ("he will, I hope, move his pen when I see him at home"), Conrad replies that he is too busy to get involved in advocacy but adds, "It is an extraordinary thing that the conscience of Europe which seventy years ago has put down the slave trade on humanitarian grounds tolerates the Congo State today. It is as if the moral clock had been put back many hours. . . . The Belgians are worse than the seven plagues of Egypt."

While still in the field gathering evidence, Roger discovers that even when punishment takes less barbaric forms, due process is entirely lacking.

Summary arrest and imprisonment—men are often taken from their homes and never seen again—are the rule. The African prisoner is given no recourse to legal aid, has no trial, and is indefinitely detained rather than sentenced to a fixed period. Some are carted off to a distant government station where, bereft of family and tribal ties, they're subject to hard labor dawn to dusk; others are dragooned into the Force Publique, some to die in a distant part of the country, others to risk desertion and flee into the forest, and still others to discharge their own rage by brutalizing strangers.

Roger insists on asking, and then asking again, what specific law has been broken, what "crime" committed—other than refusing to be a slave laborer—that warrants these capricious proceedings. He scours the penal code of the Congo statute book but finds no legal sanction that the Free State can cite—assuming it cares to bother—to justify its arbitrary policies. If punishments are to be inflicted for infractions of the law, Roger asks, *what* law has been disobeyed? *Where* are fines enumerated for given infractions, or prison terms mandated and their length specified? *Where* does it say that a certain tax is to be levied and that those who fail to pay it must work out their debt deep in the forest, foraging for rubber vines—while their wives are kept as hostages to ensure good behavior?

If, as the state claims, the native population is content—or consists solely of liars and rogues, as the state alternately insists—why are so many armed men needed to keep them in line; why are so many wearing iron neck braces or rope braces that cut deeply into the skin? "You insist that forced labor is necessary to prevent the natives from spending their days in idleness," Roger asks, but why then do the natives tell me they no longer have time to till their fields, to practice their skills in basketry and brass, to build their canoes, to fish in the waters—or to supply their children with sufficient food?

By mid-September 1903 Roger realizes that he's gathered so much damning information to refute the Congo Free State's claim to "benign intent" that further efforts would be redundant. He cables the Foreign Office that he has "convincing evidence of shocking misgovernment and wholesale repression." The point now is to return to Britain, write up a formal report, and let the facts speak for themselves. But facts never do, and Roger is about to discover that what seems irrefutable can be distorted and denied, that governments prefer to ignore what they cannot discredit, and that pious Christian gentlemen can be expert at moral evasion.

· · ·

Roger's first stop when he arrives back in London on November 30, 1903, is the Foreign Office. Passionate about the dire situation in the Congo, he expects a reception that matches his own anxious concern. When the staff response is instead tepid, Roger dismisses the whole lot of them in his diary as a "gang of stupidities in many ways." He has in fact several strong allies in the Foreign Office, in particular the sympathetic Harry Farnall of the West Africa Department. Farnall lets Roger know that his cool reception is partly due to an undersecretary who'd read Roger's heated cables from the Congo interior and announced that "the poor man must have gone off his head."

Farnall arranges a meeting with the disbelieving undersecretary, and Roger has no trouble convincing him of his sanity. Two days later word arrives that Lord Lansdowne, the foreign secretary, will personally receive him. A meeting is quickly arranged, and Lansdowne listens closely to Roger's account of the dire situation in the Congo. When Roger concludes, Lansdowne gratifyingly volunteers his opinion that Roger's evidence is "proof of the most convincing kind" and urges him to write up a formal report immediately.

Roger had begun that task while still en route home; now, having Lansdowne's encouragement if not outright endorsement, he sets to work with single-minded determination. Recently turned thirty-nine, Roger is in good health, fired up for the task, and resolved to bring to it every ounce of his strength. He hires a "typer" to take down dictation and produce clean copy, which Roger then reads over and revises. Working at a furious clip, within a week he accumulates a remarkable fifteen thousand words. He takes only a few breaks, to talk with a reporter from Reuters; to lunch with the influential, left-leaning editor of the *Spectator*, John St. Loe Strachey; and—an event that will have prodigious consequences—to meet the crusading reporter E. D. Morel for the first time.

The year before, Morel had started his own newspaper, *West African Mail*, and Roger, while still overseas, had avidly followed its reports on conditions in the Congo. Like Roger, Morel, as a younger man, had defended European expansion and had even praised King Leopold for his "foresight." At that earlier point in his life Morel had been convinced that what was good for free-trade advocates like his employer, the shipping firm Elder Dempster, was good for Africans as well.

A series of coalescing circumstances intervened that together moved Morel sharply off course: he read Mary Kingsley's *Travels in West Africa* and became her friend shortly before her death in 1900; he studied Elder Dempster's trade reports, puzzling over the large quantity of war materials being shipped to the Congo; he confronted his boss, Sir Alfred Jones, with the mounting rumors of atrocities in the Congo and was still further alarmed when Jones responded to his questions with evasion; he got hold of anti-Leopold materials that humanitarian groups like the Anti-Slavery Society and the Aborigines Protection Society had been producing; he read reports from those few missionaries who had refused to shut their eyes to facts on the ground—and in particular the unflinching accounts from Alice and John Harris of the Balolo Mission, whose horrifying lantern-slide images of atrocities aroused widespread indignation when shown throughout England. When Morel put it all together, he resigned from Elder Dempster and made the decision to wholly devote himself and his journalistic talent to alleviating the plight of the mistreated Africans.

By the time Morel and Casement meet for dinner at the Comedy Club on December 10, 1903, the two men have, by divergent routes, come to a shared conclusion: the Congo Free State is a criminal enterprise quite willing, for profit, to destroy a now helpless race. After hours of animated talk in the restaurant, the two are still so wound up with excitement, so stunned at their empathic connection, that they're unable to part. Morel accompanies Roger back to his rooms, where pages from his report-in-progress are scattered over the floor. Sitting near the fireplace in an otherwise unlighted room, Roger reads aloud in his soft, musical voice from some of the pages, spinning out the awful details of what he's personally seen in the Congo to a stunned Morel. Overcome at intervals with the harrowing images he's evoked, Roger is periodically forced to stop; he paces the room, murmuring "poor people, poor, poor people!" Then he regains his composure and continues to read.

"I can *see* them," Morel says at one point, when Roger has stopped reading, "hunted women clutching their children, flying panic-stricken into the bush . . . the quivering black bodies as the whip draws blood . . . the hands . . . the severed hands . . ." Morel, overcome, puts his hands to his face. "What are we to do, Casement? . . . What is there to *do*?"

"You've already done a great deal," Roger gently says. "And there are other sympathetic souls out there. . . . I believe it, I do. . . . Your articles have found an audience. And hopefully my report will—"

"It will tear aside the veil, of that I have no doubt. Leopold's infamy will be revealed for all to see. When do you think . . . when might you finish?"

"Soon I hope . . . within a week or so. Whether the Foreign Office will embrace my report and release it publicly, I can't predict. . . . There's opposition, that I know."

"You can't count on the missionaries for support . . . a few, maybe, like the Harrises. But most are afraid to speak out."

"I've made some strong friends among them. They helped me . . . transportation, shelter, introduced me to witnesses. . . ."

"Never forget, Casement, that they have one prime concern: conversion. Take Harry Guinness at Balolo . . . he says he favors reform, yet will do nothing to jeopardize his evangelical mission. . . . He's even spoken of Leopold's 'philanthropy'!"

"Guinness is doing some good, despite his—"

"All that organ music and hymns! I don't trust him for a minute. He views the current plight of Africans as nothing compared with their eternal salvation—or whatever he calls it. It sets my teeth on edge!"

"Well now, Morel . . ." Roger's tone is wry. "So we don't agree about *everything!*" He laughs. "We're conjoined, but not quite twins!"

"Don't tell me you're a religious fanatic?!" Morel's voice rings with astonishment.

"Fanatic, no. As regards our campaign, human rights are the only item on the agenda."

"I'm relieved to hear it. The missionary crowd wants reform only insofar as it facilitates conversion . . . cultural conversion too. I won't have it!"

Roger's voice is emphatic: "What we share is outrage over the devastation in Africa—and a determination to expose and end it. . . . Our bond is of steel."

On a personal level, the two men have taken unreservedly to each other. "The man is honest as day," Roger later writes in his journal. Morel, for his part, describes the meeting as "one of those rare incidents in life which leave behind them an imperishable impression. I saw before me a man of strongly marked features . . . graven with power and withal of great gentleness. An extraordinarily handsome and arresting face. From the moment our hands gripped and our eyes met, mutual trust and confidence were bred and the feeling of isolation slipped from me like a mantle. Here was a man indeed."

Roger completes a draft of his consular report on December 25, 1903, and before making final edits sends it for comment to Harry Farnall—who he's come to realize is a firm ally—in the Foreign Office. Farnall reads it at once, suggests a few minor changes, and tells Roger that "it could not be better, admirable both in style and substance." With Farnall's approval under his belt, Roger makes a few last-minute modifications and then, on December 28, sends off the report to the Foreign Office. He's satisfied that it's an airtight case, every assertion in the report backed with documentation and the tone throughout judicious, avoiding any hint of theatrical overstatement—to which Roger knows he is sometimes prone. As he confidently awaits official reaction, he goes back to Ireland to visit relatives and friends—and on the way stops off to see Morel again and to meet his wife; the two men again talk far into the night.

Roger also makes up for an extended period of drought in his sex life. His last encounter—itself the first in many months—had taken place back in late September, just before embarking for England, with an adult African man named Richard Koffee. Roger had spotted him months earlier, thought him unusually attractive and perhaps available, and upon returning from his trip to the interior had sought him out. He hired Koffee to do some errands for him, then engaged him in conversation; in response to Roger's explicit question, Koffee had replied—as Roger recorded in his diary—"'Yes . . . a big one and I swear God Sir'—and then bed at last."

Meanwhile, King Leopard hasn't been idle. Fearing that Casement's report is due for imminent release, he tries to preempt it. A supremely clever manipulator, Leopold shrewdly announces that the policies of the Congo Free State are entirely in line with those of the other colonial powers. The "vacant land" argument, he points out—accurately—has been used by the Germans in East Africa and the French in Angola. As for the labor question, Leopold asks, what of the British use of indentured Chinese—slavery in all but name—to work in the Transvaal after the close of the Boer War? Or, for that matter, the known fact that the chocolate magnate William Cadbury—a major supporter of Morel and Casement—has purchased large amounts of cocoa grown on the Portuguese slave plantations of São Tomé and Príncipe?

Nothing in the policies of the Congo Free State, Leopold further asserts— less accurately—has favored its own commercial interests over free competition with other governments. Moreover, he claims, the state's benevolent intentions toward the native population is exemplified by his success in having destroyed the Afro-Arab slave trade in the Congo. Yes, Leopold acknowledges, violence has sometimes occurred, and that is most unfortunate; yet physical force has characterized all colonial regimes and is sometimes necessary to maintain law and order, as well as to hold irresponsible Africans—who after all are only children—to steady work. Leopold makes the further claim—entirely inaccurate—that those few members of his Force Publique who have overstepped the bounds have all been native African soldiers; henceforth, Leopold announces, he will see to it that their white overseers hold them to stricter account.

After reading Roger's report, an uneasy Lord Lansdowne seeks advice from his predecessor, Lord Salisbury, as to the advisability of showing it to Leopold prior to publication. Salisbury tells him it's a terrible idea. In his view Leopold would attempt to strike some bargain—would promise reforms in exchange for Lansdowne burying the report, though as always with his "pledges" Leopold would soon renege. Besides, Salisbury adds, the situation in the Congo *is* "appalling" and should be exposed. He does suggest, and Roger initially agrees, that actual names be omitted from the report to avoid "the possibility that those wretched blacks will be still worse used in consequence."

Roger himself had come to that conclusion out of the belief that the "system" rather than individuals bore basic responsibility for the atrocities. Yet he soon changes his mind about naming names, deciding that abuses will be less likely to continue if individuals are singled out for their crimes—thereby scaring off other potential malefactors. He lets the Foreign Office know about his change of heart, yet when his report appears on February 15, 1904, initials have throughout been substituted for names—a decision tantamount to protecting the guilty.

To compound what Roger considers a fundamental mistake, the Foreign Office has also changed the names of agents, tribes, and villages, making it all but impossible to protect those abused and to punish the abusers. Instead of inducing tears, the report as it now stands—"N. N. and R. fought, and they killed several R. people and one R. man. O. O. O. took a man and sent him to L. L. L."—will be just as likely to produce giggles.

Furious, Roger protests to his Foreign Office ally Harry Farnall that the omission of names robs his report of much of its value and notes that in addition the printed version puts certain words in his mouth that he'd either spoken back in the 1890s, or not at all. Should Leopold and his defenders get wind of these inaccuracies, Roger angrily argues, they could righteously proclaim that the entire document is a tissue of lies. "It is disheartening, in more senses than one," he writes Farnall, "and it renders my position in regard to the Foreign Office a somewhat difficult one. I am not clear what my course should be, but it would seem that my resignation is called for. I cannot well continue to serve a Department which has so little confidence in me, and so little regard for my opinion." Eric Barrington of the Foreign Office assures him that no one wishes him to resign—"I never heard of such a thing"—and Roger somewhat simmers down.

If Leopold and his allies do pick up on items either laughable or inaccurate, they choose to ignore them in favor of mounting a much broader defense. Leopold announces that Casement's two-month tour through the Upper Congo was far too short a time to gain any real understanding of conditions. He further argues that the natives, realizing that Casement was their champion, let their imaginations run wild—and everyone knows that savages are fantasists—playing him for the fool. Besides, Leopold asks, what do Casement's charges amount to? He's noted real phenomena—depopulation and mutilation—but assigns exactly the wrong explanations for each. The depopulation is due to a ferocious epidemic of sleeping sickness, and the mutilations are intertribal, inflicted by victor over vanquished.

Leopold adds that the boy Epondo, the only case that doesn't fit the pattern, has "confessed" that a wild boar, not a state sentry, had taken off his hand. That last makes Roger grimly laugh: "The only question I should suggest to the boar," he tells Farnall, "is where he got his gun from." Roger has by then learned from a missionary that Epondo's retraction resulted from an overt threat against his life. Besides, Roger points out, the Epondo Case that Leopold is making so much of is hardly the sole instance cited in the report of severed hands, ears—and even genitals. The Foreign Office's own Congo Atrocities File contains many additional instances, and Roger now urges Lord Lansdowne to release them.

Lansdowne refuses. He claims that the cases in the file contain mostly hearsay evidence not formally attested to—which Roger calls a "deliberate lie." He feels the Foreign Office, instead of backing him up with additional evidence, is allowing the impression to take root that he's unfairly sought out and falsely highlighted what were in fact isolated episodes. Lansdowne, Roger fears, is afflicted with a paralytic loss of nerve; "the Foreign Office method of conducting the controversy with Leopold," Roger writes Farnall, consists "largely of running away from their own charges and offering apologies for my report."

At stake is not simply his own reputation but the possibility that his report will be discounted and the mistreatment of the African population will go unchecked. He's well aware that British diplomacy remains centrally focused on Europe and as regards Africa, its colonial interests congregate in the southern and eastern parts of the continent, not in the Congo. Roger innocently yearns for a foreign policy based on morality, not power and profit, and in his frustration sweepingly denounces the entire Foreign Office as a "wretched set of incompetent noodles." Having become pessimistic about prospects for reform in the Congo and uncertain about continuing in the consular service, Roger feels at loose ends, a spectator where he's recently been an active mover and shaker.

His Congo Report does produce a flood of petitions to the Foreign Office and also an inconclusive debate in the House of Commons. But press coverage is minimal, with the all-important London *Times* settling for a few cursory columns. Roger becomes convinced that without a more aroused public opinion to pressure the government, the Foreign Office will continue to procrastinate. To create such pressure, he proposes to Morel that they establish a Congo Reform Association, with Morel at its head and with himself— barred as an employee of the Foreign Office from active political engagement—helping from the sidelines.

Morel agrees to the proposition, and Roger throws himself into a sustained effort to enlist such influential figures (and friends) as the Irish peers Lord Ennismore and Lord ffrench. He also successfully solicits support from Alice Stopford Green, widow of the historian J. R. Green and herself a scholar of distinction; she will become one of Roger's closest and lifelong friends. Alice Green is as well a figure of growing consequence in the burgeoning movement of Irish nationalism, and Roger has himself by 1903 drawn the implicit and damning parallel of England's occupation of Ireland with Leopold's appropriation of the "vacant" land of the Congo.

The Congo Reform Association (CRA) soon comes to absorb most of Roger's attention. Its first public meeting is held at Liverpool on March 23, 1904, draws a large crowd, and resolves that its central task will be to "secure for the natives inhabiting the Congo State territories . . . just and humane treatment . . . by the restoration of their rights in land, and in the produce of the soil, of which preexisting rights they have been deprived by the legislation and procedure of the Congo State."

The initial launch is adjudged a huge success, and at subsequent meetings during that first year gatherings of two to three thousand become commonplace. Donations also pour in, especially from—a possible warning sign— British firms trading with West Africa. It makes some of the reformers uneasy, concerned that vested interests might gain control of the CRA and turn it into an instrument of empire. There's also the ongoing problem for Roger of having to make a living; though currently on extended leave, he officially remains a member of the consular service and that necessitates keeping a low public profile and confining most of his CRA work to providing Morel with documentary materials and bolstering his sometimes sagging spirits. For a time Roger mulls over the possibility of requesting another post in the Congo but soon realizes that he's now a marked man and that Leopold would have him closely watched—if not killed. Reluctant for now to request any other post, he continues to delay a return to active duty.

Morel proves a whirlwind of energy. The more prominent he becomes, the more witnesses appear who've previously been silent, including an increasing number of missionaries who send belated but invaluable testimony against the Congo Free State. Like Morel, Roger receives a torrent of new material and excerpts some of it for publication in the CRA's journal. The material cumulatively reveals substantially more about Leopold's Congo than previously known (Morel collects much of the testimony in a book, *Red Rubber*, which he publishes in 1904; in the next five years it will go through six editions.) The new evidence reveals beyond question that contrary to Leopold's pledge that "no indulgence will be shown towards any officials who may participate in blamable acts towards the natives," the Congo Free State is itself engaging in barbarous behavior unrivaled since the "exploits" of the Spanish *conquisitadores* in the West Indies.

Crucially, Morel is able to challenge the standard claims that Leopold's defenders have made regarding the "redeeming" features of his "philanthropic" rule, namely, that he's built railways, put up a telegraph line, placed steamers on the Upper Congo, and constructed a number of "fine stations." He has also—as the handpicked "Commission of Enquiry" Leopold had appointed alleged—"suppressed the liquor traffic" and the Arab slave trade, which are the "finest title to glory which the Congo State possesses." As one wit says during a debate on the Congo in the House of Lords, Leopold's claims to the beneficent effects of his rule seem to secure "such beatitude in this life and such a quasi-certitude of salvation in the next" that "some of your Lordships on leaving this House might almost be disposed to take a ticket immediately for the Congo."

Morel dissects Leopold's purported "accomplishments" with precision and undisguised pleasure. He acknowledges that some of the claims made for the Congo Free State are "partly true" but insists that even if entirely true they wouldn't "palliate, much less excuse the wrong-doing of the past fifteen years." To begin with, Morel argues, under previous Arab influence "the freedom of organised native communities was not interfered with," and the decades of Arab domination coincided with "some of the most prosperous in Central Africa." The slave-trading Arab may have been ruthless—but he was a "coloniser": he had permanent interests in the land and in agricultural production, creating "huge centres of economical activity"; he did not, like

Leopold, lay waste to the country. Besides, Morel argues, despite Leopold's claim of having suppressed Arab slavery, it continues to flourish west of Tanganyika. As for Leopold's boast of destroying the liquor trade, Morel quotes another expert on the Congo: "It is perfectly true that the Congo State does not pay the natives with a drink of brandy: it does not pay them at all."

Nor have the enormous profits from the ivory and rubber trades, Morel argues, benefited Africans in any way. A telegraph line? The natives have neither need nor access; their sole relationship to the telegraph is the onerous obligation of keeping the roads to it clear—decreed as a "tax" rather than a job for pay. The steamships running on the Upper Congo? The natives "use" them when being forcibly transported as laborers to areas far from their homes; they also know the ships as the hungry consumers of wood that they must continuously provide. The "fine stations"? The substantial buildings found in Boma and Matadi were erected with slave labor, as was the railway, a splendid engineering feat used to facilitate the plunder of native land— hardly a benefit to the indigenous people.

In *Red Rubber* Morel invites his readers to take an *accurate* tour with him through Leopold's Congo:

"Mingle with the people of the land. Witness their abiding desolation, their daily griefs. Wander among ruined homes and poverty-stricken hamlets, where once flourished prosperity and ease. Look how the grass almost conceals the village paths once so clear and clean; weeds overhanging the new crumbling huts; sud invading the river frontage once filled with cassava steeping pits—that sud where the mosquito and the tsetse love to breed, the purveyors respectively of malaria and sleeping sickness, whose dread ravages sweep increasingly through the land, finding ready victims in a broken-spirit and ill-nourished people. . . . Where are the native industries which once gave pleasure and occupation to these people—iron-ware, brass-ware, rude pottery, basket-making? They have 'decayed'—as everything worth preservation has decayed and withered beneath the breath of Leopoldian civilisation."

Where, Morel rhetorically asks, can Africans go to seek redress? The Congo courts have never published any record of cases involving atrocities, suggesting that few, if any, have ever been brought. How could they be when the governor general has formally reminded his agents that they're entitled to exercise "bodily constraint" on the natives, and should not concern themselves with the legality or illegality of specific acts? Additionally, every agent is required to furnish in writing the list of prisoners taken that month—not to guard against overzealousness but to ensure that recalcitrant natives are being held to account.

As much as Roger agrees with Morel's searing indictment—his own substantial contribution to the pile of evidence amounts to silent coauthorship—two items in *Red Rubber* strike him as misguided. One is Morel's censure of Irish nationalists who, he believes, tend to side with Leopold, England's adversary, out of hatred for Britain. Roger, oppositely, feels certain that his strong Irish nationalism is what has primarily sensitized him to autocratic prerogatives—and made him (and every other Irish patriot he knows) Leopold's obdurate foe.

Then there is the remark Morel makes in one of *Red Rubber*'s footnotes: "Sodomy, publicly forced upon chiefs or influential head-men whom it was necessary to humiliate in the eyes of their people has been resorted to in certain territories at the point of the sentry's gun. The practice is unknown among the natives." Roger himself, of course, is an active sodomite, and one who cohabits now and then with willing Africans. In regard to both matters, he's tempted to challenge Morel but decides that maintaining unity during the Congo struggle takes obvious precedence over issues relating to personal privilege.

Roger is now something of a public figure. The publication of his report, despite the Foreign Office having weakened it through unauthorized editing, has led to mounting controversy, forcing Leopold's begrudging agreement to appoint yet another Commission of Enquiry, this one composed of an Italian lawyer, a Swiss jurist, and the chair of the Belgian Court of Appeals. Many, including Roger, feel the commission has already prejudged the issues at stake; it will go through the motions but will in the end exonerate Leopold and repudiate Casement's report. The commission, Roger tells a friend, has been put together by Constantine Phillips, the British ambassador to Belgium and one of Leopold's cronies, along with Francis Villiers, who heads up the pro-Leopold clique in the Foreign Office. It will end, Roger predicts, with a "touching reconciliation between Leopold and Lansdowne—who will kiss again with tears." Roger—and Leopold—are in for a surprise. But the report is some months off.

In the meanwhile, the Foreign Office remains Roger's boss, as well as his sole source of income, and his funds have all but run out. When the FO offers him the consular job in Lisbon, a prestigious posting and a decided step-up in the diplomatic hierarchy, Roger decides he has no choice but to accept it, though it will remove him for some unspecified time from the Congo struggle.

He arrives in Lisbon in the summer of 1904 but hates the place on sight—
"I *do not like Lisbon at all!*" he writes to cousin Gee—and promptly falls ill.
By early fall, after only a few months on the job, he's back in London, once
again on leave. Two medical procedures become necessary, one for appendi-
citis and the other for a recurring anal fistula. The two surgeries are done
together and on January 5, 1905, Roger writes Gee that he will be recuperat-
ing in Belfast at the home of one of his new Irish nationalist friends, Francis
Joseph Bigger.

Bigger is the well-to-do Belfast lawyer and bachelor antiquarian who lives
with his mother in Ardrigh (a spacious home with a large library), edits the
Ulster Journal of Archaeology, and seems to know everyone of consequence in
nationalist circles. He holds regular gatherings that often include Alice
Stopford Green and the two young firebrands Bulmer Hobson—who though
twenty years Casement's junior will become a close associate—and Denis
McCullough, a Catholic radical and Bigger's favorite (some eyebrows *are*
raised) among the young nationalists. Bigger himself would today probably
be regarded as a celibate (or closeted) homosexual.

One of the young nationalists Roger meets at Ardrigh later describes him
in 1905 as looking like a "buccaneer of the Spanish Main. . . . He speaks in
low musical, kindly tones without a trace of arrogance, though with a great
deal of self-consciousness." It's a suggestive description, since a combination
of camouflage and hyperalertness have long been central components of a
homosexual sensibility, especially when under siege.

Francis Bigger has by 1905, when Roger becomes his guest, taken a leading
position in the "Irish Ireland" cultural movement that emerges in the early
years of the century as an alternative outlet for the expression of Irish nationalism after others have stalled or become moribund. The passage in Parliament
in 1903 of the Land Purchase Act—which, after decades of fierce agitation,
finally creates a pathway for tenants to become owners—has led to a period
of quiescence in Irish politics. Discontent with British rule shifts its focus
from political agitation to cultural affirmation—to a form of nationalism
that focuses on restoring and preserving Ireland's Gaelic heritage.

The Fenians—the secret Irish Republican Brotherhood—are also in
decline during these years. Having spearheaded armed resistance to British
rule throughout the nineteenth century, the IRB has faded in influence
in Ireland, though it's alive and well in the United States under the name
Clan-na-Gael and the leadership of John Devoy. The Fenians both in Ireland
and the United States stand in direct opposition to the Irish Parliamentary

Party, which advocates Home Rule *within* the British Empire. With the death of its leader, Charles Stewart Parnell, in 1891 and the subsequent failure of Gladstone's Home Rule Bill two years later, the issue of Home Rule has been shunted to the sidelines; Roger, for one, regards the Irish MPs as men who "have lost their souls."

His own position regarding Irish independence is in a state of transition. At this point in his life he's neither a Home Ruler content to remain within Great Britain's orbit nor a Fenian demanding total independence (and through an armed uprising if necessary). Though brought up a Protestant, Roger has scant sympathy for the insistence of Ireland's Protestant-dominated county of Ulster on continued union with Great Britain; he regards the unionists as parochial, anti-Catholic bigots. Leery of the Home Rule alternative as an insufficient expression of Ireland's unique-ness, Roger's not yet, in the early years of the century, fully committed to total separation from Britain. The advent of an Irish Ireland cultural renais-sance provides him for a time with a promising alternative and outlet for nationalist pride—"all the old hopes and longings of my boyhood spring to life again"—while he sorts through the available political options.

All the while, Roger continues strenuously to support Morel—the two stay in constant touch—and the work of the Congo Reform Association. For a time, though, his developing enthusiasm for all things Gaelic (and enthusi-asm is Roger's middle name) absorbs some of his energy. He becomes favora-bly disposed toward the Gaelic Athletic Association (founded in 1884 to cultivate national sports, like hurling) and feels especially at home in the Gaelic League, which is devoted to preserving and strengthening the native language and Irish folkways in general. Roger captures the essence of what "swells his Irish heart" in a letter to Alice Stopford Green: it is "something more than race; more than nationality; more than any reason I have yet seen put forward. There is something in the soil, in the air, in the inherited mind of a country that is as real, nay more real than the rocks, the hills and the streams. No historian defines this thing, yet it exists in all lands."

The Gaelic League issues assorted publications, runs campaigns for teach-ing Irish in the schools, and sponsors music, drama, and poetry festivals. The Belfast branch of the league—one of six hundred affiliates—is among the most active. In the nearby glens of Antrim, where part of the Casement clan has long resided, Roger joins in the first *feis* (festival) of Irishness, organized by his friend Francis Bigger in 1904. Roger cheerfully takes part in dancing four-handed reels, and he and his sister, Nina, serve as judges in a contest for "distinctive Irish clothing" (like the long-sleeved tunic and belt or the tight-fitting *truis* on the leg). He also devotes himself to the study of the Irish language and encourages cousin Gee—who will soon surpass him in literacy—to do likewise. Elsewhere, more substantively perhaps, William Butler Yeats and Lady Gregory found the Irish National Theatre, which soon evolves into the world-famous Abbey.

Such manifestations of a cultural and literary renaissance are dismissed by committed Home Rulers on the one side and the remnants of Fenian separatism on the other as trivial pastimes that divert true patriots from doing much-needed political work. Though an easy target for mockery, Roger centrally allies himself with the cultural movement for the better part of two years. Perhaps sensitized by his own sexuality, he's aware at some gut level that the assertion of "differentness" can itself contribute powerfully to political consciousness. He feels that the more awake the Irish become of the extent of their cultural separateness from the English—and the *value* of that distinctiveness—the more susceptible they'll be to a politics that demands political independence. This isn't a fully conscious position for him in 1905; rather, the importance of stressing Ireland's cultural singularity works beneath the skin. No one at the time, with a very few maverick exceptions (Edward Carpenter, say, or Havelock Ellis), is making a comparable case for the need to openly assert the valuable distinctiveness of sexual differentness.

The influential journalist Arthur Griffith is among those who mock the Gaelic League. He does so in the name of asserting that true nationalism relates to "rights, arms, freedom, franchises and brotherhood," not "singing and lute-playing," nor "mystic prose and thrice mystic poesy." At this point—and despite his occasional mention of "arms"—Griffith is no revolutionary; he enunciates a strategy of passive, nonviolent resistance that at the time still appeals to Roger. But he continues over the next few years to have conflicted feelings about the enigmatic Griffith. Roger admires his trenchant, sometimes strident, prose; his passionate devotion to Ireland; and his staunch anti-imperialism, but deplores his shadowy anti-Semitism, his lack of sympathy for labor militancy and socialism, and his eccentric insistence periodically on a "dual-monarchy" solution for Ireland (a notion that infuriates old-style Fenian separatists). By 1906, however, Roger has become sympathetic to Griffith's proposal that the time is ripe "for the Irish to organize a massive campaign of non-cooperation with Britain."

That summer Roger coauthors with Alice Stopford Green and the young nationalist Bulmer Hobson an "anti-recruitment" pamphlet, *Irishmen and the English Army,* which argues flat out that "any Irishman joining the English Army, Navy or Police forces ... is a traitor to his country and an enemy to his people." These are strong words for a man who himself remains in government service, and Roger comes in for considerable criticism for his "hypocrisy."

Yet the pamphlet's words don't in fact represent a settled militancy on Roger's part. In 1906 his politics remain insecurely moored—torn between Fenian separatism and the nonviolent solution of Home Rule. His allegiance in flux, Roger would have felt more discomfort still had he known that the mastermind behind the anti-recruitment pamphlet he'd put his name to was the old Fenian John Devoy and his American Clan-na-Gael—an organization that has long viewed Britain as the great Satan, Ireland's unwavering enemy. In any case, the majority of people in Ireland in 1906, far from being sympathetic to violent revolution, aren't even much interested in the Gaelic cultural revival—caught up as they are in surviving the harsh realities of daily life.

A piece of startling news brings Roger back to the Congo question. King Leopold's second Commission of Enquiry—which Roger had expected to be little more than a whitewash—actually takes its mandate seriously, revisits the Congo sites mentioned in his report, and talks to many of the same witnesses and missionaries. The result is a scathing denunciation of misrule and cruelty that in all essential ways vindicates Roger's 1904 report—and reenergizes the Congo Reform Association, which of late has been drifting, its funding drying up, its membership rolls static (though Morel has managed to enlist the crucial support of William Cadbury, the Quaker cocoa king, as well as St. Loe Strachey of the *Spectator*).

The commission's report is leaked to the press prior to official publication, and another round of large protest meetings follows, with the trade-union movement lending significant support for the first time. The meetings, in turn, lead to the multiplication of CRA auxiliaries and a new burst of recruits and energy for the anti-Leopold forces. Roger, along with Morel (now known to each other, respectively, as "Tiger" and "Bulldog"), try to remain cautious in their optimism. They've developed a healthy respect for Leopold's wily capacity for manipulation and aren't surprised when he arranges for the press to receive a "summary" version of the commission's report as a "courtesy" designed to relieve the reporters from the tedious task of reading through the full-length version. Roger immediately sees the "summary" for what it is: "a series of half-truths, each followed by its qualifying untruth."

Yet the press grabs at the time-saving summary, swallowing whole its endemic distortions. The *Times* commentary is typical: Leopold, it editorializes, has "on more than one occasion [made known] his desire that the whole truth, and nothing but the truth, should be told. It is significant that he's appended to the report a Royal proclamation nominating a ['yet another,' the *Times* might have added] Commission to carry out the report's recommendations. This is ... evidence of the King's desire to remove any stigma resting on his work in Africa."

Lord Lansdowne is relieved at the excuse for continued inaction. His chief concern these days is not the Congo—it has never been the Congo—but rather the conflict between France and Germany over Morocco; the threat of a European conflagration takes a far higher priority than providing succor to ignorant, probably unsalvageable, "savages." Lansdowne appoints a new ambassador to Brussels, Sir Arthur Hardinge, who promptly expresses contempt for humanitarians as "always prone to sentimentalism about slavery and other local customs to which the native populations are attached." Roger tells Morel that Lansdowne is "honest but weak and not very capable"; their only real hope for change in the Congo, Roger feels, is a victory for the Liberal Party at the polls in the upcoming 1906 general election.

Lansdowne may be weak, but he can also be an adroit tactician. Roger is stunned—and unhappy—to receive notification that His Majesty has appointed him a commander of the Order of Saint Michael and Saint George (traditionally given to people in foreign service who've performed with high merit). More incensed than flattered, Roger writes a friend, "I'm sick! Why on earth these things can be done without a man's consent I don't know; it's quite childish; like giving a poor baby a name at the font it cannot resist or discard."

Bulmer Hobson happens to be with Roger when word of the appointment arrives, and he tells Hobson that he's going to refuse it. Though at this point a more fiery nationalist than Roger, Hobson points out that refusal is tantamount to a rejection of the foreign service and thus the equivalent of a resignation. What will Roger do for income, not to mention a pension? He's always lived frugally, giving away a significant portion of his salary (when the CRA first started he donated a hundred pounds, one-third of his annual salary at the time). Yet even Roger needs *some* income, especially since his two older brothers, Charlie and Tom, continue to flounder in their assorted efforts at careers and keep turning to him for assistance.

Knowing all that, Roger still hesitates in accepting the appointment; it would mean, he tells Hobson, that in nationalist circles—the ones he now cares about most—he'll henceforth be regarded as at best a trimmer, at worst a traitor. Hobson presses him to tread cautiously, and Roger promises that he won't reject the award out of hand but will take time to mull the matter over.

As part of his "mulling" process, Roger writes to William Tyrrell, a fellow Irishman and his staunchest ally in the Foreign Office (he suspects Tyrrell urged his name for the appointment). He thanks him for his kindness but reminds him that for some time he's been openly critical of Lansdowne's irresolution in holding Leopold to account. Besides, he tells Tyrrell, "I've oft uttered contempt (that's a nasty word—but I fear it expresses literally my feeling) for distinctions and honours and principalities and powers. . . . I dislike these things profoundly" and would have felt "far happier to have been spared."

His unhappiness is genuine. Here is the Foreign Office offering him a prestigious honor while failing to offer him a consular post! And he's made it clear to Lansdowne that he needs one—that he's recovered in health, is in financial straits, and is once more available to return to service. Yet the Foreign Office hasn't responded. Sir Eric Barrington, Lord Lansdowne's private secretary, lets Tyrrell know that Roger's hasty retreat from the Lisbon assignment is viewed as an affront; the Foreign Office considers Casement a "beggar who wishes to be a chooser."

In his heart Roger has irrevocably distanced himself from the British Crown, but his pocketbook is another matter. Now past forty, his options are limited. He hasn't the talent to fulfill his earlier dream of becoming a writer (he once tried to get a collection of his conventionally sentimental poetry published but was politely discouraged). And there are no listings in the employment ads for full-time human-rights agitators—Morel is one of the few who's managed such a life, though he lives on the margin and even so has to supplement his income through journalism. "If I could get anything to do *at all,* Roger writes Morel, "I would never give the Foreign Office another thought; but nobody seems to want to employ an out-of-work Consul." The bottom line is that Roger can't afford to resign from the foreign service. And that means he can't reject out of hand the CMG appointment (known in the civil service as the "Call Me God" appointment).

He finally hits on a palatable compromise: he writes a formal letter conveying to the king his "dutiful regard and gratitude" but claiming that ill health prevents him from receiving the CMG in person on the date specified. Unhelpfully, the officer at arms, as a special favor, reschedules the investiture for a later date. Roger again demurs, again pleading poor health. When the prospect looms of yet a third date being named, he asks if the appointment can be made by post. It's a cheeky request—and a measure, too, of Roger's desperate wish to avoid literally bending the knee and being tapped on the shoulder by Britain's reigning sovereign. Surprisingly, a parcel containing the CMG ensigns does arrive by mail. Roger never breaks the seal.

That problem resolved—somewhat comically—Roger still has to secure a new consular position. For a year and a half he's been in a kind of limbo, having neither resigned nor been reassigned. The protracted stalemate is finally broken after the Liberals win a sweeping victory in the 1906 election and a new government assumes office. Sir Edward Grey, who's publicly spoken out in support of the Congo reform movement, becomes head of the Foreign Office (and Roger's ally, William Tyrrell, becomes his private secretary). Grey lets it be known that he would "like very much to see" Casement back in the service. An offer arrives: the consulship at Bilbao in Spain, soon followed by a proposed alternative: Santos in Brazil. The latter pays somewhat more, and Roger opts for it to ensure, as he tells Alice Green, "I would have money to spare for Ireland . . . to finance one or two small Irishisms of my own."

It soon becomes clear that Sir Edward Grey will disappoint those hoping for a reinvigorated stance regarding the Congo. When King Leopold issues with fanfare new "reform" degrees, Grey welcomes the excuse to stick with a "wait-and-see" policy—which amounts to doing nothing of a proactive nature to abate the criminal excesses that continue to characterize conditions in the Congo Free State. Roger is disappointed in Grey, and not deceived by Leopold's latest promises of reform. So long as Leopold remains in control of the Free State, Roger predicts, nothing will change. The British public, like Grey, chooses to believe otherwise. Morel is soon reporting to Roger that the Congo Reform Association is once again in extremis.

Departing for Santos on September 21, 1906, Roger writes cousin Gee, "I am a queer sort of British Consul," one who "ought really to be in jail instead of under the Lion and Unicorn. I must say, Gee, I *can't* stand Anglo-Saxons or Imperialists." To keep abreast of events at home, Roger subscribes to only one newspaper while in Santos—not the London *Times* but *Sinn Féin* ("We Ourselves," symbolizing self-reliance), Arthur Griffith's renamed *United Irishman*. Griffith has moved to the position that the British Parliament will never grant self-rule to Ireland, and he urges "self-reliance" instead; a coalition of organizations will form the Sinn Féin League late in 1907. Roger will read Griffith's paper faithfully and through its pages further sharpen his already keen interest in Irish history—focusing specifically on the subjection of Ireland since the union of 1800 with England. The more he learns, the more his conviction deepens that Ireland has been harmed, not helped, by its association with Britain—and the more firmly he places himself on the side of separation.

. . .

Even before landing at Santos, Roger feels a desperate longing for the Ireland he's left behind, along with considerable discomfort over the anomalous position he continues to find himself in. His profound sympathy for the underdog, the ill-treated, the subordinate—fed in part by his own secret status as a despised homosexual outsider—stands at odds with his titled role as a British functionary. Here he is on his way to serve the Crown in yet another official capacity, even as his bitterness against its policies mounts. He's in the unnatural position of having to execute instructions from the Foreign Office while deploring its arrogant sense of entitlement to dictate to others. He's the drummer in a parade he longs to see disbanded.

As Roger tries to resolve the contradictions inherent in his position, he—presciently—hits on the notion (as he writes a friend) of the British Empire becoming a "great Commonwealth of free states . . . bound together by love and interest and *fellow feeling,* not kept chained to heel." The result would be, Roger concludes "a far closer Union, and a real one." Yet he doubts that such a commonwealth can come to pass—the reason being that "it is hard to discuss these things with an Englishman, because . . . he inevitably thinks he is conferring an enormous benefit in 'anglicizing' a people or a country." Roger feels that his suggested formula will break apart on the rock of English vainglory and hauteur.

For the time being he remains caught in the same vice of contradictions that has often gripped social reformers: how to justify remaining a functioning cog in a system one finds morally repellent? Unlike many others, Roger isn't a man who can live easily with contradictions. He's too impetuous, too eager for the clear-cut solution, to tolerate indefinitely the world's everyday muddle. Periodically over the past three or four years, he's been on the verge of cutting the Gordian knot and permanently resigning from service to the Crown. But then the question of how he can survive—let alone continue to send money to those who rely on him—always blocks the clean resolve he favors.

No sooner does Roger disembark in Santos than he decides—just as with Lisbon earlier—that the place is intolerable. Literally within an hour of arriving on October 9, 1906, Roger is writing cousin Gee of his dismay—and his determination to get out as soon as possible. The "consulate" turns out to be a single rented room in a warehouse, and his living quarters a seedy hotel outside the city. Roger isn't being unreasonably grumpy about Santos. Thirty-eight years earlier the extraordinary polymath Sir Richard Burton—who, unlike Roger, was a devout imperialist—had filled the consular post at Santos, and the place had driven him into a deep depression. "The climate is beastly, the people fluffy," his wife, Isabel, had written her mother; "the stinks, the vermin, the food, the niggers are all of a piece." Her husband had added his own racist summary: "I do not hold the black to be equal to the white man."

Roger has chosen Santos over Bilbao because of the higher salary, but that proves illusory; he hasn't counted on how expensive the place would be—Santos is a major center for the coffee trade—and he learns to his horror that at the current exchange rate a pound is in fact the equivalent of seven shillings. He discovers just as quickly that he doesn't care for the people. The port is full of drunken sailors—a mark of opportunity, one might think, for those whose sexual appetite is (like Roger's) keenest when flecked with danger—but he dislikes the "half-caste" look of the populace and even more its affectations of manners and fashion; the people act, he feels, as if Santos is Paris. To make matters worse, he soon realizes that his official duties are monotonous and trivial. After a few months of trying to make the best of it, he concludes that Brazil "is the least interesting country in the world," and Santos the most "futile and absurd post he'd ever heard of, or read of, or dreamed of."

And that's exactly what he tells his superiors in the Foreign Office. Santos, he writes Sir Edward Grey, "is quite the nastiest place I've ever been in." He longs for Ireland—or Africa, where the people, despite all their sufferings, are "happy-hearted and bright-faced." He finds Brazilians, by contrast, money-mad, unsmiling, and bent on commerce to the exclusion of all else. "I don't like it here *at all, at all,*" he bluntly tells the Foreign Office, and he requests immediate reassignment. Instead, he's granted leave for most of the summer of 1907 and, after landing back in London in late July, he quickly departs for Ireland. On the way he stops off in Liverpool to visit the Bannister clan, and after greetings all around he and cousin Gee slip away for a long walk, circling past the trio of new buildings on Pier Head and settling down by the Mersey for a long catch-up on each other's lives.

"Africa," Roger tells her, "is the only place for me—if it can't be Ireland. Did I tell you I made my formal letterhead in Santos 'Consulate of Great Britain and *Ireland*'?"

Gertrude gasps with delight. "You *didn't!* Keep this up, Roger Casement, and you'll be out of a job again before you know it!"

"Wouldn't that be fine!"

"It certainly would for me. No more having to clip every mention of Ireland or the Congo and ship off the packets to you! You've made me near much of a pauper as you are!"

"The stuff you sent on the devolution offer almost put me in the hospital!"

"They think we're fools. 'Give the Micks a little more local control, and they'll be kissing our boots with gratitude.'"

"Home Rule is a bad enough compromise, but Home Rule *by installments?!* What a gracious offer!—'take some of Dublin Castle's more mundane functions off our hands, and we'll keep all the important stuff like law making and tax raising in our own!' Wouldn't you know, the Irish Party's John Redmond would grab at the deal. That man, mark me, will be our ruin."

"Griffith calls the devolution offer an insult. He's the coming man, don't you think?"

Turning more somber, Roger lowers his voice. "In truth, Gee, there's plenty of Irish who'd gladly bow the knee. For a hundred years England's been juggling the soul out of our body into its own, then left us a corpse on the dissecting table. Don't I know it myself? My Irishness dozing on all those years, almost unsuspected by myself? We have to create a governing mind again. . . . That's the ticket. . . . That's what I like about Griffith."

"He writes a fair prose too—has me laughing out loud at times."

"But he's not much for the Gaelic League. He could at least support the teaching of Irish in our schools."

"Redmond's Irish Party supports the teaching of Gaelic—if *that's* what you're after."

"The Irish Party indeed! I tell you, old girl, the Irish members of Parliament are so English, they're like a bunch of hounds leading the hunt! Leave it to the Irish Party, and we'll be attending Anglican High Mass tomorrow!"

They both laugh, and then Roger tells her that he's "off to Donegal in the morning. I'll stop for a few days at Ardrigh to see Bigger."

"Is he still busy with the neophytes?"

Roger hears the trace of sarcasm in her tone but sidesteps it. "Those youth encampments do keep him busy. He loves them with all the fervor of adolescence."

Gertrude smiles. "Isn't he the big boy himself?"

"He does good work, Gee. He's turning those lads into purebred nationalists."

Gertrude looks skeptical. "Nationalists living in medieval tents and dressing up in doublets? I know the man's done more than anyone to preserve our history, but designing costumes for teenage boys seems a bit silly, no?"

Roger is determinedly noncommittal. "He's an ardent fellow. A bit foolish sometimes, perhaps."

"I hear tell he's become a *motorist!*" Gertrude makes it sound like the most outlandish thing imaginable, as if Bigger has rocketed off to the moon.

Roger laughs. "Yes, that too. He's too corpulent now for a bicycle. Has some young fellow chauffeuring him around."

"A handsome young fellow, I presume." Gertrude's a bit startled at her own daring.

So is Roger, who works it out obliquely: "I hear a car full of them goes bouncing over the countryside, singing Irish ballads, Bigger in his saffron kilt. The man knows how to enjoy himself."

Gertrude visibly suppresses her disapproval. After a pause she heads into more neutral territory. "Is it Bigger who told you about Cloghaneely?"

"It is indeed. He says the Irish school there is first-rate."

"Have you made up your mind about it, then?"

"I'll give it a try. It's only for three weeks, and I'm way behind on my Irish studies. I know more French than I do Irish."

"And after that?"

"I still don't know. Morel thinks I'll get the Rio job. But he predicted that before, and I ended up in the hell of Santos."

"What do you make of Leopold's 'Royal Letter'? I would have thought the five-day debate in the Belgium parliament about annexing his 'property' in the Congo would have produced something more tactful."

"What can I say? The man's a malignant genius at manipulating public opinion. No sooner does it looks as if Belgium is turning against him and leaning toward annexation, and he announces yet another Congo reform package—which just happens to include the declaration that *his* personal ownership over the Congo can be shared with no one! Which puts us back to square one. And Sir Edward Grey is still 'waiting-and-seeing.'"

Gertrude shakes her head sadly. "How does Morel keep his spirits up, poor man?"

"'Bulldog'—that's Morel. Works sixteen to eighteen hours a day. Has written—if you can believe this—more than 3,500 letters just in the first half of 1906! Compared to him I'm just am angry little terrier, one that keeps disappearing overseas. The nonconformist ministers are keeping the CRA auxiliaries alive. But Morel isn't happy with their prominence. Nor am I."

"John and Alice Harris have certainly caught the public's eye. I've never seen their slides, but I'm told they're most effective."

"They are. Which is part of the problem. Morel fears the whole Congo campaign is going to take on a religious character."

"Is that so bad? Isn't Morel a God-fearing man?"

"No, he isn't. And I believe he's right in worrying about too much missionary influence."

"How can that be harmful?"

Roger smiles warmly at her. "Because, dear Gee, evangelicals care first, second, and fiftieth about one thing—conversion. They don't give two hoots for human rights or the preservation of African culture. 'Let Leopold's rule continue forever—so long as *we* remain free to preach Christianity!'"

"Let us hope that Belgium goes through with annexation," Gee rather forlornly throws in.

"Morel agrees with me that Leopold *will* capitulate and agree to annexation. But we're not convinced that will mark any real change. Annexation alone, without human-rights guarantees for Africans, will simply mean more of the same. Africa will develop not on native lines, as should be, but on European ones. We'll have to fight as hard against Belgium as we have against Leopold."

Gertrude looks so dispirited that Roger quickly shifts to a more cheerful tone: "It's all right, Gee. Morel's not giving up. Nor am I. I wish I could resign from foreign service altogether and be here steadily to support him. Come September and they'll ship me off again. I wish I knew where."

"Have you had no word?"

"My friend Tyrrell at the Foreign Office has hinted at Haiti. I should like that. I hear the living conditions are good, and not expensive. *Anything* but a return to Santos."

Haiti is not to be, through no fault of Roger's. Told that he'll be promoted to consul general for Haiti and San Domingo, one of the six top-ranked posts in the consular service, he turns down an offer he's finally been able to land for a nongovernmental, well-paying job in East Africa and accepts instead the Foreign Office post. But when he arrives in London to receive his instructions, the rug is pulled out from under him. He's told that a wounded veteran of the Boer War (and an old Etonian—i.e., "one of us") has expressed interest in the Haiti posting; the Foreign Office feels sure Roger would wish to give way to such a deserving patriot. They appeal to "my good nature to step aside," he writes Gee—"as if I have a choice."

The Foreign Office's idea of atonement is to let Roger know that whenever the consul general position in Rio becomes vacant—"probably some time next year"—he will be first in line. In response, Roger tells them that *nothing* would induce him to go back to Brazil; they can give the Rio spot to anyone they please. "I have told them pretty frankly," he writes Gee, "what I think of them, their methods, and their Consular so-called 'Service.' It is no service at all, but only robbery and corruption, and an enormous fraud on the public."

The Foreign Office is unfamiliar with outspoken independence and doesn't take to it kindly. Roger is presented with a straightforward ultimatum: either return to Brazil or leave the service. Merciful Albion does offer a choice: Santos or—Para. *Where?* Roger locates a former consul at Para—present-day Belem—and asks him about the place. "A hideous nightmare" is the reply. Can he say more? Well, Para's at the mouth of the Amazon on the Atlantic coast, with a population above a hundred thousand, and a rainy season that lasts without letup from January to June. Does it at least have a hotel? Yes, is the answer, "a superior sort of cow-shed called the Grand Hotel da Paz." And the cost of living—is it as modest as Haiti, where I could have saved half my salary? "Hardly. Prices are so high that most people wear dark clothes to avoid having to clean them often."

Roger is trapped and knows it. With Santos unthinkable, he either agrees to Para or leaves the service and again begins the long hunt for alternative work. "The truth is," he writes his old friend Richard Morten, "when one gets past 40 it is very hard to get anything decent to do." Bitter over his treatment, he swallows hard and accepts Para. At least he manages to get his home leave extended by a few months, and he returns to Ireland for long good-byes, including two weeks with his divorced sister, Nina, on the coast north of Dublin. He also gets an advance on his salary and sends money (as often before) to his brother Tom, who's been unable to make a go of it in South Africa. Worried, too, about the young activist Bulmer Hobson's employment prospects, Roger gives him the handsome sum of fifty pounds—while encouraging Francis Bigger to raise additional money to keep afloat Hobson's weekly newspaper devoted to the new Sinn Féin movement for an independent Ireland.

Roger arrives at Para, some ninety miles upriver from the coast, early in 1908. Initially, to his own considerable surprise, he finds the city more attractive than anticipated, an agreeable improvement over Santos. There are parks; one of South America's largest theaters, the Teatro do Paz; lively, bustling traffic on the streets; a trolleybus service; and some broad avenues lined with palm trees. For a dozen years, in fact, Para has been a major center for the booming rubber trade—though the boom will in a few years turn into a bust as the new plantations of the Far East begin to make wild rubber sources obsolete.

Roger's initial impression of Para soon darkens. He quickly discovers that the streets—that is, the paved ones—don't extend very far, petering out into mud puddles or swampy underbrush. The weather is foul, the rain incessant, the prices extravagant—and the state of the consulate deplorable. The files are in a state of complete disarray, commercial, personal, and official material bizarrely intermingled. And most of the office furniture is missing; apparently his predecessor sold it off to make ends meet—for which Roger feels considerable sympathy.

And then there are the people. . . . Para's elite consists of a motley international crowd of rogues, adventurers, and speculators who on striking it rich—as a fair number do—indulge in the kind of sleazy, grandiose display that Roger has always scorned, built as it is on the broken backs of Irish peasants or Brazilian Indians. Roger's distaste for Brazilians is long-standing, but in Para antipathy becomes outright revulsion. It's so pronounced that he includes it in his very *un*diplomatic dispatches: "The Brazilian," he writes the Foreign Office, "is the most arrogant, insolent and pig-headed brute in the world. Pleasure, amusement, social life, companionship all are wanting in Brazil—in a city of close on one million people I am far more alone in this sham, pretentious copy of civilization (without any of the reality) than I was away up the Congo. The Congo's naked natives were far nicer people, sincere and real, than these *overdressed,* vain, empty minded humbugs with their extraordinary vanity and arrogance."

In denouncing a large group of people on the basis of his experience with a small handful of them, Roger risks sounding like the racist he isn't—not, that is, when compared with the kneejerk bigotry of most of his white contemporaries. Back in 1901, when he was a junior consul in Lourenco Marques, he'd mounted a vigorous defense in dispatches to the Foreign Office of a local

Jewish merchant he felt was being unfairly attacked. And it was the behavior of Leopold and his minions that he labeled "savage and barbarous"—not the gentle, affectionate black people of the Congo. "What has civilization been to them?" Roger writes Morel. "A thing of horror—of smoking rifles and pillaged homes—of murdered fathers, violated mothers and enslaved children."

Even in Para, though consumed with his own unhappiness, Roger continues to remain in steady contact with Morel and to maintain his active concern with the ongoing plight of the Congolese, a "gentler humanity." By 1908 affiliates of the Congo Reform Association exist in a number of countries, including France, Norway, and Germany. As pressure for annexation increases—it will finally pass the Belgian parliament in August 1908—the cunning Leopold mounts a last-ditch campaign to avoid it. He instructs his aides to explore abuses of power in British Africa, and they have no trouble turning up enough of them to allow Leopold to advise the "hypocritical" English reformers to "clean up their own backyards." Further, Leopold commissions several books that itemize and applaud his "beneficent" rule and bribes a number of newspaper reporters to turn out stories claiming that Morel and Casement have largely fabricated their findings.

Morel, energetic and implacable, continues to lead the charge for *black* self-rule, but endemic European racism continues to work against it. As far back as 1890, the black American missionary George Washington Williams—who Mary Kingsley had so much admired—called for self-government in the Congo. Yet in 1908 Morel and Roger are among the few reformers—the black evangelist William Sheppard is another—who share the view that the land must be returned to the Congolese to use, economically and politically, as *they* see fit. The racist colonial mentality that assumes the natural superiority of the white race and the incapacity of the black race for self-governance dominates *both* sides of the Congo debate—with many "humanitarians" sharing the Leopoldian position that without compulsion black people would never work at all.

Given that reigning view, self-government is never treated as a viable political option, and Morel and Roger reluctantly shift their energy to arguing that the halfway proposal of annexation *must* include strong guarantees that Congolese human rights will be protected. But when Leopold finally does agree to relinquish his personal rule of the Congo in 1908—in return for a huge financial settlement—the transfer to Belgium marks no change at all in the oppressive conditions that have long been in place. Morel,

Casement, and other humanitarian reformers urge the British Foreign Office to press Belgium on the need for reforms, and for a time Secretary Grey does withhold recognition. But he doesn't insistently push the matter. Temporizing is Grey's characteristic stance, and the British government does little more than threaten occasionally to send out a gunboat or to stop paying duties—neither of which it ever does.

From his post overseas Roger, worried about Morel's precarious finances more than about his own, organizes a campaign to raise money for the Morel family. "My hope," Roger writes their wealthy Congo supporter, William Cadbury, "is that we may raise £10,000 to £15,000 possibly and with this sum . . . invested for the wife and children, the besetting fear and dread that weigh on his mind may be removed forever, and his whole personality released for greater good and more work for Africa, or elsewhere where such a fearless soul as his is needed." Roger presses the campaign vigorously, and though the results fall far short of his hopes, he does succeed in raising several thousand pounds for the Morels. On receiving the money, Mrs. Mary Morel calls Roger a "magician" and sends him the family's gratitude: "You will never know what your natural generosity of mind, and your unfailing sympathy, are to the Bulldog."

On his part Morel secures a remarkable number of prominent signatories for a protest letter to the *Times,* including a number of peers, newspaper editors, bishops—and no fewer than seventy-six members of Parliament. Arthur Conan Doyle, already a CRA supporter, not only signs the letter but publishes a book—*The Crime of the Congo*—warning that the Belgians seem likely to ignore the need for reform (in the book Doyle goes out of his way to praise Roger as "a man of the highest character, truthful, unselfish—one who is deeply respected by all who know him").

When King Leopold dies from cancer late in 1909, his son Alfred accedes to the throne and promises a new era of reform. For once Sir Edward Grey acts boldly: he promptly announces British recognition of Belgium's sovereignty over the Congo—too promptly, it turns out. Alfred is not as good as his word, though the public, confusing an announcement with a result, is lulled into believing that the issue is now resolved. Morel and Casement persist in arguing for the ultimate goal of returning the land to the Congolese people, but in vain. In this—and in regard as well to the protest they unsuccessfully mount against England's decision in 1909 to set up the Union of South Africa with a whites-only legislature—Morel and Casement are miles ahead of their contemporaries.

Discouragement comes from yet another quarter: some of the missionaries start to issue exaggerated reports about improved conditions in the Congo, thereby confirming Morel's long-standing distrust of religious involvement in the Reform Association. What the "improvement" actually consists of, Morel writes Roger, is the Belgian government's offer of new missionary stations for carrying out conversion campaigns. Otherwise, there has been no improvement. Morel has ample evidence that the number of atrocities still being committed in the Congo hasn't diminished at all, and he accuses the organization of British Missionary Societies of capitulation to Belgium on the basis of vague promises alone and before it has actually done anything to correct the endemic cruelties. The missionaries brush off Morel's criticism. As they have long since made clear, human rights and the preservation of African culture are not among their top priorities. The expansion of Christianity, as Morel reports to Roger, continues to take precedence over all else—with no quid pro quo asked or given for effective reform. By the close of 1909, membership and financial contributions to the Congo Reform Association have once again seriously declined.

Morel's reports do nothing to lighten Roger's misery in Para. Within weeks of arriving he decides that he *must* get away. "It rains here daily," he writes Bulmer Hobson, "and I am suffering horrors, I can assure you—in every way." He makes up his mind that "even with the loss of a pension, I should prefer immediate retirement from the Foreign Service." Within months after taking up his post, Roger comes down with a case of gastroenteritis so severe that he's bedridden for a month. On doctor's orders he's sent on leave to Barbados to recuperate. He finds it a "ghastly little Britannic Island," filled with either "princes or paupers." His health scarcely improves. "I have shrunk to a shadow," he writes Hobson, "and neither eat, sleep nor walk but lie on my back all day." Granted leave, he returns to England for further convalescence.

PART 3

The Putumayo

WHILE ROGER LIES FEVERISHLY ILL IN ENGLAND, entirely unbeknownst to him, two young Americans, Walter Hardenburg and Walter Perkins, both of whom have been working as engineers on the construction of the Colombian Pacific Railroad, confidently head off for an adventuresome journey into a region of the Amazon Valley disputed between Colombia and Peru and known as the Putumayo. The trip proves far more prolonged and perilous than they'd bargained for.

After a number of hair-raising episodes—from devouring gnats to suicidal rapids—the two arrive at the Colombian rubber station at La Reserva. Perkins goes off to see to repairs on their canoe, and Hardenburg meets with the station head, David Serrano, an agreeable, middle-aged man who tells him that as a result of Peruvian invasions, La Reserva is one of only three rubber stations that remain in Colombian hands. He also warns Hardenburg that the agents of the Peruvian Amazon Rubber Company treat the Huitotos, the local aboriginal tribe, "very harshly"; if the Indians do not bring in the specified amount of rubber, they're "flogged, shot, or mutilated." "Do the Colombians also engage in such practices?" Hardenburg asks. "They do not," Serrano firmly replies.

When Hardenburg suggests that perhaps Peruvian brutality is confined to just a few renegade employees, Serrano recounts his own recent experiences. He tells Hardenburg a jarring tale of how, just a few weeks before, agents of the Peruvian company had invaded La Reserva to collect a small sum of money that Serrano owed the manager—"a notorious brute, Miguel Loayza"—of the El Encanto branch of the company. They chained Serrano to a tree, ransacked his stock, and dragged off his screaming wife and young son. Hardenburg is horrified and asks if he can help in any way. No, Serrano tells him, he's appealed to the Colombian authorities and at this very moment is awaiting the arrival of a police inspector.

In the meantime Hardenburg, with the instincts of an anthropologist, spends considerable time getting to know the Huitotos and exploring their culture—and he keeps meticulous notes about his impressions: "The Huitotos are a well-formed race, and although small are stout and strong.... Their hair, long and abundant, is black and coarse, and is worn long by both sexes.... These Indians are humble and hospitable to a marked degree.... They [are] always cheerful, willing, and reliable. They call Serrano their father, and, indeed, treat him as such.... The houses of these aborigines are generally large and circular in form, covered with a well-woven thatch roof, capable of lasting for years, made from the leaves of the *yarina* or vegetable-ivory tree.... [They sleep] in light *chambira*-palm fibre hammocks...but the unfortunates employed by the Peruvian Amazon Company are worked so hard by their taskmasters that the great part of them are obliged to sleep on the ground, on account of not having time to make their hammocks.... Those Huitotos enslaved by the 'civilising company' are so constantly employed in the extraction of rubber, the only food they get—omitting the extremely meagre and irregular supplies furnished by the Company, which are not worthy of consideration—is the small quantity of *yucas* and plantains that their women have time to cultivate, and a few products of the forest, such as certain large worms they extract from the bark of different trees, the tender tops of the *chonta*-palm, a few wild fruits, etc. The result is that many die of starvation.... A custom very general not only among the Huitotos but also among many of the 'whites' is the use of the coca ... a powerful stimulant, and the Huitotos when out in the forest collecting rubber find it very useful, especially as they often have to carry the rubber they gather several leagues on their backs with practically no food at all to sustain them.... The numbers of these Indians are diminishing to an alarming degree and, unless something be done to protect them, this noble race of aborigines will, in my opinion, soon disappear completely, as have so many others in the region of the Upper Amazon."

The Huitotos have amply confirmed for Hardenburg the account Serrano had earlier given him. When police inspector Orjuela arrives, he suggests that a "good, friendly, man-to-man talk" with Loayza, the Peruvian agent, will set all to rights. Hardenburg shares Serrano's skepticism; yet for want of options, Serrano decides to put himself in the inspector's hands. Loayza's headquarters is agreed on as the rendezvous point for a meeting, and Hardenburg and

Orjuela set off together on a steamer for the long trip down the Putumayo River, leaving Serrano to clear up a few business matters before joining them.

Partway into the journey a Peruvian river gunboat fires on the steamer, barely missing Hardenburg's head, and then takes crew and passengers prisoner. They're kicked, beaten, insulted—and forced to watch the rape of a Colombian woman who'd also been on board. To Hardenburg's astonishment, he finds his friend Walter Perkins among the other prisoners. Perkins recounts the story of his recent capture at a nearby Colombian station—and the horrors he witnessed as the Peruvians murdered the employees, stole everything in sight, and then burned down what remained. Hardenburg is stunned to learn that among the twenty-eight killed was David Serrano.

Miguel Loayza appears the next morning, learns that Hardenburg and Perkins are Americans, and orders them—"as protection from the Colombians"—transferred to another Peruvian vessel, the *Liberal;* police inspector Orjuela is locked up in a small cage. The tough-minded Hardenburg, convinced that he and Perkins will be killed, decides to brazen it out. He tells Loayza that they're employees of a "huge American syndicate" sent out to open a "large mercantile establishment" in Iquitos; should they fail to arrive, their employer will instantly investigate and, given the syndicate's great influence, will demand that the U.S. government intervene.

Loayza reacts with gratifying alarm and says he'll send them to Iquitos in a few days on the *Liberal;* in the interim he allows them, under guard, freedom of movement. Though still uncertain of his fate, Hardenburg distracts himself by investigating the condition of the Indians he sees loading and unloading the vessels that pull into port. He describes them in his notes as "practically naked, their bones all but protruding through their skins, staggering under their heavy loads, fed at most once a day with a handful of *farina* and a tin of sardines—and all branded with the infamous *marca de Arana*" (the mark of Julio César Arana, head of the Peruvian Amazon Rubber Company). Hardenburg also comes across a terrified group of a dozen young girls ranging in age from nine to sixteen due for shipment to El Encanto (where Loayza is superintendent) to serve as concubines for Peruvian agents. Hardenburg sees one Peruvian *comisario* openly dragging off a small Huitoto girl of seven to sell as a "servant."

The two Americans arrive safely in Iquitos, where Hardenburg—alarmed at what he has seen and heard—decides to conduct a number of eyewitness interviews to add to his own knowledge of the region. Reviewing the evidence, he comes to an unequivocal conclusion: "This state of affairs is intolerable ... a living hell—a place where unbridled cruelty and its twin-brother, lust, run riot, with consequences too horrible to put down in writing. It is a blot on civilisation. ... Why is it not stopped?"

The question becomes still more haunting when Hardenburg meets an intrepid journalist in Iquitos, Benjamin Saldana Rocca, a Peruvian Jew and committed socialist, and learns that since the summer of 1907 he's been publishing articles in his newspaper, *La Sanción,* exposing conditions in the Amazon—even daring to name Julio Arana and to directly indict the Peruvian Amazon Rubber Company. Saldana Rocca's valiant efforts lead not to an official investigation but to threats on his life. Forced to flee to Lima, he instructs his son to turn over all the material he's gathered to Walter Hardenburg.

Adding Saldana Rocca's eyewitness accounts to his own interviews, Hardenburg combs through the material and prepares a series of articles that will ultimately appear as an explosive pamphlet titled *The Putumayo: The Devil's Paradise.* He's well aware of Roger's parallel experiences in the Congo and keeps his 1904 report at his side as a model and guidepost. Hearing rumors that Julio Arana has him in his sights, Hardenburg decides to finish his work in a safer climate and leaves for England in June 1909.

Roger, meanwhile, has recovered from his bout with gastroenteritis and is trying unsuccessfully to resuscitate the private-sector job he'd earlier turned down when told—falsely, it had turned out—that he'd be appointed consul general in Haiti. He's surprised when the Foreign Office in December 1908 belatedly comes through with the offer of consul general in Rio de Janeiro, and Roger's financial straits force him to eat his earlier words about *never* returning to Brazil. He accepts the position—one of the most desirable in the service—and arrives in Rio in March, 1909, just a few months before Hardenburg returns to England.

As if physically allergic to Brazil, Roger responds to Rio with an immediate attack of high fever. He recovers quickly, but his impression of the country doesn't improve; within a week he's writing cousin Gee, "I hate Brazil." He does acknowledge that Rio is a cut above Para; much of the consulate's routine work is done by vice-consuls, and the climate is pleasanter—especially after he starts to commute, like many of the region's diplomats, to the mountain resort of Petrópolis, seventy miles from the capital. But the upgrade doesn't improve his mood, and the boring routine of his duties further feeds his discontent. He characterizes the Rio consulate as a "hot stuffy office in a noisy tropical street," and in September his discontent overflows in a letter to Gee: "Brazilian life is the most perverted, comfortless and dreary of any in the world . . . the people uninteresting, pretentious shams beyond conception."

That same month of September 1909, Walter Hardenburg publishes in the influential weekly, *Truth,* his first article: "The Devil's Paradise: A British-Owned Congo." A week after the article appears, *Truth*'s editor, Sidney Paternoster, receives a letter from the London headquarters of the Peruvian Amazon Rubber Company, denying all its allegations: "The Directors have no reason to believe that the atrocities referred to have in fact taken place, and indeed have grounds for considering that they have been purposely mis-stated for indirect objects. Whatever the facts, however, may be, the Board of this Company are under no responsibility for them, as they were not in office at the times of the alleged occurrences."

In response, Hardenburg, with Paternoster's strong support, publishes the full names and affiliations of the seven members of the Amazon company's board, along with a brief history of its operations. "Of these seven directors," Hardenburg writes, "at least two"—the Peruvians Julio César Arana and his brother-in-law Abel Alarco—are not only "well aware of the state of affairs in their 'possessions,' but actually encourage the atrocities." The other five directors, Hardenburg points out, are Englishmen who "are either dupes who have been taken in by the slick tongues" of Arana and Alarco and "are not aware of the awful and appalling crimes committed in their names by their employees," or else they are "hardened ruffians, deliberately pocketing the products of slavery, torture, and crime."

To support his charges, Hardenburg has gotten signed affidavits from ex-employees of the Peruvian company, prints them in *Truth,* and summarizes their content: the company, Hardenburg writes, "works the natives day and night at the extraction of rubber, without the slightest remuneration . . . gives them nothing to eat . . . robs them of their crops, their women, and their children . . . sells these people at wholesale and retail in Iquitos . . . flogs them inhumanly, until their bones are visible . . . gives them no medical treatment, but lets them die, eaten up by maggots, or to serve as food for the chiefs' dogs . . . cuts them to pieces with *machetes* . . . grasps children by the feet and dash their heads against walls and trees . . . have the old folks killed when they can work no longer and, finally, to amuse themselves, to practise shoot-ing or to celebrate the *sábado de gloria,* they discharge their weapons at men, women, and children, or, in preference to this, they souse them with kerosene and set fire to them to enjoy their desperate agony." Such instances of extreme savagery, Hardenburg insists, are not occasional excesses but endemic to the system.

Truth has a considerable readership of some twenty thousand, and its influence is broader still. It continues to run Hardenburg's articles through November 1909, and in their train charges and countercharges proliferate. When questions are raised in Parliament, the government's sole response is to express entire ignorance of the company and its activities—which, as *Truth* emphasizes, should itself be something of a source of embarrassment, since the Peruvian Amazon Company is registered in Britain. Some two hundred black Barbadians, moreover, are said to be employed by the company as overseers—and Barbados is under the British flag. Does it not follow, asks one MP, that the British government has the right, nay the duty, to investigate conditions in the Putumayo?

The right, perhaps, reports David Cazes—who serves in a semiofficial capacity and at a tiny salary as the British consul in Iquitos—but not the necessity. Cazes has lived in the Putumayo for some years yet has never once reported a word to the Foreign Office concerning the mistreatment of the Indians—for the good reason, he now assures the Foreign Office, that the allegations published in *Truth* are wild exaggerations. He insists that the Putumayo Indians have, in his experience, been well treated and the company attentive to their needs. As for reports that the company employs Barbadian overseers, Cazes implies that they are no longer in the area. One fact that he fails to mention is that his own chief source of income derives not from being the part-time British consul but from the rubber trade.

Unlike Cazes, others who know the Putumayo step forward to back up the veracity of Hardenburg's reporting in *Truth*. The most forceful among them is Capt. Thomas Whiffen, scion of a wealthy English family and a veteran of the Boer War, who sends a blistering series of letters to the Foreign Office in 1909, confirming in detail Hardenburg's gruesome articles in *Truth*. He gives, as one representative account, the boast made to him by the head of the Abisinia rubber station, Abelardo Aguero, "that no female—child or woman—is ever allowed to pass his door," unmolested, that is. Whiffen himself had to rescue a little Indian girl of eight or nine, whom Aguero had already violated, and return her to her tribe. In apologizing to Roger for the delay in sending him a copy of Whiffen's letters, a staff member of the Foreign Office explains that they were "of too indecent a nature to send to our female typewriters, so I had to copy them myself."

While Roger studies the material, the Foreign Office inquires of the governor of Barbados whether "negroes still work for the Peruvian Company." "No," the answer comes back, "they haven't for some three or four years." The Foreign Office seems relieved at the news: it decides that any further inquiry on its part might be viewed by Peru, and perhaps Colombia too, as "interference in their internal affairs." But whether as a result of ignorance or malfeasance, the governor of Barbados is soon proven wrong. Louis Mallet, an undersecretary at the Foreign Office, takes it on himself to interview Whiffen and discovers that the captain omitted from his account the fact that several dozen British West Indians, including Barbadians, are still indentured to the company—some of them "practically slaves" due to their accumulated indebtedness—and that the Peruvians use them as "enforcers."

Mallet recommends that a letter of inquiry be sent directly to the Peruvian Amazon Company in London, a suggestion Sir Edward Grey adopts. "It is clearly highly discreditable," the letter reads in part, "as your Board will doubtless admit, that a British Company should be in any way responsible for the present disgraceful state of affairs, the existence of which there is unfortunately no reason to doubt." In responding, the company denies any knowledge of so-called atrocities and accuses both Hardenburg and Whiffen of being blackmailers; Julio Arana includes a personal affidavit claiming that the two men have come forward because he earlier rejected their attempts to extract money from him. Arana further denies "absolutely . . . that lawlessness has of late existed in the Putumayo Region."

Unfortunately for Arana, another eyewitness now steps forward: John Brown, Captain Whiffen's guide during his trip to the Putumayo. Brown fully confirms not only the endemic ill-treatment of the Huitotos but the active presence of Barbadians, whose contracts have expired and who want to leave but are trapped by indebtedness. Here is exactly the justification the Foreign Office needs to press forward—yet still it hesitates. The (now combined) Anti-Slavery and Aborigines' Protection Society sends letter after letter to the Foreign Office, demanding that something be done, and additional questions in Parliament add to the pressure. Yet it will take until spring 1910 before the sluggish Foreign Office is finally driven to a proactive position.

In the interim Roger, still in Rio, closely follows events—in regard both to the Putumayo and to developments in Ireland. The reports from the Amazon seem to him the Congo all over again, though perhaps in more depraved form still. As for Ireland, he keeps up through regular correspondence with such close friends as Alice Green and Bulmer Hobson. He hails Alice's 1908 historical work, *The Making of Ireland and Her Undoing*, with its emphasis on the vitality and richness of the Irish past, as an immense contribution to present-day Irish nationalism. To Hobson (and others as well), he sends money he can ill afford.

Roger's political views have by this point consolidated and will not waver again: he no longer feels *any* attraction to Home Rule and instead favors Ireland's full independence from Britain. When the general election in January 1910 results in giving the Irish Parliamentary Party (IPP) the balance of power in the Commons, with the "deplorable" (Roger's word) Home Ruler John Redmond at the IPP's head, Roger is underwhelmed. Nor is he pleased that the hotheaded Hobson is openly speaking out against the leadership of Arthur Griffith; Roger is at best a lukewarm fan of Griffith—he deplores his "narrowness" as exactly the quality "we cannot stand in our far too narrow Ireland"—but believes a unified opposition to England is essential.

Amid his political activities, Roger, now in his midforties, manages to find time to satisfy his ample sexual needs. In January 1910, for the first time in seven years, he starts a new diary and in it he dutifully—there's a mild obsessive-compulsive thread in Roger's personality—records his robust round of amorous adventures in Rio. He makes only occasional entries and writes in his usual erotic shorthand: for the month of January there are only five entries relating to sexual encounters and for February but two—though the pace quickens thereafter. All the entries that relate to sex continue to be abbreviated, bare-bones summaries, like this one for February 28: "*Deep Screw and to hilt . . . Mario* in Rio . . . Lovely, young—18 and glorious . . . Perfectly huge." An enthusiast in all things, Roger is often rapturously transported by his pickups (most of whom he pays, with most of the sex taking place outdoors, often in known cruising spots): "Splendid *testemunhos* [testicles in Portuguese]—soft as silk and big and full of life"; "Perfectly huge. *'Nunca veio maior! Nunca!'* [Never seen bigger! Never!]."

Occasionally, Roger arranges for repeat engagements. In this regard, "Ramón"—who he first meets in March 1910 while vacationing in Buenos Aires—is a standout. Roger sees him some fourteen times over a three-week period and in his diary waxes eloquent over his "splendid erections." He takes Ramón out for meals, to visit the zoo and clubs, and to walk in the gardens of Palermo. When it comes time to part, Roger writes of the leave-taking sadly, even sentimentally, in his diary: "Saw last time at Belgrano. Never again." After returning to Rio, Roger writes to Ramón several times.

Later that same year, when on leave in Belfast, Roger meets a bank clerk in his midtwenties—Joseph Millar Gordon—with whom he continues to have intermittent contact over the next few years. And there will be a few other Ramóns—that is, casual contacts that evolve into mini-romances. But Roger's dominant pattern will remain casual, semi-anonymous sex—reminiscent somehow of the predominant fantasy Masters and Johnson will discover some seventy years later in the heterosexual men they study, namely, being "taken" by "groups of unidentified women." It's a suggestive finding: Roger's multiple orgasms with multiple partners may represent how most people would behave sexually, at least when young, if freed from the constrictions of middle-class morality that glibly equate frequent sexual contacts with an incapacity for intimacy. If one defines "intimacy," as most people do, as "close, warm, caring, long-term relationships," Roger's capacity is irrefutable—though in his case, the relationships revolve around nonsexual friendships with a few relatives (like Gee Bannister) and a few friends (like Richard Morten, Herbert Ward, and Alice Green).

In June 1910 the Peruvian Amazon Company finally bows to mounting pressure and agrees to appoint a commission to go to the Putumayo and investigate conditions. The commission's mandate is cleverly broadened to include "the exploration of possibilities of commercial development"— thereby providing a built-in excuse for any member of the commission who prefers *not* to focus on the treatment of the Indians. The company chooses Reginald Bertie, younger brother of the British ambassador to France, to head the group. The other four appointees are Henry Gielgud, the Amazon company's own secretary; Louis Barnes, a specialist in tropical agriculture; Walter Fox, knowledgeable about rubber plants and affiliated with the Royal Botanical Gardens; and Seymour Bell, an economist. It's agreed that the British Foreign Office will be allowed to name one of its consuls to accompany the delegation—but with his jurisdiction specifically confined to investigating the status of subjects of the Crown, namely, the unknown number of Barbadians employed by the company.

The Anti-Slavery Society, after first asking Roger's permission, lobbies for his appointment to the consular slot. He goes to the House of Commons to consult with Charles Dilke, his Congo ally, as well as Josiah Wedgwood and Noel Buxton—both from families long associated with antislavery causes. He has what he calls "splendid" talks with all three, after which he writes his trusted ally at the Foreign Office, William Tyrrell, that he's heard he "was to go to Putumayo and was ready if Sir E. Grey wanted it." Tyrrell wires him to call at the Foreign Office the next day, and when he does Grey makes the appointment official. He lets Roger know that although his public mandate is confined to the Barbadian question, he should discreetly investigate as well the general issues that have been raised about the treatment of the Indians. He tells Roger further that he's free either to travel to the Putumayo with the commission or to make his own arrangements. Roger decides to go with the commission, feeling that he'd be at a disadvantage if he joined them after they'd already gotten to know one another.

Roger spends the next two days reading through the Putumayo files at the Foreign Office, then goes to Ireland to make his good-byes. Joining the other commissioners at Southampton, the group leaves on the *Edinburgh* on July 23, 1910. The first stop is Madeira on the twenty-seventh, and Roger takes literally the four-day "layover" and has several pleasing sexual encounters. Reembarking, the commission reaches Para on August 8, where Roger, as he puts it, "blushes to roots of hair with joy" at running into an old trick, João, who, equally delighted, presents him with roses. The commission changes vessels and proceeds upriver in a launch to Iquitos, where it's formally due to begin its work.

During his time on the launch, Roger strikes up a conversation with one of the independent rubber traders aboard and later writes down their exchange:

ROGER: "I sometimes wonder why this vast tropical garden is empty of all human life. . . . Where have the Indian inhabitants gone to? I have a good idea, of course, but don't like to entertain it."

TRADER: "I myself have 100 free laborers on the land the Peruvian government granted me. But no Indians."

ROGER: "Why is that?"

TRADER (WITH A SLY SMILE): "Isn't that what you people are here to investigate?"
  Roger is surprised. "So word of our mission has preceded us."
  The trader grins broadly. "You haven't been moving about in secrecy."
  Roger laughs. "No, a bit clumsy I suppose. Not that we have anything to hide."

TRADER: "Others might. And you've given them ample opportunity to do so. But you're wrong, you know."

ROGER: "Wrong about what?"

TRADER: "There are still many tribes of savages up the feeder rivers to the Amazon, like the Caqueta or the Ucayali. And they can be handled properly, as Julio Arana has done."

Roger involuntarily reacts with a start. "You speak well of Arana?"

TRADER: "These tribes in their unconquered state are no use to anyone. They have to be conquered, made to work. The whole forest region has rubber, but no labor save its Indian tribes and the only means of starting labor is to force the Indians to work."

Roger tries to conceal his anger. "Arana's system for 'employing' the Indians amounts to slavery."

The trader smiles. "Arana is a wealthy man."

ROGER: "The Indians don't abandon their forest freedom voluntarily and gladly present themselves to collect rubber for Mr. Arana."

TRADER: "Oh, there is fighting of course. Some Indians resist . . . but in the end they are reduced."

ROGER: "And the Peruvian government looks on with approval?"

TRADER: "Of course—it is the only way the tribes can be civilised—how would *you* do it?"

ROGER: "In Britain's African colonies, the white settlers cannot take lands from the natives—nor can the government itself. Our government purchases land from the native chiefs." (Roger's conscience whispers in his ear: "Oh really? You mean like the Zulus in South Africa? I thought you hated England?" "Don't bother me now!" he shouts back. "I do hate England but it's better than Peru!")

"After all," Roger tells the trader, "it's Britain that applied pressure to King Leopold!"

TRADER (HIS TONE UNRUFFLED): "Really? I heard a different story."

ROGER: "Above all, the natives must be protected in their rights over the land. Whether in Africa or Europe, a people must be rooted in the soil for social and economic development."

The trader laughs. "Aren't you Irish?"

"I am." Roger knows what's coming.

"I know a bit of history. Parnell and the Irish Land League had to fight a long war before the English would allow ownership of the land by those who till it."

"You have a point," Roger acknowledges, his voice begrudging. "But we got it back, didn't we? Plenty of English saw the justice of the cause. They knew we weren't their property. Unlike Arana. He owns the rubber trees, and he owns 'his' Indians. The Lima government agrees with him."

"Of course it does. Conquering a savage tribe is a patriotic act. The conqueror deserves territorial rights. Arana turns useless savages into useful labor."

"Not useful when dead."

"They're a weak people. They'd rather die than work."

"That's absurd." Roger no longer tries to conceal his anger. "You'd die too if given 200 lashes—and no food."

The trader laughs. "That's just foolish propaganda. What would you do if the government gave you a large tract of forest inhabited by wild Indians?"

"I would refuse the gift."

"Which means you're a fool. There's no point discussing the matter further."

"I agree with you."

The launch arrives in Iquitos on August 17. By this time, after nearly a month spent with the commission members, Roger has formed tentative impressions. He tries to hold himself somewhat apart, in line with his distinct mission regarding the Barbadians, but he's affable by nature, and Bertie, head of the commission, is (as Roger writes Morel) "very anxious to rope me into his councils, and already is trying to get me to regard myself as one of his party" rather than the commission's "guest," which officially he is. Roger was initially unimpressed with the "very harmless" Colonel Bertie, but just as he comes around to rather liking him, Bertie falls ill and on doctor's advice returns to England.

Louis Barnes, the agricultural specialist, replaces him as leader of the investigation—and will become Roger's staunch, if sometimes phlegmatic, ally. The botanist Walter Fox, pipe smoking and rotund, acts as if he's just emerged from his London club for a breath of air and, like the economist Seymour Bell, seems with each new experience to change his estimate of the situation—every situation. The youngest commissioner, the thirty-year-old Henry Gielgud, is the only member (other than Roger) ever to have set foot in South America; the year before, as a hired accountant, he spent three months in the Putumayo auditing the company's books and turned in an entirely positive report of its "many accomplishments." According to the pugnacious Gielgud, the allegations of atrocities published in *Truth* have no credence.

Roger is not optimistic about the commission's prospects; he predicts to Morel that it will be "fairly well hoodwinked." It doesn't help that their instructions include an investigation of "commercial prospects"—thus providing a readymade excuse for focusing on financial rather than moral issues. All of this propels Roger early on to a more active role on behalf of the Indians than his instructions officially warrant. As early as August he's writing Gerald Spicer, an undersecretary in the Foreign Office, "I fully realise that the surest hope of getting permanent good for the people of the region we are visiting is to convince the Commission and carry it with me so far as possible."

Roger is in no doubt from the start that Hardenburg's and Whiffen's accounts of barbarous conditions in the Putumayo are accurate; his previous experience in the Congo has shown him all too clearly what greed, in combination with the conviction of racial superiority, can engender. In a region like the Putumayo where, as Roger reports to Tyrrell, "there is practically no administration save that of the Company itself . . . and no sense of justice at all when it comes to dealing with these poor, docile forest tribes of Indians," corrective measures are all but out of reach. "We are up against 400 years of Latin American dealings with the conquered," Roger later jots down.

Lacking authority to compel evidence on oath, and without interpreters or guides, the commissioners fail—willfully, in Roger's view—to utilize what power they do have actively to challenge the evasions and lies that everywhere confront them. He wants the commissioners to start asking difficult questions: What cargo—including troops—does the Peruvian government send in the company's steamers to and from the Putumayo? Does the company ever charge the government for such services? If not, isn't that tantamount to proving Hardenburg's contention that Peruvian officials are in the pay of the company and receive "benefits" from it? And, if so, doesn't it follow that the company, as a quid pro quo, gets the Peruvian government to look the other way while it conducts its "civilizing" mission? Roger doubts that the commissioners have either the interest or courage to ask such hard questions.

After arriving at Iquitos, the capital of Arana's enterprise, and discovering that the commissioners will be housed in a company-owned building, Roger gives way to a burst of (temporary) despair: they "shall only touch the fringe of the matter," he writes in his diary. Roger himself is the guest of David Cazes, who he soon discovers is an "honorary" consul only, his income deriving almost entirely from his business as a local rubber trader—another dire omen, in Roger's view, especially since Cazes is slated to be his official interpreter. In an attempt to minimize the potential damage, Roger takes a room in the local hotel, Le Cosmopolite, telling Cazes that he wouldn't dream of burdening him with a guest. But the hotel is so "dreadful" and his room so hot and full of mosquitoes that he gives in and retreats back to Cazes's "very pleasant" home.

On the very first day in Iquitos, Roger meets with the local Peruvian prefect, Dr. Paz Soldán, who assures Roger that Hardenburg's articles in *Truth* are "fables, originating with blackmailers." He adds that the "House of Arana" has performed distinguished service to the state and stands "high in the opinion of the Government." Roger makes a mental note to himself to distrust anything further that Soldán might tell him. As if on cue, and in response to Roger's question as to who he should address himself to in the Putumayo should he find that the condition of British subjects is deplorable and requires intervention, the prefect comes up with three names—all of whom turn out to be principal agents of the Peruvian Amazon Company. No, Roger tells Soldán, he does not think it prudent to present potential complaints against the company to an agent of the company. "Very well," Soldán says, "then I suggest the *Comisario*"; the magistrate, it turns out, is a Señor Burga, a relative of Pablo Zumaeta—another of Julio Arana's brothers-in-law. Soldán either believes I'm a total fool, Roger thinks, or he's letting me know that *all* roads of access in the Putumayo lead to Arana.

The very next day Roger locates two Barbadians in the employ of the company and does preliminary interviews with them. One, clearly frightened, says in essence that everything is just fine. The other, Frederick Bishop, confirms all of Hardenburg's charges—"the Indians are enslaved, pure and simple"—and even acknowledges that to save his own life he himself has had to flog and brutalize them. Bishop will become one of Roger's key witnesses, the only Barbadian whose testimony he learns to fully trust. Not without fear for his safety, Bishop is determined to clear his conscience and over time will provide Roger with firsthand accounts of how the chief agents of the company, and especially the "monsters" Alfredo Montt and Armando Normand, have killed—"by shooting, flogging, beheading, burning, and starvation"— hundreds, if not thousands, of Indians. Bishop assures Roger that he's willing to repeat his testimony in front of those he accuses, and Roger decides to take him into his employ as the best means of protecting him. He pays Bishop twelve pounds a month, plus food and board.

Given his experience in the Congo, Roger has learned how to bluff and conspire with the best of them. He writes out all of Bishop's depositions in detail and sends the statements to the Foreign Office for safekeeping. He dutifully plays bridge, evening after evening, with the members of the commission, the better to insinuate himself into their confidence. And he even puts together a dinner party consisting of the commissioners, David Cazes—and some of the devils themselves, Pablo Zumaeta, and Julio Arana's brother Lizardo Arana. At the dinner Roger offers a toast to "the health and prosperity of Peru."

Despite a tenacious and troublesome eye infection, Roger, with Bishop's help, continues to locate and interview a number of Barbadians—and continues to hear horror stories. One of the men, Joseph Labadie, recounts an incident he witnessed involving Carlos Miranda, a company agent; as Roger transcribes it, Miranda, having decapitated an old woman, "then seized the head and holding it up by the hair to the assembled Indians, compulsory witnesses of this tragedy, told them to look well at it for that was what would happen to all bad Indians."

Bishop reports that several Barbadians refuse to let Roger interview them, out of understandable fear of the consequences. Roger tries, through Bishop, to persuade them that his mission is designed to help them, not put them in jeopardy, but for now he decides not to press the case, fearing "I may do more harm than good." A few of the recalcitrant Barbadians do come around, including a man named Adolphus Gibbs; he tells Roger that he's seen the notorious Armando Normand kill Indians "in all sorts of ways," including burning them alive. In total, before setting off with the commission for the Putumayo in September, Roger manages to do six interviews during the two weeks in Iquitos, and he sends off detailed accounts to the Foreign Office. ("As anything may happen to me up there," he writes to the undersecretary, "it is as well you should have these statements to know how things look to us before starting.") He also passes along Bishop's warning that they're not likely to see any "active wrongdoing"; the Arana clan is too clever for that and will have cleared away most of the evidence.

As they set out on the company's flagship, the *Liberal,* for the thousand-mile journey, Roger decides to expand his second, nonsexual diary into a fuller account; his earlier jottings now ripple out into a cascade of words, not in journal entries alone but also in letters and official reports as well. The commissioners have by this point taken on an interpreter, fluent in Huitoto, and Roger is relieved not to have to rely on David Cazes's translations any longer. He's never trusted Cazes, feeling certain that he knows far more than he's admitted about Arana and the company. Roger's angry, too, at Cazes's tendency, like almost all the traders in Iquitos, to "talk of *his* Indians, just as if they were sheep or cattle—or rubber trees."

Accommodations aboard the *Liberal* are primitive, the journey a hard one from the beginning. Roger initially tries sleeping in a hammock on deck but promptly develops a sore throat and fever. Yet he marvels at the vegetation and wildlife all along the riverbank—herons and macaws, tapirs and wild pigs, and five different kinds of palm trees, including the unfamiliar *pona,* which, he writes, "shoots up its graceful stem from 6–12 inch magnificent fronds like those of a hart's tongue fern on top." He's captivated by the sight of a young tapir swimming midstream "at a tremendous rate" and is crushed when a man jumps from a canoe and, after a long chase, catches the "poor little chap" by the hind leg and hoists it on board; "I *should* like to save him," Roger writes in his diary, "and take him home to Ireland. He richly deserves his life."

After a nine-day trip, the *Liberal* arrives on September 22, 1910, at La Chorrera, Aranas's major trading post. Victor Macedo, its chief agent, and Juan Tizon, a resident of Iquitos and one of the company's managers (and a man who'll play a major role in Roger's life over the next few months), are among the welcoming party that comes aboard, as do seven Boras to carry the baggage. The Boras are one of the principal tribes of the Peruvian Amazon region, and the males wear nothing but a *fono* (a small bark strap to cover the penis). The Indians all show a multiplicity of scars on their bare buttocks, some of which, Roger notes, are one and a half or two inches broad; "this is their welfare, their daily welfare," Roger writes. Five Barbadians also come aboard to stand over the Boras and "drive them." Roger's first impression: "The whole place is a Penitentiary."

He wastes no time. The very next day he calls in the five Barbadians at La Chorrera for interviews and asks Juan Tizon and Louis Barnes, head of the commission, to attend. Three of the five claim to have seen nothing out of the ordinary; everything is "just fine." The other two speak out boldly (though as Roger writes, "*obviously* under great mental stress") about the terrible conditions at La Chorrera, divulging that not only have they often seen men flogged and killed but have themselves participated. Tizon, a company manager, tries to shake their story, but the two are adamant. In Roger's opinion, "Tizon did not like it at all, but bore it and in the evening began flattering me after dinner and saying nice things about me and how glad he was my Govt. had sent a man like me. Is it sincere or is it part of the game?" Time will tell, as Tizon begins his own tortuous journey toward the truth.

The following day Roger calls back Joshua Dyall, one of the three recalcitrant Barbadians, for further questioning and again invites Tizon and Barnes to witness the interview. This time around, for whatever reason, Dyall releases a torrent of self-incriminating testimony. He confesses to killing five Indians himself—one he flogged to death, two he shot, two he beat to death (as ordered by Armando Normand) by "smashing their testicles" with a stick, Normand participating. Dyall also describes another common punishment: when Indians fail to bring in their quota of rubber, Normand puts a chain around their necks, hauls them high off the ground, then drops them suddenly—some are merely knocked out, others break bones, one bites through his tongue.

Tizon again attempts to challenge and weaken Dyall's statement, but Roger will have none of it. "What possible motive," he asks Tizon when the two are alone, "would lead a man to charge himself with grave and dastardly crimes, unless he was confessing? The man may be a brute, but he's been employed by greater brutes. If a question of punishment arises, I will defend Dyall and indict those who ordered the punishments."

Tizon flushes with a confused mix of anger and guilt. "The commission is not a judicial body," he says, "and nobody else in the Putumayo is empowered to investigate criminal acts. There are no Peruvian magistrates or courts."

"All the more reason," Roger insistently replies, "to take Dyall and others with us to confront each guilty agent as we move from station to station."

"And then what?" Tizon persists. "I accept the Barbadians' charges in the main, but you have no legal means to enforce penalties. Can't you see that?"

"I will put it up to the commission members," Roger concedes. "I'll call a meeting for tomorrow."

That same evening Tizon knocks on Roger's door and asks if they can talk further about the day's events. Roger cordially invites him in, and the two men mull over the best course of action till well past midnight. Tizon argues that "anything might happen" if Roger continues to insist that "black men"— the Barbadians—directly accuse Arana's agents of criminal acts. He reiterates that no legal channels exist to process the accusations and—knowing what the agents are capable of—warns Roger that he's putting the Barbadians' lives in danger. (Tizon doesn't mention the considerable mystery, or miracle, that Roger himself hasn't been directly threatened or killed.) Tizon's warning that the Barbadians are in danger is an argument difficult to refute, and after several hours discussing possible alternatives, Roger reluctantly concedes the point. He does so only after Tizon swears that he'll move mountains to see that the guilty agents are somehow gotten rid of—though not, Tizon strenuously argues, the company itself, since a "far worse state of things" would replace it. Though Tizon has earlier been a defender of the company, Roger believes that he's now sincere in his desire to cleanse the system. Yet he continues to doubt whether Tizon has either the ability or the strength to see the matter through.

At the meeting of the commission the following day, with Tizon present, Roger conveys to the members the gist of the discussion he and Tizon had the previous night. "I regret," he says, "that, as an official of the British government, I cannot put the Barbadians' testimony to a judicial test, but given the fact that the Putumayo is a 'very peculiar region' and lies outside the jurisdiction of civilized authority, I've bowed to Tizon's argument that if the company itself is somehow dissolved, Arana and his horde of infamous ruffians will nonetheless remain and will fasten the bonds of slavery over the Indians more securely than ever." He tells the commissioners further that Tizon has pledged to do everything within his power (Ah, Roger thinks, there's the sticking point) to see to it that flogging and other brutal forms of punishment will henceforth be abolished.

"My country's honor is at stake," Tizon himself adds. "If I fail, I will resign—I wish to God I had never been associated with the company. But please, gentlemen, I beg of you to use your influence in London to help me. If the London shareholders and the board of the company withdraw their support, Arana will lose his critical source of cash."

"And let us not forget the Indians," Roger stresses. "Any sincere inquiry must begin with the Indians themselves. If ever there was a helpless people on the face of this earth it is these naked forest savages, mere grown-up children. Their very arms show the bloodlessness of their timid minds and gentle characters." Roger's passionate humanitarianism is uncommon in his day, but his characterization of the Indians as timid savages is utterly mainstream—yes, even among Irish nationalists. No less an Irish patriot than John Mitchel had much earlier defended American slavery and white supremacy; the view that people of color are innately inferior remains strong. Roger transcends his times in characterizing Indians and Africans as people rather than as beasts but is *of* his times in tending to see them as a breed apart—an enviably gentler, simpler, more emotionally open breed: a form of stereotyping, still, but one many cuts above the model of "brutal, immoral primitives" then current. Roger isn't among the tiny few in every generation—like Mary Kingsley—

able to adopt in advance the *next* generation's perspective (though his sympathy approximates it).

Roger's sense of outrage extends to the commissioners themselves. Why aren't they doing more? he asks himself angrily. Why haven't they made the slightest effort to find out how and why the Boras got those deep welts across their buttocks? "It is proof of lawlessness," Roger writes in his diary, "and of extreme lawlessness, for the marks are deep, and yet everyone takes it as a matter of course. Then there's the case of the Indian I found who'd been chained for two months; when I ask Tizon about it, he replies that the Indian is 'a bad man.' Regrettably, I grew angry with Tizon—after all, he's our best hope for change—and asked him 'where it will end'? If you chain up a 'bad man' at this station, at another with a more violent agent in charge, he'll shoot the Indian rather than chain him. Another Indian here was labeled a 'bad man,' I just learn, because he tried to stir up a revolt against the white man. I'd call him a very good man, a hero."

At the next stop, Occidente, purportedly the company's "best" station, Roger discovers that a new form of flogging has been invented: beating the Indians across the back and shoulders with the flat of a machete—an advantage over the whip in that it is both more painful and leaves no marks. The innovative agent, Eugenie Acosta, also employs the "discipline" of having an obstinate Indian held under water until he's half-drowned—a hundred years later the technique will earn the term "water boarding." Roger brings these practices to the attention of the commissioners, but they profess their powerlessness to remedy the situation—with only Barnes expressing indignation. The Indians understand. One abruptly comes up to Roger, lays his head against his chest, puts his arm around his waist, and embraces him; he does the same to Barnes.

One afternoon the commissioners rouse themselves enough to go some way into the forest, where they observe at firsthand how rubber is collected. Upon returning they tell Roger how surprised they were to find only two Indian tappers and only three rubber trees. "I'm surprised you're surprised," Roger replies, trying to keep his voice nonjudgmental. "The Indians need to search constantly for the trees because the supply is nearly exhausted, thanks to the reckless destruction of the forest—yet the agents take no account of that when they beat and torture the Indians for failing to bring in the fanciful quotas set them. Roger tells the commissioners, "In my estimate 90 percent of the Indians bear marks of having been flogged."

Both Seymour Bell and Walter Fox protest the figure as too high. "I urge you," Roger solemnly says, "to ask the Indians themselves. I am myself forbidden from questioning any employee of the company who is not a British subject."

"Please don't misunderstand," Fox earnestly tells him. "It is thanks to the testimony you've gotten from the Barbadians that has provided most of the information we have."

"There is a great deal more to be gathered," Roger tersely replies.

"I'm afraid we lack your skill," Fox meekly offers.

"It takes no special skill. Interest perhaps, but not skill." Roger realizes he's on the verge of an outburst and abruptly excuses himself: "I need to take a swim.... Swimming is my salvation."

"Do keep an eye out for crocodiles," Fox calls out to Roger's receding back, the concern in his voice sounding genuine.

On his way to the river, Roger passes three Indian boys lying in a hammock, playing with one another's genitals—without concealment or embarrassment. It's not the only time Roger has come upon such a scene, and he periodically notes them in his diary: "the beautiful muchacho showed it, a big stiff one and another muchacho grasped it like a truncheon. Black and thick and stiff as a poker"; A native boy "pretending to do it with small boy with huge *thrust*"; "After dinner talked to two . . . muchachos, one a fine chap. He pulled stiff and fingered it laughing." Roger sees similar playful pleasuring among some of the older Indian porters and boat hands and is delighted at the lack of any apparent guilt or shame. The undisguised erections that he frequently sees delight him still more, since sublimation has been his only companion since the mission began.

By early October Roger is finding that he actually *likes* Tizon and believes he's "the only honest man in the Company"; more than that, he contrasts the Peruvian's energy and his capacity for moral indignation with the commissioners' lazy acquiescence. Fox, the botanist, seems more interested in the rubber trees than in the Indians who tap them; the curiosity of Bell, the economist, is primarily aroused when investigating the Putumayo's commercial prospects; as for Gielgud—secretary and previous apologist for the company—he does seem, occasionally, to be opening his eyes to the plight of the Indians, but not in any consistent, reliable way. "For any serious purpose," Roger writes in his diary, "I fear Gielgud is useless. The whole question doesn't strike him as serious. I am disgusted with the lack of character and humanity of these shifting, vacillating men. *It is not a Commission* at all."

Roger pours out his discouragement to Tizon, telling him that he doesn't see how conditions are going to change. He believes Arana has successfully deceived the company's board of directors in London. And so far the only evidence of any direct and open kind has come from the Barbados men, not from the commission's investigations. The only real question remaining, Roger tells Tizon, "is which will be exhausted first, the Indians or the rubber trees. . . . I do not think the Indians will outlive the trees." Tizon nods his head sadly. "I fully agree with you," he says.

But Roger's temperament is essentially optimistic. He can fall into periods of despondency, yet isn't rooted there; inherently buoyant, he's quick to find or invent enough evidence to restore his hope for a favorable outcome. He finds that in fully venting his misgivings to Tizon, he's cleared away some of his own gloom, and within days he's again convening the commissioners to try and convince them to adopt a more proactive role.

They gather in one of Occidente's sheds for storing rubber, and Roger opens the meeting with a calculated confession. "I realize," he says, "that every time I approach one of you gentlemen, it's with a new crime on my lips or with tears in my eyes. Today I'm determined to turn over a new leaf and to—"

Gielgud interrupts with loud applause: "Here's to that, old man! A good turn, I'd call it!"

Roger swallows hard but retains his smile. "I'm glad you approve, Gielgud. It gives me the idea of starting with the exchange you and I, and Mr. Fox, had just yesterday about the issue of contracts."

"Excellent idea!" Gielgud enthusiastically responds. "As you all know, my connection to the company has made me especially sensitive to this whole question of what is or is not a *voluntary* contract."

"Pardon me," the economist Bell interjects, "but who are we talking about? What is at issue here? A contract with *whom?*"

"With the *Indians,* of course!" Gielgud blurts out impatiently, then catches himself. "Excuse me, Bell. I don't mean to be rude, but I thought that was obvious."

"Not to me," Bell replies. "But carry on."

Roger tries to reinvigorate the discussion. "The issue as I see it," he says, "and as I presented it yesterday to Gielgud and Fox, hinges on whether the Indians can be said to have entered into a voluntary contract with the company, as the company claims, when they accept advance 'payment' in the form of various trinkets—the very few trinkets carried in the company store. My position is that there is no such contract, no proof that the Indians are aware that by accepting such trinkets they've obligated themselves to bring in a certain amount of rubber from the forest. Still further, there's no evidence that they even *want* such trinkets, let alone that they've been warned in advance that a failure to bring in a specified amount of rubber will lead to floggings—or worse."

Walter Fox takes the pipe out of his mouth long enough to say, "The Indians may have no idea what a contract is, but they *are* familiar with the barter system. They know that when accepting an item they must give something back in return."

"They also know what a 'gift' is," Roger replies. "If I give a tin of sardines to a hungry Indian, he doesn't assume he has to fetch me clean bed linen in return. Nor should he."

Louis Barnes—all six feet six of him—rises from his chair, towering over even Roger. "Just a minute here . . . if I may, as head of this commission— aren't all of you simply *assuming* what the Indians do or do not know?"

"Exactly, Barnes, exactly," Roger replies excitedly. "That is really my whole point. That is why I've been all along urging the commissioners to *interview* the Indians. Only the Indians can tell us what they believe they're agreeing to. But so far, gentlemen, you've refused to take their testimony."

"That would upset the whole show," Gielgud throws in, with some heat. "It would create chaos."

"How so?" Roger asks. "Doesn't the 'show' *need* to be upset? Isn't that why we're here?"

"It's certainly not why *I'm* here," Bell tosses in. My expertise is economics. When I accepted the company's invitation to join this commission, I did so with the expectation that I'd be exploring the commercial potential of the Putumayo region. And that is what I've been doing."

"That was *one* part of your mandate," Roger responds, aware that he's becoming agitated. "The *second* part of your mandate is to survey and report on the general conditions you find here. I don't see how you can fulfill that obligation without inquiring into the condition of the indigenous tribes."

"Look here, Casement," Bell replies, "I don't speak Huitoto, not to mention Andokes or any of the other languages spoken here."

"If you wish, I can find interpreters. Not that you need them." (Roger can hear the anger in his voice and gives himself a scolding: Damn it, watch your tongue! You won't get anywhere this way.) "All you need to do," he hears himself saying, "is *to look at the Indians' buttocks and thighs.* That language is testimony enough, easy to understand—and eloquent."

Gielgud is on his feet. "I don't defend flogging, but *something* has to be done to get the Indians to work! Whipping is the rough and ready way of dealing with defaulting creditors. Besides, you're confusing the deeds of a few mavericks with company policy."

Roger can feel his anger building. "And the beheadings and the shootings?" he shouts, "Are they also designed to get the Indians to work? How about kidnapping and raping their wives, will that do the trick? Or maybe burning down a few villages?! Bishop told me that when news arrived that we were on our way here, the bones of four muchachos killed in January were dug up and buried in the forest!"

Gielgud's agitation matches Roger's own. "You're confusing the Putumayo with the Congo!" Simmering down a bit, he adds, "we all appreciate the good work you did there, but Arana is not King Leopold."

"Slavery in the Putumayo is *worse* than in the Congo, though on a smaller scale, affecting thousands not millions! In the Congo there are at least judges and police. There are missionaries. Here we have slavery without *any law,* and slavers who are the scum of the earth, ruffians, brutes, jailbirds! . . . In the Congo there is payment, *food*—here people die of starvation. The only thing the two regions have in common is that their defenders use the same kind of perverted logic!"

Gielgud rises from his chair and, directing the remark to Barnes, heatedly says, "I think this has gone far enough."

"Perhaps so . . . yes, I think for now. . . . But gentlemen, I also think . . . I think Mr. Casement has raised a number of issues that we must consider at greater length . . . but yes, for now I think we can profitably close this session."

Gielgud and Bell quickly leave. Fox lingers behind, touches Roger's arm, and quietly says, "I'm so sorry, Casement. . . . I mean, I feel out of my depths about all this . . . not quite able to grasp everything. . . ."

Touched, Roger tries to reassure him: "You have a kind heart, Fox. . . . Human sympathy . . . that's all one needs, finally. . . . I'm too hotheaded, for which I apologize. . . . I *try* to keep my temper in check . . . but often fail."

Fox gives Roger a warm smile, softly says good-bye, and leaves. Barnes sits back down in his chair and motions to Roger to do the same.

"Roger, Roger . . ." Barnes quietly begins, "your heart is perhaps *too* warm. . . . You cannot win men over by denouncing them."

"No, of course not . . . you're quite right to reprimand me. . . . I did get carried away."

"In a good cause, a good cause. That is your saving grace. . . ."

"What are we to *do,* Barnes? I know you share my views. But the others . . . one day they denounce the horrible treatment of the Indians, the next they tell me the system isn't *all* bad. They say we can't intervene because this is Peru, another country; then they say it isn't Peru, that no authority exists here, that we can't bring criminal charges because there's no one to arrest the criminals. Gielgud, an Englishman educated at an English University, should be able to *smell* right from wrong in a case of this kind." (Good Lord, Roger thinks to himself, I sound like Lord Salisbury!) "Gielgud insists that I exaggerate everything. . . . Do I?"

"Not as I see it. Frankly, I don't understand how they manage to look away. . . . Oh, Gielgud I understand. . . . He's young and coarse, and he knows where his bread is buttered."

"He passed through this same region—I'm sleeping in the bed he used!—a year ago. He reported that all was well, a little 'rudimentary' perhaps—I believe that was the word he used—but 'quite suited,' as he put it, 'to the surroundings.'"

"Try and be a bit more patient, Roger. I know that's difficult, given the scale of injustice here—"

"But I'll be leaving before the rest of you! As soon as I finish interviewing all the Barbadians, I *have* to leave; those are my instructions. Then what will happen?!"

"I believe they'll come round, I do. . . . As you just said to Fox, 'he has a good heart,' and he does. . . . As for Gielgud, perhaps even he . . . eventually. . . . Time will tell."

"I hope you're right, though I doubt it. You're the only one, Barnes—you and Tizon—who fully sees the situation here for what it is."

"My mind is as fixed as yours. I can assure you of that."

"I should never forgive you, Barnes"—Roger's voice is solemn and emphatic—"if you go back on your promise. . . . If you fail to condemn this damned system lock, stock, and barrel when you get back to England . . . I should never forgive you. . . ."

Finding himself near tears, Roger gives Barnes a fierce embrace, then hurriedly leaves.

Back in his room, he takes down his diary and writes furiously in it: "Can I count on Barnes? He's ill and exhausted. . . . Perhaps I can count on him more when he gets home, when he has to deliver a summing up.... The world, I am beginning to think—that is, the white man's world—is made up of two categories of men—compromisers and Irishmen. I might add 'and Blackmen.' Thank God that I am an Irishman, that I am not afraid to 'assume,' that I won't shirk the charge of 'exaggeration.' Let that be. I shall drive home this nail, and if these unhappy, these enormously outraged Indians of the Putumayo, find relief at last from their cruel burden, it shall be through the Irishmen of the earth."

. . .

Through most of the next two months, the commission, accompanied by Roger much of the time, moves from station to station in the Putumayo. What they find is what they already know, multiplied many times over, the only variables being the degree of horror, the depths of deception, and the attempts at justification. Roger himself moves back and forth between the tactics of anxious diplomacy and frustrated outrage—but is unvarying in his determination to bring the culprits to justice. He shreds the official instructions that confine his mission solely to determining the status of British subjects (though Sir Edward Gray *had* informally encouraged him to keep an eye out on conditions in general) and unapologetically enlarges it to include nothing less than wiping out the "most hideous form of slavery on the planet." Over time Louis Barnes, initially allied with Roger, grows convinced that their mission is futile and retreats into a kind of apathetic weariness. Walter Fox moves in the opposite direction, shifting from bumbling inconsequence to full-throated indignation that's a match for Roger's own.

In mid-October the commission arrives at the Último Retiro station, where the smooth-tongued Augusto Jimenez is the agent in charge. In response to direct questions, he slides effortlessly into formulaic responses:

> "How is the rubber collected?"—"The *blancos* 'advise' when quotas are due and which techniques for extraction are best."
> "Are the Indians paid?"—"Yes, of course; indeed, they're paid in *advance* in goods they choose from the company store."
> "Who fixes the price equivalents between, say, a kilo of rubber and a pair of pants?"—"I do. Who else?"

Roger's inventory of the company store takes less than five minutes. There's almost nothing in it beyond rifles—off-limits to Indians—matches and a few iron pots and plates. Only a couple of tins of food—the item most craved—are on the shelves. He next inspects the *cepo,* the stocks in which "bad" Indians are put, often for days, without food. Roger measures the circumference of the stocks and finds the openings are so small that the holes can fit only "the emaciated legs of these poor Huitotos, whom even the neighbouring tribes call 'mosquito legs.'" For others, their legs become deeply infected after a single day. In Roger's view, the cepo is "not intended as a place of detention, but as an instrument of torture." He learns that there are double cepos, one for the legs, the other for the head and arms, as well as a cepo that moves up and down to accommodate the small size of children. He suggests that the commission should order the cepo in Último Retiro publicly burned. Only Fox agrees with him. The others think it wiser "not to do anything quite so glaring."

On a trip through the forest to see the condition of a small group of Indians in the interior, the commission finds that the path has been cleared away the previous day; as Roger describes it in his diary, all the rough spots on the six-mile road have been made smooth: "trees felled, saplings and trunks laid over wet spots, and bridges made over many streams with a liana rope banister to hold by." Who did so much heavy labor in so short a time? The answer is obvious: enslaved Indians—in this case, women. For Roger, it goes without saying that they got neither pay nor food.

Bishop investigates and confirms Roger's assumption. "They *never* get any food. . . . They've got to find it as best they can. . . . That's why they chew the coca" (the leaves of the plant from which cocaine is distilled, which kills the appetite). Coming across a group of "starving wretches," Roger can stand it no longer: he empties out most of his own supply of meat and fish tins; it comes to half a tin for each Indian in the group. Roger watches, with a mix of horror and gratification, as the Indians squat down then and there and "literally wolf down with the loudest 'begorrahs' I've got yet, and such smiles of delight." One boy swallows the greasy paper around a sheep's tongue inside a tin; another opens a tin with his teeth.

Though Fox has become "furious and disgusted," a residue of perplexity remains. "Isn't it possible," he asks Roger, that "the evil system we see all around us isn't a sort of natural and inevitable growth based on the fact that the first 'settlers' had to hold their own against the Indians by terror . . . the cruel necessity for self-defense?"

"No," Roger tells him, "that is not how it happened. Those who arrived here four hundred years ago came not as settlers to trade with the Indians but to *appropriate* the Indians." It wasn't the rubber trees they wanted back then; it was the Indians themselves—slaves to "feed them, build for them, run for them, carry for them, and supply them with wives and concubines." Until the rise of the rubber trade in the 1890s, white men made no attempt to form permanent settlements in the Putumayo; the early trade was primarily in sarsaparilla (an aromatic plant distilled as an herbal tonic) and "Peruvian bark" (used to distill quinine, the preferred treatment for malaria). When the Indians resisted, they were massacred or enslaved. "What we see today," Roger tells Fox, "is merely the logical sequence of events—cowed and entirely subdued Indians, reduced in numbers, hopelessly obedient, with no refuge and no retreat and no redress." Fox declares himself persuaded.

The commission's next stop, the station of Entre Ríos, stands in the center of a large clearing of some 250 acres. Roger is amazed at the "splendidly built" station house and other small buildings—which turn out to be entirely the work of the Huitotos. Using not a single nail, they've peeled off the tree bark and lashed together the boards with liana; the walls and floors are made from *frona* palm bark. "Only another tribute to the skill and knowledge of these poor Indians," Roger writes in his diary. While the Indians sweat away, it outrages Roger to see the handful of *blancos,* "of lazy cut-throats armed to the teeth and living in absolute idleness, wandering around barefooted, dressed like 'beachcombers,'" each with his harem of "wives," usually women forcibly removed from their Indian husbands.

Bishop hears a story about one of the prime cutthroats, Elías Martenengui, and passes it on to Roger. Martenengui spotted an attractive Indian woman one day and told her husband that he intended to keep her until the man returned with a stipulated amount of rubber. It took him fifteen days to collect it—only to be told it wasn't "enough" and to be sent back for more. This went on three or four times, and Martenengui finally told the husband that he was keeping his wife in his harem for good and gave him a young girl as a replacement. When the husband protested, he was beaten and driven off. He then refused to work rubber at all—and was killed for insubordination.

Roger hears about ongoing resistance among other Indians. He learns that the young Bora chief, Katenere, only recently murdered, had refused to work any longer for Armando Normand, the most notoriously violent of all the station agents. Captured, Katenere was put in a cepo and his wife dragged in and raped before his eyes. Katenere later managed—with the help of an Indian girl who raised the top beam of the cepo when no one was around—to escape. He then stole some Winchester rifles, armed members of his clan, and waged open war. Overwhelmed by Normand's forces, Katenere was put to death. "The world," Roger writes in his diary, "thinks the slave trade was killed a century ago! Yet the worst form of slavery . . . has been in full swing here for 300 years, the dwindling remnant of a population once numbering millions, now perishing at the doors of an English Company, under the lash, the chains, the bullet, the machete, to give its shareholders a dividend."

By mid-October the commission reaches Maranzas, lair of the archvillain himself, Armando Normand. He turns over his sitting room for Roger to use as his bedroom, a silent acknowledgement that he's aware Roger is the most vocal of the "complainers" and is to be handled with kid gloves. Roger scans the walls of the sitting room; they're pasted with pictures of the Russo-Japanese War of 1904 cut out from the *Graphic,* a popular magazine, along with photos of "a lot of cocottes [prostitutes] taken," Roger writes in his diary, "from some low-class Paris paper" as well as several photos "of brutal-faced South American people"—members, Roger surmises, of Normand's own family. Also hung on the walls are certificates from the London School of Bookkeepers; who would have guessed, Roger muses, that the dreaded Normand is an *accountant!*

That same evening Roger is summoned to dinner and presented formally to his host, who meets all his expectations: "a face truly the most repulsive I have ever seen, I think. It was perfectly devilish in its cruelty and evil. I felt as if I were being introduced to a serpent." Some half dozen other people are also guests at dinner, including Barnes and Bell. The bland, noncontroversial talk is conducted entirely in Spanish, in which Roger isn't fluent. On the few occasions when a remark is directed at him personally, he somehow manages to grasp the meaning—and makes a point of replying in English.

Roger decides that as soon as he interviews the two Barbadians at Matanzas, he will end his mission. He now has more than enough evidence of Normand's assorted crimes, and "it makes me sick to look at him." The interview with one of the Barbadians, James Lane, is brief. He claims not to have witnessed "many gross crimes," nor to have himself flogged any Indians, saying he has no "arm" for it and that the other Barbadian, Westerman Levine, does most of the flogging. Roger takes one look at the strapping young Lane and his "very fine, muscular arms" and realizes that he won't get much truth out of him. Yet somewhat to Roger's surprise, Lane does acknowledge that he's seen three Indians flogged to death, two of them at Matanzas, one of whom, a man named Kodihinka, was brutally beaten for running away, then put in a cepo with his back and limbs bleeding profusely and with his wife and children pinned in irons alongside him, where he died three days later.

Roger, on sight, dislikes Westerman Levine—his mean face with a smirk smeared across it and a "lurking grin always in the eyes." It rapidly becomes clear that he's intent on lying his way through the inquiry. When Roger asks him directly about Kodihinka, Levine denies that the man died in the cepo from flogging. Outraged at the flagrant lie, Roger determines to call Levine's bluff. He has James Lane brought back into the interview. Lane sticks to his initial story and openly accuses Levine of lying.

"Will you now tell me the truth?" Roger angrily asks Levine.

"I forgot about that episode," Levine replies with a grin.

"What?!" a furious Roger yells. "Forgotten—and only a month ago!"

Roger calls Tizon in to witness the rest of the interrogation, and Levine, apparently now intimidated, does finally admit that he'd given Kodihinka "a *few* cuts—maybe three. He was dead anyway. I gave him the cuts, sir, because he no pay me for a box of matches I gave him."

"I see," Roger spits out. "You gave him three lashes with his hands tied, his back and limbs bruised and bleeding, and himself, as you say, in a dying condition?"

"Yes, sir, but it wasn't from these three cuts he died; he died from the beating on the road."

Roger can't contain his rage—"You are a coward and a scoundrel!" he shouts. "If we were in Barbados, I would see to it that you were hanged!"

"I did it on orders, sir," Levine smirks, as if to say, "Yes, I'm lying, you fool, and you can't do a damned thing about it."

Roger reads the message clearly and orders both Barbadians from the room. When they've gone, Tizon looks dazed and tells Roger, with a groan, that he cannot go on. "To think I am mixed up with this!" he cries.

"You are *honorably* mixed up with it, Tizon. And you must remain so. You have a duty to Peru and to these Indians. You must keep a brave heart. I will give you all the moral aid I possibly can, though my job here at Matanzas is done."

After leaving Tizon, Roger runs directly into a long line of exhausted Indian men, women, and children, "dear little bright-eyed boys—tiny girls—mothers with infants," staggering up the hill under the burden of their large *tulas* (canvas road bags carried on their backs and secured with a strap around the forehead). The loads they carry are huge, often in excess of seventy kilos, weighing as much or more than they do, and often carried for distances of sixty or seventy miles over roads that, in Roger's words, "even a mule cannot traverse."

He tries to speak to several of the men and boys, with Bishop translating, but (as he later writes in his diary) "all seem half dazed and wholly frightened." One older woman, stark naked, crying and groaning, is trembling all over and "the most pitiable sounds arose to the poor creature's lips." So wretched is she that Roger can't hold back his own tears. He removes the *tula* from her beaten, whip-marked back; when he tries to lift the load himself, he can raise it for only a second or two, and just barely off the ground. The woman keeps repeating to Bishop that "Normand will kill me, Normand will kill me." Roger reassures her that she'll be safe and has her taken to the house he sleeps in. She collapses in a "groaning heap by the fire"; Roger gets her "rigged up in pajamas" on his bed sack, puts a warm coat over her, gives her food and medicine, and treats her bruised limbs and back with lanolin and pads of cotton wool.

Other Indians follow them into the house, and Roger, until he runs out of supplies, gives them whatever food and medicine he has. He looks at the Indians' "big, soft-eyed faces, averted and downcast" and wonders "where that Heavenly Power can be that for so long allows these beautiful images of Himself to be thus defaced and shamed." A commission of "botanists and commercial experts isn't what's wanted here," Roger writes in his diary. "What's needed is a Hanging Commission with a gallows."

It's Barnes's job, as head of the commission, to file a final report, but Roger doubts that he's up to it. He seems to have no capacity for sustained effort, and he admits as much. He's told Roger several times that he considers the system so corrupt from top to bottom that the Indians are doomed to extinction. As Roger writes in his diary that night, "There is no Commission. There are four decent men walking about together, but there is no point of common union and action.... There cannot be said to be any real collective enquiry. Fox alone, to my mind, fully realises his responsibility."

Roger, too, despairs at times of finding a solution for the plight of the Indians. The situation in his view "far exceeds in depravity and demoralisation the Congo regime at its worst. The lowest Belgian," he writes in his diary, "is a gentleman compared to Normand and the others." Further complicating the problem, Roger feels, is the contrasting temperaments of the South American Indian and the native African. Their weapons alone tell the tale. The Indians' "childish spurs and deadly blowpipe—noiseless, stupefying and not bloodletting"—versus "the heroic Zulu's six-foot spear and an 18 inch blade fit for beheading." The Zulus rose up against their oppressors and matched them in ferocity. In contrast, Roger feels, the South American Indian—the Huitoto more so than the Bora—is "hopelessly obedient. What the white man orders they are only too prone to execute."

"If only we were in British territory," Roger tells Tizon, "with a hundred men, what pleasure I should take in scouring the place clean!" Roger's brief spasms of "brutality" are a compound of profound frustration and a streak of romantic derring-do. In truth, he never wore a revolver when in the Congo, and in the Putumayo he either has a servant carry his pistol or keeps it locked up. Roger's innate gentleness is not so distant from that of the Huitotos and in part accounts for their sympathetic kinship.

Unable to bear Matanzas and the wanton cruelty of the Normand crowd, Roger leaves after only three days and returns to Entre Ríos. Once there he spends much of his time writing—despite the stubborn eye infection that forces him to sleep with pads soaked in boracic lotion and to keep his left eye bandaged during the day. But he's determined to record as many details in his diary as soon as possible. He wants to avoid the perils of memory and is so committed to producing as full a record as possible that he sometimes writes straight through the night.

While wrapping up loose ends, Roger comes up with the idea of bringing one or two native Indians back home with him as the best possible way of getting the Anti-Slavery people and the various missions "interested in the fate of the whole race out here in the toils" and the more willing to undertake a public campaign on their behalf. He knows it's a "wild thought" but also feels that it's "the last hope of these poor beings."

The idea becomes a concrete possibility one day when Roger is in the company store at La Chorrera, buying a case of salmon tins to distribute among some of the emaciated Indians ("they clicked their tongues and lips with joy, poor souls"). Noticing that a young boy is fixedly staring at him, Roger makes inquiries and discovers that the boy's parents and older brother have all been killed and that he's indentured to one of the agents. The "dear little chap" has a few words of English, and when Roger asks if he'd like to leave the Putumayo and travel across the waters to another land, the boy, named Omarino, clasps both Roger's hands and whispers excitedly, "yes." It isn't that simple, of course. His "owner" demands that Roger "buy" the boy and names his price: a shirt and a pair of trousers. The deal is sealed.

Soon after, Aredomi, a married man about twenty years old, begs Roger to take him along as well. Roger reluctantly agrees only when it becomes clear that Aredomi has no compunction about leaving his wife and that she is indifferent to his plan. Roger works out an agreement whereby Aredomi will "send for her if he elects to become a European, or to return if he wishes it." He and Roger start to develop a shorthand way of talking to each other: Roger learns to name certain items in Huitoto, and Aredomi does the same in English. Aredomi goes to his village for final good-byes and returns with a feather headdress for Roger—a gift of gratitude.

When Roger interviews the remaining eight Barbadians at La Chorrera, they speak their minds freely about the horrors they've witnessed—and to some degree participated in—and express their fear that once he departs from the region they'll be left to the tender mercies of Armand Norman. It turns out they're all deeply—and fraudulently—in debt to the company. Tizon advises Roger that the simplest solution, if he wants the Barbadians to leave with him, is to pay off their debts. Roger spends many days going over the account books and becomes outraged over the discrepancy between the Barbadians' low wages and the exorbitant prices charged them for purchases—"they have been robbed incredibly."

The steamer *Liberal,* which will carry Roger, Omarino, Aredomi, eighteen Barbadians, and several others away, is unaccountably delayed, and for a week Roger frets over his suspended state. He isn't feeling well, hasn't had any news from Europe for four months, nor had his hair cut and his beard properly trimmed for two. "I am sick of this horrid atmosphere of crime," he writes in his diary; he longs to get away. He's only slightly cheered up when Tizon reports that he's received full power of attorney from the prefect at Iquitos to "dismiss any employee of whatsoever rank and to appoint others." Roger professes to be pleased but confides his real feelings to his diary: "I wish I could think that any sincere and honest enquiry by Peru was likely," but he very much doubts it—"after waiting 3 years and when the fat is in the fire and all is known, she begins tardily to move."

Roger is fearful that the Barbadians—the only real witnesses he has to the company's criminality—will be arrested and jailed when the steamer reaches Iquitos. He manages to persuade Gielgud—whom Roger continues to regard as a "cold-blooded, selfish guzzler"—to see to it that passage orders for the Barbadians are made out as if for Iquitos, but with the proviso that they have the liberty "to break the journey at intermediate ports." To Roger's immense relief, Gielgud agrees to the plan—but that doesn't change Roger's opinion of him.

On November 16, the *Liberal* finally boards its passengers, clears off the ropes, and moves into the stream. With immense relief Roger records how the steamer "slipped down the still water between the sandbank and the shore and with our nose in the downward current were in a moment swept out of sight.... My last view of the scene of such grim tragedy as I believe exists nowhere else on earth today." He realizes, too, that his own escape from injury and death was hardly foreordained; speaking one's mind in the Putumayo isn't a recommended passport to safety.

Five days later, with Roger's encouragement, all the Barbadians except Bishop and one other debark at two separate points on the Brazilian side of the Amazon, before the steamer reaches Iquitos, where they would have risked arrest. His witnesses are safe, but the drama far from over.

Arriving in Iquitos on November 25, 1910, Roger rents quarters in town for Bishop, Aredomi, and Omarino and stays himself, once again, with the trader and part-time British consul David Cazes and his wife. Upon meeting the Indians, Mrs. Cazes (Roger writes in his diary) "sniffs at their being here, and suggests a bath. I said the Indians are, generally speaking, much cleaner than whites as regards their bodies." His contact with her husband is even less satisfactory. Roger is more certain than ever that Cazes knew a great deal early on about atrocities against the Indians but did nothing to inform the Foreign Office.

In Iquitos, a comparatively urban spot, Roger ends his long stretch of celibacy with a shipboard steward named Ignacio Torres, who first catches his eye while polishing the brass with a "huge and stiff" erection; he laughingly looks over at Roger—and contact is made. He sees Ignacio nearly every day for more than a week—and will remain in touch with him through letters for more than a year. While continuing to see Ignacio, Roger also takes up in Iquitos with a "strong-limbed, very sturdy chap about 22 or 23 years of age" named Julio and sees him too with some frequency—interspersing both "regulars" with a few anonymous contacts on the side. After a period of famine, he indulges in a feast.

In regard to his public duties, Roger makes an official call on Dr. Paz Soldán, the Peruvian prefect in Iquitos, who tells him that a government Commission of Justice is about to sail for the Putumayo to investigate conditions. He assures Roger that the commission will set all to rights and implores him, in the interim, not to make public any report that he submits to the British Foreign Office; publication would be a "crushing weight on the guiltless shoulders of Peru."

Guiltless shoulders, indeed!—Roger thinks to himself. What he tells Soldán is more politic: his chief concern is getting safely home, not in speaking truth to a complicitous prefect. "I intend to write two distinct reports," Roger tells Soldán. The one will be a report on the Amazon company's general treatment of the Barbadian subjects of the British Crown and will in no way implicate the government of Peru. The other, dealing with charges against various Peruvian citizens for their ill-treatment of the Indians, he has "every hope" can be kept confidential.

When the prefect overflows with unctuous gratitude, Roger adds that should the pending Commission of Justice fail to gather sufficient evidence or recommend sufficient corrective action, he *will* publish his second report as well. Though he's mastered the art of an "iron fist in a velvet glove," Roger's all but certain that he'll have to use the whip hand, that the pending "inquiry" will prove, as before, a "sham." When the prefect assures him several times over that the commission is determined to avenge past wrongs, Roger smiles wanly as he thinks to himself, These people will do nothing unless forced to. Publicity is their fear, their haunting dread.

It becomes clear even before Roger leaves Iquitos that the inquiry will indeed be a travesty—if it comes to pass at all. Bishop tells him that Arana's brother-in-law, Pablo Zumaeta, has also paid a visit to Paz Soldán and has managed to get himself and one of his cronies appointed to survey conditions in the Putumayo *before* the Commission of Justice arrives—to ensure, in other words, that the path of evidence is swept clean, potentially hostile witnesses intimidated, and their own minions duly rehearsed. Well, Roger concludes, the truth *will* come out; if the Peruvian government is bent on dissembling, he'll take whatever public action is necessary.

When the day finally arrives to depart Iquitos for the long voyage to London, Roger writes in his diary that "the only people I regret leaving are the Indians"; only they have managed somehow to preserve "morality of mind, gentleness of demeanour, and simplicity of heart." The "big question" remains—"the future of the South American Indians and Native people generally."

When they reach Para, Roger sees to it that Aredomi and Omarino, along with Bishop, are transferred to a vessel bound for Barbados and the care of the Jesuit Father Frederick Smith at the Catholic church in Bridgetown; Roger's hope is that under Smith's tutelage they'll gain some knowledge of English folkways before he brings them to London. Having been the British consul at Para, Roger also takes advantage of his knowledge of the town's cruising grounds, especially the Big Square near the palace, and during the four-day layover he manages at various times to have sex with several different men.

When it comes time to depart for Southampton, Roger summarizes in his diary the tumultuous months now safely behind him. The crimes of the Putumayo, he writes, the "crushing enslavement of a hapless subject people," are not solely due to four hundred years of Latin brutality but due as well to Christianity's "zeal to convert" and to the value "modern commercialism" places on profits over people.

Roger arrives in London on January 4, 1911, and by the next day is at work preparing an official report for the Foreign Office.

He's determined on a reckoning.

. . .

Within a day of his arrival back in London, Roger learns from Louis Mallet, the sympathetic undersecretary at the Foreign Office, that the Peruvian minister in London has conveyed his government's determination to act "with due energy" in regard to the Putumayo. Mallet also passes on Lord Grey's congratulations to Roger for "good work" that has borne fruit so rapidly and suggests that he submit a short preliminary report as soon as possible for transmission to Lima as a further way of encouraging speedy action.

As Roger works away on the report, he's astonished to receive a note from Julio Arana, then in London, suggesting they meet to work together on a program of reform. "Rather cheeky!" Roger writes to Mallet; he wouldn't mind meeting the "rascal" if he thought it would do any good, but Mallet agrees that there's nothing to be gained. Receiving no reply, the belligerently self-confident Arana writes again, and Roger ignores him again, simply writing in his diary, "the swine!" Roger turns his hand full-time to producing the preliminary report Grey has requested, and turns it in on January 7, 1911. He includes a warning to the Foreign Office that Peru's promise of "due energy" is no guarantee, judging from its past performance, of any corrective action. Peru, Roger believes, is more interested in muffling Britain's protest than redressing it. On the last day in January, Roger hands in his full-length report to the Foreign Office, a searing indictment that names names.

Grey submits it to the Peruvian government through the British chargé d'affaires in Lima, "tactfully" adding that the British government will refrain from publishing the report if it has Peru's assurance that judicial proceedings against the guilty parties will be inaugurated.

Week after week goes by with no response from Lima. Word spreads that a Casement Report exists, and a Liberal MP raises questions about it in the

House of Commons. Consul David Cazes reports from Iquitos that there is no sign of a judicial commission—not even a rumor from Lima of pending appointments. Juan Tizon writes from La Chorrera that he's used the official power Prefect Soldán had earlier given him to discharge several of the company's chief agents, including Armando Normand, from their posts, but none have been arraigned and all continue to roam about freely. The various reports outrage Roger, who thinks such appalling criminals should be in prison—and at once. "Full up" with the horror of it all, he goes to Dublin in February to catch up with family and friends, including sister Nina and cousin Gee.

On his way back to London, Roger stops off to visit Morel and his wife, with whom he's stayed in touch throughout his time in the Putumayo. Morel updates him on the latest developments in the Congo, and none of it serves to dilute Roger's current mood of futility.

"Yes," Morel tells him, "the flag of Leopold's Congo Free State has been lowered, and the Belgian tricolor now waves over Boma, but every other promise of change is still on paper."

"And the new Colonial charter . . . the new system of governance? I thought the Belgian parliament had—"

"The parliament handed over policy to a so-called minister of colonies, which would be amusing if it wasn't so sad, since Belgium has exactly one colony: the Congo."

Roger looks puzzled and upset. "But didn't I hear something about a new colonial council set up to advise the minister? From what I read in the press, it looked promising. . . ."

"They left out the fine print. Eight of the fourteen members are appointed by the king. Albert's an improvement over his father. Less brutal. But he's just as devoted to royal prerogatives."

Roger feels a comingled mix of anger and agitation. "Look here, Morel . . . I mean, are you telling me that *nothing* has actually changed for the better? Surely, the Africans, at least, no longer have to—"

"I didn't mean to sound quite so bleak," Morel breaks in. (The picture *is* bleak, but he doesn't want to burden Roger with all of it at once.) "Administratively, governance of the Congo is now in the hands of cautious bureaucrats—better than rule by a capricious monarch. The colony is practically crawling with bureaucrats. . . ."

"But what are they *doing?*" Roger persists.

"Not much, I fear. Didn't I write you about the Permanent Commission for the Protection of Natives?"

"It sounds a mouthful. Is it *doing* anything?" Roger's mournful look makes it clear he already knows the answer.

"Well, apparently . . . I mean, it seems the commission hasn't been . . . been meeting very often. . . ." Morel's effort to soften the blow is transparent.

Roger groans. "Like every other damned commission I know of . . ."

"Gross abuse of the natives," Morel adds encouragingly, "*has* greatly diminished, but they . . . they can't move about as freely as they once could."

"What in heaven's name does *that* mean? Are they being held captive?"

"No, no, nothing like that. But, as you know, the bureaucratic mind favors *neatness*. . . . They've been organizing everyone into tribal units with more distinctive identities than in fact exist. You now belong to one particular tribe living in one particular place and . . . and you're supposed to stay there."

"That's an absolute mockery! . . . The Congolese people don't rigidly separate themselves . . . especially the Bantu or . . . or the Bakongo and Baluba in the savannas where . . . where several languages are . . ." Roger suddenly collapses into a chair, his hand covering his face. Morel goes over and pats him repeatedly on the back, about the best he can do by way of comfort, though he feels Roger's pain acutely.

"Now, now, old Tiger . . . let's have none of that. . . . Things aren't all *that* grim, you know. . . . Surely it's better to be confined to a small area than to be beaten to death!"

Roger raises his head. "The mines will take care of that."

"Yes, the mines . . . I did write you about the mines. Yes, when the price for rubber began to collapse, the discovery in Katanga of copper, gold, coal—all kinds of treasure—took up the slack. Which are where most Congolese men are now working. . . ."

"I'm sure they are, and just as sure that not a drop of the fabulous profits are trickling down to them."

"All too true, I'm afraid. It takes a huge investment, after all—foundries, rolling mills, crushers. . . . No African could possibly afford—"

"I see, I see. But many a white European *can*. . . . Yes, the rest of the picture is all too clear. The miners work long hours, are paid a pittance, live in filthy huts with no sanitation, probably not even fresh water . . . and the European mine owners build castles even larger than Leopold's."

"We do what we can, my dear old friend," Morel says somberly. "What more can we do? . . . People are no longer being flogged to death. That's something, is it not? It's something. . . ."

"If you say so, old Bulldog, if you say so." Roger gets up from his chair and impulsively embraces Morel. "Let's hope I can manage to do at least *that* much in the Putumayo, eh? I wouldn't wager any bets. . . ."

Returning to London in March, Roger submits his final report to the Foreign Office and, appalled at what Morel has told him about the Congo and deeply frustrated at the lack of movement in regard to the Putumayo, requests a private meeting with Lord Grey. His request granted, he's told that Louis Mallet will also attend the meeting. As Roger enters the huge Italianate building, which houses the Foreign Office in Whitehall, and climbs the imposing Grand Staircase, with its towering naves, brilliant chandeliers, and marble pilasters, he can't help but wonder, half-amused, at how the most powerful nation on the face of the earth finds itself humbly petitioning a third-rank South American country to please, oh please, be kind enough to respond to our request for information.

And he says as much—politely—at the very start of the meeting.

"I don't understand," Roger begins with feigned innocence, "how the authorities at Lima dare to ignore what is, after all, a most restrained request that Peru provide *some* evidence that it's taking action in the Putumayo. Are Arana, Zumaeta, Normand, and their ilk still in control of the situation? If so, *why*? Why haven't they been removed and arrested? Why has no investigative or judicial commission arrived? . . . But I needn't go on. You honorable gentlemen are surely as well informed as I. . . ."

After some general clearing of throats, Lord Grey obliquely remarks, "You have done most exemplary work, Casement. Your reports are models of clarity and insight."

"Thank you, m'lord."

"I do feel that now and then—only now and then, I assure you—your passion somewhat overcomes your objectivity."

Roger is genuinely surprised. "Really, m'lord? I struggled very hard to control my personal feelings in the matter, which to be sure *are* passionate."

"As well they should be," Louis Mallet throws in. "I myself would like to see every one of the scoundrels hanged." Catching Grey's frown, Mallet quickly adds, "Beg pardon, m'lord."

"I dare say," Grey roundly responds, "that we all feel rather strongly about this matter. But if we wish to achieve our objective, I believe patient diplomacy is the best path."

"Were the 'offending' passages in my report removed, m'lord?" There's a slight edge to Roger's voice.

"Yes. By my order. Mr. Mallet objecting." A wry half smile crosses Grey's lips.

"Can you give me an example?" Roger asks, determined to press the matter.

"I doubt I can remember specifics. . . . Do you, Mallet?"

"I believe the word 'scoundrels' was omitted . . . also a direct accusation of lying. I don't seem able to recall other examples. . . ."

"All of it true, and much more," Roger says, not entirely succeeding in controlling his exasperation.

"Doubtless," Grey drily replies. "But you will remember, Mr. Casement, that your orders strictly speaking were to report on any wrongs being done to British subjects, to the Barbadians, not to address the condition of the Indians."

Roger is flabbergasted at what amounts to a misrepresentation. "But you *did,* m'lord, more than hint that I should keep my eyes open as to what you called the 'general situation.' I trust my memory is correct in that regard."

Roger's boldness, somewhat to his surprise, pays off. "Well, yes," Grey acknowledges, "certainly something to that effect . . . and I must say, I'm glad you did. What an appalling situation. Something must be done."

"Thank you, m'lord. I was hoping for exactly that response."

"The trouble is *what* should be done. My inclination is to let the Peruvian government know that we expect prompt action and, absent such, will make your report public."

"But m'lord! . . ." Roger's alarm is transparent. "I've been assuming all along that the value of my report lies in its publication—its ability to arouse public indignation—which alone would force the Peruvian government's hand. Just as my Congo Report did. Or should I say—having recently seen Mr. Morel—was at least designed to do."

Grey looks apprehensive. "We do what we can, Mr. Casement, we do what we can. . . . Belgium is a sovereign nation, after all."

"I understand from Morel," Roger says, his tone bristly, "that a number of England's wealthiest financiers have invested in the Congo mines, and that conditions there are appalling. I trust these financiers, as British subjects, can be urged to take corrective measures."

Grey flushes with annoyance. "His Majesty's government, Mr. Casement, is not in the habit of handcuffing our overseas investors."

Alarmed at the turn in the conversation, Mallet hurries to bring the subject back to the Putumayo. "It is our feeling, Casement," Mallet says, aiming for a calming effect, "that to publish your report now might jeopardize our chief leverage with Lima. We have no legal jurisdiction, after all, in the Putumayo; it is not British territory. Our best weapon is to hold in reserve the threat of public embarrassment."

Since it's obvious to Roger that Grey is wedded to a hands-off policy on the Congo, he lets Mallet steer him back to the Putumayo, where he still has some residual hope of action. "What about pressure from the United States?" he throws in. "Could this not be a joint effort?"

"We wish it were possible," Grey civilly replies. "James Bryce, our ambassador to Washington—"

"Yes, I know him," Roger breaks in enthusiastically. "He was chief secretary for Ireland. A very decent sort . . ."

"And most sympathetic on this matter. He informs us that the U.S. government would also welcome the publication of your report, but Peru is its main ally in South America, and it doesn't wish to risk a rupture. Even more important, it doesn't want to jeopardize the Monroe Doctrine's long-standing interdiction of interference from Europe on the North American continent."

"Ah yes—the bloody Monroe Doctrine! The USA's insistence that Latin American is *its* vassal, and no one else's!" Roger impulsively bursts out, then quickly draws back. "Excuse me, m'lord. But that doctrine, I've always felt, is the height of national arrogance. '*We* can do whatever we like on the continent, but nobody else dare interfere!' As if the United States is any less of a threat to Latin America's indigenous population than other powers in the world!"

"I see your point," Grey genially replies, then adds with just a hint of impishness, "but dare not acknowledge it publicly."

His waggish remark breaks the tension.

Grey presses his advantage: "I don't think you've learned this yet, Casement, but as of just yesterday Lima does seem to have reawakened from its long slumber."

"Really? Meaning, I presume, that it's reinvigorated border wars against Colombia and Ecuador?"

"Yes, but not only that. Lima is apparently sending out to the Putumayo not a commission, as previously thought, but rather the respected jurist Romulo Paredes. He'll be armed with warrants to arrest the six major culprits you name in your report. That's some ground for optimism, is it not?"

"Forgive me, m'lord, but, eager as I am to share your view, Mr. Mallet here—I do hope I'm not out of line, Louis—told me on our way into the room that word has arrived that only one of the miscreants is any longer *in* Iquitos, and he's already been released on bail."

"Alas, that's quite true, Mr. Casement. And Mr. Mallet did right to inform you of it. You are, after all, at the heart of this matter. Like you, I am losing patience. Lima seems always to have some excuse at hand to prevent them from taking energetic action. Yet just today our consul in Lima wired that he does still believe in the good faith of the Peruvian government. Isn't that so, Mallet?"

"It is, m'lord. But . . ."—Mallet seems hesitant—"we've had additional word since, that the rainy season has disrupted all telegraphic communication between Lima and Iquitos. So apparently yet another delay looms."

Grey rises abruptly from his chair. "I can hardly believe it. I really *am* losing patience!" Scowling, he shakes Roger's hand vigorously. "You have my pledge, Casement. We will *not* let this matter die. You will excuse me now: I must immediately get word to Consul Jerome in Lima. We will be back in touch very soon. . . . Mallet?"

Mallet dutifully follows Grey from the room, then, looking back at Roger, shrugs his shoulders as if to say, "Who knows?"

Roger thinks the odds are slim that the Foreign Office will press Lima vigorously. Yet he's unprepared for Mallet's shocking phone call soon after the meeting with Grey. In a state of great distress, Mallet tells Roger that the Foreign Office has gotten news that the Peruvian government is planning to name *Julio Arana* as its representative to the *International Rubber* exhibition due to open in June at Islington's Agricultural Hall.

"I've never *heard* of the *International Rubber* exhibition!" Mallet shouts over the phone to Roger. "Damn those Peruvians! It's an outrage! We're going to protest directly to the director of the exhibition. We want Arana declared persona non grata."

It never comes to that. Getting word, apparently, that his appointment has angered the British, the wily Arana seizes the initiative. He tells the Peruvian government that, much to his regret, he must decline its kind offer. He is far too busy, he says, with putting the affairs of the Peruvian Amazon Company in order.

Though Lord Grey is by temperament irresolute, his patience isn't infinite. Soon after the meeting with Roger and Mallet, Grey is shown an issue of *El Diario*—the Peruvian president's personal organ—that contains a reprimand to the British government for having insulted and defamed its distinguished citizen Julio Arana and for believing the atrocity stories circulated by Colombia, Peru's enemy, and spread by the gullible Roger Casement. Within days Grey calls Roger back in for another consultation.

"The matter has become intolerable," Grey tells him straight-out. "The Peruvian government has all but told us to stop 'meddling' in their affairs. The effrontery! They seem to have forgotten that the Peruvian Amazon Company is a *British* Company, with a *British* board of directors! It is subject to *our* jurisdiction, not theirs! The company's malfeasance reflects on our good name, and we will not sit idly by while a bunch of brigands tarnish it."

Startled and delighted at Grey's unexpected vehemence, Roger decides to curtail his own, lest Grey seize on "excessive Irish ardor" as an excuse for retreating yet again to a more temperate position. "I couldn't agree more," Roger quietly says.

"I'm sick and tired of their excuses," Grey grumbles. "They're wasting our time and theirs."

"And wasting still more Indian lives," Mallet throws in.

"Quite so." Grey sounds somewhat abashed at the reminder.

"If I may, m'lord?" Roger asks, with calculated hesitation.

"Yes, Casement?"

"Our goal, I believe, should not be the destruction of the Peruvian Amazon Company but rather its reformation."

"Why not just close the company down?" Mallet asks. "How do you reform a gang of thieves?"

"Closing it down," Roger responds, "will get rid of the company, but not the depredations of Arana and his cronies. They'll continue to enslave and brutalize the Indians—even more so, since no authority will any longer exist above them. If, on the other hand, we can persuade the British members of the company's board of directors—a majority—actively to take up their responsibilities, there's some hope for a change in policy."

"I see your point," Grey says. "It's a good one. However, the question remains: how do we activate the board and bring it under the control of the Foreign Office?"

"I've thought a great deal about that, m'lord." Roger's tone is as sycophantic as he can manage. "I believe control is best exercised indirectly. I thought perhaps one way forward would be for the Foreign Office to let the board know, unofficially, that my services are available to them for consultation."

"Excellent idea, Casement! I like it very much." Lord Grey is actually grinning, an expression not previously known to be part of his muscular repertoire.

"As do I," Mallet chimed in. "Perhaps we might push it just a bit further and suggest that you attend the next board meeting."

"No, not 'suggest,'" Grey added—"strongly urge!"

And so it is done—in a matter of speaking. Grey does write to the board, urging the advisability of Roger attending its next meeting. But he also states his belief that its members have been "wholly ignorant" of "the appalling state of affairs in the Putumayo." Informed of Grey's gratuitous exoneration of the board—for that's what it comes to—Roger's temper again flares. Ignorance is no excuse, he writes Mallet; besides, Arana is a member of the board and surely *he,* at the least, has long been aware of—has indeed sponsored—the brutality.

Mallet passes on Roger's objection to the foreign secretary, and Grey, in the apparent belief that he's toning down the exoneration, lets the board know that what he meant in his initial communication was to excuse only the British members from responsibility. The board then dutifully invites Roger to attend its next meeting, and he accepts the invitation—though "reluctantly," he replies (continuing with the sycophantic strategy), "not wishing to intrude but cognizant of your need for my expertise in affairs relating to the Putumayo." He does, cleverly, request that the board hire an experienced expert in taking down shorthand to ensure the accuracy of his remarks.

During this same four-month period—April to July 1911—another development further brightens the picture. The commissioners who Roger had accompanied to the Putumayo issue a report that confirms his own account in all significant respects. Still, Roger isn't entirely pleased with it. As he tells the Foreign Office, the report fails to acknowledge that the indigenous Indians, and no one else, have title to the land; their "long-established methods of existence are to him of vital importance" and must remain intact. To acknowledge such a claim—far in advance of its time—would be to undercut the entire logic of imperialism, and no imperial power, perhaps least of all Britain, is about to acknowledge it. Roger's complaint is ignored.

By then, Roger has attended the Amazon Company's board meetings—and his doubts have once more blossomed. The directors strike him as "all at sea"; they don't know what to do, nor even, should they ever decide to act, whether they have the legitimate power to do so. Roger urges the board to better inform themselves by sending one of its own members to the Putumayo to work with Juan Tizon, the Peruvian reformer, and to hear from him a detailed account of conditions in the area. But . . . but . . . the directors reluctantly reveal that, far from being able to afford such an expenditure, the company is in dire straits financially.

The news astonishes Roger. He informs the Foreign Office that the board has apparently been characterized all along not only by "criminal neglect" but by "business incapacity" as well. *Why* is the company in such bad shape? In large part, though Roger doesn't fully credit the fact, for reasons out of its control—in particular, the market shift since 1908 from "wild" rubber harvested from trees in Africa to the cheaper plantation rubber grown in the Far East. By 1910 the production of rubber in the Putumayo has fallen off 20 percent and continues thereafter to drop precipitously. None of this means that the huge commissions taken by Arana and his associates aren't contributory to the company's plight, but their depredations alone aren't sufficient to explain the firm's dangerously high level of debt. When Arana finally attends one of the board meetings, he urbanely offers to take a cut in his director's salary; the sham offer makes Roger's blood boil. He's later able to convince the other board members that Arana's real intention, now that pressure against his influence has built, is to destroy the company and exploit the Putumayo free from any supervisory power.

The "solution" that the board comes up with is essentially a plea for Roger to work miracles. The company can be saved *and* cleansed, they tell Roger, if only he will go to his "humanitarian" friends and raise enough money to buy out Arana. Long attracted to miracles, Roger agrees to try. He appeals to William Cadbury and other wealthy reform-minded folks, but they're far too business savvy to assist their impractical friend. "Don't you see?" Cadbury asks him. "Don't you understand that rubber production in the Putumayo is doomed, that British and Dutch plantations in the East have essentially taken over the trade?"

In the midst of his futile attempt at fund-raising, Roger gets a confidential note from Sir Edward Grey. Its contents make his head spin: "It gives me great pleasure to inform you that the King has been pleased, on my recommendation, to confer upon you a Knighthood in recognition of your valuable services in connection with your recent Mission to the Putumayo District. Yours sincerely, E. Grey."

Roger's reaction is to write a single word in his diary: "Alack." While mulling over the ghastly/thrilling news, his head whirling with a flywheel of opposing feelings, he doesn't even tell cousin Gee the news. During the three-week period that ensues from the day of notification to the scheduled date for the ceremony, Roger careens from side to side in an inner debate so intense that he almost forgets about pursuing sex—though he catches himself in time and makes his usual round of outdoor cruising spots. His tastes expand along with his pending role of imperator ("Japanese youth 25, G. Miyagawa"; "Donald Ross of Egypt"; "Lovely French lad or Italian. 20. Dark cap, fair, very tall . . . and then thick young German or Italian sailor round Gardens").

When the king's Birthday Honours list is published, and the cat let out of the bag, Roger is inundated with congratulations. In response to a letter from Alice Green, Roger thanks her for having seen through to "the Irish side to it all"—meaning, that his nationalist friends are likely to react negatively. If he accepts the award, they'll denounce him as a traitor, and with cause he believes: "I feel always that until Ireland is safe and her outlook happy no Irishman has any right to be accepting honours or having a good time of it anywhere." Nor does it matter, he feels, that he's done nothing to pursue the honor and has been "in reality, deeply desiring *not* to get it."

And yet . . . . how can he possibly "fling back something offered with gracious good will"? Grey is, after all, his boss; Roger, after all, basically likes him—and has chosen to remain in His Majesty's service. Perhaps, he acknowledges, that too is hypocritical, yet he remembers his frustration at trying to find a job outside the consular ranks that paid a decent wage. He can himself live on very little, caring nothing for ostentation or possessions. But others rely heavily on him—especially his two brothers, Charlie and Tom, the one struggling financially in Australia, the other in South Africa—including as well any number of Irish activists like Bulmer Hobson, publications like *Irish Freedom,* organizations like Sinn Féin, and schools like Patrick Pearse's Irish Ireland Saint Enda's in Dublin or the Gaelic institute at Cloghaneely.

Perhaps Roger, who has a decidedly theatrical streak, is overdramatizing—there's been no rush to judgment among Irish nationalists—but his conflicted feelings are real enough, and he has to find a way to cut through them. (A few years later William Butler Yeats will suffer from no such ambiguity; he'll straightforwardly refuse a knighthood on the grounds that the Irish people would feel "only for a ribbon he left us.") Roger's deliberations are a good deal more labyrinthine. It helps that Alice Green, whose Irish patriotism no one doubts, urges him to accept the award and assures him that it's okay to *want* it. And so it is that on July 6, 1911, Roger presents himself for knighthood—letting it be known, as a rearguard action, that he can't locate ("so little does he care for it") his earlier award, the CMG badge, and has to borrow one from the Foreign Office for the occasion.

Three weeks later the state-appointed Peruvian judge Romulo Paredes, having completed his tour of the Putumayo, releases a preliminary report that agrees in all particulars with Roger's previous account of widespread criminality. Paredes issues some 215 warrants for arrests (while later confiding to Roger that he fears assassination), and Peru announces its intention to send the respected jurist Judge Valcarcel to Iquitos to hear the indictments. Roger's reaction is that the news is "almost too good to be true."

It is. Most of the main culprits immediately escape to Brazil, and only three of the warrants, for minor figures, are executed. In Roger's view, too wide a net has been cast; to topple an infamous system, he feels, it makes more sense to focus on rounding up the half dozen or so men who set the pattern for their underlings.

It gradually dawns on Roger that perhaps this is the moment to return to Iquitos. He's failed to raise enough money to stabilize and purify the Peruvian Amazon Company, and if it goes under, as seems imminent, the British Foreign Office will no longer be able to justify intervention on grounds that the well-being of British subjects—the few Barbadians who remain in the company's employment—is at stake. Roger has already succeeded in pushing the Foreign Office to appoint a full-time consul in Iquitos to replace the untrustworthy amateur, David Cazes. Roger's recommendation for the job, George Michell, an old friend who previously served as consul in Boma, has been appointed but isn't due to leave for his post until the fall of 1911. In the interim Roger suggests to the Foreign Office that he fill in for Michell: "I am quite ready to go," he writes Gerald Spicer, "and should be glad to try and put a square ending to what has begun . . . and were I in Iquitos I could influence things a good deal in the right direction." Sir Edward Grey enthusiastically accepts the idea.

Shortly before embarking for South America, Roger writes to tell his old friend Morel about his new mission: it's "a continuation of my work of last year and I hope to make a clean sweep this time." He hopes to be "an instrument of good and maybe the means of ending a ghastly system of wrongdoing." Yet, at age forty-seven, he's determined that "this is my last external effort on behalf of others. Henceforth and for aye I shall concentrate on Ireland alone." A fellow passenger on shipboard during the second leg of Roger's journey thinks him already the very personification of the Irishman:

"The temperature was floating around ninety-six in the shade [but] he wore a thick and very dark brown suit of Irish homespun. How he stood it I do not know. . . . The final touch was a tremendous and very knobbly walking stick—a shillalah that must have been two inches in diameter at the very least."

Roger takes with him the two Indian youths, Omarino and Aredomi, he'd brought to England. They seem to have been happy enough during their stay—Roger brought them to the Anti-Slavery Society, William Rothenstein painted their portraits, and Roger's sister, Nina, served as their combined chaperone and governess. But Roger came to realize that their presence in England served no significant purpose after all. Although the two had for the most part seemed content, they'd been slow to pick up English, and he felt they'd probably be better off returning to their homes. Upon arriving in South America, Roger sees to it that Omarino and Aredomi are well taken care of; a few months after their return, the new consul, George Michell, employs them as household servants—though ultimately they tire of the work, resign, and disappear back into the forest.

Once in Iquitos, Roger plunges into a maelstrom of activity and soon learns that Armando Normand has absconded to Argentina and that two other prime villains, Jose Fonseca and Alfredo Montt, have retreated to a Brazilian frontier town—forcibly taking with them ten Boras. One major criminal, Aurelio Rodriguez—who'd burned alive some forty Indians in a single day—*had* been arrested, but Pablo Zumaeta had quickly put up bail, and both had fled to Peru. Roger attempts to get the Brazilian authorities to extradite Fonseca and Montt, planning to then arrest them once they land on the Peruvian side of the border—but the two police officers assigned to make the arrest "somehow" manage to get stupefyingly drunk, and the scheme is aborted.

Before long Roger is raging at the "perfectly insane way time is wasted" and feeling impotent to effect any change. With far more leisure than he'd hoped for or wants, Roger avails himself of the ready availability of sexual partners in Iquitos ("Tram inspector . . . entered Kiosque, I followed and he put hand at once softly fingering and milking—I put hand and found, in dark, a *huge* stiff one—long and thick and firm as poker," etc.) But Roger's good-luck charm is for the first time tarnished: during one erotic encounter he's robbed, and during another he comes close to being arrested—standard dangers of the subterranean homosexual life that previously he'd somehow managed to avoid. Roger turns uncharacteristically cautious, aware that his newfound political notoriety has made him vulnerable to scandal. This is not what he came back to Iquitos for. Not wanting to risk compromising his mission, Roger decides that he will have to "sacrifice love to fear."

But his mission has in any case been derailed before it can begin. He learns that the Peruvian Amazon Company has gone into liquidation—and none other than Julio Arana himself has been appointed official liquidator. When the company expires, so too will the legal grounds for British intervention to protect its subjects. Nor will Roger's vow of sexual abstention alone be a sufficient guarantee of his personal safety. Judge Romulo Paredes tells him—as others have before—that his unmasking of the Putumayo perpetrators has put his life in serious jeopardy; he, too, Paredes says, has received so many threats that he lives in constant alarm.

He also confirms what Roger has all along feared: that the situation in the Putumayo is almost certainly beyond redemption, that the Peruvian authorities will do nothing to arrest the criminals or to rock the boat. In a last-ditch effort to apprehend Fonseca and Montt, Roger tracks them to the Javari River, but after more than a week in pursuit fails even to catch sight of them. Roger implores the Foreign Office to enlist the United States in pressuring Peru to publish the Paredes Report, but to no avail. He's hit a brick wall.

By this time, early December 1911, George Michell and his family have arrived in Iquitos to take over the consulship; Roger helps them settle in and then boards a steamer for Para. "Left Iquitos! Hurrah!" he writes cousin Gee—"that vile and pestilential hole is finally behind me!" In Para he feels safer and resumes his search for sexual pleasure, doubling up for lost time: one pickup "worked fiercely and hugely" and later "still more furiously and inquired 'Ebon?' [Do you like it?] when putting in with awful thrusts."

Roger assumes that in Para he'll change ships and then take up his old post again in Rio. But a startling letter arrives from the Foreign Office: he is not to be redeployed; the Rio post has gone to someone else. Rather than return to England and cool his heels while awaiting another belabored Foreign Office decision about his future, Roger is suddenly seized with a daring, perhaps foolhardy, impulse: he will take ship to Barbados, and from there to the States, where he will use his personal acquaintance with James Bryce, the British ambassador, to open doors for him—open them wide enough to attempt a personal appeal (or, as he puts it to a friend, "a sort of personal assault") on President William Howard Taft and the State Department, urging them to join Britain in pressuring Peru for reforms—though it's not at all clear that the Foreign Office would cooperate with such a scheme. Leaving

Para on December 24, Roger sails for Barbados, where, on New Year's Eve, he boards the SS *Terence* for New York.

. . .

Upon arriving in the city, Roger immediately contacts James Bryce, the British ambassador to Washington since 1907, who, falling in with Roger's plan, invites him to come to the Capitol. Roger could hardly have found a more congenial spirit. Born, like Roger, in County Antrim, Bryce shares his deep sympathy for the oppressed; during the Boer War he'd been a strong critic of Britain's actions in burning down farms and herding civilians into concentration camps. In his 1888 masterwork, the 1,500 page *The American Commonwealth*—still regarded as a classic—Bryce deplores the mounting inequality of wealth in the United States and its plague of venal politicians, yet expresses optimism about the country's future.

Bryce gives Roger a warm welcome and does exactly as Roger had hoped: he puts him into personal contact with those American officials most responsible for U.S. policy on South America. Bryce's right-hand man, Alfred Mitchell Innes, is, like Bryce, also a sympathetic figure, and he and Roger take to each other immediately. Bryce and Innes share with him several recent communications from Lima declaring that a number of arrests have been made, that the Peruvian police are in hot pursuit of the remaining malefactors, and that Pablo Zumaeta has *not* absconded but is in fact under lock and key. Roger politely tells them that their information is outdated at best and fabricated at worst. He shares with them his own recent discovery in Iquitos that all the leading malefactors have already fled the country. Neither Bryce nor Inness has any trouble accepting Roger's version of events as the accurate one, nor in acknowledging that their own so-called informants may well have been paid propagandists.

Innes, like Bryce, is well connected and helps to smooth Roger's path with introductions. They arrange for Roger to meet with various South American specialists in the State Department and even manage to effect a private dinner with President Taft. Bryce reports to the British Foreign Office that Roger impressed one and all: "He was able to create a personal interest among the higher authorities, which gives strong grounds for believing that publication of his report will be welcomed by the United States Government." A member of the embassy staff has a more dramatic take on the meeting with Taft: "A queer picture they made—the tall Celt haggard and livid from the

Putumayo swamps, fixing with glittering black eyes the burly, rubicund Anglo-Saxon [Taft]. It was like a black snake fascinating a wombat."

Roger's own dispatch to Lord Grey is a good deal less melodramatic: he simply reports that by the end of the cordial dinner, President Taft, though previously skittish, seemed persuaded that a joint effort by the United States and Britain *would* put maximum pressure on Peru to take action. And Taft does follow through. He directs the U.S. secretary of state to notify Lima that strong evidence exists that the local authorities in Iquitos have made no effort to press charges against the Putumayo perpetrators. The State Department dispatch characterizes the situation as "unacceptable," and lets Lima know that unless Peru cleans up the "iniquitous system," the world will be forced to conclude that it is "unable properly to exercise sovereign rights over disputed regions"—the diplomatic version of an outright threat that the United States will be forced to side with Colombia in its contested border dispute with Peru.

Bryce cables news of the strong U.S. position to the British Foreign Office, and a gratified Sir Edward Grey leans to the view that the propitious moment has finally arrived to publish Roger's now two-year-old report. Grey has been hoping that the mere threat of publication would be sufficient to move Peru to salutary action. It hasn't been—as Roger had predicted all along—and Peru must now suffer the consequences. A lighthearted Roger sets sail for home, well satisfied that his mission has been a marked success. He feels confident that the publication of his report will lead to an explosive public outcry.

Once back in London, Roger tries to strengthen the Foreign Office's resolve through a long memo arguing that publication of his report (and Paredes's as well) is the only remaining option for bringing the Putumayo criminals to account—for letting "the civilised world know how Peru has used her primitive, defenceless, innocent populations in this greedy rush for rubber." Yet Roger is realistic enough to add that actual trials of the perpetrators can be expected to take place only "long after we are dead, and the last Putumayo Indian has been gathered in fragments, to his fathers." Grey responds with a note commending and "entirely approving" the role Roger has played in Washington.

The hosannas are premature. It isn't long before politicians in the United States raise a storm of protest over the presumptive breach of the Monroe Doctrine, and the U.S. State Department, in reaction, begins to backslide. Roger learns, too, that the U.S. minister in Lima has strongly urged against publication of Roger's report as counterproductive. Alarmed, Roger writes heatedly to Bryce that if the rumors are true and publication is delayed or abbreviated, "it will be a sin—and a sin of selfishness that God will not forgive." That Roger takes to invoking theological authority—more typically he alternates between secular humanism and a vaguely Christian spirituality— is a measure of his exasperation.

Up and down the adrenalin goes, back and forth the contradictory rumors, the slivers of news, the rarified tall tales (the tallest, that Pablo Zumaeta had been made acting mayor of Iquitos, turns out to be true). Liberal members of Parliament such as Joseph King and Josiah Wedgwood are reportedly organizing a well-orchestrated demand for the publication of Roger's report, and a seemingly official rumor spreads that Lima is poised, yet again, to appoint a new investigatory commission. Roger, like a human seismograph, internally registers every blurb on the ticker tape—each alloyed bulletin producing a parallel rise in anxiety.

Then news arrives that looks definitive: in late March 1912 Bryce cables the Foreign Office that the United States will defer to whatever decision the British government makes about publishing the Casement Report. Roger exhales, "At last, it will come to pass!" Well, not quite, not tomorrow, not even next month probably. Why *not*, for God's sakes! What *now* stands in the way?! Well, Roger is told, it seems that Paredes is willing after all to return to the Putumayo to gather more conclusive evidence. More—*what?!* From Hardenburg through Whiffen, from Casement to Paredes, thousands of pages of testimony have accumulated, and all of it points in one direction. Short of Moses returning with another set of tablets, the evidence is as conclusive as death and taxes. Cannot the Foreign Office understand when it's being hoodwinked? Cannot Whitehall see that the Peruvian government is, once again, simply playing for time?

Apparently not. But Louis Mallet can, members of the press can, Liberal MPs can—even the pope can! (He issues an encyclical deploring the ongoing suffering of the Peruvian Indians.) Unaccountably, the Foreign Office remains frozen in place. Weeks pass into months, until mounting public pressure for the release of Roger's report becomes so concentrated and sustained that in response to the umpteenth question in Parliament, Sir Edward Grey finally announces on July 2 that the report will be published "very shortly—at any rate before the end of the month." This time Grey—as if to atone for the endless delays—comes in *under* deadline. On July 13, 1912, Roger's report is finally released. Two days later the London *Times* headline reads, "The Putumayo Atrocities: A South American Congo—Sir Roger Casement's Report Published."

A host of other publications follow suit—including the prestigious *Spectator* and *Economist*—and, via Reuters and the Associated Press, news of the report travels around the world. It's left to a U.S. newspaper, the New York *Sun,* to put its particular, and highly peculiar, slant on the story: "Negroes of British Company Commit Terrible Crimes"—in other words, the Barbadians, not the Peruvians, are the prime villains. (In that same year of 1912, sixty-two blacks are lynched in the United States.)

The *Sun* isn't alone in hawking a prejudicial message. Julio Arana and his brother-in-law Abel Alarco make themselves amiably available for press interviews. Alarco tells one interviewer that the Casement Report is a tissue of lies; it's based on Hardenburg's distorted earlier account, still further embellished after the Colombian government provided Casement with a substantial bribe in exchange for discrediting Peru, its antagonist in the border dispute. In truth, Alarco announces, Peru has brought the many blessings of rubber to the world *despite* having to rely on "the savage, an unintelligent and unproductive being."

On one matter Alarco is straightforward: "We need not hesitate to declare, we who have opened the Putumayo to commerce and the world, that we have used force when force was indispensable. One does not conquer by caressing." After all, he points out, Peru is neither singular in this regard, nor the pacesetter: *all* the European powers have been subduing indigenous populations by force for centuries. True enough, but no European power, Peru's critics insist, has used force on so large a scale or with such ferocity. Oh really? Peru responds. The slave trade to the Americas? The German massacre of the Hereros in South West Africa? The French in Algeria? Or, for that matter, the British denial of food to the starving peasants of Ireland during the potato famine?

By midsummer 1912, a considerable groundswell has developed in Parliament for the appointment of a select committee—"Oh, no!" Roger groans—to inquire into the extent of responsibility the British directors of the Peruvian Amazon Company bear for the Putumayo atrocities and to suggest changes in the law to prevent such behavior in the future. Prime Minister Herbert Asquith declares himself in favor of such a committee and the House of Commons formally establishes it in October, with the highly regarded Liberal MP Charles Roberts in the chair. During its deliberations over the next few months, Roger will appear before it a number of times.

From the day of the publication of his report, Roger is inundated with praise—and with an assortment of offers and requests. Several publishers proffer book contracts. The London *Times* declares that Roger Casement deserves well "of his countrymen and of mankind" for the "ability and zeal with which he has investigated under very difficult conditions an appalling iniquity." The *Daily News* hails him as "man of the week" and prints a glowing tribute from his old friend E. D. Morel: "To denounce crime at a distance is a relatively simple task. To track the criminal to his lair in the equatorial forest . . . this is different. And to retain, through all, your clearness of vision, capacity to weigh evidence, self-control and moral strength—this is to pass through the highest test of mental and physical endurance, to attain the most conspicuous point of human achievement."

"Good heavens, Morel!" Roger writes him in embarrassed gratitude. "Next thing I know you'll be listing me as a jewel in the Crown of Empire! Stop it at once!" The reprimand is mocking, but the discomfort real: Roger dislikes overcharged praise, aware he's a mere mortal and of a "peculiar" sort typically denounced as sinful rather than held up as a candidate for sainthood. Besides, he's well aware that in commending him, the British are congratulating *themselves* as morally superior to the rest of the world. Yet two awkward facts remain: the Putumayo horrors have been committed under the aegis of a British company, and the British government dithered interminably before allowing Roger's report to see the light. He feels some sympathy for the attack on Britain's role mounted in the German press: "These butcheries remain an indelible blot on the British name." Roger—and Germany—seem to have forgotten that only a few years earlier Germany had savagely put down a revolt of the Khoi and Herero tribes in its South West Africa colony, killing some hundred thousand and herding survivors into concentration camps.

With his report now in circulation, Roger feels there's only one outstanding item on his Putumayo agenda: establishing a Christian mission in the area that—like at least a *few* of those in the Congo—might serve as a refuge and source of solace for the Indians, even, perhaps, a rallying point for resistance. Himself an ambiguous Christian who rarely enters a church—other than to view the architecture—conversion of the Indians is not among Roger's significant priorities. As he writes Morel, "I think there is mighty little Christianity in any of these 'Churches'; a good dose of severe heathenism would be good for mankind."

But that outburst marks the apogee of Roger's agnosticism. By both temperament and life experience, he *is* an apostate—a defector from official morality, a renegade—yet he is never attracted to atheism: something amorphous resides in the mist and could crystallize under sufficient pressure into a credo. Still, sectarian prejudice and antagonism have always puzzled and displeased him. Though reared Protestant and secretly baptized by his Catholic mother, Roger will all his life view denominational hatred as an atavistic outlet for a host of concealed enmities of a nonreligious nature.

That opinion is confirmed when—soon after his Putumayo Report appears—he launches an appeal to raise £15,000 for establishing a Putumayo mission and finds himself smack up against a host of suspicious orthodoxies. Roger accepts the reality that Peru is a Roman Catholic country; ergo, it will allow the establishment of a Catholic mission only. The Anglican archbishop of Canterbury, on the other hand, though a supporter of Roger's humanitarian work, is among the many who distance themselves from what they call his "Papist" fund-raising.

The prominent Protestant missionary John Harris is another. In soliciting Harris's support, Roger reiterates his unassailable argument that Peru will agree only to a Catholic mission, and a mission, in turn, is the only external agency that *might* be able to protect the Indians; it "would give these poor, hunted people," Roger writes Harris, "*some* ray of hope into their lives." But Harris is unbending, and the organizers of the Putumayo Mission Fund face strong headwinds in trying to gather contributions.

In Ireland, Protestant sectarianism is strongest in the county of Ulster. It's Roger's own birthplace, but that's no reason, as far as Roger is concerned, for sanctioning Ulster's anti-Catholic bigotry. Writing to cousin Gee in September from Belfast, he sums up his feelings: "The Church parade has begun past my windows—heavens, how appalling they look, with their grim Ulster-Hall faces all going down to curse the Pope and damn Home Rule in Kirk and Meeting House and let their God out for one day in the week—poor old man with his teeth broken with the cursing."

Within a few short years, as Ulster's fierce determination to remain part of Protestant Britain deepens, the more Roger will move away from the Protestantism that typifies the county—and edge toward the Catholicism that predominates in the "disloyal" rest of Ireland. His politics will determine his religious affiliation to a greater degree than the obverse (that is, his faith decreeing his politics). In any case, despite a concentrated funding drive throughout the summer of 1912, little more than £2,000 is raised—though ultimately a single benefactor will allow for a skeleton mission to go forward.

Averse to (excessive) adulation and satisfied that his role in the Putumayo scandal has pretty much played itself out, Roger feels the need to take stock as he approaches fifty. He knows that he wants to devote the bulk of his energy for the foreseeable future to the Irish struggle for independence but doesn't know—that long-standing, unresolved conundrum—whether, morally, that means he has to resign from the British consular service or whether, financially, he must remain in it to support himself and his needy siblings. Brother Tom has now opened a mountain inn in South Africa; Roger isn't surprised that it doesn't fare well—he thinks Tom's business sense is even worse than his own—nor surprised when Tom once again appeals to him for financial help. Roger, of course, says yes, though he confesses to Gee that "I wish he would either grow up or revert to infancy. In one case you could reason with him—in the other smack him."

In part because of his openhandedness, Roger is feeling badly squeezed. The stress of unpaid bills may be contributory to the proliferation of physical symptoms he now suffers. His joints ache; he has pain in his back, hips, and legs; his appetite is poor; his bowels are constipated. He submits to a series of X-rays. Nothing tangible shows up; hints are made about an "old adhesion," an "ovoid swelling" around the appendix, a "tender" liver. (How very sweet, Roger thinks. I didn't know "tenderness" showed up on X-rays.) He makes the rounds of various specialists and is told, variously, that he has arthritis, rheumatism, and lumbago. Is that three conditions or three words for one condition? Do they differ causally or merely linguistically? When he asks the doctors for clarification, they scowl and shrug. Roger draws the obvious conclusion: they don't know. He decides they're using different terms to describe the same affliction.

But what then is the treatment? The medical fraternity has a host of disparate answers. "A return to regular work habits," a doctor in Dublin recommends. "Do you mean," Roger asks, "that I should again take up the consulship in Rio?"

"Good heavens no! That's in Latin America!"

"Yes. Rio is the capital of Brazil", Roger laconically confirmed.

"I see. No, I would stay closer to home. The regularity in diet and so forth. You take my meaning?"

Roger doesn't, but nods yes.

"Rest," another specialist tells him; "after so much excessive activity, you must replenish your vital fluids with total rest." Roger accepts the advice and goes on a peaceful month-long holiday to Donegal; he feels briefly better, then worse ("the rheumatism is settling down on me like a winter cloud," he writes Gee). Perhaps, he wonders, he didn't rest long enough, though he's never felt comfortable with free time. He asks the Foreign Office to extend his leave and heads off to the Canary Islands, where he does improve—so much so that he decides to continue on to Cape Town and pay a visit to brother Tom and his family. That proves even more restorative: he's always been fond of his extroverted if indigent brother and finds his second wife charming. Finally returning to England, Roger feels greatly restored and in excellent spirits.

The Foreign Office soon takes care of that. He discovers from his bank that the FO did indeed extend his leave—but on half pay as of July 1, 1912. The news comes as a considerable shock; his income is already stretched thin. What had been a salary of £528 a year has been cut to £264—in today's income somewhere around $15,000. Feeling, with reason, unappreciated and aggrieved, Roger cautiously writes his Foreign Office ally William Tyrrell, asking if the cut in salary is designed to force him to return to "that infernal hole" Rio—against both his wishes and the advice of his doctors. He asks Tyrrell to inquire about an alternative assignment and also to find out from Treasury what his pension would be if he chose to retire rather than continue in the service—though he makes it clear that he prefers *not* to retire (what comes through just as clearly, though Roger doesn't explicitly say so, is that he's deeply wounded at the Foreign Office's cavalier treatment).

In his reply, Tyrrell tries to sooth his hurt feelings, but there's no gainsaying the message he delivers: so sorry, old chap, we will miss you, but you must do as you think best, and you seem to have settled on retirement. Your pension will come to £440 a year. "I can quite understand the wrench you feel, but I also know," Tyrrell rather airily adds, "that it will not make any difference to those happy relations which you have established with everybody you have had to deal with from my Chief downward." The words are kind, but formulaic—at least that's how Roger reads them. The "absolute Anglo-Britannic swine," he writes angrily to Gee—"those pigs!" He moves yet another step closer to declaring full independence—for himself, for Ireland—from all that England represents.

But first he feels obligated to perform one last service for the Putumayo Indians: to testify before the House of Commons' select committee, chaired by the Liberal MP Charles Roberts. Before the committee hearings even begin, Roger and Roberts consult frequently, both in person and through the mail, Roger providing documents, advice, and suggestions for witnesses—even particular lines of questioning to pursue. The two men are as one in their determination to bring to justice the guilty parties—preeminently the archcriminal Jose Arana and the London board of directors who lazily failed to inquire into, let alone ameliorate, the plight of the company's Indian slave laborers. The inquiry, held in the Palace of Westminster and jammed with spectators, has thirty-six sittings over a period of nearly eight months, interviews twenty-seven witnesses, is widely covered in the press—and accomplishes very nearly nothing.

Roger himself testifies twice. He carefully walks the select committee through the process whereby the company's agents, working on commission and assuming that the white man has a natural claim on the labor of "savages," obliterate morality in the name of maximizing profit. He nicely turns on its head the company's claim that it has brought "civilisation" to a primitive people by arguing that "there are *no* civilised authorities in that part of the country." A "civilised" company would surely compensate its workers, but instead of salaries the Peruvian Amazon Company offers its Indian laborers what it calls "the equivalent" in trade goods. Roger holds up some of those goods for everyone in the courtroom to see.

"I have here a hat, a pair of pantaloons, and a shirt. The Peruvian agents assess the worth of these three items," he declares, "as the equivalent of 60 kilos of rubber—whereas their actual worth is more like 60 pence." He holds up a belt made of cardboard, some fishhooks, and beads. "They are all things," he tells the courtroom, "of very trifling prime cost indeed, and of very inferior quality. What I have produced here represents . . . more than three years' work to an Indian; and, besides, he would have to feed himself and his wife and children . . . would have to carry the heavy loads of rubber on very long journeys. . . . I do not think he would voluntarily and willingly have worked for this trash except under compulsion."

Urged on by chair Roberts, Roger also produces photographs, most of which he himself took. One is of a woman, all skin and bones, lying near death in a hammock; others are of children bearing deep scars across their thighs and buttocks from flogging; still others are photos of Indians carrying huge sacks of rubber on their backs, their emaciated bodies bent out of shape, some of them dying during "the long journeys and the heavy weights imposed upon them."

The evidence is graphic and appalling, and the directors' attorney, Raymond Asquith, the prime minister's son, offers no line of cross-examination or contradiction. "What responsibility do the London directors bear for this wretched state of affairs in the Putumayo?" chair Roberts asks Roger while he's in the witness box. "I told them what was going on," he responds. "They did not seem to resent the information. Nor did they act upon it. They were—and are—Arana's dupes. That is the choice they've made." In corroboration of Roger's view, Roberts puts a London reporter on the stand who went, when Hardenburg's articles in *Truth* first appeared, to the offices of the Peruvian Amazon Company to ask the directors for comment. He was told that Hardenburg was a blackmailer, and when the reporter returned the following day, he was handed an envelope with a banknote in it—an action one would justifiably label "attempted blackmail." The reporter refused the envelope.

Week after week the inquiry proceeds. Several of the company's English directors are themselves put on the stand. One says—as if ignorance is the equivalent of exoneration—that he knew nothing of atrocities until Hardenburg's articles appeared. And then? "Mr. Arana assured us that such incidents were rare—and wholly the work of Colombians attempting to destroy Peru's claim to the region. We saw no reason to doubt his word. He is an honourable man. We trusted Mr. Arana more than we trusted Hardenburg."

Why then, another director is asked, did the board decide to send a commission to investigate conditions in the Putumayo? "Cannot you understand the immense anxiety we feel toward our stockholders?" the director indignantly replies. "The commission's mandate was to explore commercial prospects, not to inquire into the features of the labor system." In the face of such stupefying smugness, all that Roberts can manage by way of response is a disbelieving shake of his head.

Almost three weeks into the inquiry, Julio Arana himself appears before the select committee. He's in London to wind up the affairs of the company and willingly presents himself to testify, massively confident in his own ability to play the role that the company's directors have assigned him: the sensible, quietly reserved, dignified man of affairs. Over a two day period of questioning, Arana successfully manages to give evasively complex answers to straightforward questions, parrying with panache any effort to corner him (Why did his agents carry guns? Why to protect the Indians from wild beasts, of course) and sidestepping every direct question with an opaque non sequitur (Why were his laborers not fed? Oh, aren't you aware? They dislike our cuisine, much preferring the diet provided by their wives).

Soon after his testimony, Arana leaves London; he never returns, but is hardly silent, issuing a number of statements and open letters in which he claims that he's a victim of "a campaign of defamation instigated by forgers and blackmailers." Arana sees to it that Juan Tizon's good work in the Putumayo is undone and that demonstrations are mounted in Iquitos to protest Paredes's presence and to threaten him with lynching; he's forced to flee for his life, leaving Arana once more unopposed in the region. His fortune intact, Arana will have a long life—and continue to be regarded in his native Peru as an accomplished, greatly admired citizen.

After the select committee finally completes its grueling investigation, it hands the House of Commons a six-hundred-page report that singles out Arana for condemnation and censures as well the British directors of the company for "culpable negligence." The report further calls the Foreign Office to account—a gratifying touch, from Roger's point of view—for its ineffective guardianship over how British capital is invested abroad and how British subjects are treated. The committee recommends to the House of Commons that it pass legislation to prevent any comparable undertaking under British auspices in the future. Charles Roberts requests a debate on the matter—a request that Prime Minister Asquith rejects. Roberts and the Anti-Slavery Society refuse to let the matter die and diligently organize a petition drive to put pressure on the government for action. Signed by a large number of notables, the petition is formally presented to Prime Minister Asquith, who ignores it. No old law is changed, no new law written.

A page has been turned, but from Roger's perspective it remains blank. Within a few short years, and in a different context, he will once again hear from Arana.

There the matter rests—until the Great Powers, in 1914, decide to start killing one another instead of Indians.

PART 4

Ireland

EDWARD CARSON, FORMER CROWN PROSECUTOR—and defense attorney for Lord Queensberry in Oscar Wilde's libel suit against him—is a fiercely determined combatant, as brilliant as he is pugnacious, his powerful oratory a match for his intelligence and his presence on a stage commanding enough to silence a crowd of thousands. As of 1910, Carson is the undisputed leader of Ulster, the northeastern-most province of Ireland and the only one with a Protestant rather than Catholic majority—though the margin is slim and there are sizeable pockets of dissent in the province, especially in Ballymena and County Antrim, Roger Casement's birthplace.

Ulster is Unionist—that is, determined to remain part of imperial, Protestant England, and it strongly resents the growing call for Irish Home Rule; to Ulster that would mean being submerged in a poverty-stricken, Catholic-dominated Ireland. Class snobbery as well as religious antipathy color Ulster's view. The province is distinct from the rest of Ireland in having early on developed linen and shipbuilding industries; capital accumulation and industrialization are far more advanced in Ulster than elsewhere on the island, and economically the province is more centrally connected to the English cities of Manchester and Liverpool than to the predominantly rural areas of Catholic Ireland to the south. The prosperous, English-identified "Protestant Ascendancy" in Ulster likes the status quo. It doesn't want its thriving image tarnished by undue association with what it regards as the rampant "Papism" and the uneducated, unemployed minions endemic to the rest of Ireland. Issues arising from poverty—like trade unionism—are for the Carsonites less important than issues relating to the protection of property.

Edward Carson himself is no bigoted reactionary or one-dimensional demagogue: he favors the creation of a Catholic university, women's rights, and an end to capital punishment. But the fear, subliminal or otherwise, of Catholic tyranny in a unified Ireland is a potent undercurrent in Ulster's resistance to Home Rule. If Irish Catholics are not bent on hegemony, Ulster Protestants ask, then how else do you explain the pope's recent *Ne Temere* decree requiring that non-Catholic members of mixed marriages agree to raise their children as Catholics? And what of the 1911 papal ruling that no layman can bring a Catholic cleric before a civil court? Is a privileged class of citizens to be above the law? In short, isn't a Home Rule Bill tantamount to establishing a Catholic theocracy?

John Redmond is head of the Irish Parliamentary Party (IPP) in the House of Commons and a fervent Home Ruler. He's himself the product of a mixed marriage (his mother Protestant, his father a well-to-do Catholic barrister); educated at the Clongowes, the exclusive Jesuit school that (like Roger Casement's) steers clear of "extravagant" nationalism, Redmond regards Gaelic as "the language of the kitchen." He tries to appease Protestant Ulster's fears by cautioning against too quick an equation of the views of certain "extremist" Catholics with the political intentions of the Roman Catholic majority. Those "extremists," in turn, remind Redmond that as far back as the Emancipation Act of 1793, the Reformed Presbyterian Church of Ireland openly lamented the extension of the franchise to Catholics.

The issue of Home Rule reemerges as a major issue with the January 1910 election, in which the ruling Liberal Party in Parliament loses its majority. To form a government, Prime Minister Herbert Asquith is forced to turn to John Redmond's IPP. As part of the bargain for its support, Asquith agrees to the IPP's main demand: a Home Rule Bill for Ireland. Two previous attempts in 1886 and 1893 under Gladstone's sponsorship had failed, the first in the Commons, the second vetoed in the House of Lords, both times overwhelmingly. If a new bill is to succeed, the Lords, obviously, must first be brought to heel—and Asquith dutifully sets himself to the task. After a protracted series of stormy maneuvers and crises, the Parliamentary Act of 1911 succeeds in emasculating the Lords' veto power, and the way is now open for Asquith to introduce a new Home Rule Bill.

The result embitters Carson, who now feels certain that for Ulster to remain part of imperial Britain, it will have to take matters into its own hands. In his first big speech following the passage of the Parliamentary Act, Carson heatedly tells the gathering of some fifty thousand, "I now enter into compact with you, and with the help of God you and I joined together . . . will defeat the most nefarious conspiracy that has ever been hatched against a free people. . . . We must be prepared to become responsible for the government of the Protestant Province of Ulster." Carson's inflamed rhetoric isn't simply designed as a crowd-pleaser; he's no less adamant privately, writing to a friend that his mind is implacably set on "very drastic action in Ulster."

Asquith introduces the new Home Rule Bill in the House of Commons on April 11, 1912. It is unrecognizably tepid when compared to Carson's ferocious advance description. The measure doesn't offer Ireland anything like the full independence that nationalists like Roger have long dreamed of. It sets up instead an Irish parliament of limited autonomy, its powers essentially confined to local matters; the imperial Parliament in London would continue under the bill to exercise control over all issues relating to international affairs, custom and postal duties, taxes, pensions, and decisions relating to defense. This seemingly bland little pudding of a bill in fact contains the ingredients to imperil a whole set of competing dreams, ranging from the wish for a wholly free Ireland (Roger Casement) to one moderately independent (John Redmond) to one immoderately attached to Britain (Edward Carson).

Carson is quick to throw down the gauntlet. In a speech at Blenheim on July 24, 1912, he starkly denounces the new bill: "We regard the Government as a revolutionary committee which has seized upon despotic power. . . . They may, perhaps they will, carry their Home Rule Bill through the House of Commons. . . . If such an attempt is made, I can imagine no length of resistance to which Ulster can go in which I should not be prepared to support them, and in which, in my belief, they would not be supported by the overwhelming majority of the British people."

The implication is clear—and palpably unconstitutional. Carson is saying that if the House of Commons passes the Home Rule Bill, the Protestant majority in Ulster is prepared to resist it—even, by implication, with force of arms. Asquith's response is equally stark: he denounces Carson's speech as "reckless rodomontade—a declaration of war against Constitutional Government, furnishing forth the complete grammar of anarchy."

Roger's sympathy is with neither man. The policies of both are inimical to his long-standing dedication to the idea of an Ireland entirely free from British domination *and* united as one people. In Ireland he's in a distinct minority. John Redmond and his Irish Parliamentary Party at Westminster fervently applaud the Asquith bill and urge Ireland to accept it "not with a grudging or lukewarmness but with alacrity and enthusiasm." Redmond knows that this time around passage is not only possible but likely; in stripping the House of Lords of its veto power in 1911, Redmond believes the country "has given a clear and unequivocal mandate to the Premier to settle the Irish question."

According to Roger, it settles nothing of the sort. He, along with Sinn Féin ("We Ourselves")—the conglomerate organization of radical Irish separatists—and its counterpart in the United States, Clan-na-Gael, take sharp issue with Redmond's support of Asquith's bill. Roger, for one, sees the bill as confirming Ireland's vassalage status, as guaranteeing that Ireland, in all essential ways, will remain an appendage of Great Britain instead of becoming the independent nation he longs for. Carson's insistence that Ulster remain part of Britain is equally anathema to him. When Carson refers to "our own splendid folk," Roger (and many other nationalists) know the reference is to Anglo-Irish Protestants and that Carson's Unionists (if not Carson) would relegate Irish Celts and Catholics to a subordinate status. Yet, in Roger's view, Ulster is indubitably Irish, no matter how busily it denies the fact; this is especially true, he feels, of independent-minded *Presbyterians* of Ulster, once writing, "I *love* the Antrim Presbyterians.... They are good, kind, warmhearted souls." Roger can also, in some moods, be critical of Catholicism, referring at one point to "this great official Church with its preposterous claims to be the beginning and end of all life."

Of late, his dream of an independent, unified Ireland has been further weakened by the sharp decline of interest in the Irish Ireland cultural movement. Roger himself has lost some of his enthusiasm for it; at one low point in 1911, he writes Alice Green that "chanting nouns and verbs in Dublin streets" is about "as useful as chopping turnips." For the moment about all he feels sure of is embodied in a Sinn Féin resolution that firmly rejects "any arrangement which leaves a single vestige of British rule in Ireland." Both Sinn Féin and the secret Irish Republican Brotherhood (IRB)—"extreme" nationalists with roots in the nineteenth-century Fenian movement and willing to use physical force—are in 1912 mere remnants of their former selves, though far stronger among Irish Americans belonging to the powerful Clan-na-Gael in the United States.

Though born an Ulster Protestant, Roger's priorities are different from Carson's: he's more attuned to issues relating to class than to the divisions based on religion. For Roger, the Gaelic-speaking islands off Connemara become a case in point. Reading a newspaper account about the wretched living conditions there of the rural peasantry and the devastation being wrought by typhoid and typhus, he decides to raise a relief fund and to go there himself to better understand the plight of the people. He manages to collect some £2,000—enough to make sure that every infant on the islands gets a free meal every day for a year—but comes away from the scene appalled at what he calls an "Irish Putumayo"; its "white Indians lie more heavily on my heart than all the Indians of the rest of the earth."

The islands, he knows, are not uniquely destitute. He reads with alarm the Poor Law Commission survey that reports more than six thousand families of seven or more living in single rooms in Dublin, a city where the infant mortality rate is 142 per 1,000 as compared with 103 per 1,000—high enough—in London. In Roger's view, Ulster's identification with Great Britain is tantamount to an alliance of the "haves" against the "have nots." He sees Ulster as ambitious to emulate London's prosperous hauteur—and to keep clear of Connemara's poverty.

Though Asquith, himself Protestant, has endorsed Home Rule, he's also expressed equivocal support for Ulster's wish to remain part of Great Britain and *not* be included in any Home Rule Bill, no matter how diluted its powers. The defeated Conservative Party, with Andrew Bonar Law now at its head, is still more emphatically and categorically in Ulster's camp. Bonar Law creates a storm when, directly echoing Carson, he declares that he "can imagine no length of resistance to which Ulster will go in which I shall not be ready to support them."

Carson, for his part, is busy solidifying his ranks. He chooses a vast outdoor meeting in Ulster in September 1912 to introduce his notion of a "Covenant"—a solemn oath—to resist "the present conspiracy to set up a Home Rule Parliament in Ireland." Carson announces that he's ready to resist Home Rule "by any and all means"—a threat that promptly brings down on his head the charge of treason. "I do not care two pence whether it is treason or not," he responds; "it is what we are going to do." Carson has the strong backing of Sir James Craig, the wealthy heir to a distillery and a Unionist MP since 1906. Craig, in December 1910, sets up a secret committee to buy arms from abroad to ensure—should the Liberal Asquith government refuse to exclude Ulster from Home Rule—that the province is prepared for armed resistance.

By the summer of 1911, arms have begun to arrive in the province, and the process accelerates from that point on. Carson insists that his determination to arm Ulster is ultimately grounded in a wish to prevent Ireland's partition. He declares that he, too, wants a unified Ireland—but one that remains in the old union with Britain. Tactically, Carson urges Ulster to stand firm on the assumption that an adamant posture will wreck the entire Home Rule enterprise and thereby prevent Ireland's partition.

The Solemn League and Covenant (the biblical overtones deliberate) that Carson introduces at the huge outdoor gathering in September 1912 calls on all the province's Protestants to affix their signatures to a document that declares Home Rule "disastrous to the material well-being of Ulster . . . subversive of our civil and religious freedom, destructive of our citizenship, and perilous to the unity of the Empire." The covenant concludes with the "sure confidence that God will defend the right, we hereto subscribe our names."

"I presume," Roger writes Gee, "you read the Covenant? You see He is trotted out there. They are confident He will 'defend the Right.' Supposing He doesn't! How awful if God should turn out to be a disloyalist!" If sheer numbers are a reliable indication of God's will, then Carson may with impunity claim divine sanction: the response to his proposed covenant is overwhelming. At a ceremony on September 28—henceforth known as "Ulster Day"—Carson becomes the first signatory to the covenant, and the ensuing ten days are set aside for comparable ceremonies throughout the province.

Carson himself speaks at many of the meetings, accompanied by processions, bands playing "Protestant Boys" and the like, streamers, drill parades, and a sea of earnest, cheering multitudes often breaking into choruses of "O God Our Help in Ages Past," which becomes the unofficial anthem of the Ulster Unionist movement. "The mental atmosphere," according to one eyewitness, "isn't that of a political meeting but of a religious service—and in fact the proceedings open with prayer, as has become the inevitable custom on such occasions. . . . Protestant Ulster has set apart a day of self-dedication to a cause for which they are willing to make any sacrifice."

And so it goes all over northeast Ireland. By the time it's over, some quarter million men have signed the covenant—and an equal number of (unequal) women sign a separate declaration. Yet Ulster itself—though its leaders avoid emphasizing the fact—is home to a substantial minority of Catholics, and they lean toward Home Rule. Ulster's Protestants themselves, moreover, do not monolithically support Unionism—Roger himself being but one example of opposition. Comparably, the other provinces of Ireland contain significant pockets of Unionists, despite their Catholic majorities. The terrain is jagged and shifting, the factional leaders in a constant state of readjustment as their opposite numbers unexpectedly reposition themselves.

John Redmond, for one, publicly reaffirms his desire "to live in brotherly love with all our countrymen of whatever class or creed." Privately, though, he anguishes over the assorted oppositional voices that range from a rejection of a Home Rule Bill of any kind to hailing (or opposing) the Asquith version—which fails to provide for *real* self-government. Redmond manages to convince himself that Ulster Unionists are mostly bluffing and will in the end accept a Home Rule arrangement that swears to protect minority religious beliefs—and commercial privileges.

Redmond sees no reason in 1912 to accommodate any of the suggestions currently being floated for excluding the province of Ulster from Home Rule. He shares with Roger a strong preference for a united Ireland but—unlike Roger—one that remains part of the British Empire. The Conservative leader Bonar Law stakes out yet another position. Like Roger, he's well aware that there are, in his words, "two Irelands separated from each other by a gulf far deeper than that which separates Ireland as a whole from the rest of the United Kingdom." But he differs from Roger in championing Carson and Ulster Unionism—as do a host of other powerful allies, including much of the officer class in the British army, Lord Alfred Milner (he who, as high commissioner for South Africa, canceled Roger's planned expedition during the Boer War), and the poet Rudyard Kipling.

Asquith has at times sounded sympathetic to the Ulster cause, but he's a man of indecisive temperament; "wait and see" is his trademark stance. When introducing the Home Rule Bill in the Commons on April 11, 1912, he acknowledges the "strong and determined hostility" of Ulster to Home Rule. Yet he also reminds the Commons that in every test of public opinion since the 1880s "four-fifths of the elected representatives of the Irish people" (males, that is) have favored a separate Irish parliament linked to Britain—though not, Asquith fails to mention, the watered-down version of Home Rule he's now offering, which allots that parliament only marginal power. Instead, Asquith denounces "the right of a minority of the people, and relatively a small minority . . . to veto the verdict of the vast body of their countrymen."

John Redmond consoles himself with the notion that Ulster Unionism will gradually dissipate, yet the opposite seems to be happening. Carson hasn't invented—though like all politicians he *has* manipulated—anti–Home Rule sentiment in Ulster. With each passing day it seems to be growing more passionate, with feelings becoming so entrenched by the closing months of 1912 that the danger of an armed uprising in Ulster begins to loom as an actual prospect.

The threat becomes manifest with the formation of the Ulster Volunteers. If signing the covenant was a theoretical pledge to resist Home Rule, joining the volunteers is a concrete decision to present oneself for training in the use of arms should the pending bill not exempt Ulster. In honor of Ulster's deepening defiance, Rudyard Kipling writes a poem that concludes,

> Believe, we dare not boast,
> Believe, we do not fear—
> We stand to pay the cost
> In all that men hold dear.
> What answer from the North?
> One law, one land, one throne,
> If England drive us forth
> We shall not fall alone.

Taken together, the nine counties that make up the province of Ulster, unlike the overwhelmingly Catholic population in the rest of Ireland, is closely divided, with Protestants making up a narrow majority—56 percent of the citizenry. Yet, even in Ulster, only four of the nine counties—Derry, Down, Armagh, and Antrim (home of the Casements)—have *large* Protestant majorities. Edward Carson—supported by Bonar Law—on January 1, 1913, presents an amendment to the pending Home Rule Bill, proposing that all of Ulster's *nine* counties be excluded. The justification for such an amendment seems flimsy to many, but Carson's rhetoric is menacing: "Can any man measure beforehand—if once you try to drive people out of a Constitution they are satisfied with into another—where the forces of disorder if once let loose will find their objective, or what will be the end of it?"

Carson's amendment seems to embody a shift in his position from "No Home Rule" to "Home Rule, Except for Ulster," but Asquith is hardly pleased. He accuses Carson of knowing in advance that his amendment for a nine-county exclusion will fail and has decided to push it to suggest an opposition so widespread that Home Rulers will be cowed. If so, the tactic fails. The Asquith Liberals and Redmond's Irish Party hold firmly together and defeat the amendment by a substantial margin of 97 votes. In a gratuitous statement that needlessly minimizes Ulster's grave opposition, Redmond declares, "I, for my part, am not seriously influenced by the threatened danger of civil war in Ulster."

Two weeks later the third reading of Asquith's Home Rule Bill passes the Commons by the large majority of 110. Jubilation reigns in Liberal and Redmonite circles. The House of Lords, as expected, promptly tries to throw the bill out by a still larger majority, but the Parliamentary Act of 1911 has removed the Lords' veto power, and the bill is automatically set to become law some time in 1914. Or so it appears.

The Carsonites are a stubborn lot. Local groups in Ulster have been drilling and undergoing military training for some time, and in January 1913 the Ulster Unionist Council consolidates the groups into the Ulster Volunteer Force; it limits the UVF to a hundred thousand men, and only those who've signed the covenant are eligible. The group grows rapidly in strength; tens of thousands of men, hoisting wooden dummy rifles, are seen parading in all sorts of public venues, from parks to meeting houses. The dummy rifles for a time cause some hilarity—among the Redmonites, that is—but the UVF is in deadly earnest and intends to substitute real rifles in the near future. Sir George Richardson, a retired general of the British army in India, agrees to serve as the UVF's commander in chief. He sets up an efficient staff structure and within a short time takes the salute, as some fifteen thousand volunteers pass in review at the Balmoral grounds near Belfast.

Matters now move swiftly. A commission is appointed to draft a constitution for an Ulster provisional government, and two months later a letter of support appears in the London press, signed by some two hundred peers and Conservative Party adherents. The letter insists that nothing less than the integrity of the British Empire is at stake: should the "dangerous" precedent be established of certain powers "devolving" to local authorities, the empire as centralized in an imperial Parliament will gradually crumble to dust. If any doubt remained, the signatories to the letter have made it abundantly clear that the cause of Ulster has influential champions in England.

John Redmond, against the evidence, continues to declare himself unimpressed with what he chooses to call the Carsonites' "bluff." He's insistent that UVF drilling is merely a tactic designed to stampede the Asquith government into excluding Ulster from Home Rule; so long as Asquith stands firm, Redmond asserts, the opposition will fade away. Standing firm, however, isn't among Asquith's core qualities—as Carson, for whom adamancy is second nature, is well aware. "The Prime Minister," Carson tells an Ulsterite audience, "knows perfectly well that so long as we are in the position of having behind us ... the active co-operation and sympathy of certainly one-half of the population of Great Britain [that is, the Conservative Party and its adherents], that he is in as helpless and hopeless a position as regards this bill as ever was a Minister in regard to any bill in the House of Commons."

Strong words. Stronger than any Asquith can summon up in reply. Sympathetic to some sort of compromise with Ulster, Winston Churchill, first lord of the admiralty (though not yet forty), records a conversation in which Asquith tells him that he "always thought (and said) that, in the end, we should probably have to make some sort of bargain about Ulster as the price of Home Rule." The prototypical Asquith phrase is "in the end"; marking time, dawdling, and delay are as central to his personality as his accent. Roger, like many radical nationalists, believes that the Liberal government's hemming and hawing has been tantamount to coddling the Ulster unionists, confirming their belief that intransigence will ultimately bring success. As the *Irish Times* puts it, "the most stubborn community in Europe [Ulster] waits for the feeblest Government in Europe to take up its challenge."

Redmond takes it up instead. He accuses Carson of jeopardizing a Home Rule Bill that the large majority of the Irish people desire—of throwing them "back into the inferno of disappointed hopes, despair and madness of heart.... [This] is not statesmanship, it is criminal folly." His accusation is based on the undeniable premise that in a general election the majority of Irish voters would cast their ballots for Home Rule. Carson, for his part, chooses to believe that a general election would return the Conservatives to power and Bonar Law to the post of prime minister—which in turn would put an *end* to the agitation for Home Rule. Yet Carson is realistic enough to know that, alternately, an election could result in the retention of the Liberals and their Irish Party allies. Carson's champion, Bonar Law, drives the point home: should a general election, he tells Carson, register a majority for Home Rule and should Ulster reject the verdict, that would amount to "rebellion"— if *armed* rebellion, then the government would have to meet force with force.

During a debate in Parliament in the summer of 1912, Bonar Law insists that Ulster is not bent on denying Home Rule to the rest of Ireland, if that is what Ireland wants; Ulster asks only that it not be included. Despite this reassurance, Redmond continues to insist that Ulster wishes to "coerce and overbear" all of Ireland, and he argues strenuously that "twenty-eight counties will not permit themselves to be intimidated by four." Carson, for his part, lets it be known that should an attempt be made to *force* Home Rule on Ulster, its provisional government will at once assume control of the county, and the now-powerful Ulster Volunteer Force will stand guard over the decision.

Roger is no fan of Home Rule. He continues to hold out for the dream of a united Ireland entirely free from British control—an Irish parliament that genuinely rules rather than one subservient in most important matters to Britain. In the current debate between Redmond's and Carson's contending forces, he's unsympathetic to both sides, though he can't help but admire Ulster's spunk (the province, he tells Alice Green, is "the best part of Ireland in many ways"). He even has occasional spasms of admiration for Carson—though he describes him in a letter to Gee as "a cross between a badly raised bloodhound and an underfed hyena, sniffing for Irish blood in the track, and whooping 'Rule Britannia' in the streets."

But if Roger marginally sympathizes with Ulster's rejection of Home Rule, he feels no sympathy at all for its devotion to the British Empire—and is downright alarmed at the growth of the Ulster Volunteer Force. His apprehension puts him into a natural alliance with a new set of associates at least as colorful and as temperamentally adversarial as he. One of them is his old friend, Bulmer Hobson, for whom he's earlier served as a kind of mentor and who's become a leading figure in both Sinn Féin and the Irish Republican Brotherhood. When Hobson and Arthur Griffith become antagonistic over the latter's continued insistence on the feasibility of a dual-monarch scheme, Roger's sympathies are with Hobson. Roger doesn't doubt Griffith's credentials as a devoted Irishman, but his difficult personality—reserved, enigmatic, opinionated—is foreign to his own open-handed, receptive nature.

Through Hobson, Roger meets a vivid group of Irish radicals that includes Countess Constance "Con" Markievicz—close to Roger in age and in her energetic, theatrical style—and the equally notorious labor leader "Big Jim" Larkin. Con grew up as Constance Gore-Booth, the highly privileged eldest daughter of a wealthy, aristocratic Anglo-Irish family with a forty-eight-room manor house, Lissadell Court, in County Sligo. Surrounded by servants and tenant families, she was showered with admiration for her striking beauty, passionate intensity, and daring feats of horsemanship.

Her closest friend while young was her more reserved, introspective sister, Eva, who becomes a poet, involves herself in suffragist and labor politics, and lives her adult life with another politically engaged woman, Esther Roper. The concurrent protest movements at the turn of the century—Irish independence, feminism, socialism, trade unionism—enlist a significant number of sex radicals in their ranks. Among the notably unconventional figures are Rosamond Jacob, who declares her belief that "promiscuity in both sexes is better than the double standard of morals" and writes in her diary that she loved one man of her acquaintance "not spiritually and patiently and unselfishly, but physically and impatiently and selfishly, as a man loves a woman—the idea of his being happy apart from me has no charms for me at all"; Ella Young, who combines lesbianism and goddess worship—and, perhaps predictably, ends up in a commune in California; Hannah and Francis Sheehy-Skeffington, whose atypical heterosexual marriage demotes sex to insignificance and elevates political engagement as the couple's prime binding force; Maude Gonne, who openly accuses her republican-hero husband, John MacBride, of sexually abusing their daughter; and Edith White, who confesses to an overwhelming desire to go about Dublin dressed as a man. Their counterparts on the male side include the poet and schoolteacher Patrick Pearse and Roger's old friend Francis Bigger, who sublimate their same-sex passion in the creation of all-male, homosocial environments—and Roger, who refuses to sublimate his. None of this makes pre–World War I Ireland comparable in sexual unconventionality to the hothouse bohemianism of Bloomsbury (or, later, of Weimar Germany)—but closer to both than to the restrictive puritanism that will reengulf the island during the 1920s.

As a young woman, Con Markievicz stays pretty much in the traces, surrounded by a veritable posse of suitors, attending the usual round of parties and balls and mingling in the social life that centers on Dublin Castle, the viceregal seat of British rule. But Con is more willful and has a more skeptical cast of mind than most young debutantes; she feels less comfortable with their conventional routines. In 1893, when twenty-five, she wins over her parents to the then scandalous idea of attending art school and is accepted at the prestigious Slade. There she mingles with a bohemian group of young people and becomes involved with the women's suffrage movement.

She also falls in love. Count Casimir Markievicz, too, is a painter, and a handsome, high-spirited Ukrainian; the two marry in 1899. Breezy, fearless, the young couple actively sample a variety of interests and causes. After a time, when Casimir begins to focus more on theater than politics and Constance on Irish nationalism, their relationship evolves into a comfortable friendship, with long periods of absence from each other. By her midthirties, Con has given up a traditional married life, her career in painting, and whatever shreds of aristocratic respectability still cling to her. All have been surrendered to her serious, this time lasting, commitment to Irish independence.

Bulmer Hobson meets Con Markievicz in 1908 and becomes her mentor; he gives her books to read about Irish history and introduces her to fellow radicals, including two of the senior figures of an older generation, Tom Clarke and James Connolly. Clark has served fifteen years in prison for his part in a dynamiting plot and is on the Supreme Council of the IRB, the publisher of *Irish Freedom,* and the proprietor of a tobacco shop on Great Britain Street in Dublin that's become a center of radical ferment. Though Clark believes in Con's sincerity, he doesn't on her behalf challenge the IRB's policy of excluding women. Earlier Con had approached Arthur Griffith about joining Sinn Féin, but he'd brusquely rebuffed her, convinced (so she learns) that she's a British spy.

Bulmer Hobson knows better and encourages Con to start attending Sinn Féin meetings, where women (despite Griffith) are treated with respect and even elected to the organization's executive committee (nationalist goals, however, are the group's undisputed priority, and the suffrage issue is downplayed). Though Con appreciates Hobson's help, she gradually distances herself from him. The more radical she becomes, the more she questions his inability to stick to anything for very long; she also senses and deplores the gap she perceives between Hobson's fiery speeches and his refusal to join in demonstrations that might lead to injury or arrest.

With James Connolly, the trade unionist and committed socialist, the story is very different. A warm, sympathetic man and a strong supporter of Jim Larkin's campaigns on behalf of unskilled labor, Connolly's revolutionary words and actions are of a piece, and he and Con become deeply attached. Connolly gives her copies of his books, *Labour in Irish History* and *Labour, Nationality and Religion,* which emphasize (and somewhat mythologize) Ireland's communitarian Celtic past. Connolly also strongly supports, as does Jim Larkin, the militant women's movement, in which Con Markievicz and her sister, Eva, are becoming increasingly active.

With Connolly's support, Con joins Inghinidhe na h-Eireann, the women's organization founded by the stunning, imperious Maud Gonne, Yeats's unrequited love. Con is elected to a committee putting out a new paper—*Bean na h-Eireann* (Women of Ireland), founded in 1908 and edited by the redoubtable Helena Molony, who's devoted to "militancy, separatism and feminism." The emphasis is on "militancy." The Inghinidhe and *Bean* strongly identify with the far left wing of Irish nationalism, insistent that Ireland will win its independence only through physical force. In an article as early as 1909, Con writes, "Arm yourselves with weapons to fight your nation's cause. . . . Arm your minds with the histories and memories of your country and her martyrs, her language, and a knowledge of her arts, and her industries."

It's a position Roger is also edging toward, though a bit more slowly than Con. He occasionally writes for *Bean,* as does the poet George Moore (AE).

All share contempt for Redmond's Irish Parliamentary Party, and none are surprised when it proves instrumental in defeating the so-called Conciliation Bill, which would have extended the vote at least to women of property. When *Bean* ceases publication in March 1911, Hobson and some of the other young radicals start the paper *Irish Freedom,* dedicated to the "total freedom" of Ireland . . . untrammeled and uncontrolled by any other government in the world."

Two years earlier, when still close comrades, Hobson and Con Markievicz had worked together to form a national organization for boys—the Fianna—to "weld the youth of Ireland together to work and fight for Ireland." Robert Baden-Powell's 1908 book, *Scouting for Boys,* had launched the scouting movement in Britain, but where Baden-Powell was intent on justifying and inculcating the virtues of imperialism, Markievicz and Hobson focused on combining physical culture with militant Irish nationalism. The Fianna trained young men in drilling, signaling, and—through Irish-language and history classes—devotion to the cause of Irish liberty. Many of the Fianna scouts will subsequently join the Irish Volunteers—the counterpart to Carson's Ulster Volunteer Force—and some, later still, will end up in the IRB as leaders in an armed struggle for independence.

Almost simultaneously, Hobson and Con Markievicz, along with Helena Molony and several others, embark on the establishment of an agricultural commune a few miles north of Dublin; it's designed all at once to serve as a base for the Fianna boys and as a respite from the exhausting demands of organizational work. In theory, a live-in agricultural expert was to teach them the ("surely simple") techniques of cooperative farming, but nothing proved at all simple, and within a short time the would-be communards give up the experiment and decamp in various directions. Hobson and Molony head back to journalism, and Markievicz openly admits that her theatrical temperament makes her far less suited to raising sheep than to raising hell. She and Casimir promptly join up with the radical Theatre of Ireland, a breakaway group from (as they saw it) the insufficiently political Abbey Theatre, the preserve of Yeats, the playwright J. M. Synge, and Lady Augusta Gregory—none of whom are exactly slouches when it comes to Irish nationalism.

Roger, from the start, considered the agricultural commune ill-advised. He assures Hobson that "there is no one I should wish to help more than you—for your sake and the sake of Ireland," but his practical sense tells him that Hobson is spreading himself too thin, that his impulsive gusto is diluting his effectiveness. Having previously been generous in responding to

Hobson's requests for money, Roger now pleads a tighter purse and turns him down. "I feel a brute saying this and putting you off," he writes Hobson, "but I can't help it for the time." This rebuke (as the egotistical Hobson sees it) leaves him feeling unappreciated and resentful. To follow Roger's advice, he'd have to curb his outsized ambition; instead, he extends his activities still further, setting in motion the formation of "Freedom Clubs" designed to unify the scattered forces of Irish separatism.

Sean O'Casey, the playwright and political radical (he's a member of the IRB), is among those who take a dim view of Hobson's growing prominence, referring to him scathingly as "head bottle-washer of all Nationalist activities." O'Casey regards Hobson's paper *Irish Freedom* as a rag and its editor a man devoid of literary talent. He thinks it's "pathetic" that a true patriot like Tom Clarke actually admires "this Protestant shit." O'Casey is increasingly drawn instead to Jim Larkin's focus on the appalling lot of working-class Ireland. He wants to move the IRB into an alliance with "Larkinism"—a policy Hobson and others reject as a "dilution" of the nationalist cause.

Con Markievicz is also profoundly attracted to "Big Jim" Larkin and the syndicalist vision embodied in his union, the Irish Transport and General Workers Union (ITGWU). She first hears Larkin speak at a meeting in Dublin and is overwhelmed by the power of his oratory: "I realised," she later wrote, "that I was in the presence of something that I had never come across before, some great primeval force rather than a man." Larkin, she discovers, not only is against Asquith's Home Rule Bill but—much less common—is in whole-hearted support of women's suffrage.

Larkin never wavers in his defense of a free and united Ireland, and even as regards unionization he asks (in the words of the ITGWU preamble), "Are we going to continue the policy of grafting ourselves on the English Trades Union movement, losing our identity as a nation in the great world of organised labour? We say emphatically, No. Ireland has politically reached her manhood." Larkin wants "one big union"—skilled and unskilled workers alike—with the ultimate goal of worker control of the means of production. In this he's directly echoing the Wobblies—the Industrial Workers of the World—in the United States, a movement that in 1912 has twenty-five thousand members, carries out the famed Lawrence strike, and is brutally attacked by both federal and state authorities.

Roger is more ambivalent than Con about Larkin's syndicalist vision, with its call for worker control of industry, but he rejoices in Larkin's disgust with John Redmond and the other "sell-outs" of the Irish Parliamentary Party. He welcomes, too, Larkin's encouragement of Irish Ireland and all forms of cultural nationalism. And it isn't just words with Larkin: he enrolls three of his sons in Patrick Pearse's uniquely nationalist—and child-centered—Saint Enda's school, to which Roger has long sent donations, usually ones beyond his means.

Larkin is as controversial as he is magnetic. A large man with a decided swagger to his walk, he's an immensely complicated figure—all at once deeply empathic and brashly egotistical, as selfish as he is generous, a humanist who expects deference, a paternalist who inspires brotherly love, a Catholic who despises priests, hot-tempered, passionate, impulsive—Larkin is a truly larger-than-life figure, and one who refuses ever to minimize the sufferings of the working class. Sean O'Casey is among those who idolize the man for speaking "not for an assignation with peace, dark obedience, or placid resignation; but trumpet-tongued of resistance to wrong, discontent with leering poverty, and defiance of any power strutting out to stand in the way of their march onward."

In his newspaper, *Irish Worker and People's Advocate,* Larkin focuses on Dublin to illustrate the wretched conditions in which workers and their families live. He publishes the facts and figures: in 1911–12, eighty-seven thousand people in Dublin, out of a total population of three hundred thousand, live in slums, with twenty thousand families surviving in one-room flats. They are barely surviving, with sanitation confined to the occasional toilet, a water tap outside in the yard, and the cost of food up 15 percent since 1900 with no accompanying rise in wages—all in contrast to English workers, whose wages have been steadily rising. The mortality rate in Dublin has become the same as that of Calcutta. Yet for all Larkin's passionate denunciation of injustice, the *Irish Worker* indulges in the kneejerk anti-Semitism of the day; one typical cartoon in the paper features a bovine capitalist by the name of "Ikey O'Moses" and the caption "Gentlemen of the Jewry."

By 1912 Larkin's ITGWU has some ten thousand members, but the employer class is led by the formidable—and intransigently antiunionist—William Martin Murphy, president of the Dublin Chamber of Commerce. The crucial test of will between Larkin and Murphy comes in 1913. Having by that point won a substantial pay raise for dockworkers and even an increase for agricultural hands, Larkin shifts his aim to unionizing Dublin's tramway company—which Murphy happens to own (along with a hotel, a department store, and a chain of newspapers). Murphy is determined to thwart Larkin's plans; he demands that all his employees sign written agreements pledging not to join Larkin's union, and he locks out the hundred or so who already have. In response, seven hundred tram workers go out on strike.

Murphy calls a meeting of the powerful Employers Federation. Indignation reigns and the decision taken to lock out every single employee—twenty-five thousand in all—who has joined *any* union, including those in industries as diverse as coal, building construction, and large-scale farming. Led by Murphy, the employers set as their goal the destruction of the entire union movement in Dublin—and for good. If that brings on starvation, so be it; the workers have only themselves to blame.

While out on bail, and in defiance of a police ban on "seditious" gatherings, Larkin is in the process of addressing a large crowd in Dublin when mounted police, using their batons freely, charge into the crowd, leaving two dead and hundreds injured. A warrant is issued for Larkin's arrest; the charge is "seditious conspiracy." Larkin publicly burns the police poster banning protest meetings and announces, "I recognize no law but the people's law." He further promises, even as he decides to go into hiding, that "I will address the people of Dublin on Sackville Street on Sunday." Con Markievicz offers her house as refuge.

Larkin is determined to fulfill his promise to appear publicly the next day, and to that end Con, Helena Molony, and others prepare an elaborate masquerade. Larkin is dressed up in a frock coat and top hat, his hair blackened and a fake beard attached, and he's coached in the stooped gait appropriate for an elderly man. A reservation is made for a "Reverend Donnelly" at the Imperial Hotel—the conspirators relishing the irony that its owner is William Martin Murphy. The theatrics come off in style. As Con and the others watch in high glee from across the street, Larkin enters the hotel without incident, then a few minutes later throws open a window on the second floor of the building and shouts out to the crowd, "I'm Larkin!—I'm here today in accordance with my promise!" It's a triumphant moment—but short-lived. Before Larkin can get out more than a few words, the police seize him and move quickly to a waiting van in the street.

When they pass Con, she impulsively jumps forward, grabs Larkin's hand, and shouts, "Good luck!" A police inspector punches her in the face, and as if mobilized by the act, scores of officers charge into the peaceful crowd, batons drawn, savagely beating anyone in their path. James Connolly, leader of the small Irish Socialist Party and a close associate of Larkin's (and Con's), later describes the scene: the police "came steadily like mowing machines, and behind them the street was like a battlefield dotted with bodies. Some of them still lying twisting in pain."

Several sympathetic men move Con, bleeding from her mouth and nose, down a side street, away from the fray. In all, some 430 people are treated in Dublin's hospitals for assorted injuries, the large majority unaffiliated with the union movement. The workers remain defiant, though disappointed when the English transport union fails to call a sympathy strike—and when John Redmond remains adamantly silent, refusing to offer a word of comfort or support, even though the Irish Party in Parliament has in the past shown empathy toward striking workers. Bulmer Hobson is no less silent—thereby completing Con's alienation from him—and the "moderate" nationalist Arthur Griffith, not to be outdone, is overheard saying that the strikers ought to be bayoneted.

Yet a number of English intellectuals and radicals side with the Irish workers, and several raise a pointed question: "Why is it that Carson and his Ulster Volunteer Force are left unmolested as they drill and train for implicit combat, while Larkin and his cohorts, who refrain from directly threatening violence, are beaten and jailed?" Larkin's words, to be sure, are often incendiary, and violent words can transmute into violent action. Still, the Larkinites remain a step removed from any straightforward commitment to physical force. They never make a declaration equivalent to the one Conservative Party leader Bonar Law has issued—"if Ulster fights, she will not fight alone"—nor, from the opposite camp, to Lord Lansdowne's (Roger's old nemesis when foreign secretary) dictum, "We have Ireland, and we mean to keep her."

Larkin is sentenced to seven months at hard labor, but popular indignation—in England as well as in Ireland—is so strong and sustained that he's freed after a month. He embarks at once on a series of rallies he calls the "Fiery Cross," his megalomania deepening in tandem with his notoriety ("I have got a divine mission, I believe, to make men and women discontented"). Meanwhile, Con Markievicz and others are trying to deal with the immediate problem of how to feed the multitude of people thrown out of work. They set up a large-scale basement kitchen that doles out soup and potatoes to over three thousand people a day; it's a grueling, mind-numbing routine—and essential for keeping up the strikers' morale.

Yet Sean O'Casey can't see beyond the stereotype of Lady Bountiful. He caricatures Con posing for pictures "in a spotless bib and tucker, standing in the steam, a gigantic ladle in her hand, busy as a beebeesee whenever a photographer shows up." O'Casey's class hatred, understandable enough, has narrowed his vision to caricature. Less understandable is the reaction of the many middle-class nationalists like Bulmer Hobson who show scant support for Larkinism (the poet AE is a major exception), seeing trade unionists not as natural allies but as competitors for political loyalty. By early 1913 the destitute, starving strikers reluctantly sign the hated antiunion pledge and gradually return to work. James Connolly speaks for the bitterness of many: "So we Irish workers must go down into Hell . . . eat the dust of defeat and betrayal."

Resistance hasn't died; it's gone underground. With the failure of peaceful protest the idea begins to take hold that the time has come to form a citizens' army capable in the future of combating the violence of the police, the employers, and their strikebreaking minions. A precedent and model is near at hand: the paramilitary Ulster Volunteer Force. Hasn't Edward Carson, many ask, set the tone when telling his followers, "Don't be afraid of illegalities"? And hasn't the British government implicitly sanctioned Carson's threat of physical force when, instead of rebuffing him, it starts to bargain with him—in the process seeming to accept the right of a minority to undermine the will of the majority? Asquith ignores the questions and reminds his critics that his government *had* resisted Ulster militancy early on. As far back as December 1910, when the Ulster provisional government began its gunrunning (the initial runs were small-scale), the British government had raided the Unionist arms depot at Leith in Scotland and had also confiscated a large consignment at Hammersmith. The unintended consequence, however, had been to persuade Ulster's leaders to embark on a still more ambitious and better planned round of arms smuggling. The fits and starts have been many, and on all sides of the equation, yet the trajectory of the Asquith government now seems clearly pointed to acquiescing in the exclusion of Ulster from Home Rule.

Up to this point, Roger has been flirting around the edges of the mounting conflict. In October 1913 he moves out from the sidelines.

. . .

When Edward Carson and his followers describe themselves as "Unionists," they mean the coupling of Ulster and Great Britain, to the exclusion of Catholic-dominated southern Ireland. When Roger uses the term he means the coalescence of Ulster and the rest of Ireland, to the exclusion of Great Britain. In 1913 Roger, who despises religious bigotry, has seized on the fragile hope that Presbyterian (not Anglican) Ulster might bring the province into a union with Catholic Ireland, the two combining to form an independent republic that henceforth will deal with England not as a vassal but as an equal. To bolster this hope, Roger harkens back to the tradition of "1798," when Ulster Presbyterians had joined in rebellion against the Crown—and Ulster Anglicans had joined in defeating and hanging them.

A meeting is called for October 24, 1913, at the town hall in Ballymoney, located in Roger's home county of Antrim—which is part of Ulster but with a population nearly 80 percent Protestant. The theme of the meeting, Roger writes cousin Gee ahead of the event, will be to "proclaim the great fact that Protestants of Co. Antrim are standing out to fight Carsonism and proclaim their faith in a united Ireland." He holds to the hope, uncommon among Irish leaders, that Ulster might yet be won to the cause of a united Ireland— might even take the lead. The hope is faint—the Carsonites are powerful and rigid in opposition—yet had it come to pass, Ireland might have avoided partition and decades of bloodshed.

Roger and Capt. Jack White, a socialist landowner, are announced as the principal speakers at Ballymoney. After Roger urgently describes the upcoming meeting to Alice Green as potentially one "of *extraordinary* significance . . . a protest from the heart of Antrim," she agrees to attend. On the day of the meeting, a large banner is stretched across the proscenium arch of the hall, reading, "No Provisional or Provincial Government for Us," and the Rev. J. B. Armour, a prominent Ulster Presbyterian, is in the chair. The hall is quickly packed to overflowing, with some five hundred people—"smiling, good-faced farmers . . . and a magnificent table of *reporters*"; as Roger later writes, "I never saw so many in a small hall."

Speaking for the very first time from a political platform, Roger emphasizes his local roots: "I have lived amongst Ulster people many years of my life and in quiet and daily contact with them I have learned to know them well." He mocks Asquith's Home Rule Bill for the insignificant and demeaning crumbs of power it concedes to an Irish parliament and denounces any plan to exclude any part of Ulster from Home Rule as "unacceptable"—though he nonetheless manages to praise Carson for being "the first in this generation to teach Irishmen to fight." Further, he insists that "Catholic Ireland, Nationalist Ireland" desires "no triumph over Ulster. They seek only the friendship, the goodwill, and I believe *even the leadership of Ulster.*"

The entire event, Roger writes Gee the next day, proved a "*grand* success." And the reporters present largely agree. Roger is widely hailed for his eloquence and daring, though the London *Times* insists that the meeting represented "only a small and isolated pocket of dissident Protestants" and refers to Roger patronizingly as the "romantic nationalist." The Belfast press also throws a partial damper on the event by pointing out that Ballymoney Protestants are more divided in their political loyalties than is true elsewhere in Ulster, where Carsonism reigns supreme. That assessment seems confirmed when Roger—eager to "light a fire that will set the Antrim hills ablaze"— tries to follow up on the Ballymoney success with repeat performances elsewhere. Carson Unionists stymie his efforts; they dominate many of the Ulster town councils and consistently thwart Roger's attempts to hold additional meetings.

He is, after all, something of a drummer without a parade. A knight of the realm, a British civil servant and public hero, he yet rejects the desire of his Ulster countrymen to retain their affiliation with the empire. Raised Protestant, he insists on allying with the faith's historical enemy, Catholicism. Devoted to the suspect mythology of the Celtic past, he creates unease among secular radicals like Jim Larkin, as well as the nonmystical revolutionary Irish Republican Brotherhood. A sexual renegade, the ultimate outsider who can never come in from the cold, Roger stands one-legged on a balance beam that stretches between two nonexistent poles. One need only imagine Edward Carson, the antagonist of Oscar Wilde, in possession of *all* the facts of Roger's life, and one can begin to measure the risky audacity of his determination to play a public role in Ireland's future. Risky or not, he insists on joining the ongoing debate about "what to do about Ireland."

He does realize pretty quickly the futility of his hope, never very plausible, that Catholic Ireland and Ulster, left to their own devices without British interference, could "settle this question, man to man." The English public, it becomes clear, is "actually in love with 'Rebellion in Ulster,'" while in Ulster the pulpits, as Roger puts it, "resound with yells for a Holy War—these infuriated and selfish bigots, who have suffered no wrong, no threat, no injury to a hair of their heads, go out in thousands to break the law, to arm and drill."

An irresistible conclusion dawns on Roger. If Ulster can take up arms to defend its right to stay in the empire—and do so to English applause (from Bonar Law) or acquiescence (from Asquith)—perhaps the time has come for the rest of Ireland to take instruction from Ulster and start arming as well, but with the goal of *separating* from the empire and creating a wholly independent Irish Republic. Others are reasoning along similar lines, in particular young radicals like Bulmer Hobson, who have taken over the Irish

Republican Brotherhood (IRB). Small groups begin springing up here and there to practice drilling, and as their numbers multiply the umbrella name "Irish Volunteers"—in deliberate opposition to the "Ulster Volunteers"—is increasingly applied to them.

It strikes Roger and others that an ideal candidate to head up the Volunteers would be the moderate Eoin MacNeill, one of the founders of the Gaelic League and a professor of early and medieval Irish history at University College. MacNeill isn't a member of the IRB, nor sympathetic to its advocacy of "physical force separation." Nor, for that matter is he particularly sophisticated politically, or resolute: as late as March 1914, he will write Roger that "It would be simply heavenly if the Government undertook to suppress our Volunteers and Carson's together. Is there any way of getting them to do it?"

MacNeill thinks he can guide the Volunteers along a temperate path that might ultimately lead to a rapprochement with Ulster, and he accepts the offer to head up the group. Alice Green, for one, has strong doubts about his capacity for leadership: "I have seldom seen a man more unfitted for action, less fit to lead others in a difficult crisis, and less wise in his judgment of men." It's an opinion she conveys to Roger, who nonetheless decides to back MacNeill, at least for now. When, in short order, the IRB will move to capture control of the Irish Volunteers' governing Provisional Committee for the purpose of armed insurrection, MacNeill will only belatedly become aware of its intentions.

From the start, the Provisional Committee, of which Roger is a member, represents a broad range of nationalist sentiment, including on the Far Left Bulmer Hobson, now a committed advocate of physical force; Roger in the center, though leaning in Hobson's direction, despite his long-standing abhorrence of violence; and on the right, several members of Redmond's Irish Parliamentary Party, whose main interest is in capturing control of the committee to prevent any prospect of armed insurrection. John Redmond, the IPP's leader, has long opposed physical force; though he regards the Irish Volunteers as a passing phenomenon, a minor detour on the road to a peaceful transition to Home Rule, he wants to keep a hand in—just in case.

The Irish Volunteers grows much more rapidly than Redmond expects or wishes. His own popularity, until now immense, has somewhat declined in the face of concessions that both he and Asquith have been making of late in regard to Ulster's exclusion from Home Rule—proposals ranging from letting the decision be made on the county level to exempting the four Ulster counties with large Protestant majorities. In contrast and in direct response to the wavering resolve in the Redmond-Asquith camp, Carson's attitude hardens—shifting from verbal ferocity to the open sanctioning of armed resistance.

The thirty-member Provisional Committee of the Irish Volunteers chooses Roger to represent it in a series of London press interviews. The message he carries is that—unlike the Ulster Volunteers—the Irish Volunteers "will be defensive and protective, and will not contemplate either aggression or domination." In truth, the Provisional Committee is not uniformly in favor of a defensive strategy. The committee includes an IRB contingent that *does* advocate "physical force separatism," a position that Roger himself feels increasing sympathy for, though he is not yet fully committed. (Even as late as mid-1914—in the context of a pending European conflict—Roger will send a letter to the *Irish Independent,* declaring that "our duty as a Christian people is to abstain from bloodshed"; he does add, though, that "our duty as Irish men is to give our lives for Ireland"—in other words, not for Great Britain.)

For the next six months Roger plunges into a recruiting campaign for the Volunteers, traveling widely throughout Ireland, exhorting young men to join up. At Cork he reports to cousin Gee, "I had a grand reception, a hurricane of cheers and embraces too from workmen, and 700 men enrolled Volunteers!" In Galway the town hall fills up with young men "clinging like limbs of ivy to the rafters and wings" and "storming" to the platform in their eagerness to enroll; during his speech Roger includes, not for the first time, some peripheral praise for Ulster's "manly steadfastness." Apparently a few embers still burn amid the ashes of his earlier belief that Ulster Presbyterians could be persuaded to choose unity with Ireland rather than with Britain.

. . .

Following Larkin and Connolly's failed attempt to wring concessions from William Martin Murphy and the Employers Federation, yet another militia—the Citizen Army—emerges. It doesn't attract widespread support, never numbering more than a few hundred members. The nationalist emphasis of the Irish Volunteers—defend "sacred Ireland!"—turns out to have far more appeal to the working class than does Larkin's attempt to unite them behind the banner of class struggle. Yet Con Markievicz—though she does join the Volunteers—devotes most of her energy to the Citizen Army, not least because she deeply admires its head, James Connolly, but also because of its welcoming attitude toward women (the Volunteers confine their female members to a separate auxiliary, where they perform traditional supportive roles). Con, the born aristocrat, adopts more fervently than many workers do, the Citizen Army's pledge "to sink all differences of birth, property and creed under the common name of the Irish people." Con is elected treasurer, and Jim Larkin chair.

Almost all those who join the Citizen Army look favorably on the far more powerful Irish Volunteers, but the chief exception is (as so often before) the playwright Sean O'Casey. He denounces the Volunteers as "bourgeois" and as "suspiciously aloof" from the terrible conditions that afflict the working class; "let others prate about rights and liberties common to all Irishmen," O'Casey writes. "We are out for the right to work and eat and live." Despite the best efforts of O'Casey, Markievicz, and Larkin, the Citizen Army remains small-scale, pretty much confined to the Dublin area.

John Redmond's public reason for distrusting the Irish Volunteers centers on the commitment of its IRB members to the tactic of physical force. Yet Redmond is no pacifist—as he will soon demonstrate when World War I erupts, and he will strenuously exhort young Irishmen to enlist in the British army. Nor does his distrust have anything to do with the Volunteers' "bourgeois" or masculinist ethic. No, Redmond's hostility, as he *privately* acknowledges to a trusted few, rests on his fear that a rapidly expanding Volunteers poses a potential threat to the preeminence of his own Irish Parliamentary Party.

Two episodes give a particularly strong boost to enrollment in the Irish Volunteers and further exacerbate Redmond's fear of a rival political force. One is the so-called Curragh Mutiny. In the early months of 1914, the Asquith cabinet learns from police reports that the *Ulster* Volunteer Force is undergoing a sudden spurt in growth and that plans are afoot to equip its members with real, not wooden, guns—to be attained through a series of raids on local arms depots. This policy flies in the face of the Asquith government's recent announcement of a ban (weakly worded, to be sure) on the importation of arms—by any faction—into Ireland. A five-man cabinet subcommittee is formed to look into the rumors of possible UVF raids (one of the five is Winston Churchill, then first lord of the admiralty), and it recommends "as a precautionary measure" that the local depots be reinforced with additional troops and that warships be sent to patrol the coastal waters off Ulster.

The recommendations are a bombshell. Alarm spreads through Ulster that the Asquith government has decided to *coerce* the province into accepting Home Rule. Edward Carson leaves at once for Belfast to make sure that unionist hotheads don't precipitate a misguided riot. The heat goes up another notch when the cabinet decides to send Sir Arthur Paget, commander in chief in Ireland, to oversee the dispatch of additional troops to Ulster. King George V himself—who's "not unfavorable" to excluding Ulster from Home Rule—warns Asquith about predictions he's heard that some officers are likely to disobey any instructions to use coercion against the province. Accordingly, Asquith accepts Paget's recommendation that officers with direct family connections in Ulster be excused from duty—though he announces that others who refuse to comply with orders are to be dismissed. Yet when Paget convenes seven senior officers to explain the pending operation, he does an inept job of it, apparently telling them that troop movements *will* include active military operations and that he "expects the country to be in a blaze by Saturday."

And it quickly is. That same day the commander of the English cavalry brigade at the Curragh camp near Dublin lays out Paget's confused and inflammatory instructions to his staff, and of the seventy-seven officers no fewer than forty—including the commander himself—declare on the spot that they prefer dismissal to taking part in any military action against Ulster. News of the "Curragh Mutiny" sweeps the country. The Tory leader Bonar Law declares in the Commons that the planned troop movements "are part of a concerted plan either to provoke or to intimidate the people of Ulster." Charges and countercharges fly. Rumors have it that the officers can't—or won't—carry out their duties; that a misunderstanding has, or hasn't, occurred; that the cabinet does, or doesn't, intend to issue a written statement; that the army will, or won't, forcibly impose Home Rule. "What loyalty can any Irishman with brains and heart have," Roger plaintively writes Alice Green, "for *any* English Government? I have none." Alice Green has held out more faith in the Asquith administration than Roger, but the bungling at Curragh persuades her that it's misplaced.

When the (imaginary) smoke finally clears, the saber rattling leaves behind a very real residue: Ulster can now rest assured that the Asquith government will *not* impose Home Rule by force—which further means that John Redmond's Irish Party can no longer plausibly argue that "in the end" all of Ireland will come under Home Rule. The implausibility is confirmed a month later, when the UVF (with Carson's blessing) successfully carries out a gunrunning operation. It has been preceded by several secret, small-scale importations dating back to 1910, as well as, in 1913, two major seizures by the British authorities that convince hard-core Carsonites that a more ambitious and sophisticated operation is needed.

The Larne gunrunning expedition of April 1914 is the direct result of that conviction—and its consequences prove ominous. Purchasing arms in Hamburg, Germany, the UVF's rented ship, the *Clydevalley*, successfully circumvents Churchill's naval cordon and on the evening of April 24 smuggles ashore at Larne and two other Ulster ports some thirty-five thousand rifles and three million rounds of ammunition. They're quickly distributed by motorcar across the province. The event puts to rest for good Redmond's notion that "Ulster is bluffing." As Carson exultantly tells an audience a few days later, "For years we were jeered at.... But there is no longer jeering." Carson, sworn defender of the constitution, has sanctioned—and now jubilantly hails—a large-scale act of law breaking. The action buries beyond retrieval Roger's once-hopeful view that *somehow* the two rival groups—the Irish Volunteers and the Ulster Volunteer Force—might join together to achieve a united, independent Ireland. Given the religious antagonisms involved, the hope has always been remote. Now it is stone dead.

Roger goes into a huddle with Eoin MacNeill and Alice Green; they meet in the privacy of the inexpensive Belfast hotel room that Roger keeps as a home base while he crisscrosses Ireland drumming up support for the Irish Volunteers. The room is overstuffed and drab; frayed velvet chairs, an ancient table with chipped legs, and a large, sagging bed take up most of the cramped space.

The talk is initially as dispirited as the surroundings, skirting the central issues that have brought the three together. They mostly commiserate, in a halfhearted sort of way, about the escalating crises that have kept them reeling of late. Then Alice Green alludes approvingly to the recent suffragists' protest of lying down across the roadway to stop Asquith's car—and the conversation heats up.

"Such extreme behavior," MacNeill says sternly, "will never move the prime minister, no more than did the ill-considered railway and coal-mine strikes. Asquith does not respond to immoderate gestures."

"Asquith does not *respond*, period," an annoyed Alice replies. "And *moderate* gestures have gotten us nowhere."

"I was surprised at Con Markievicz's reaction," Roger adds. "Surprised that she'd insist Irish nationalism takes precedence over women's suffrage."

"I'm surprised at *you*," Green scolds. "Markievicz has put herself on the line over and over during the strikes. And her very presence, along with her sense of entitlement, speaks volumes about what women can contribute, if allowed."

"Sorry, but on that point," MacNeill says, "I go with Asquith. "As the PM said in Commons, he can see no way our public fabric would be strengthened, raised, and refined, if women were politically enfranchised."

Roger laughs. "Meaning, I suppose, that English standards are already as high and refined as possible! Sorry, Eoin, *I* go with Con and Alice on this one. But really, friends, I've asked you here, as of course you know, to help me think through an effective response to the Larne gunrunning. I presume you've heard Carson's dictum that 'All government rests on force; and all law rests on force.'"

"He was speaking from the passion of the moment," MacNeill asserts, with an edge to his voice.

"Which is usually the moment of truth," Roger responds.

"I don't understand why Carson can't see," MacNeill says, as if talking to himself, "that a united Ireland would certainly be dominated by Ulster, given its economic superiority."

"Carson is a prisoner of his own damned covenant!" Roger energetically replies. "He's gotten tens of thousands of men to denounce Home Rule as destructive and perilous. He couldn't compromise now if he wanted to. Which he doesn't."

"At least Carson," Alice adds, "doesn't push the religious issue front and center—like James Craig's stupid remark that a united Ireland would leave Ulster at the mercy of 'an ignorant Catholic majority.' Carson's better than that. Nor does he want armed conflict either."

"He may not want it," Roger says firmly, "but he's determined to be prepared for it. Shouldn't we be as well?"

"Of course we should," Alice promptly replies.

"If you organize people for armed conflict, you will get armed conflict," MacNeill counters. "Look at what's happening in Europe today. The Great Powers racing to outdo one another in building up their armies, and that means—"

"*And* navies," Alice interjects. "The kaiser seems determined to challenge Britain's supremacy on the seas."

"And why not?" Roger asks, "Did God decree an English monopoly? Did he mandate the English Empire—and its inviolability? I'm no fan of the kaiser, but the English match him in arrogance and self-righteousness."

"If I may," MacNeill interjects with some irritation, "I can stay only for another few minutes, and I believe we should stay focused on the issue at hand: the gunrunning at Larne and what to do about it."

"Quite so," Roger quietly agrees.

MacNeill looks directly at Roger. "I've heard you quoted as saying that if we only had the needed rifles, we could have a splendid army of 150,000 Irish Volunteers within six months. Is the quote accurate?"

"More or less. Who quoted me?"

"Erskine Childers."

"I see. A good Irish nationalist. Alice knows him well."

"I do indeed. And think most highly of him."

"Childers and I have had some serious conversation of late," Roger adds. "But more of that some other time...."

"No, I think the time is now, right now," MacNeill says with visible force, surprising the other two.

"I must say straight out, Roger," MacNeill continues, "that I don't recognize you of late. You sound more and more like Hobson, though I thought you had limited sympathy for the IRB's insistence on physical force."

Taken by surprise, Roger fumbles for a response: "Yes, I ... you and I both, Eoin, have stood out against ... against any glib call for ... bloodshed ... but—well, this is just why I asked you here today, I feel at sixes and sevens ... conflicted in my own mind. I mean, if Ulster can go to Germany to negotiate an arms shipment to Larne, doesn't the question automatically arise about the Irish Volunteers doing the same?"

"It doesn't arise in *my* mind," MacNeill says firmly. "What about you, Alice? Where do you stand on this?"

"With Roger. Very much so. But I'd welcome a frank discussion of the matter."

"*I* stand with John Redmond." MacNeill's tone is bristly. He turns toward Roger: "He wants a united Ireland as much as we do; he's just going about it differently."

"Oh, Eoin!" Alice's reprimand sounds more like a moan. "How *can* you be so naive? Redmond wants a united Ireland, does he? Yes—united in slavery to our English masters!"

"Asquith's refusal to take action against the gunrunning at Larne," Roger adds, "has hardened many of us.... Enrollments are way up at the Volunteers...."

"I thought you and I," MacNeill says directly to Roger, "have been negotiating in good faith with Redmond about bringing the Irish Party and the Volunteers into closer alignment."

"We have been. Until Redmond made what he calls his 'modest request.' "Modest!'" Roger snorts. "He insists that we put twenty-five Redmonites—twenty-five!—on the Volunteers' Provisional Committee—in other words, give them an absolute majority! Then he 'modestly' suggests that if we don't agree to his proposal, he'll form his own organization of Volunteers! It's blackmail, plain and simple!"

"Really, Eoin, it's absurd!" Alice adds emphatically. "The Redmonite members of the Volunteer's Provisional Committee would represent the Irish Party—and that means accepting Asquith's insulting version of Home Rule."

"What the hell does Redmond want with the Volunteers, anyway?" Roger angrily asks. "Up to now he's been ignoring and patronizing us—now suddenly, now that we're a hundred thousand strong, he wants to make sure we're in *his* pocket!" Roger's agitation has brought him to his feet, but the room is too small to pace, and he sits back down again.

MacNeill responds in a voice of controlled temper. "If you object, then you should resign from the Volunteers. You and Bulmer Hobson both."

"Which is what we had decided to do," Roger calmly replies. "Until today, that is."

"Is this some sort of jigsaw puzzle that I'm supposed to piece together?" MacNeill angrily asks.

"If we leave the Volunteers, and Redmond gets control of the Provisional Committee, then any arms we import would be Redmond's to dispose of . . . a chance we're not willing to take. We are *not* resigning." Roger has revealed more than he intended and is quick to backtrack. "Never mind, all that. . . ." he says unconvincingly. "That's not why we're here today. . . . We're here to . . . to—"

Seeing Roger falter, Alice chimes in: "We're here to try to convince you, Eoin, that you're wrong to place faith in John Redmond. Not if you still hold out hope for a truly free Ireland."

It's now MacNeill's turn to jump up from his chair. "No one questions my devotion to Ireland!" he thunders. "Not in my hearing! Oh no, not in my hearing!"

Alice feels she's overstepped and tries to soothe the waters. "Really Eoin . . .," she says, "You know perfectly well that Asquith's version of Home Rule is like offering a poor man a pence, when he wants and needs a pound. We want an Ireland that really *does* rule itself—you want that, too—not the watered down Irish parliament that Asquith and Redmond support."

MacNeill remains standing but has to some extent calmed down. "It's a start, that's what I say. . . . It's a start. After a century of struggle, a *start!* It'll evolve over time, evolve into a totally independent Irish parliament, a free country that—mark my words!—Ulster will come clamoring to join. . . . Redmond has made a start. . . ."

"Redmond needs to get us a general," Roger says quietly.

A shocked MacNeill stands stock-still for an instant, then moves toward the door. "You . . . you really go too far, Roger. . . . Are you advocating violence? If so, this is a parting of the waves between us."

"What I advocate is the *threat* of violence. It's the only way to get England's attention. It's what Carson and Ulster have done. And what we must do too. Your Redmond will never understand that. . . ."

"I *welcome* Redmond's takeover of the Provisional Committee," MacNeill says in a theatrically subdued tone. "His is the voice of sanity. Of reason. No romantic posturing . . . no foolish Fianna boys jabbering about gunrunning."

"Have it your way, Mac." Roger attempts some version of a warm smile. "I hope I may still regard you as a friend."

MacNeill is momentarily disarmed but quickly stiffens. "Time will tell, Roger. I personally bear you no ill will."

"I'm glad of that," Roger softly replies.

"Nor you, Alice." She nods her head curtly but says nothing. At the door, MacNeill turns back into the room. "In any case, I take my leave. And . . . wish you well. . . ."

After the door closes behind him, Alice turns to Roger: "And good riddance, I say. I never trusted the man. Not even his scholarship!"

Roger laughs. "That *is* the supreme insult!" He shakes his head in disbelief: "I don't understand—Eoin's a good-humored man, no vanity in him."

"He and Redmond deserve each other. Now Roger . . . please explain to me why you think staying in the Volunteers and arming them will somehow outflank Redmond? He's a clever one. . . ."

"He won't touch a group willing to resort to physical force—even theoretically. *He'll* be the one to abandon the Volunteers. In truth, though," Roger adds pensively, "I think we should try and keep him *in* the organization."

"Honestly, Roger, I can't keep track of these strategic twists and—"

"Bulmer agrees with me. He feels a knockdown factional fight—or, I should say, *another* factional fight—and the Volunteers will splinter into irrelevance. Which would mean that if we do manage to import guns, we'll have no intact organization to distribute them. There—is that clear enough, my Good Woman of the Stern and Unbending Manner?"

"Oh no—don't try your charm on me, Mr. Casement! Not this time!"

Roger bursts out laughing. "Ah, my dear Heroine of the Irish Ballads!—'"

"*Stop* it this minute!" Alice makes a halfhearted effort to frown. "*Let us kindly return* to the very serious matter at hand."

"You mean how to kill people?"

"You're giddy, Roddie! MacNeill would be furious. You're supposed to be crestfallen at his disaffection."

"There are many worse sorts than old MacNeill. I suspect he'll come round."

"He's a Redmonite through and through."

Roger suddenly turns serious. "There's no clear path, Alice. I can't see in front of my own face."

"Well," she says firmly, "I can tell you who's standing there: Erskine Childers. And he's beckoning to you. And, for that matter, to me."

"I've talked to him once, as I said. I like him, and I agree with much of what he had to say, but—"

"But?"

"Well . . . he's so damned *English!* My distrust kicks right in! Then I remember that Winston Churchill called him a 'murderous renegade,' and I feel a good deal better about him."

Alice laughs. "Childers can't help it, poor fellow. It isn't his fault he was born into the English upper class. At least he's managed to break away."

"To incompletely break away."

"Meaning what?"

"Oh, come now, dear Alice! Describing his experience during the Boer War to me, he kept referring to the South African natives as 'Kaffirs' or 'niggers' or 'boys.' . . . It quite threw me."

"They all sound like that—those Etonians."

"And not just Etonians. Childers got quite passionate defending the Boers' rotten treatment of the natives. He simply assumes—they all do—the rightness of white supremacy. He'd have felt entirely at home in Leopold's Congo."

"As bad as all that?"

"Until I compare him to everyone else. Everyone white, that is. Frankly, I wouldn't care to poll any of our Irish comrades on the subject. Africans are 'them,' never 'us.'"

"That struggle is untouched. You and I probably harbor some of Childers's smugness, at least unconsciously, maybe a less rabid version. . . . But Ireland won't wait while we perfect ourselves, Roddie, or hold out for spotless allies. We have to work with what we have. . . ."

"My wise Alice . . . you *are* the 'dear old woman.' . . ." Roger gets up and moves to hug her.

"What's this, what's this?! There's no time for *affection,* for heaven's sake!" They embrace, and laugh.

"Besides," Alice says, "you'll adore Erskine's wife, Molly. She's American, a rich Bostonian, but don't hold that against her. She's physically frail, what they call a 'diseased hip,' but I've never known a purer soul."

"Present company excepted."

Alice smiles. "Meaning me—or you?"

"You, of course. Men aren't supposed to have pure souls. Warriors," he says mockingly, "are *not* sob sisters."

"Nor is Molly! Nor, for that matter, is her close friend Mary Spring-Rice. These are *vital* people, fearless. A match for any of your so-called warriors. It's Mary who's come up with the idea of using private yachts for running the guns."

"I know that name. Spring-Rice."

"Of course you do. Her cousin's Cecil Spring-Rice, diplomat son of a diplomat. And as of two years ago, our ambassador to the United States."

"Yes, of course . . ."

"Eton, Balliol, peer of the realm—Cecil has all the usual stigmata. Except he's a strong Home Ruler. An *English* Redmonite."

"Just the man I need!"

"For what?"

"Bulmer wants me to go to the States to raise money for the Volunteers."

"Spring-Rice is close to President Roosevelt. Meaning he's definitely *not* your man. He views John Devoy and Clan-na-Gael as the enemy— 'irresponsible revolutionaries.'"

"Devoy is furious with Bulmer, probably with me too, for even *considering* letting Redmond's people join the Provisional Committee. I doubt my trip will happen."

"You have more than enough on your plate already. And now the Childers expedition."

"What was that about 'private yachts'?"

"It's Mary's idea. She's volunteered to be a crew member—Molly Childers too—with not a drop of experience as a sailor. It would mean a three-week voyage in a small boat trying to evade the Royal Navy's cordon, likely to be shot at—not to mention the prospect of drowning. Is that 'warrior' enough to earn your respect?"

"I'm rightly chastised. As if I didn't know my own mother had the heart of a lion—not to mention my cousin Gertrude. But when is 'yachting' to happen? Tell me *more,* for heaven's sakes!"

"It might not happen at all. First, money has to be raised to buy the arms. Then we need to find an arms dealer willing to sell. After that—"

"We?"

"Of course 'we'! Did you expect me to hang back? Between the three of us, we've already raised—"

"Which three?"

"The women, my dear. The women. Me, Molly, and Mary. We've put up half the money needed—£1,500 in all."

Roger's face lights up with admiration. "My God, you're something!"

"Save your applause until we carry it off—*if* we do." Alice laughs. "After all, you might end up delivering a eulogy instead of an encomium!"

Roger jumps out of his chair with excitement. "I can help! I can help, Alice! I'm in touch with the London agent of a Hamburg arms dealer—it's part of my possible trip to the States. I can introduce Childers!"

"Really? That *would* be marvelous! It might solve our biggest problem. . . . How soon? There are so many details to work out. The slightest slipup and . . . well, it would be a huge help to know that the arms are *there* in case we actually manage to get to Hamburg!"

"The dealer is rock solid. The name comes from Tom Clarke—that should be guarantee enough!"

"None better. Good heavens, Roger—this could really happen!" Suddenly Alice's spirits sag. "Maybe it's all madness. . . . We're talking about violence . . . shedding blood."

"No, we're talking about self-defense. *Responding* to violence. The English shed blood all over the world and without the slightest twinge of conscience. . . . Demonstrating our *ability* to arm ourselves is the best guarantee of a peaceful solution . . . the only guarantee."

. . .

The yacht may weigh twenty-eight tons, and Childers may have sailed the *Asgard* more than a thousand miles within just the last year, but the combined solidity of boat and skipper make at best for an even match with one of the worst storms to hit the Irish Sea in thirty years. The voyage had begun on July 3, 1914, with a crew consisting of Erskine and Molly Childers, Mary Spring-Rice, and several other friends connected to the Irish Volunteers—all Home Rulers, *not* revolutionaries (though within a few years Childers will become an uncompromising nationalist).

Roger has been centrally involved in planning the risky venture. It hinges on a crucial rendezvous on July 12 at the Roetigen lightship in the North Sea between the Childers yacht and a German tugboat bringing the nine hundred rifles and ammunition from Hamburg (which Roger has arranged for and which Alice Green has helped to finance). Neither boat has a radio, yet remarkably the assignation takes place as planned. But that marks only the midpoint, not the climax, of the *Asgard*'s ordeal. Ninety huge bales of armaments need to be transferred from the tug to the yacht, and the Childers crew has to unpack every bale and unroll every gun from the straw that encases it.

"Our hearts sank in despair," Molly Childers later writes. "The six of us and about six of the tug hands worked like galley slaves [from 7:00 P.M.] until about 2 am at the job"—all the while relying on lamplight that barely pierces the darkness of the night, with the yacht constantly lurching from side to side in the storm and with the petroleum jelly that protectively covers the guns smearing everyone and everything. The twenty-nine boxes of ammunition prove especially difficult to handle, the men sweating and panting under the weight. Except for quickly stuffing some chocolate into their mouths and passing around a jug of water, there isn't enough time to eat—or to sleep. As Molly later writes Alice Green, "I nearly slept as I stood and handed down guns. It was all like a mad dream, with a glow of joy and the feeling of accomplishing something great at the back of it to keep the brain steady and the heart unperturbed."

Once the transfer is finally completed, the *Asgard* is so crammed with armaments and the crew has so little room to move that to get around at all they have to crawl on their knees or, when standing, inch forward hunched over, their arms pulled tight into their sides, their heads lowered on their chests. Everyone gets badly bruised from constantly banging into the guns that fill every nook; soaked to the skin, during the worst of the storm they vomit regularly over the side of the yacht. And they must remain on board for another two weeks—until the scheduled landing on July 26 at Howth, north of Dublin. Conditions are so difficult that when a newspaper later writes up the voyage, it assumes that no fragile female could have been involved and refers to "two men on board dressed as women."

Ever since the Ulster Volunteers' Larne gunrunning three months prior, the Royal Navy has been very much on the alert for additional attempts. Yet somehow the *Asgard* avoids the cordon—it sails straight through a naval review at Spithead, where King George V is saluting the ships—and successfully lands its cargo, in broad daylight, on the agreed-on date of Sunday, July 26. At the time Roger is in the States on a fund-raising mission for the Irish Volunteers, but before leaving he enlists Bulmer Hobson in the gunrunning scheme and together they devise a clever strategy to avoid police scrutiny. For weeks before the actual landing Hobson makes a point of conducting frequent drills of sizeable contingents of Volunteers to instill the impression that such mobilizations are utterly routine. As a result, when the *Asgard* docks and a thousand Irish Volunteers are standing at the ready in port, they attract no special attention and proceed to unload the Mauser rifles and forty-five thousand rounds of ammunition, without police interference.

It takes only half an hour to empty the yacht, and the assembled contingent of Volunteers each puts a rifle on the handlebars of his bicycle—the ammunition is loaded into taxis—and heads back to Dublin, mission apparently accomplished. But at Raheny, Hobson decides that the men need a break to rest, a decision that gives the Dublin Metropolitan Police, finally alerted, just the extra time they need to catch up with them. Most of the Volunteers are able to disappear through the hedges, but a brief tussle ensues with one contingent, during which the police manage to seize some two dozen rifles.

That test weathered, another lies directly ahead. As the police march back to their barracks and a crowd continues to jeer at them, the infuriated officers fire directly into the onlookers, killing three and wounding thirty-eight. The incident comes to be known as "Bachelor's Walk," and it epitomizes for Irish separatists like Roger the sharply divergent way the Asquith government treats militant nationalists like himself and the no-less-militant Carsonites— the one is assaulted, the other coddled. The previous day an infantry brigade of five thousand Ulster Volunteers had marched fully armed through Belfast without the slightest protest or interference from His Majesty's government.

Roger is in Philadelphia when he hears about Bachelor's Walk. He writes the Irish politician Bourke Cockran that the first news he received was of a "massacre," and as a result "two companies of Irish Volunteers here in Philadelphia put up, then and there, 3000 Dollars—from about 160 to 200 poor men—for arms for Ireland." He tells an interviewer, "I put the blame for the murder of women and children at Bachelor's Walk fair and square on the shoulders of Mr. Asquith."

Public outrage over the incident combines with the huge amount of publicity given the *Asgard*'s sensational voyage, to produce within weeks a 25 percent increase in the ranks of the Irish Volunteers and a sizeable number of donations to its coffers; the day after the Howth landing, John Devoy's radical Clan-na-Gael in New York cables the substantial contribution of $5,000. Though the successful gunrunning episode gives the Volunteers a significant shot in the arm, the group remains small potatoes when compared to the resources in arms and cash of the Ulster Volunteer Force. The Irish Volunteers may have succeeded in landing £1,500 worth of arms at Howth, but the guns are antiquated and the ammunition of dubious value. The Ulsterites had landed £60,000 worth at Larne (and carted them off in "motor cars," not bikes). The UVF is clearly the far more formidable outfit of the two, better trained and financed (its specialized branches include ambulance and commissariat contingents) and—headed by the truculent, sardonic Carson—with tougher, more resolute leadership.

. . .

The month before the Howth landing, Redmond's contingent of twenty-five members succeeds in gaining tenuous control over the Irish Volunteers' Provisional Committee. Just how tenuous becomes apparent when Redmond's supporters on the committee try, and fail, to exercise control over the new supply of guns from the *Asgard;* the armaments remain well hidden, mostly in the hands of the IRB, and are destined to reappear at a crucial point two years later.

The battle over seating the twenty-five Redmonites on the Provisional Committee has been long and bitter, and it creates a lasting division within the IRB itself. Bulmer Hobson is a major casualty. His IRB comrades accuse him of having taken a bribe from Redmond, force his resignation, and never forgive his "apostasy." Roger isn't a formal member of the IRB, but during the crucial vote to seat the Redmond contingent, he's persuaded by Hobson's argument that if the Redmonites *are* seated on the committee, they'll be easily neutralized—a fanciful prediction. Though Roger votes for seating, he's torn in his decision and soon after refers to the vote as an act of "*Hara Kiri!*" Eoin MacNeill also votes to seat, but unlike Roger does so wholeheartedly, with no ambiguous regrets.

Seating the Redmonites produces the very split in the Irish Volunteers that the gesture was meant to avoid. The hard-bitten old Fenian Tom Clarke denounces Casement as a British spy, the "master hand" in the "betrayal" (he assigns Hobson the subordinate role of Roger's "Man Friday"). Roger defends the vote as an "act of larger patriotism—not of small surrender"—a necessary step in winning Redmond's support for the further importation of guns; it's "the young men with the rifles," Roger claims, that "will make the new Ireland." Within just a few months, his argument will have lost all force: Redmond will remain adamantly opposed to the importation of arms. As for "unity," the Provisional Committee, riven by antagonism, is secretly taken over by its IRB members. They swiftly ally the Irish Volunteers with the Larkin-Markievicz Citizen Army. The Redmonites, in reaction, sever their ties and form an entirely new group, the far larger National Volunteers.

. . .

Roger leaves Philadelphia and arrives in New York to raise funds for the Irish Volunteers on July 18, 1914—eight days before the landing at Howth and ten days before the assassination of Archduke Franz Ferdinand of Austria-Hungary throws the European continent into turmoil. The hardheaded, puritanical John Devoy, leader of the radical Clan-na-Gael, is still furious about seating the Redmonites on the Provisional Committee—so furious that he tries to cancel Roger's journey to the States, but he's already left—and gives him a cold reception in New York. In the week preceding Howth, Devoy treats Roger with bare civility, and is unyielding in his denunciation of Bulmer Hobson's "treachery." When Roger tries to explain that he and Hobson gave way to Redmond's demands "to save the Volunteers from disruption and Ireland from a disgraceful faction fight," Devoy remains unconvinced and implacable.

John Quinn, the wealthy Irish American lawyer and a leading patron of modernist writers and painters, becomes Roger's primary host during his month-long visit to New York, inviting him to stay at his spacious, book- and art-lined apartment at 58 Central Park West. Quinn is very much an Irish patriot—though a Home Ruler, not a Devoy revolutionary—and his home has become a central destination for visiting Irishmen trying to pry American funds loose for assorted Irish causes. He very much takes to Roger and, along with contributing money, provides introductions and helps to arrange speaking engagements.

On the day of the Howth landing, Roger is on a fund-raising side trip back to Philadelphia—and in a fever of anticipation about the fate of the *Asgard*. Alice Green has kept him informed about developments—"our friends are on the sea," and so forth—but the first word he gets about the actual landing comes from a local reporter, and it feeds his worst fears: "British troops have seized the guns and killed several Volunteers." Tormented at the news, Roger spends a sleepless night. In the morning a corrected account arrives: the arms have been successfully unloaded and safely hidden. "How can I tell you all I have felt since Sunday!" Roger cables Alice Green. "I can never tell you. I was in anguish first—then filled with joy—and now with a resolute pride in you all. We have done what we set out to do! And done it well." He further reports that John Devoy's rage has given way at news of the Howth landing to sunny high spirits (or his dour version thereof). He is now, in Roger's words, moving about in "a glow of joy," calling the Howth landing "the greatest deed done in Ireland for 100 years."

It makes all the difference in Roger's reception. Devoy continues for a time to hold him at arm's length, constantly probing to see whether, underneath his charming, handsome veneer, he's truly a committed Irish patriot (meaning, as defined by Devoy, someone committed to the use of physical force to win freedom for a unified Irish Republic). The testing is continual, and Devoy is never entirely won over. But, in the aftermath of Howth, Roger is showered with so much attention and praise that Devoy's occasional coolness doesn't register as harshly.

Roger reports to Alice Green that everywhere he goes, "the Irish here would make me into a Demi God if I let them"; he's told "you are the man we want, the leader we yearn for, the *Protestant* leader of Irish nationalism." "Possibly the most distinguishing thing about him," one interviewer writes, "is his utter kindliness. It shines from his blue-gray eyes and radiates from him like an aura." This amounts to *modest* praise when compared to the delegation in Philadelphia that tells Roger that he embodies the spirit of the early nineteenth-century Irish hero Robert Emmet. Joe McGarrity, one of the three-man executive of Clanna-Gael, becomes an especially enthusiastic convert to the cult of Roger Casement, calling him a "reincarnated Wolfe Tone" (the Irish revolutionary who died of his own wounds before the British could hang him), and he urges Roger to undertake a national tour across the States in an effort to unify contending Irish factions. Occasionally, McGarrity trades in Wolfe Tone—who after all lived *long* ago—for Charles Parnell, leader of the Irish Parliamentary Party and champion of Home Rule in the late nineteenth century.

No one seems to have brought up Jesus Christ, but Roger can be forgiven for feeling suspicious that some of the photographers who trail him everywhere might in fact be British hirelings keeping him under surveillance. That his fears are grounded in some reality becomes still more plausible after the assassination of Archduke Ferdinand, heir to the Austro-Hungarian throne, on July 28, 1914. As the long-simmering tensions among the European powers seem likely to erupt in war, as fear (and in some quarters exaltation) mounts, and as Roger's sympathies and hopes seem to go toward Germany, England's chief antagonist, his loyalty to the Crown comes sharply into question.

"England's difficulty is Ireland's opportunity" has long been a watchword among Irish patriots, and Roger makes no effort to hide those views. In an article on the causes of the current conflict, he portrays England—"shaken by the discovery that in the first half of 1914 German exports had almost caught up with British"—as eager to grasp onto the current crisis as a chance to carry out "the destruction of German sea power, and along with it the permanent crippling of German competition in the markets of the world."

In fact, powerful voices in England are calling not for war but for calm and restraint; Sir Edward Grey, the foreign secretary, twice suggests mediation, but the German chancellor, following the kaiser's instructions, twice sabotages the effort. As late as August 1, 1914, the *majority* of ministers in Asquith's cabinet, led by chancellor of the exchequer Lloyd George, declare their opposition to intervening in any conflict that might break out on the continent.

Nor is opposition to an armed struggle confined to England. Socialists and pacifists are working across national lines to prevent a conflagration, with socialist leaders particularly outspoken in reminding workers everywhere that their class interests do—or should—trump their national loyalties. Socialists have of late been gaining traction throughout Europe: in the election of 1912 the German Social Democratic Party wins 110 seats in the Reichstag, making it the country's largest single party; in 1914 the French socialists hold on to 103 seats, and the British Labour Party elects 42 socialist members of Parliament. Yet in every country the divisions within socialism are profound, with orthodox Marxists advocating armed revolution as the most effective path to change, while social democrats insistently rely on the ballot box.

Kaiser Wilhelm has long denounced Germany's Social Democratic Party as the "Jewish Party," and when the SDP deputies in the Reichstag refuse to vote war credits, he furiously brands them an unpatriotic collection of "traitors." Yet in other moods—and the kaiser's abrupt mood swings are legendary—Wilhelm insists that he continues to oppose a general war. Tsar Nicholas of Russia and Foreign Secretary Grey in England also seem reluctant—and changeable.

In the kaiser's mind the maintenance of peace hinges on the willingness of Serbia to meet the series of harsh demands that Austria issues in late July. Yet the kaiser also views a divinely willed death struggle between Teutons and Anglo-Saxons (where France fits in is conveniently ignored) as at some point inevitable; he urges Austria to seize the current opportunity to expand its borders into Serbia—despite the fact that Russia has sworn it will come to the aid of its fellow Slavs (just as Germany has pledged its full support to Austria). Dutifully following the kaiser's lead, Austria does give Serbia an exacting ultimatum that includes the right of Austria actively to intervene in Serbian internal affairs to suppress "conspiracies."

Despite a conciliatory response from Serbia, on August 1, 1914 Germany mobilizes, with France quickly following suit. The kaiser declares that "the sword has been forced into our hand" and promptly demands unopposed access to France through Belgium, whose neutrality has been guaranteed by a European treaty that dates back to 1839. King Albert of Belgium rejects the demand, and on August 4 German troops invade. The Asquith government promptly declares war against Germany for its "flagrant violation of international law." The die is cast.

From Philadelphia Roger writes John Quinn that, as he sees it, "with John Bull pulled in . . . I think we should lose no chance to arm the Volunteers. . . . Bull will want our help, and it should be given *only* on terms that we get freedom at home, and if we have the men armed we can ensure a greater measure of respect for our claims." In saying as much, Roger is speaking for the small minority in Ireland that continues to hold the issue of Irish independence at the top of its agenda. But it is John Redmond who speaks for the overwhelming majority when he declares loyalty to Great Britain. The Home Rule Bill in the preceding months had been moving steadily forward in the Commons despite ongoing and spirited debate over which, if any, Ulster counties should be exempted. With the onset of war, Asquith meets privately with Bonar Law and Carson, and the three men agree that the Home Rule Bill should be postponed indefinitely "in the interests of national unity."

Redmond—unlike Carson, who couldn't be happier with the prospect of an indefinite postponement of Home Rule—still wants and hopes to get the bill enacted into law, and he fights a rearguard action to that effect. (In the upshot, after a series of backstairs maneuvers even more elaborate and tricky than what has preceded, Home Rule is placed on the statute book—but simultaneously suspended—and thereafter shelved again and again.) In a speech in Belfast, Carson openly boasts that the Home Rule Bill is now "nothing but a scrap of paper," and he predicts that at the end of the war even its paper status will be repealed in a matter of ten minutes.

Redmond chooses to believe otherwise and in any case doesn't want his loyalty to Great Britain questioned. Rising in the Commons on August 3, 1914, he declares his "honest belief that the democracy of Ireland will turn with the utmost anxiety and sympathy to this country in every trial and every danger that may overtake it. . . . I say to the Government that they may tomorrow withdraw every one of their troops from Ireland. I say that the coast of Ireland will be defended from foreign invasion by her armed sons, and for this purpose armed Nationalist Catholics in the South will be only too glad to join arms with the armed Protestant Ulstermen in the North." The crowded benches in the House of Commons break out in waves of enthusiastic cheering, and the chorus of approval is echoed in the press. Redmond is widely hailed as "a true patriot and a wise statesman."

But he is not universally hailed—not by Roger, not by the IRB, nor by Sinn Féin or the Clan-na-Gael. From New York City Roger writes Alice Green that "my heart bleeds for those poor people [Germans] beset by a world of hatred, envy and jealousy. . . . This is England's war—she has plotted it and planned it for years." He characterizes the large number of Irishmen signing up for the English armed forces as being "dragged at their heels" to aid "in assassinating the one great, free people of Europe." In fact, Redmond needs to do very little "dragging." Recruitment efforts in Ireland meet with considerable enthusiasm—more so in Ulster, predictably, than elsewhere, and Roger has to fall back on other arguments to account for the willingness of many Irishmen to serve; he favors the explanation that "99 cases out of 100" enlistments are due to "dire poverty and absence of work," preferring "the devil-may-care role of a soldier to misery and idleness in the slums of Dublin or Cork." He also credits the large number of enlistments on the English government's campaign of vilification against Germany, including charges that German soldiers are engaging in the systematic violation of "Catholic Nuns, Virgins, married women and girls."

John Devoy is no less vehement in his support of Germany. The August 8 issue of his New York *Gaelic American* carries a front-page banner: "Redmond's Open Betrayal of Ireland." In the body of the piece Devoy insists—against the evidence—that if the means of transportation were made available, half a million Irish Americans would at once offer their services to Germany. In other fringe developments, the Supreme Council of the tiny Irish Republican Brotherhood pledges to rise in arms to create an Irish Republic independent of Britain; the government suppresses publication of the IRB paper, *Irish Freedom,* as well as Arthur Griffith's *Sinn Féin;* the Irish Volunteers demand that Home Rule be implemented before agreeing to commit to the war effort; and James Connolly replaces Jim Larkin—who decides to migrate to the States—as head of the Irish Citizen Army and offers Con Markievicz a commission. The two lead a training exercise—twice—to "occupy" Dublin Castle. The poet and educator Patrick Pearse (like most men in the Citizen Army) disapproves of women drilling and marching but "sees no reason" why they shouldn't learn to shoot.

Roger's admirers regard his optimistic temperament as a core strength, his detractors as an encumbrance to seeing things as they "really" are. The reputation of revolutionaries across the centuries seems to hinge on whether or not they reach, or at least approximate, their goals: George Washington comes down to us as a far-sighted patriot, John Brown as a misguided idealist. For good or ill, Roger's sanguine temperament in 1914 is at high tide. Like so many others in a Europe that hasn't experienced a major war in fifty years, he initially regards the outbreak of hostilities as something of an opportunity for Ireland. Yet unlike Patrick Pearse (and so many others) who claim that "bloodshed is a cleansing and a sanctifying thing," that "from the graves of patriot men and women spring living nations," Roger's initial reaction to the outbreak of war (as he writes Alice Green) is a lament: "I don't see anything clear. It is a ruined old world I see." His attitude is closer in spirit to Sean O'Casey's words than to Patrick Pearse's: "war is all guns and dreams but no wounds."

The special value of this particular war from the point of view of Irish nationalists lies in the hope it holds out for an independent Ireland. Roger has never bought into the common assumption that in the event of war with Germany, Britain and Ireland would inexorably link arms. As early as 1912–13 he'd written a series of articles arguing that the opposite would come to pass—that Germany would welcome an Irish alliance as holding out the promise of wresting supremacy on the sea from England and in return would offer Ireland its full independence. England's enemy, in Roger's view, should be seen as Ireland's friend.

He wonders too about the rest of Britain's colonial possessions. None of them—including India, Canada, Australia, New Zealand, and South Africa—

have been consulted in the decision to go to war; the dominions are simply informed, through their governors general, that they, too, are at war with Germany. Not all of them dutifully march off to serve the Crown. There's a short-lived anti-British rebellion in South Africa, and the performance of some of the Indian troops in Flanders is considered subpar, leading one English general to scornfully declare that the colonial troops are "only fit to feed pigs."

Roger's focus, of necessity, stays on Ireland. The idea of personally serving as an unofficial envoy to Germany gradually seizes him as a potentially useful undertaking. While en route to Washington in late August 1914, he writes John Quinn a "strictly confidential" letter, asking him to join others in signing a document he's drafted expressing "sympathy and admiration for the heroic people of Germany." An outraged Quinn refuses his signature—and thereafter cools noticeably toward Roger. Quinn has no sympathy for those who blame England for "forcing" war on Germany and sardonically suggests that it might be a good idea to have Germany occupy Ireland for a year or two—"it would shut up a good deal of the mouths-almighty." He tells Roger plainly that if he wants to serve Ireland then his place is in Ireland.

Those more inclined to revolution than John Quinn enthusiastically sign Roger's statement of sympathy for Germany, including John Devoy and Joe McGarrity. In Ireland, the *Irish Independent* prints it—drawing praise from a number of well-placed IRB leaders, including the rising star Sean McDermott. John Devoy is even more explicit than Roger; he writes in the *Gaelic American* that a German victory is the best guarantor of Irish freedom, and he leads a delegation to consult with Germany's ambassador to the United States, Johann Count von Bernstorff.

The count has long encouraged the kaiser's antipathy to England; as far back as 1905, he won Wilhelm's approval with a memo that exactly expressed the kaiser's view: "instead of recognizing the living forces in history," von Bernstorff wrote at the time, "and getting on good terms with us," the British government is attempting a policy that "throughout the entire course of world history has always failed," namely, to "stand in the way of a rising nation." In Devoy's view the "rising nation" is of course Ireland; he persuades von Bernstorff—and the count transmits the information to the German Foreign Office—that "an Irish leader (unnamed) who just returned from Ireland declared with certainty that the Irish were disloyal and declining to offer volunteers [for military service]. . . . Looked at from here, nothing could be said against a [German] declaration in the way the Irish wish it" (that is, a declaration that favorably views Irish independence).

As war fever rises, the Germans—who pride themselves on having invented the "scientific" study of the past (Leopold von Ranke's *wie es eigentlich gewesen*)—confidently cite the "lessons of world history" as a way to promote morale on the home front. The most favored "lesson" is that history "proves" that "again and again England takes everything from her vanquished and treats the poor, robbed people just as slaves." The Irish are the case in point usually cited: according to the German Foreign Office, the British have turned Ireland's "once so blooming a land" into a "hunger state" and have destroyed half the population "through murder, hunger and forced deportation." Certain British statesmen, preeminently the belligerent first lord of the admiralty, Winston Churchill, obligingly provide confirming rhetoric: should the Irish take up arms against Britain, Churchill bellows, he "would pour enough shot and shell into Belfast to reduce it to ruins."

In furtherance of Roger's growing conviction that he should become a secret envoy to Germany, Devoy offers to introduce him to Ambassador von Bernstorff. Roger jumps at the chance. He's grown tired of the United States, likes it less the longer he stays. He finds the average person "ignorant and unthinking," far too dependent for their views on what they read in their "rotten press," which in his opinion is "the worst in the world—uninstructed, fumbling, stupid and unenlightened on everything but baseball, American finance and politics."

As for Quinn's sardonic advice that Roger's place "is in Ireland," Roger feels that he wouldn't be able to hold his tongue in advising "some of the poor boys" against the "abominable sacrifice of Irish manhood to English mammon" and as a result would be "in jail within a week, or in a Concentration Camp or in flight to the hills." In a manifesto that he writes in September 1914—the slaughter in Europe by then well underway—Roger denies the commonplace assumption in England (and in much of Ireland) that Irishmen owe Great Britain military service. "For what?" Roger asks. For a "Home Rule Bill of limited scope and subject to amendment and still suspended after thirty years of public promises by the Liberal Party"—in other words, for a "promissory note (payable after death)." Ireland, Roger argues, has no reason to quarrel with the German people; it's England, not Germany, who has destroyed Irish liberty.

While in Washington, Roger has an interview with Theodore Roosevelt and warns the ex-president that England will "inoculate" the United States with "the virus of her own disease. You will become Imperialists, and join her in the plunder of the earth." (The prediction is apt enough, though the timetable askew: as early as the late nineteenth-century annexation of the Philippines, the United States had already caught the imperialist bug; Roger prefers to view England as a unique carrier.) As for Roosevelt, he wrote a friend that he found Casement "charming."

Roger himself describes his manifesto as if written by a "caged animal"— another way of saying, by a man longing to be active yet stymied on all fronts. His fund-raising campaign—now that John Quinn with his multiple contacts has moved to the sidelines—is not going well; he's raised only a tenth of his initial goal of $50,000. It's time for a change, time to make a move—and for the large-hearted, audacious Roger that means something suitably reckless.

When he broaches his plan to go to Germany, even John Devoy expresses uncertainty about the vagueness—and thus the wisdom—of such a mission. Devoy believes—and has conveyed that belief to Count von Bernstorff— that once Britain is pinned down on the western front (at this early stage in the war, German troops have overwhelmingly won the day), there will be an armed uprising in Ireland. It is at that point, as Devoy sees it, that the Irish should turn to Germany for arms and officers to ensure success, with Clan-na-Gael providing all the needed funding. Berlin is impressed with Devoy's "pragmatism" and with his follow-through. He uses his paper, *Gaelic American,* to advertise pro-German meetings (often drawing large crowds, with the rally in Celtic Park on August 9 producing a crowd of ten thousand) and to carry articles praising Germany's military leadership.

With his usual gruff directness, Devoy asks Roger precisely what he hopes to accomplish in Germany. To Devoy's surprise, Roger—having seriously mulled the matter over—comes up with a concrete answer: he hopes to persuade the Germans to let him raise a brigade from among the Irish soldiers captured in battle and currently incarcerated in German prison camps. Devoy flashes at once on the earlier precedent of John MacBride, who in 1899 raised a small "Irish Brigade" to fight on the side of the Boers—though it existed for barely a year. (The more uncomfortable precedent, as Devoy may well have remembered, were the several Irish regiments who fought with distinction on the *British* side throughout the Boer war.)

In response to Casement, the hardheaded Devoy raises a cautious eyebrow—he's already discounted Roger as an emotional, soft-headed romantic, "as trusting as a child"—but holds his tongue; he sees nothing to lose in letting Roger have a go at recruitment and to that end introduces him to his several contacts at the German consulate in New York. He even agrees formally to accredit Roger as Clan-na-Gael's representative and to provide him with $2,500 in gold—a tidy sum in 1914.

Roger books passage for Oslo on the Norwegian liner *Oscar II,* sailing from New York on October 15, 1914. He books passage for two—not mentioning the fact to anyone, not even to his close confidant Alice Green. The second person is a twenty-four-year-old Norwegian sailor named Adler Christensen, who'd earlier jumped ship and found himself penniless in New York. He and Roger had initially met in Montevideo some years before and quite by chance had run into each other again on a Manhattan street. Roger had fond memories of Adler from their first encounter—a large-penised, beefy roughneck with a penchant for women but who, for cash, performed admirably with men.

Roger sees him with some regularity in New York and listens attentively to his tales of penury and misfortune—erotic attraction has a way of focusing the attention, even as it blurs awareness of pathological fabrication. Roger has long prided himself on trusting his "instincts for an honest heart," but in Adler's case they seem to have taken a hike. The pathetic stories he pours forth of starvation and homesickness (somehow made more moving by the impressive bulge in his crotch) arouse Roger's intense empathy. When he discovers that Adler speaks some German, which Roger doesn't, he comes up with the idea of taking Adler along as a kind of Man Friday and to stop off in Oslo (then Christiania) to make it possible for the poor man to satisfy his aching wish to see his family again after a twelve-year absence. Roger's version of caution is to book separate cabins for them on the ship.

Arriving at Oslo, Roger goes off to the German legation and Adler—skipping that urgently desired reunion with his parents—goes to the British one. He explains to the official on duty that he's just off the boat from New York, having accompanied an English "nobleman" on his way to Berlin to hatch some sort of German-Irish intrigue. Adler serves up copies of several documents he's pilfered from Roger and steamed open, including a sketched plan to land a group of armed men in Ireland in preparation for a subsequent German invasion. Adler feels no hesitation in telling the British official that he and the nobleman—over whom he claims to exert "great power"—are involved in a sexual relationship of an "improper nature" and that the nobleman trusts him completely. The British minister in Oslo, Mansfeldt Findlay, has little doubt that the "nobleman" in question is Roger Casement.

Believing that Adler's material is of "extreme importance," Findlay forwards it to Sir Edward Grey, the British foreign secretary, as well as to Prime

Minister Asquith, Field Marshal Kitchener (secretary of state for war), Winston Churchill, and the chief secretary for Ireland, Augustine Birrell. Findlay has in fact disliked Adler on sight, describing him to Grey as having a "fleshy, dissipated appearance"; he subsequently learns that Adler is wanted by the police in New York "as a dangerous type of Norwegian-American criminal." Still, Findlay thinks Adler could well prove a valuable informer— so valuable that on a second visit he offers Adler a written guarantee of a £5,000 reward for information leading to Casement's capture, as well as immunity from prosecution.

Adler is a good deal more clever than he appears. With an eye to turning double agent, he returns from the British legation with a creatively melodramatic tale for Roger. Drawing on stray bits from penny dreadfuls, Adler regales him with morsels of invented intrigue: how a complete stranger handed him a phone number to call; how the call produced an address to proceed to; how the address turned out to be the British legation, where a man in a tweed suit announced himself as the British minister, assured him they knew all about the Irish-German plot, and further told him how it would be "worth a great deal"—since Casement couldn't be arrested in a neutral country—if Adler could simply arrange for the nobleman to "disappear." (Findlay will later categorically deny that he ever proposed bodily harm to Casement.)

Roger apparently swallows Adler's story whole and even expresses gratitude for his integrity. Outraged at "perfidious Albion," he decides to speed up their departure from Oslo for Berlin, where they arrive on October 31, 1914.

. . .

Ireland isn't exactly at the center of anyone's attention when Roger arrives in Berlin. The single largest battle of the war to date is entering its third week at Ypres, with massive losses to the combatants and no decisive result in sight. The German assault on British, French, and Belgian troops, initially deemed a success, has lost momentum, and a costly stalemate has ensued. Successive attacks and counterattacks, marked by the taking, surrendering, and taking again of a few feet of land, has been accompanied by ferocious close-quarter fighting and the maiming and killing of huge numbers of soldiers on all sides.

Late October, when Roger arrives in Berlin, marks the bloodiest period in the month-long battle. Over three days the six German divisions under command of Gen. Max von Fabeck suffers 17,500 casualties—bringing the total to 80,000 overall. Fabeck realizes that there's no longer any hope of an out-right victory, but the kaiser insists otherwise; word comes down from on high: the soldiers' suffering must be borne. Ultimately, the Allied armies succeed in holding back the German onslaught, but they too lose tens of thousands of troops. Both sides lose their innocence as well, the expectation of a glorious, short-lived "adventure."

Any number of Roger's Irish friends have tried to persuade him that Germany cannot be trusted to bother itself with the affairs of a small island rent by factions whose men are signing up in droves to fight the "Huns." Arthur Conan Doyle, who knows a thing or two about intrigue, puts it to Roger this way: "On the face of it, would any sane man accept an assurance [from Germany] about Ireland which obviously has been already broken about Belgium?" Roger has an answer: he's relying on Germany's self-interest, not benevolence: an uprising in Ireland that forces Britain to fight on yet another front inevitably weakens its efforts against Germany.

In the diary he briefly starts up again, Roger formulates his goals in a tone all at once touching, bleak, and borderline grandiloquent: "I thought of Ireland, the land I should almost fatally never see again. Only a miracle could bring me to her shores. That I do not expect. . . . But victory or defeat, it is all for Ireland. And she cannot suffer from what I do. I may, I must suffer—and even those near and dear to me—but my country can only gain from my treason. Whatever comes that must be so. If I win it is a national resurrec-tion—a free Ireland, a world nation after centuries of slavery. . . . If I fail . . . still the blow struck today for Ireland must change the course of British policy towards that country. Things will never be quite the same. The 'Irish Question' will have been lifted from the mire and mud and petty, false strife of British domestic politics into an international atmosphere. That, at least, I shall have achieved."

Roger's reception on arrival in Berlin gives him every reason to believe that, despite Germany's preoccupation with the war, his expectations are not unrea-sonable. Within twenty-four hours of arriving, Count Arthur von Zimmermann, undersecretary of state and a close adviser to the kaiser, arranges to meet with him at the German Foreign Office. The two men imme-diately take to each other and discuss at some length how Germany might best help Ireland win independence. He then takes Roger to meet Count George von Wedel, head of the English Department in the German Foreign Ministry. That also goes well and von Wedel obtains from the secret police a special identity card for "Mr. Hammond of New York" to protect him from being stopped and interrogated. Following the meeting von Wedel reports to Chancellor Theobald von Bethmann-Hollweg that "Casement made a reasonable and trustworthy impression" on him. Roger, in turn, telegraphs the Clanna-Gael, "Here everything favourable, authorities helping warmly."

Feeling that he's passed muster, Roger makes haste to capitalize on his success. Secluding himself in the Continental Hotel—room 219, with Adler discreetly billeted a few doors down at room 240—Roger goes through draft after draft of what is in fact a brief memorandum that he hopes will persuade the German Foreign Office to issue publicly "a declaration of friendly intentions" toward Ireland.

Satisfied at last, Roger brings the finished memo to Zimmermann's office and reads it aloud to him. When he finishes, Zimmermann assures him that he agrees with every sentence, and he takes possession of the document to pass on first to von Wedel and then to Chancellor Bethmann-Hollweg. The memo focuses on two proposals—the formation of an Irish brigade recruited from British prisoners of war and a formal German proclamation declaring the government in favor of Ireland's independence. Von Wedel approves the proposals and appends a note to the chancellor: "My personal impression of Sir Roger Casement inclines me to give them serious consideration."

Bethmann-Hollweg agrees. On November 20—to Roger's immense satisfaction—a public announcement is made to the world press: "The Imperial Government formally declares that under no circumstances would Germany invade Ireland with a view to its conquest or the overthrow of any native institutions in that country. . . . Should the fortune of this great war, which was not of Germany's seeking, ever bring in its course German troops to the shores of Ireland, they would land there, not as an army of invaders to pillage and destroy, but as the forces of a Government that is inspired by goodwill towards a country and a people for whom Germany desires only *national prosperity* and *national freedom.*"

The "goodwill declaration" is widely published—though not in England. It also appears as a leaflet designed for Ireland and the United States, with Roger's accompanying preface stating that he has sought a "convincing statement of German intentions" regarding Ireland to serve as a counterweight to widespread English propaganda warning the Irish people that in the event of a German victory, their "homes, churches, priests, and lands would be at the mercy of an invading army actuated only by motives of pillage and conquest."

Remarkably, Roger also persuades Chancellor Bethmann-Hollweg to append to the leaflet an additional comment: "The German Government repudiates the evil intentions attributed to it in the statements referred to by Sir Roger Casement, and takes this opportunity to give a categoric assurance that the German Government desires only the welfare of the Irish people, their country, and their institutions."

"Everything goes splendidly," Roger writes Devoy's close associate Joe McGarrity the next day. To Devoy himself Roger sends, along with a copy of the German goodwill declaration, a request that it be "published throughout Ireland, by every possible means"; "I am entirely assured," he adds, "of the good will of this government towards our Country." It's a triumphant moment for Roger, an achievement beyond what almost everyone expected. Devoy is uncharacteristically impressed. He's all along harbored doubts about Roger—a case of the tough-minded pragmatist's leery suspicion of the "soft-headed" visionary (in combination with the straitlaced prude's disapproval of "degenerates"—Devoy has somehow learned that Roger is homosexual).

All that is now put to the side. The *Gaelic American* praises Roger to the skies for having secured a pledge that "will remove any doubt which may have existed regarding German goodwill by a section of the Irish people." Along with the bouquets, however, comes a body blow: Alice Green, long Roger's intimate friend and political ally, declares herself horrified at his "treason" and tells him directly of her "profound and heartfelt sorrow." She breaks off all communication.

Another unsettling—though less devastating—bit of news reaches Roger almost simultaneously: the British Foreign Office has announced the forfeiture of his pension. The *New York World* is quick to follow up with a story that Roger is in the pay of the German government. Incensed, Roger contacts John Quinn in New York and asks him to institute a lawsuit against the *World* for slander; he insists that the British government has planted the lie, again proving itself willing to utilize "the elemental weapons of British warfare against an Irishman—the Black Lie and the Silver Bullet." Well aware that Quinn has cooled to him, Roger sends him an impassioned plea: "I have never received one cent from the German government. . . . They knew I was poor and that John Bull had collared all I possessed and they offered privately to bear all that expense. I refused. . . . I have refused every form of 'assistance.'"

Roger is being truthful with Quinn. Devoy's Clan-na-Gael *is* sending him money, but he's not had a cent from the Germans, not even from nongovernmental sources. A variety of offers *have* come his way—from publishers to lecture agents to a tobacco company eager to issue a new cigar bearing his name and image, but Roger has turned them all down. He's long since learned how to live frugally and is determined not to hand his enemies any ammunition that could compromise his mission.

Quinn writes back to say that a slander case against the *World* is hopeless. He also writes to the German ambassador, von Bernstorff, giving his reasons at length: U.S. libel law is "most unsatisfactory"; such litigation would be "particularly expensive" and Roger would have to come to New York to testify; and the *World*'s statement may be annoying but isn't necessarily libelous—"it would be no crime for Sir Roger to have been paid by Germany. It does not reflect upon his integrity or his honour or his personal reputation. He is acting for Germany. He is doing it openly and not secretly. It would be the most natural thing in the world if Germany did help him out, particularly as he has lost his pension." In a letter to a third party (who sends it on to Roger), Quinn simplifies his basic reason for turning Roger down: he is "acting for Germany."

Roger lets Quinn know that he's seen his letter to von Bernstorff, is incensed by it, and insists on responding to some of its "extraordinary statements": "I should have thought it was abundantly clear that I was acting not 'for Germany' but for Ireland," Roger writes Quinn. "No action of mine since I arrived in Europe has been an act for Germany—anymore than, say, to cite a very notable case, Wolfe Tone [the eighteenth-century Irish hero] acted 'for France' when he tried to get French help for Ireland in a previous great Continental war [Roger might have added that the Founding Fathers also turned to France for help during their revolution]. However different the circumstances may be in many respects, my action and the motives inspiring it have been the same." He adds, in a body blow aimed directly at Quinn, "I would have thought that every Irishman would understand at least that much, even if a restricted patriotic development might not permit him to sympathize with the end in view." Nor, Roger adds, has he "lost" his pension: "I ceased to use it when I embarked on my present line of action; and I no more 'lost' it than I did my rank in the British service. I gave both up." In the future Roger will rarely write to Quinn or see him. But Quinn is a man of integrity; he deplores Roger's current course but remains convinced that he's an "honourable" person—and Quinn will, unbidden, later rise to Roger's defense.

Having gotten an official statement from Germany of its benign intentions toward Ireland, Roger now addresses the obverse side of the coin: establishing England's *evil* intentions. He believes that all of Anglo-Irish history supports the claim, give or take an occasional gesture of noblesse oblige—like Gladstone's land reforms. But now, with so many Irishmen heeding John Redmond's call to defend the empire against German "aggression," Roger wants to remind Ireland of its history and wants in particular to reemphasize British treachery. He chooses to point the moral with the example of his own case—the recent attempt by Mansfeldt Findlay, the British minister to Norway, to arrange for his "disappearance" through the agency of Adler Christensen. Roger has continued to trust Adler and to enjoy their sexual relationship, but he regretfully decides that the plot he's hatched to entrap Findlay requires Adler to return to Norway.

After dining in the hotel one late November evening, Roger tells Adler that he needs to talk privately with him about an urgent matter that's arisen. The two adjourn to Roger's room and in a rare indulgence—befitting, in Roger's mind, the solemnity of the occasion—he orders a bottle of port sent to the room. Once they've settled in, their glasses full, it's Adler who opens up the conversation.

"It's about Findlay, isn't it?"

"How did you know?"

"I'm nobody's fool."

"Germany's 'goodwill declaration' seems to worry His Majesty's government more than a little." Roger allows himself a smile of satisfaction. "Just two days ago the Foreign Office instructed its representatives in neutral countries to keep watch for my appearance."

"Are you going somewhere?"

Roger laughs. "So they seem to think. And that I'd travel only through neutral ports. But I'm not going anywhere. *You* are."

"Thanks for telling me." Adler sounds more surprised than annoyed.

"I decided only today."

"I thought the big news was that I'd be leading the German-Irish invasion force."

"*What* invasion force?"

"Isn't that what the Brits are afraid of? Germany announcing it won't conquer Ireland means the Huns do plan an invasion."

"Not this early in the war. No, no, you're off the mark. And please, Adler, don't use that term."

"What term?"

"'Huns.' It's deeply disrespectful. Germany is a highly cultured, civilized country. You've been reading too much English trash about Prussian atrocities."

"I've been reading the *German* press—which is more than you can. Lotsa stories about French and Belgian civilians ambushing the 'brave' German troops, shooting at them from windows and cellars. And how the noble Huns are responding. It isn't pretty."

"I suppose you mean Louvain."

"Is that the one with the library?"

"Yes. A library that still stands, despite allied claims to the contrary."

"If it still stands, why do the *German* papers praise their troops for torching it?" Adler is pleased with his sly perception.

Roger's reply is vague: "War is a ruthless business. Keep in mind that every nation behaves badly at times."

"The Germans are murdering hostages. It's a matter of policy, not some shell-shocked soldier suddenly shooting a civilian."

"I've been to Louvain. It's nonsense. The town's still there, bustling with commerce."

"From what you told me about the Congo, it's pretty easy to cover up evidence of atrocities." Adler's hit the mark, and Roger changes the subject.

"Enough about that. I need to fill you in on Findlay. You leave first thing in the morning."

"Oh swell! Twelve full hours from now. Thanks a lot for the notice."

"This is a mission of the utmost importance, Adler. I need to feel that you fully understand it. And are fully committed to carrying it out."

"I can handle Findlay. Haven't I handled him already? I told him to go fuck himself. I bet nobody ever talked to him like I did! He was right pale in the face. That bastard I will get."

Roger is both relieved at Adler's vehemence and offended by it. "I trust you completely," he says—and means it. "I hope you know that."

"Yeah, yeah . . ."

"You'll be carrying two fake letters that I've written. You're to tell Findlay that you stole them from me."

"Am I allowed to know what's in them?" Adler sarcastically asks.

"One is a purported letter to my dear friend Joe McGarrity in New York, in which I—"

"What's 'purported' mean?"

" . . . uh—'reputed' . . . 'professed' . . . so a letter reputed to exist or a letter that—"

"I get it, I get it! So what's it *say?*"

"I praise the Germans, make fun of the British—"

"Oh Findlay'll love that!"

"I want to get him good and angry. And then I want to scare him to death. The letter goes on to describe a planned conspiracy—a fake one. It's all in code, but code easily deciphered—like 'our friends here are prepared to go the whole road with us,' and—" Roger interrupts himself: "Here, I'll read you a bit of it." He retrieves an envelope from the desk and, extracting the letter, starts to read from it: "'The *sanitary pipes* will be furnished and on a big scale, with plenty of—'"

"Sanitary pipes? What the hell does *that* mean? Am I supposed to play like I'm some kind of plumber?"

Roger laughs. "It's code, Adler. 'Sanitary pipes'—*guns*—a big supply of guns! Believe me, Findlay will understand."

"So you're saying Findlay's smarter than me?"

"Now, Adler," Roger's tone is warmly coaxing. "Stop being so difficult."

"I can beat the shit out of that creep!"

"It's your third glass of port."

"So? What's the problem?"

"You start sounding vulgar."

"I *am* vulgar, Roddie lad. That's why you like me so much!"

Roger smiles sheepishly, waves the letter in his hand. "No point going on with this, I suppose. You're not concentrating."

"'Course I am. Go on, go on. . . ."

"The gist of it is—in code, of course—to let him think we've gathered fifty thousand troops—purportedly—and ends with 'We shall be fully prepared here by Christmas.'"

"Who's the second letter to—Woodrow Wilson? What's all this supposed to accomplish?"

Trying to placate Adler, Roger keeps to an even-tempered tone. "The content is much the same. It's to invented friends in Philadelphia, telling them preparations here will be completed at the end of December and that in the United States they should plan to be ready no later than January. That's the gist of it. You can read the letters yourself when you . . . feel better. Just be sure to reseal them."

"I can't go," Adler says petulantly, "not until I get my tooth looked at. It's a piss of a lotta pain, I'll tell you."

"We can get that attended to. I'll make an appointment for tomorrow. I want you to leave for Norway the day after."

"Who's gonna fill your butthole while I'm gone? The Germans all look like blonde pussies to me."

"That's because you're blonde." Roger isn't at all sure what he means, and Adler certainly isn't. "Blonde men are always looking for a father," Roger adds, more enigmatically still. "You, at least, have found one."

Adler starts to hiccup. "A fuck of a lotta difference it makes!"

Good Lord, Roger thinks. Maybe I'm drunk too.

The next two months career between the audacious and the absurd. At times it's difficult distinguishing between deceiver and deceived, traitor and patriot, drama and farce. The emphasis depends much on the sight of the beholder and on which part of the narrative is highlighted or down-played. Adler, shifting between reluctance and zealousness, and back again, threads his way through the central scenario in precarious balance, one day appearing in the guise of a stage villain, the next as a master of the high wire, the third as the confused orphan in a storm. Roger, for his part, ranges, even in his own mind, from master manipulator to neophyte schemer. Neither man stays in a role or holds to a solid strategy for very long—though Roger, unlike Adler, has a fixed star: freedom for Ireland—and both men shift in mood on a hairbreadth from fierce independence to adolescent longing, the stouthearted warrior abruptly giving way to the forlorn waif.

The journey begins when Adler—dental work completed—returns to Norway and meets again with Findlay on November 26. Adler shows him the two fake letters from Roger, and the British minister reacts with satisfying alarm. Perspiring and pale, he paces the room—having carefully drawn the blinds—muttering about Casement's "dastardly" treachery. His agitation inspires Adler to further invention. What the letters don't disclose, he "confides" to Findlay, is that Roger is actively fomenting rebellion not only in Ireland but in India and Egypt as well. Adler inventively describes German generals and admirals dancing constant attendance on Roger at his hotel, where they pour together over maps and charts of Ireland in an effort to pinpoint the ideal spot for a coastal assault. The more distressed Findlay becomes, the more Adler insists that the £5,000 previously offered for "removing" Casement is grossly insufficient.

Describing the meeting in a letter to Roger, Adler gleefully reports that in the two-hour-long interview he "got him going now all right," with Findlay promising that at their next meeting he'd let him know for sure "how mutch [sic]" the British government would be willing to pay for delivering Casement to them. Adler also reports that Findlay thinks Roger is a "gentleman," though a "very clever, very dangerous son of a bitch. 'They must get you.'" Adler is certain that he has Findlay wrapped around his little finger.

And he's right: Findlay has been entirely taken in. He sends a "Most Private and Secret" dispatch to the British Foreign Office, declaring that "I believe the information he [Adler] has given to be genuine. He is not clever enough to invent it." But Adler *is* clever enough, and he adds some impromptu fabrications that go beyond anything in Roger's letters—including an elaborate description of Roger's grand reception by Kaiser Wilhelm; a top-secret project relating to an invasion of Ireland that involves six hundred men now training at the Krupp munitions plant; and a "picked band" of tested German officers ready at a moment's notice to accompany the invasion force.

The authorities in London react to Findlay's dispatch with alarm. Word goes out to British representatives around the world to keep an eye peeled for the infamous Casement and his plot to destroy the empire. Britain's highest security officers, including Basil Thomson of Scotland Yard and Capt. Reginald Hall, head of naval intelligence, are also put on alert. Sir Edward Grey himself ensures that copies of Findlay's report go directly to Lord Kitchener at the War Office and to Winston Churchill at the admiralty. Kitchener approves the payment of £5,000 in gold to Adler, and the Foreign Office so notifies Findlay.

"When I served them," Roger writes in his diary, "I was a 'hero'—the most chivalrous public servant in the service of the Empire etc. etc. Now that I dare to cut myself off from them and to do a far braver thing and surely a more chivalrous one I am at 'the most charitable view' a lunatic." For their part, Basil Thomson and Reginald Hall become convinced that Roger is himself headed imminently for Ireland to lead an armed rebellion, and they urgently put out an "all-points" alarm.

At Adler's next meeting with Findlay, he spins a few more tall tales— "Casement receives news of any event that transpires in Ireland within three hours"—which alarms Findlay enough to up the ante, on his own say-so, from £5,000 to £10,000 pounds. He also, remarkably—Adler must have been a consummate liar—gives Adler a key to the back door of the legation, which will allow him entry at any time. Roger responds exuberantly to the elevated price on his head—"I am mounting up in value!"—but in fact he's growing more uneasy about the situation. He sometimes wonders if all the effort being expended on Findlay might be diverting him from his next primary task: forming a brigade of Irish prisoners of war. He also feels high-minded regret at the need "to intrigue and tell lies," wishing, unrealistically, that he could deal with Findlay directly, as one gentleman to another.

He's concerned, too, at the disquieting information his German contacts have begun to relay about Adler's roguish, spendthrift ways. Roger himself has noticed a change in Adler's demeanor: "The old, boyish eyes and smile are gone and he does not look me openly in the face." Adler, in turn, picks up on German distrust of him and feels that his clever manipulation of Findlay is underappreciated. The once-exuberant adventure is giving way for Roger to periods of doubt and depression. "I am very lonely often—and get most miserable," he writes at one low point. Toward the close of 1914, he confesses that he feels "an outcast with no place to lay my head when this present war is over. The enemy [England] would hang me—that I know—and he dominates so much of the earth that I shall not be very safe in many parts of the world—even could I get there." He feels "broken-hearted" that in all likelihood he'll never see Ireland and his friends again.

The intrigue with Findlay, in any case, is drawing to a semicomic close. In a meeting at the end of December, Adler tells Findlay that, even as they speak, a substantial body of German troops is readying itself for an invasion of Ireland. A few days later Adler throws a calculated tantrum in front of Findlay, complete with threats of "revealing all" to Casement, a generous sprinkling of "fuck you's," and several dramatic stormings-out from the conference room. Findlay, still in thrall, coaxes Adler back, formally guarantees him both money and free passage to the United States, and the right as well to retain any portion of Casement's purported cache of £20,000 that he can lay his hands on.

Findlay's lavish promises to Adler draw a rather sharp reprimand from the Foreign Office. "Nothing," Findlay is told, "should ever be given to the informer in writing"; he can be *told* that he can keep any money found in Casement's possession, but it must be made "perfectly clear that he is on no account to have any harm or injury caused to Casement's person." That this dispatch shows far more consideration for Roger's safety than the Foreign Office has previously demonstrated is due entirely to Sir Edward Grey, who, despite everything, retains considerable admiration for Roger's past accomplishments in the Congo and the Putumayo.

By February 1915 the assorted, interlocking conspiracies of the past few months begin to disintegrate. Findlay, despite his instructions, does put in writing the promise of £5,000 in gold to Adler should Roger be captured. Adler tells Roger about the written promise, which Roger characterizes as "the most damning piece of evidence, I suppose, ever voluntarily given by a Government against itself!" He feels that he's "caught the British Government in flagrante delicto" and is eager to bring formal charges against it; his anger flares when von Wedel vetoes the idea. Roger has looked forward to, has even counted on, a direct confrontation with the British Empire, and from this point on his distrust of German intentions begins to grow, as does the feeling that he occupies a kind of no-man's-land. He fully burns one bridge with a lengthy letter to Sir Edward Grey rehearsing the entire Findlay Affair "in detail," holding the British government directly to account in its "lawless effort" to destroy him—and returning the insignia of the Order of Saint Michael and Saint George, the coronation medal, "and any other medal, honour, or distinction conferred upon me by His Majesty's Governments, of which it is possible to divest myself."

During the four month period in which the "Findlay Affair" comes in and out of focus, Roger's attention is increasingly consumed by another matter entirely—the effort to form a brigade from the Irish prisoners of war idling in German camps. As planned, the brigade's mission would be to attempt—with the aid of German arms and English-speaking officers—a landing on the Irish coast, there to be joined by the Irish Volunteers, with the resulting outbreak of a full-scale rebellion.

As a first step, Roger secures German cooperation in sorting out Catholic Irish prisoners from the rest and uniting them in a separate prisoner-of-war camp at Limburg. In a partial reversal of his own earlier belief in the staunch nationalism of Presbyterian Ulsterites, he now feels that "speaking generally Irish Protestants are anti-National and pro-English," whereas Irish Catholics, he's come to believe, have enlisted in the English army only from necessity and "are *not* proud to be fighting England's battles."

In late December 1914 Roger makes a formal proposal to the German Foreign Office about forming a brigade, stipulating that such a unit would be "pledged to fight solely in the cause of Ireland and under no circumstances shall it be employed or directed to any German end." The brigade would fight under the Irish flag, wear a "special distinctively Irish uniform," and as soon as possible "have only Irish officers." Roger's emphasis on pro-Irish rather than anti-British intentions can't be as cleanly separated as he sometimes pretends.

He realizes that the Irish coast remains "ringed round with English ships, mines—and spies" and that a direct descent on Ireland might not be possible. If that proves the case, Roger suggests—taking a decided leap off the deep end—then the brigade "might best help the Irish cause, *morally, spiritually,* and materially by helping to drive the British out of Egypt"; in Roger's view that would be a "blow struck for a kindred cause to that of Ireland." But when the remark is repeated to John Devoy, his slumbering distrust of Roger reawakens; he denounces any notion of Irishmen fighting in Egypt as arrant nonsense.

The Egypt alternative fades into the background when Count Zimmermann, the German undersecretary of state for foreign affairs, promptly conveys his government's agreement to the formation of the Irish brigade. At Roger's urging, the Germans even release some 150 Irish civilians who had been detained and arrange for their speedy return to Ireland as a gesture of goodwill. As Roger puts it in a letter to Joe McGarrity, "Everything goes splendidly."

That burst of optimism is short-lived. Upon arriving for his first visit with the Catholic Irish prisoners at the Limburg camp and escorted to the barracks in which the captured men are being held, Roger tries to conceal his initial shock: the prisoners seem in deplorable shape, ill kempt and dispirited, huddling for warmth in the poorly heated building. Nor do they greet him with any notable enthusiasm; many are youngsters still in their late teens, and the name "Roger Casement" prompts no recognition; most of the older men have heard of him but aren't quite sure why and in any case aren't in the mood for the high-flown, patriotic speech Roger spontaneously offers up about the "trap" of Home Rule and the noble history of the Fenian patriots. He's brought with him copies of Devoy's *Gaelic American* and also some pamphlet material, but most of the prisoners barely glance at it. It is decidedly *not* an auspicious beginning.

When Roger returns to the barracks the next day, things go a bit better. Most of the men remain indifferent or hostile, but 2 of them (out of 383) show at least marginal interest in the notion of a brigade—one, Corporal Quinlisk, is only eighteen years old, but the other, Sergeant MacMurrough, is in his thirties and tells Roger that he enlisted only because he'd been up to his neck in debt. Sensibly, Roger doesn't share the fact that at the moment he himself is very nearly penniless; he's pretty much used up Clan-na-Gael's original stake of $2,500, and several months have gone by without any word from New York. (What he doesn't know is that the faithful Joe McGarrity is working hard to overcome Devoy's growing doubts about the feasibility of Roger's mission.)

Quinlisk and MacMurrough aren't optimistic about winning over more recruits. They tell Roger that most of the Irish prisoners are fiercely anti-German and deeply suspicious of their motives for sanctioning a brigade ("Is it a trick?" "Will we in fact end up fighting for Germany?"). Roger himself feels real alarm for the first time. Why haven't the Germans done a better job preparing the prisoners for his visit—and message? Can Quinlisk be trusted? He comes from a family with historical ties to the Royal Irish Constabulary, which in Roger's eyes has always been profoundly loyal to the Crown. As for MacMurrough, Roger suspects—the man seems like a "rogue"—that his civilian crime had been much more heinous than indebtedness.

By mid-January 1915 Roger has become deeply dispirited, and he toys with the idea of entirely abandoning the notion of trying to form a brigade. He's frank with Count von Wedel about his misgivings, writing him that the prisoners "seemed very ill disposed, and declared they were much worse treated at Limburg than at the other camps where they'd been held." Impulsively candid as always, he confides to von Wedel his worst fears: "a sham corps of sorts could be formed by tempting the men with promises of money; but an appeal to their Irish 'patriotism' is an appeal to something non-existent." He even shares the dark fear that "all thought of enrolling the men must be abandoned."

Discouraged though he feels, Roger lacks alternatives. He can't get back into Ireland—and if he could, he'd almost certainly be quickly apprehended and locked up. Perhaps, he thinks, he should try to find his way to the United States and, once there, apply for citizenship. But then what? The Clan-na-Gael's long silence suggests that they've come to regard him as persona non grata; he'd be without a political home, without friends. Just as a profound depression threatens to engulf him, a twenty-five-page letter arrives from John Devoy. It's so unexpected and so full of cheering news that Roger's frame of mind instantly shifts. Devoy reports that he's sent (through the German embassy) an additional $1,000 and praises Roger for "the splendid way in which you have done your work." Devoy's letter does include one caution: "The proper place for an Irish brigade is *in front of* the English"; under no circumstances should Roger entertain the idea of sending the brigade to fight in Egypt. Though he bows to Devoy's wishes in this regard, Roger doesn't consider the idea basically unsound: a staunch anti-imperialist, he feels that it's entirely reasonable to see the struggles in Ireland, India, and Egypt for independence from Great Britain as interwoven.

Within a few days of Devoy's letter, one arrives from Joe McGarrity, full of additional appreciation. "You are my *brave, brave,* man," McGarrity writes, and he recounts a mass meeting celebrating Irish-German friendship that filled every seat in New York's Academy of Music, with hundreds turned away. When Roger's name was mentioned, McGarrity reports, cheers resounded in the hall. In almost the same mail, Roger receives a long-delayed, misrouted letter from his beloved cousin, Gee. It adds greatly to the store of much-needed sympathy: "Keep well and a brave heart," Gee writes. "Ireland needs you, and your work for her is bound to live in the long run. Never despair—you are the salt of the earth, a righteous man, and it is to you that all of us over here look for inspiration and uplifting."

Roger's mood again soars—and he shares that, too, with von Wedel. He's come to believe, he writes von Wedel in mid-January 1915, that the wretchedness of the prisoners' physical condition is what has most depressed their spirits and put a damper on their incipient patriotism. After all, he reports, the men, poorly clad, are being worked very hard, often in bad weather, up to their knees in mud, and at the end of the day "slouch back to their not too sustaining diet"—none of which, Roger suggests to von Wedel, "is calculated to put them in any 'heroic' frame of mind." Perhaps "if a little more meat could be put in their soup," if they were a "little happier in their bodies," the chance of awakening a "better spirit would improve."

But the Germans are having doubts of their own. Roger's initial enthusiasm about the prospects for forming a brigade had been infectious—but so too is his more recent pessimism. Von Wedel's response to Roger's letter is perfunctory, as if he now considers him some sort of peripheral nuisance. To make matters worse, Roger falls ill with influenza, and the doctor orders him to bed; on medical grounds alone, he's unable for a time to get to the camp at Limburg. He then discovers that none of the suggestions he'd earlier made to von Wedel for improving conditions at Limburg have been implemented. He writes him again and, with his usual frankness, tells von Wedel that he can "see no object in my return to Limburg under these conditions."

Soon after, Roger learns that the German guards at Limburg have been physically punishing the Irish prisoners. That rouses Roger to send yet another letter to von Wedel, this one more peremptory: "It is to my mind not only an act of ill will, but an act of cowardice for armed men to strike unarmed men, under their guard; and unless I receive clear assurance that it shall be instantly stopped I shall be compelled to desist from all further effort." Roger still regards von Wedel as "a gentleman and a friend," but he puzzles over why this once-magnanimous supporter is now treating him in so distant a way. Zimmerman, too, seems more eager to avoid him than to hear him out. Roger still trusts both men—but that's more a tribute to his generosity of spirit than to his perspicacity: he tends to trust people long after they've ceased to warrant it.

Adler Christensen is the chief case in point; Roger continues to refer to him as "my faithful companion," but in March 1915, with the Findlay escapade having played itself out and with nothing left to occupy his time, Adler decides to return to Norway. From there he soon emigrates to the United States, and Roger, "still trying to help poor Adler to live a better life," urges John Devoy to secure employment for him. Devoy promises that "we will do all we can," and he hits on an assignment for which Adler, with his language skills, seems especially well qualified. The mission, in essence, is to help Robert Monteith, a captain in the Irish Volunteers, somehow make his way to Berlin. Devoy has gotten word that Roger's efforts to form a brigade are going badly, and his hope is that Monteith, with sixteen years in the military behind him, including service in the Boer War and in Egypt, can set things to right.

In truth, matters have of late been going worse for the brigade than Devoy even knows. Most of the Irish prisoners have remained indifferent, sullen, or suspicious—and a few have become overtly hostile. When Roger, feeling that he's on the mend from his prolonged bout of illness, decides that he's well enough to visit the Limburg camp again, the experience proves a shock. One detainee shouts at him, "How much are the Germans paying you?" and several of the prisoners work up a cheer for John Redmond. On a follow-up visit one of the men "accidentally" shoves Roger; in humiliation and anger, he walks out of the camp.

. . .

Robert Monteith, a sturdy, sensible man, is thirty-six years old in 1915, married with three stepchildren, and a seasoned veteran of military service, having been twice wounded. His disillusion with Britain and its empire began during the Boer War, when (as he later wrote) "in the smoke and red flame of the first Boer farmhouse I saw burned, there appeared to me the grisly head and naked ribs of the imperialist monster." During the 1911–13 labor strife in Dublin, Monteith had been a strong supporter of Jim Larkin, and when the Irish Volunteers formed, he joined immediately, becoming a drill instructor with the rank of captain; he was among the small minority who stayed loyal after John Redmond and his followers split off to form the much larger National Volunteers. In Dublin, Monteith met and impressed Tom Clarke, the hard-nosed old Fenian who told his longtime comrade John Devoy that Monteith, with his military background and his devotion to Ireland, might be just the man to help Roger form and train the brigade.

Monteith is decidedly available: after World War I breaks out, he's offered a commission but refuses to serve—leading not only to his discharge but to a "deportation" order under the Defence of the Realm Act that gives him thirty-six hours to get out of Dublin. Through a ruse that has the authorities believing he and his family are permanently emigrating to the United States, Monteith arrives in New York City and promptly links up with the Clan-na-Gael; John Devoy takes the man's measure and agrees with Tom Clarke's favorable assessment.

The challenge now is to get Monteith to Germany and at work helping Roger salvage some kind of functioning brigade. Roger has been urging the Clan for some time to send him someone with military experience who might be able to rouse the Irish prisoners of war from their torpor and, not so incidentally, pull him out of his own doldrums as well. He blames no one but himself for his failure to mobilize and inspire more than a few of the men; the end of the Findlay Affair, in combination with the loss of Adler ("I cannot get your face out of my head," he writes him, and "in life and death I will never forget you and your devotion, affection and fidelity to me"), has reduced Roger's passionate engagement with life to a kind of forlorn inertia. He feels isolated, devoid of meaningful activity, prey to yet another round of physical ills and depression.

When in the doldrums, Roger tends to overaccuse himself—surely the result in part of having internalized to some inevitable extent the current view of homosexuality as "degeneracy." Though austere and self-denying, he becomes convinced that he's squandered the Clan's investment. Generous to others—he continues somehow to send money to Adler (and to his siblings)—he rejects the solace of self-pity, instead repeatedly berating himself for his "idleness," his uselessness, and his failure to help Ireland ("I simply tried too much—flew too high and fell").

Roger condemns his "failures" more rigorously than do most of the leading figures in the Clan—at least publicly. His dear friend Joe McGarrity picks up on the self-deprecating tone of Roger's recent letters and writes from New York that he needs to "brace up, you owe it to yourself to be proof against the vile attacks of your enemies; the more they attack you the more we will love and admire you." Even John Devoy, who from the beginning has doubted the viability of an Irish brigade and wavered in his estimate of Roger's reliability—Devoy equates pessimism with "weakness of character"— even he not only continues to send Roger money but praises the diplomatic skills "for which you are eminently fitted and in which you have achieved splendid success—a success which will go down in history as a great achievement." Devoy's superlatives, of course, are ascribable in part to his wiliness—as well as to his implacable determination to salvage *something* positive from a bad situation.

Roger hasn't entirely given up on the prospect of forming a brigade, though the odds remain poor. He recruits a U.S. priest, Father John T. Nicholson, to give the men a pep talk—and Nicholson does succeed in rallying an additional dozen to the cause. Roger himself continues to pester the Germans relentlessly about fulfilling at least *some* of their assorted promises—like agreeing to provide officers and arms, keeping the lists open at Limburg, and helping to actively recruit members for the brigade.

Further encouragement comes with the arrival from New York of the wealthy young poet and mystic Joseph Mary Plunkett, who also happens to be a militant IRB emissary. Plunkett treats Roger like a valued comrade, which raises his spirits, and freely confides highly restricted information; he even shares with Roger the IRB's secret password ("Aisling") and sign (a stylized Irish cross). But when Plunkett goes on to tell Roger that plans are afoot for a military uprising, the news shocks and horrifies him. He emphatically warns Plunkett that no rebellion could possibly succeed in Ireland without the support of a Continental power. To attempt anything short of that would be "worse than folly"—it would be "criminal stupidity." He's even further alarmed when Plunkett tells him that the IRB leader, the charismatic Patrick Pearse (head of the famed progressive school Saint Enda's and a rumored homosexual), is among those firmly committed to the use of force.

Plunkett tries to calm Roger with the news that his sometime-associate Eoin MacNeill, who heads the Provisional Committee of the Irish Volunteers, is firmly opposed to armed insurrection. But he then adds that MacNeill is blind to the fact that the IRB members of the committee have secretly seized control of the Volunteers—and Roger's anxiety soars once more. He despairingly tells Plunkett that if the plotters are foolish enough to proceed, he will feel the moral obligation to "come and join you, to stand and fall beside you." Plunkett's news of a likely uprising unexpectedly galvanizes Roger's determination to try yet again to shape up the brigade—however forlorn the hope that it might help to lessen the pending carnage. He urges Plunkett to try his hand at rallying the Irish prisoners of war. Plunkett does and has some success, raising the total number of prisoners committed to the brigade—after six months of intense recruitment pressure—to some three dozen men.

The point now is get Robert Monteith from New York to Berlin and actively engaged in shaping up the brigade. Given the enveloping war, with it naval cordons, air and sea bombardments, and submarine activity, traversing the Atlantic has become a highly problematic and dangerous business. Making it still more so, is the Clan's inability to secure a U.S. passport for Monteith, leaving him no choice but to stow away on a neutral Norwegian ship in a second-class stateroom booked for his assigned helpmate—none other than Adler Christensen. Adler is pleased with his new assignment but tells Devoy that he considers Monteith's chances of getting through as at best six out of ten. Adler agrees to provide Monteith with food and to keep an eye peeled for unwanted cabin stewards or ship inspectors, but—ever one to cover his tracks—he makes it clear that should trouble arise, he will disavow Monteith rather than face arrest himself.

The voyage proves harrowing. At one point a British cruiser comes alongside and sends a search party aboard; in an attempt to avoid detection, Monteith races through the ship from one empty cabin to another while Adler scouts the passageways. Coming into one cabin on the run, Monteith crashes into a pile of furniture in the middle of the room, making an awful racket; he lies still in the dark, fearing discovery—but no one comes. On another evening a drunken passenger, confusing the cabins, mistakenly pushes into the one where Monteith is currently hiding under the bunk. The man plops himself down and falls heavily asleep, his weight pressing Monteith so close to the steam-heat pipes that he ends up badly blistered.

The worst moment comes when the ship docks at Cristiania, and the passengers are told to have their passports and papers ready for examination as they descend on to the dock. Not speaking Norwegian, there seems no way for Monteith to avoid arrest. But in a stroke of creative genius, he plays at being drunk, careens down the gangplank, and smashes directly into the soldier checking passports; the soldier courteously helps him to his feet—and on his way.

Adler refuses to continue on to Copenhagen, as previously agreed, insisting that he must remain in Cristiania to await the next ship heading back to the States so he can be present at his wife's delivery—her existence, not to mention her pregnancy, is news to all concerned. When Adler arrives back in New York, the Clan discovers that he has not one wife but two, each unaware of the other's existence; he's also embezzled the money Roger entrusted to him for his sister, Nina. Joe McGarrity breaks the news to Roger is a lightly coded letter: "Our hero has done certain things that has made matters very unpleasant and has made Uncle John [Devoy] lose confidence in him. . . . Were it not for his splendid service and loyalty to you, a break would have been created recently." The news forces Roger, deeply saddened, to acknowledge that he's been a "fool."

Monteith continues on alone to Copenhagen and then to Berlin, where he immediately rings Roger up at his hotel—though Roger, unsure of when Monteith will arrive, happens to be in Munich. Before joining him there, Monteith pays a courtesy call at the German Foreign Office on the Wilhelmstrasse. The city is crowded with troop movements, regiments of men marching through the streets on their way to the front, with tearful scenes of farewell playing out on every corner. Monteith feels very much the conspicuous alien, awkwardly out of place.

At the Foreign Office, Count von Wedel greets him with a cordial handshake—and a hint of amazement that Monteith has managed to arrive safely. Quickly putting him at ease and without much prelude, Von Wedel turns at once to the topic of Ireland. Monteith tells him that John Devoy and the Clan have instructed him to report directly to Casement and to take his orders from him. Von Wedel says he entirely understands and doesn't press for further details, relieved that Roger will be otherwise engaged for a spell and leave off his constant importuning of the German authorities. Von Wedel does let Monteith know that Casement has been ill off and on for some time and "takes too little care of himself." The count advises Monteith to remain at his hotel until he can arrange for passports—which he does that very day.

Monteith leaves that same night and arrives in Munich early the following morning. He goes straight to Roger's hotel, and the two men settle down over breakfast for what turns into a lengthy talk. They take to each other at once. Monteith admits to feeling a bit starstruck: Roger has long been a hero of his, and he's not disappointed when finally meeting the man himself: "If ever a man looked a knight," Monteith later writes, "Roger Casement did. I have known no eyes more beautiful than Casement's, eyes that seemed to search the heart and read one's very soul. . . . His lithe, wiry figure, his sinuous, panther-like movement," make him seem like something more than just a man. What could von Wedel have meant by Roger's "poor health"? To Monteith he seems remarkably *alive*.

"It's nothing serious, I assure you," Roger says, after Monteith repeats von Wedel's concern. "I suffer from a bit of anxiety now and then. And with good reason, as I'm sure you'll agree—I mean what with the war absorbing all attention and the fate of poor Ireland withering away at the margins."

"England does finally seem united behind the war effort." Monteith says somewhat blandly, as if a lack of affect will protect him should Roger disagree.

"Yes, thanks to Asquith's coalition government. What a farce! Can you believe it? Lloyd George—the *leading* proponent of neutrality—now minister of munitions! Bonar Law at the Colonial Office! And Carson—who's broken the law over and over and gloried in it—named attorney general! The world's turned upside down, Monteith."

Monteith swallows hard, tries not to sound too authoritative: "The Germans do seem to have lost the initiative somewhat, don't you agree?"

"Everything hinges on the United States. If they can be kept out of it, I still rate Germany's chances high." Roger is indulging in a bit of calculated optimism: just the month before he'd written Joe McGarrity that "Germany *cannot* beat England. . . . It will be a miracle if she [Germany] wins."

"Doesn't the sinking of the *Lusitania* greatly increase the chances of the United States entering the war? On England's side, of course."

"Twelve hundred innocent souls, lost at sea . . ." Roger shakes his head sadly. "Frankly, I don't understand it. Unrestricted submarine warfare is *bound* to bring the Americans in. And if that comes to pass, we can forget about Irish independence."

"Devoy insists the American people don't want war and won't permit it."

Roger shakes his head sadly. "A democratic vote will not decide the issue. Woodrow Wilson wants an English victory. *That's* what counts."

"They say the kaiser is out of touch."

"Who says?"

"Devoy and the others. That he has only a vague idea of what's going on at the front, and his authority with his own generals is gone."

"I think that's about half right. As I hear it, anyway—and my sources are limited—Wilhelm is more out of touch in regard to domestic matters than military ones. After all, it's the kaiser who got rid of Admiral Tirpitz for refusing to restrict submarine warfare."

"I meant more what's going on in the trenches . . . the awful loss of life . . . the terrible stalemate."

Roger lowers his voice. "It's all ghastly beyond measure . . . appalling. So much pointless carnage . . ."

Monteith sighs. "Everyone was expecting a short war, a lightening victory . . ."

"Well, not everyone ... but certainly most people.... Destroying England's imperial power, alas, isn't done in a day. Germany's worst mistake, it seems to me, was thinking the British might remain neutral—then they could romp to victory over France and hold on to Belgium permanently. And now the Americans ..." Roger lapses into silence.

"About the brigade, sir?"

"Yes, yes, of course—the brigade. Frankly, I've pretty much soured on the Germans. They don't care a damn for our cause.... I tell you frankly, Monteith, that I've come close to giving up, leaving Germany and somehow making my way to America, where I might do some good. This inactivity is killing me. I've been an active person all my life. I want to get some place where I can *do* something—anywhere, anything!"

Taken off guard at Roger's intensity, Monteith finds himself mumbling some platitude about "Oh, it can't be long, sir, before we get the men in shape...."

"I hope so.... You'll get used to my moods," Roger says, managing a weak smile. "I'm truly thankful you've arrived, Monteith. I fear my standing with the Irish prisoners isn't high. My own fault, my own fault ... I made the foolish assumption that all Irishmen were nationalists. Most of these men are working class. What they care about is a job, a decent wage. Who can blame them? Home Rule's an abstraction to them—a piece of privilege that doesn't affect their lives."

"I know many a working lad—lasses, too—who put Ireland above everything."

"Do you?" Roger sounds genuinely surprised. "I'm glad to hear it. I think politics is a luxury for most people, a game to keep their idle minds occupied. I know most of the Limburg men see me as some sort of dreamer ... someone who never had to work for a living, no family, no responsibilities.... I came at them at much too high a pitch, Monteith, all that blabber I spilled out about Wolfe Tone and the grand old Fenians.... They've never heard of Wolfe Tone. And why should they have? ... Yes, I made quite a mess of it, I fear. I've been trying to inch my way back into their confidence but ... but I'm sometimes sorry I ever came to Germany." Roger tries to shake off his gloom: "Well! I'm damned glad you're here, Monteith. Perhaps together we can make a whole new start of it, eh?"

Monteith, shy and reserved, actually blushes. "I certainly hope so, sir. I'm here to follow your lead," he adds briskly.

"*You're* the military man, Monteith! I'll look to you for guidance. I'll try not to be a burden. Devoy's lost confidence in me, I can tell, no matter what dear old Joe McGarrity writes to cheer me up."

"I don't think that's true, sir." Somehow Monteith doesn't sound convincing.

"You can't tell with Devoy. He seems to agree with you. Until he doesn't—and then it's like trying to turn a stone into a snowflake."

"All that he said to me was, 'I think Casement ought to push for more recruits.'"

"Of course—but *how?!* I can hear Devoy now: 'If the Boers could raise an Irish Brigade of three hundred to fight England, why can't Casement manage a hundred?' Why? Because the Boers were painted as a small nation of democrats fighting Goliath. The Irish *are* a small nation of democrats—but don't want to fight on the side of Prussian aggressors who invade another small nation like poor little Belgium."

Monteith doesn't want to argue with his idol. Besides, having just arrived, he still feels buoyantly optimistic. "Let's see if we can't light a fire under the lads, eh?"

"You're certainly welcome to try. . . . But prepare yourself for a good deal of weariness and disappointment."

The very next day the two men head back to Berlin and from there to the camp at nearby Zossen, where the Irish prisoners who've already joined the brigade, or seem plausible recruits for it, have recently been moved. That amounts to some 50 or so men—out of a total number of Irish prisoners now swelled to 2,200. As they enter the camp, Roger tells Monteith that he's been repetitively pressing von Wedel to publicly announce the formation of an Irish brigade but that von Wedel keeps politely telling him that before Germany can issue such an announcement, "'The brigade must be large enough in numbers to persuade the world that it's of some consequence.' He does have a point."

When the men are assembled, Roger introduces Monteith to them, and then Monteith, in a brief speech, inventively tells them that many folks back in Ireland are centering their hopes for independence on the brigade and are making sacrifices, unspecified, in its behalf. (The man's got a gift for blarney, Roger thinks to himself.) He and Roger then inspect the barracks, and Roger is surprised to find them comfortable and well heated, to learn that "excellent discipline" reigns, that interpreters have been giving classes in German, and that another instructor is offering one on the Irish language. Just a few weeks before Roger had protested yet again to von Wedel about the poor living conditions and the bad effect on morale, and both he and Monteith are greatly encouraged at the seeming improvement. Monteith jots in his diary that he's deeply touched at Roger's "obvious paternal love for the men."

After a few days of rest and consultation in Berlin, Monteith heads off to the main camp at Limburg to try his hand at recruiting additional men for Zossen. He talks to as many as fifty men a day and does so without any Germans hovering nearby. He tells the men that he has little he can offer them materially but that joining the brigade will give them the chance to fight for Ireland *in* Ireland. The men are friendly enough, but unpersuaded. They'd rather live under an English Parliament, they tell Monteith, than the autocratic rule of a kaiser. When he protests that the brigade's goal is solely to fight for Ireland, not Germany, one Irish prisoner tells him that he's kidding himself. "To fight *for* Ireland," one bold young man points out, "means fighting *against* England—so no matter how you cut the mustard, that means you're fighting *for* Germany. No thanks!" Out of the hundreds of men he talks with, Monteith comes away with a single recruit.

So it's back to Zossen and to training those already more or less committed to the brigade. In his own mind Monteith divides the rank and file into three groups: soldiers of fortune out for adventure and uninterested in politics; men who feel guilty at having served in the armed forces of the "enemy" (England) and seek to make amends; and men who are carelessly indifferent, equally willing to idle away time in the camp or to jump into a trench. Since the brigade is a unit unto itself, with its own command structure, barracks, and parade grounds, Monteith is free to set his own pace in training and drilling the men.

The pace he sets is brisk, with Roger joining in when his unreliable health allows. Monteith becomes so concerned about Roger's bouts of weakness and exhaustion that he persuades him to leave Berlin and take up lodging in Zossen's comfortable inn, the Golden Lion. The change agrees with him. He often accompanies Monteith and the men during training routines and occasionally—his special favorite—the long marches. Roger has all his life been an impressive walker—in Africa he's said to have sometimes covered up to forty miles in a day. Aged fifty-two, with silver streaking his hair and beard, he can't manage that kind of feat any longer, though he and Monteith often walk ten to fifteen miles on a given hike, absorbed in conversation about Ireland, about Roger's hope to visit India one day, and about his love for the "honorable simplicity" of the black people of Africa. When he accompanies Monteith on some of the brigade's marches, the two men, walking at the head of the column, get so lost in animated conversation that by the time Monteith becomes aware of it, Roger has inadvertently picked up their pace—and they find themselves a full mile ahead of their men.

As the cold weather sets in late in 1915, Roger's health worsens. It isn't due to weather alone. He feels the German Foreign Office has become increasingly indifferent to him, rebuffing requests for meetings or restricting them when they do take place to brief, vague exchanges of platitudes. Roger thinks he knows why. He discovers that an employee of the *Gaelic American* named George Freeman, a man of no standing in New York's Irish nationalist circles, has been sending a series of letters to the German Foreign Office, informing them that the Irish leadership in the States has lost confidence in Casement, regrets having ever sent him to Germany, urges the German authorities to disregard his importunities and—most damaging of all—implying that he is not a "fitting" representative of the Irish people due to a hereditary condition of "degeneracy"—a common code word for homosexuality.

Roger suspects that Freeman is in fact Devoy's creature, doing his bidding while protecting his master's anonymity. Roger writes directly to Devoy, insisting on an explanation. The wily old man professes total surprise—and ignorance. He has no idea, he informs Roger, why Freeman has written to the German Foreign Office asserting that "everybody regrets that Casement was sent over"; Devoy claims that he's confronted Freeman, who tells him he meant to say that "a number of people regretted"—to which modification Devoy claims he thundered—"*It is not true of anyone at all!*"

To calm the storm, Devoy writes directly to Germany's chancellor, Bethmann Hollweg. Employing the subtly ambiguous phrase "my colleagues have requested me"—which allows for the interpretation that the initiative is not his own—Devoy provides "an emphatic and categorical contradiction" to Freeman's statement. "We have the fullest confidence," he continues, "in Sir Roger Casement; there has never been since he went to Germany any lack of confidence in him on our part"—an assertion patently untrue in regard to Devoy's own long-standing distrust of Roger. Devoy concludes his letter with a flourish: "Sir Roger Casement's work in Germany is recognized by all Irish Nationalists as of the first importance." He "has authority to speak for and represent the Irish Revolutionary Party in Ireland and America."

If so, the Clan continues to show remarkable indifference to its purported spokesperson, writing to him less and less and failing to keep him abreast of political developments. The German Foreign Office, perhaps reading between the lines of Devoy's equivocal endorsement, makes no adjustment whatever in its detached, unresponsive attitude toward Roger. To the contrary, the office starts to pester him with an increasing number of complaints about the behavior of brigade members—their drunkenness, their disobedience, their unauthorized leaves of absence.

The complaints are based on a modicum of truth—some Irishmen do drink—but the indictment as phrased is all-encompassing. It infuriates Roger and leads him to despair about the prospects of *any* additional German assistance. He feels that although the brigade's very existence has generated pro-German propaganda and been "enormously helpful to their public cause"—surely an exaggeration—the Germans have failed to respond in kind: after their initial announcement of "goodwill" toward Irish independence, they haven't, in Roger's view, performed "a single *act* of goodwill to drive home the truth or purport of the public statement."

Meanwhile, the members of the brigade housed at Zossen are becoming increasingly dispirited at the lack of action—or even the promise of action—and what seems like the endless, pointless repetition of drilling and marching. Roger shares their frustration. In December 1915 he writes to a member of the German staff that he cannot stand much longer "my present position of utter uselessness. . . . I have been accustomed all my life to action and the strain of this long period of hopeless idleness is more than I can longer bear."

In his desperation, Roger proposes to Count von Wedel in January 1916 that "since the possibility of any direct action on behalf of Ireland in the Western war field is now recognised as more than remote," the brigade be employed in assisting Turkish forces in expelling the British from Egypt—and that he himself proceed at once to Constantinople to lay the proposal in person "before the Imperial authorities of the Ottoman Empire." Thirty-eight members of the brigade, he reports, have volunteered "for active service on the S.E. front i.e. EgyptAsia" and have signed an agreement to that effect. (John Devoy, had he learned of the proposal, would have gone apoplectic; he'd long made it clear to Roger that the Irish brigade was to be employed *only* in Ireland.) Two days after Roger's approach to von Wedel, Capt. Rudolf Nadolny, a member of the Political Section of the General Staff who's become Roger's leading detractor, sends a secret memo to his superiors reporting that Monteith has told him that only twenty-four members of the brigade have volunteered to fight on the eastern front—and that Roger Casement "has had a nervous breakdown and is staying in a sanatorium near Munich."

The diagnosis, coming from an antagonist, may have been deliberately overdrawn, but there can be no doubt that Roger's depression has deepened. Soon after Nadolny sends his memo, Monteith receives an urgent message from Roger to come at once to the Golden Lion. Entering his room, Monteith finds the heavy curtains drawn, the room overheated, and Roger himself "prostrate," his nerves (in Monteith's words) "gone to pieces." He lies still on the bed, his color ashen, his breathing barely perceptible. Monteith wants to send for a doctor, but Roger begs him not to. He calls Monteith to his bedside and tells him in a whisper that he's become utterly useless to anyone—the Clan distrusts him, the Germans patronize him, and most of Ireland is supporting England in the war, either not realizing or not caring that an English victory will doom Irish independence and all but guarantee a future civil war. To Monteith, Roger sounds free of self-pity or even of recrimination against those who've belittled his efforts. Monteith tries to reassure him that the people of Ireland do understand and appreciate all that he's done. Roger is unpersuaded.

Ignoring his wishes, Monteith does send for a doctor, who, after examining Roger, orders a period of extended rest. In mid-January 1916 Roger enters a sanatorium at Neu Wittelsbach, just outside of Munich. He and Monteith will not see each other again for nearly two months.

. . .

Returning from a brigade training session one day early in March 1916, Monteith is startled to find a message from the German General Staff marked "Urgent." The communiqué is brisk: "Please appear without delay at headquarters in Berlin." The preemptory tone doesn't bother Monteith; he's a soldier's soldier and can follow orders as well as give them. He leaves Zossen at once, reaching the Foreign Office that same afternoon. A scowling Captain Nadolny, Roger's hostile liaison officer, is impatiently awaiting his arrival and wastes no time in blurting out the news: "A coded dispatch arrived from New York this morning saying that an armed rebellion is planned for next month in Ireland. Do you know of this?"

Stunned, Monteith manages to control his alarm at the news. "No—no, I do not. Nor does Sir Roger, or he would surely have told me."

"Why would *he* be informed?" Nadolny's disdain is transparent. "We all know that *Sir Roger*"—Nadolny spits out the words contemptuously—"is not currently abreast of developments. His purported 'breakdown,' and all that."

Monteith wants to slug the popinjay but contains his anger. "Sir Roger has been most unwell. As you're aware. But he's decidedly on the road to recovery."

"Far enough along the road to appear at the Foreign Office?"

"That would be up to him and his doctor to decide. Are you requesting that he appear?"

"Only if he wishes to find out what is going on in his native land." Nadolny's superciliousness is too much for Monteith.

"Sir Roger's illness is due in no small measure to the imperial government's failure to fulfill its promises to Ireland. That failure may have convinced him to withhold certain information from you."

"You just told me he did *not* know about a planned uprising." Nadolny looks smugly pleased at having sprung what he assumes is a trap.

"What I should have said is that Sir Roger hasn't informed *me* of any plans for an uprising. That isn't the same as his not knowing of such plans. He is very protective of his subordinates, doesn't wish to place any of us in jeopardy."

"Cleverly answered," Nadolny says.

"Beg pardon?"

"Never mind. I would very much like to speak to Casement. Please convey the message."

"I shall do so. Whether he is able—or willing—to travel to Berlin will of course be his decision."

"Oh come now, Monteith, why not be straightforward about all this, eh? We both know that Sir Roger's failure to create his brigade has forced us to turn to the New York group surrounding Mr. Devoy for a viable Irish-German connection."

"Roger Casement is the official representative in Germany of John Devoy and the Clan."

"Official, yes. But *actual,* no. Which is presumably why Devoy has taken to writing to us directly, not through Roger Casement."

"Presume what you like," Monteith replies, trying to conceal his surprise.

"Devoy reports that his information about an uprising comes directly from the Supreme Council of the Irish Republican Brotherhood, the group—as you can see, we *are* well informed—securely, if secretly, in control of the Irish Volunteers."

"What makes you certain the IRB is conveying the full truth about this uprising to Devoy? Or for that matter to the Volunteers? I myself know very little; I'm a soldier, not a politician. What I do know is that Devoy is on record as saying that the liberation of Ireland must await Germany gaining the upper hand on the western front. That doesn't sound like a man expecting an uprising next month."

The implied slur on Germany's military performance isn't lost on Nadolny, though he tries to conceal his anger. "Our army," he says stiffly, "is poised for a breakthrough at any time."

"Whatever information *you* have, I'm confident Sir Roger has as well. He has many close contacts in the Volunteers."

"I doubt he has more information than Devoy—"

"You will have to ask him yourself—"

"Devoy feels it was a mistake ever to have sent Mr. Casement to Germany. As he put it to us, 'You cannot expect much from a man whose personality is, uh, 'unstable.'"

"There is no finer human being in Germany *or* Ireland than Sir Roger Casement." Monteith says, in a tightly formal voice. "It's a pity you cannot see that."

"Your loyalty is highly commendable, Monteith."

"I will give your message to Sir Roger. He'll send a reply as soon as convenient."

Instead of returning to Zossen, Monteith boards the next train to Munich. He finds Roger out of bed and feeling more animated. After being fully briefed on the exchange with Nadolny, Roger's first thought is to comfort Monteith about the German's high-handed tone. "You have to understand that they operate from a rigid sense of hierarchy," Roger explains. "They regard you, a 'mere' sergeant, as a person of neither rank nor pedigree—and therefore of no consequence, an underling to be treated with disdain."

"Thank you for your concern. I didn't take Nadolny's manner personally."

"I'm glad of it. Now as to this supposed uprising—I don't know what to believe."

As Monteith feared, the news comes as a considerable shock to Roger, despite having had an earlier warning of its possibility from Joseph Mary Plunkett. It's clear that neither Devoy in New York nor the IRB in Ireland has kept him abreast of developments; he's out of the loop by design, not inadvertence. What neither man knows is that Devoy has told a confidante that he's come to regard Roger as a creature of "utter impracticability," a man with a "loose tongue" who will "tell everything to every fellow who calls on him."

Devoy has in fact made up his mind that should a German expedition ever embark for Ireland, Casement must be kept in Berlin—"officially" as the Clan's representative but actually to keep him from "bungling interference."

In Ireland, too, Roger's detractors are in control of events. The radicals who dominate the Supreme Council of the IRB (and, secretly, the Irish Volunteers as well) have never forgiven Bulmer Hobson, Roger's closest contact in the IRB, for having engineered the seating of the Redmond contingent on the Volunteers Provisional Committee; Hobson's been shunted to the sidelines, no longer a figure of significant influence. As for the titular head of the Irish Volunteers, the nonviolent moderate Eoin MacNeill, with whom Roger has an on-again, off-again relationship but basically respects, MacNeill isn't aware until too late that the IRB radicals are running the Volunteers behind his back.

Unaware of the full extent of Devoy's animosity, Roger greets Monteith's news about a planned uprising with momentary euphoria—"some action at last!"—and for the moment lets his excitement overcome the now-undeniable confirmation that he's no longer in the loop and has learned of the plan not from the Clan or the Volunteers but secondhand from the Germans. Yet for the first time in months, Roger feels a surge of energy ("I jumped to life—or tried to—for there was not much jump in me").

When Monteith subsequently adds other details from his conversation with Nadolny, Roger's initial euphoria trails off into alarm. Instead of the hundred thousand rifles requested in support of the uprising, the Germans are now offering only twenty thousand—and rejecting entirely the call for trained German officers to accompany the shipment. Monteith reluctantly relays as well Nadolny's claim that Devoy wants the Germans to keep Roger in Germany rather than let him join the landing party. In response Roger simply says that without more substantial German help, the chance for success is slight.

What neither man knows is that the Germans have made it clear to Devoy that their terms of twenty thousand rifles and no officers are not subject to negotiation—and Devoy has already accepted them. Devoy characterizes the German offer in a coded letter to Joe McGarrity as "favorable . . . the salary is not as big as I expected, but it is a living wage and I am certain I would get a raise soon when they [see] I could make good." When Roger finally learns of Devoy's decision to go ahead despite only skimpy support from Germany, he considers it a grievous mistake, a cause lost from the start.

Devoy, not "romantic" Roger, dons the rose-colored glasses. He claims that although forty thousand British troops are stationed in Ireland, a full thirty thousand are "poorly trained, have few competent officers, no trained non-commissioned officers, little artillery and a few machine guns"—in other words, no match for the forty thousand Irish Volunteers and fifty thousand National Volunteers (Redmond's group) that Devoy feels sure will flock to the banner of rebellion once it begins. His evaluation of the British troops is accurate enough, but his estimate of the number of Volunteers who would fly to the colors is wildly off the mark—a decided case of wishful thinking by a man who thinks all Irish nationalists *should,* and therefore *do,* share his belief in armed struggle. The hard-nosed pragmatist has entered the realm of starry-eyed fantasy that he's long accused Roger of inhabiting.

At that point in Roger's recovery, his doctors have been allowing him out of bed for no more than four hours a day. Yet he's determined to confront Nadolny directly, and he tells Monteith that he's decided to make the trip to Berlin. Monteith tries to dissuade him, but to no avail. Despite his weakened condition, Roger does somehow manage to reach Berlin for a prearranged meeting with Nadolny. Getting straight to the point, he tells Nadolny that without greater German support, the uprising in Ireland is bound to fail. Nadolny's contemptuous retort is that Germany in fact isn't much interested in Ireland and its fate; it has decided to send the arms—on a large merchant ship named the *Aud*—on the off chance that an uprising might prove a useful diversion, leading the British to shift troops from the western front to the coast of Ireland. When Roger angrily accuses Germany of having played a double-dealing game all along, Nadolny warns him to watch his tongue—or Germany might cancel the shipment of twenty thousand rifles altogether. Roger tells him to watch *his* tongue—and terminates the meeting.

He comes away convinced that Nadolny is a "complete and perfect scoundrel," the "biggest fool" he's yet encountered in Germany—which is saying a great deal, given his nearly complete turnaround from being a profound admirer to a severe critic of all things German. His loss of faith in Teutonic ways has, as a counterpart, led to a slight resurgence of admiration for Anglo-Saxon England, at least when contrasting "the individual candour, truthfulness and straightforwardness of the Englishman with the absence of these qualities in the governing classes here—or indeed in almost any section of the people." Nadolny, for his part, reports to the German Foreign Office that he found Casement "very agitated and unpredictable."

As for Devoy's belittling attempt to keep him out of the loop, Roger, generous by nature, is quick to give him the benefit of the doubt. He acquits Devoy of personal ill will, charging him solely with—out of ignorance—placing excessive faith in the "double-dealing and faithless" Germans. At the same time Roger has no intention, despite being ill, of being left behind in Germany as the *Aud* and its shipment of arms makes its way to Ireland's Tralee Bay. He has always opposed any attempted armed revolt "unless backed up with strong foreign military help," and he feels certain that the niggling amount of armaments the Germans are sending dooms the whole enterprise in advance—he calls it "the most ill-planned undertaking in the entire history of Irish attempts at independence," one "wholly futile at the best, and at the worst something I dread to think about." Yet he insists on participating. He calls it a "matter of honor." "My instinct as an Irish nationalist," he tells Count von Wedel, "is to be with my countrymen in any project of theirs, however fool-hardy, to stand or fall with them."

Roger presents a plan to the German Foreign Office designed to supplement the mission of the *Aud* (which is to be disguised as a Norwegian ship carrying timber). He submits a memo in which he points out that "since the programme for the proposed landing of arms has not been elaborated in any way" other than noting that the ship should be at the Irish port of Fenit on Easter Sunday night, he, Monteith, and a sergeant chosen from the brigade should be dispatched at once in a submarine "with a detailed plan for the landing of the arms." Roger himself calls the scheme "mad" but can think of no other way to give those planning the uprising advance warning that the *Aud* will carry only twenty thousand rifles—and to adjust their plans accordingly. He's unaware that Devoy and the IRB already know that the number has been reduced to twenty thousand.

The *Aud*, of course, may never reach Ireland. One member of the German admiralty predicts that a British cruiser will almost certainly seize the vessel en route; Roger even thinks it possible that the Germans *want* the *Aud* captured as a way of ridding themselves of the whole Irish problem. He feels that the odds of his own survival are slim and makes the irrevocable decision not to send the brigade to Ireland; he refuses to expose the men to almost certain capture and death—or to put them in the path of temptation to turn "king's evidence." When Captain Nadolny learns of Roger's decision, he threatens to send the brigade to Ireland on his own orders. A defiant Roger tells him that he's welcome to try but predicts that the men will ask "but where are Casement and Monteith in all this?"—and the game will be over. After what Roger characterizes as a "long and exhausting" argument, Nadolny begrudgingly relents.

On the evening of April 7, 1916, Roger and Monteith meet with the German General Staff at the Hotel Saxonia. They're told that after considerable debate the decision has been reached to grant their request and send them by submarine to the Irish coast, to arrive before the *Aud*, thereby allowing time (as Roger has suggested) to organize a detailed plan for landing the arms—and, hopefully (given the minimal German support), to rethink the notion of an uprising. They're also told that along with twenty thousand rifles, the *Aud* will carry a million rounds of ammunition and ten machine guns and that it will arrive off the coast of Ireland sometime between April 20 and April 23—no greater precision is possible, the General Staff points out, due to the assorted cordons that will have to be circumnavigated. The *Aud* will be met on the coast by a pilot boat identifying itself by flashing two green lights. What Roger is not told is that the rifles are fifteen years old, part of a large batch seized from the Russians on the eastern front of the war. Nor is he told that although the submarine is equipped with a radio, the *Aud*—incredibly—is not, meaning it will be unable to communicate after leaving its berth.

The day before departure, Roger writes to both Count von Wedel and Chancellor Bethmann Hollweg about his concern for the plight of the Irish soldiers who'd volunteered to join the brigade but are now, for their own protection, being left behind. Their situation in Germany has become precarious: thanks to the machinations of Captain Nadolny, the Political Section of the German General Staff is attempting to have the initial agreement of December 1914 declared null and void, which could reduce the fifty-three Irish soldiers now at Zossen to the status of "enemy aliens" or "deserters."

Roger solemnly protests what he calls a "betrayal" and in the time remaining does everything in his power to protect the brigade members. He turns over to St. John Gaffney, the U.S. consul general in Munich, a considerable sum of money that he's gathered from various sources and pleads with Gaffney to use it to put the Irish soldiers "to some useful occupation here in Germany until the war is over, and then to send them to America"—where Roger has arranged with the Catholic priest who spent some time at Zossen "to provide for their future there."

On April 12 Roger, Monteith, and twenty-seven-year-old Sgt. Daniel Beverley, chosen to represent the brigade, board the U-20—the submarine that sank the *Lusitania*—and are given a cordial welcome by the three dozen or so officers and crew, most of whom speak English. The hatches are battened down, and the sub heads out to open waters, traveling at a speed of nine knots an hour when submerged and twelve when on the surface. It carries four torpedoes, and in the limited space available the three men are allotted bunks where their heads are just under the torpedo tubes. The first day and a half are uneventful, but then the crank that drives the diving fins breaks, and they have to head into the port of Heligoland. Told that the repairs could take some time, Roger, seasick and unwell, momentarily fears that the Germans have deliberately sabotaged the trip. He's relieved when the captain immediately requisitions another submarine and within hours everyone is transferred to the U-19.

The trip from Heligoland to Tralee Bay off the west coast of Ireland's County Kerry lasts five days and, despite rough weather, is otherwise without incident—or so it appears. What the sub's passengers don't know is that the British have earlier cracked the German code and have been reading every one of Devoy's messages from New York to Berlin. Nor do they know that U.S. secret service agents on April 18 raided the German consulate in New York and among the papers seized found a telegram from Devoy to Berlin spelling out the exact date for the planned uprising in Ireland.

All of that is calamitous enough, yet there's more: in response to an April 14 message from the IRB in Dublin stating, "Arms must not be landed before night of Sunday, 23rd—This is vital," Devoy sends word to Patrick Pearse, a central figure in the IRB leadership, that the *Aud* might reach Tralee Bay as early as April 20. Somehow the message never reaches Pearse, and the *Aud* does arrive on the afternoon of April 20—thanks to the expert seamanship of its captain, Karl Spindler, who's managed to elude British ships sent to the bay after Devoy's messages to Berlin had been decoded.

That same evening, the submarine carrying Roger, Monteith, and Beverley reaches the spot where the expected pilot boat should have been waiting. It isn't there. The sub circles the area for some two hours searching for the boat and straining to catch sight of flashing green lights—the signal agreed-on in Germany. All three men come up on the conning tower and join the members of the crew in anxiously scanning the skylight for either pilot boat or signal. They do spot the *Aud* two miles on the starboard beam, try sending a radio message—and are puzzled at their inability to make contact. All hands are literally stumbling around in the dark. On the sub they keep up a kind of hollow gaiety, singing Irish songs and swapping stories, but Roger, weak and full of foreboding ("I feel that all is indeed lost and the sooner my life is taken from me the better"), retreats to his bunk.

On board the *Aud*, Captain Spindler is no less anxious and puzzled. Why is there no signal light from shore? Why no pilot? Why no contact with the submarine? What neither those on the *Aud* or the submarine can know is that the IRB leaders in Dublin, having received no word to the contrary, are assuming that the arms shipment won't arrive before April 23 and that there's therefore no reason to be paying premature attention to the sights and sounds of Tralee Bay. In the early morning hours of April 21, the *Aud* circles the area for several hours; then Spindler decides he must obey his orders, leave the bay, and head south. When he does, the *Aud* is intercepted by two British warships and ordered into Queenstown harbor for inspection. Spindler has other ideas. He booby-traps the *Aud,* gets his men into lifeboats, and, when they've pulled off to a safe distance, blows up the ship, sending the IRB's cargo of arms to the bottom of the sea.

Unaware of the *Aud*'s fate, those on board the submarine have reason enough for heartbreak. The sub's commander tells Roger that he cannot remain in the same locale and risk the safety of his vessel any longer. If the three Irishmen are determined to get ashore, they will have to manage it on their own. Roger looks so ill that Monteith fears he might collapse, but Roger insists he's well enough to make the effort, and the other two fall in behind him. Each is issued a pistol, but Monteith doubts if Roger knows how to use one.

"Do you understand how to load a Mauser?" Monteith asks him.

"No, I've never loaded one," Roger replies weakly. "I've never killed anything in my life."

"Well, Sir Roger," Monteith says, "You may have to start very soon. It is quite possible that we may either kill or be killed."

Monteith carefully instructs Roger on how to open and close the breech to eject a charge and then hands him the empty pistol. Roger practices the routine until he masters it but then—with a look of intense antipathy—asks Monteith to please load it for him. He does so, then places the gun in the holster and hands it back to Roger, along with a cartridge belt and sheath knife. They then pack kits containing a few basic items and bring them on deck, where the sub's small, collapsible boat is lifted from the forward hatch. Shivering in the cool morning air—it's 2:30 A.M.—the three men fasten on life vests and climb into the boat, which is then lowered over the port side.

Monteith is suddenly seized with a wave of anger over their plight. "Good Lord!" he calls out, "they are going to run a revolution and cannot have a pilot boat out for a shipload of arms!"

Roger makes a stab at humor: "It will be a much greater adventure going ashore in this cockleshell."

"You're simply not up to this," Monteith almost snarls. "It's inhuman. Beverley and I could have managed without you."

"Now, now," Roger says soothingly, "it's all going to be fine, you'll see"— even while feeling precisely the opposite.

As the submarine slowly disappears into the thick fog, the three men take stock. Each carries a .37-caliber Mauser pistol, a thousand rounds of ammunition, an overcoat, a change of underwear, flashlamps, a pair of Zeiss binoculars, and a sheath knife. They're a mile or so offshore and none of them are seamen. Roger takes the steering oar, and Monteith and Beverley pull on the other two—but, try as they might, the boat keeps going around in a circle rather than forward. Monteith finally realizes that the oars aren't a matched pair—his is far heavier and longer. By shortening his grip, they finally succeed in moving forward until the outline of a beach becomes faintly visible. To their surprise, the closer they get to shore, the rougher the sea becomes, and they have increasing difficulty in keeping the boat from capsizing. Then suddenly, out of nowhere, a wall of water comes rushing forward, upsetting the boat and pitching all three men into the sea.

Fortunately, they're wearing life vests. The sturdy Monteith surfaces first and is able to grab the boat and turn it right side up. All three then manage to get back into it and are relieved to discover that the oars, secured by cords to the rowlocks, are still in the boat. They start off again, but fate is not in a kind mood: before getting very far, the boat gets stuck on a sandbar. They try to pull it loose, but the large waves that continue to crash over them frustrate the effort—and further sap their energy. Monteith is finally able to free one of the oars and with it succeeds in prying the boat off the sand; he then manages, with difficulty, to haul his drained, deathly looking "Chief" into it. Heading toward shore, the boat strikes land within just a few minutes.

They crawl out onto Ireland's Banna Strand beach, Beverley half-carrying Roger, who sinks down into the sand like deadweight. Meanwhile, Monteith is unsuccessfully trying to scuttle the boat by punching holes in it with his knife. Due to an injury sustained while on the sub, his right hand has become painfully swollen and useless, and, unable to pierce the boat, he gives up and lets it drift offshore. Roger, his eyes closed, is stretched out on the sand so close to the water's edge that the waves wash over his entire body. Fearing Roger will lapse into unconsciousness, Monteith drags him to his feet, massages his body, and makes him move about a little to help restore circulation. Beverley is in a bad way too. None of them has eaten or slept in more than twenty-four hours.

By dawn, the three have wrung out their clothes, rested a bit, and feel some of their strength returning—though Roger remains in bad shape, barely able to stay awake. Monteith and Beverley decide to bury the kits—except for the overcoats needed to ward off the cold—and they then head inland toward the town of Tralee. Due to the fog, visibility is limited and the direction uncertain. About half an hour in, they have to wade across an inlet, plunging waist deep in the marshy mud and slush. Roger's condition is pitiable, and Monteith decides he's unable to proceed. Over Roger's protest, Monteith and Beverley hide him in an old earthwork, "McKenna's Fort," that they've spotted, while they continue on to Tralee to seek help. Before leaving, Monteith gives Roger a paper with the communications code that the German General Staff provided to pass on to the Volunteers in Dublin.

By 7:00 A.M., numb and stiff, the two men reach the outskirts of town and look in vain for someone wearing the Irish Volunteers tricolor badge or for a public house where they might find food and news. But it's Good Friday, and nearly every store is closed for the religious holiday. Overdue for a bit of luck, they finally find a sympathetic store proprietor and, after some dodgy soundings-out on both sides, are given food and put in touch with some of the men associated with the local branch of Volunteers. Several of them recognize Monteith from his days as an organizer for the Volunteers, and they vouch for him to the others; from then on, cooperation is full. The first priority is to send a car to bring Roger to safety; the second is to alert Dublin of their arrival and of the shipment of arms that the *Aud* is carrying—so they still think—offshore.

Back on Banna Strand, a prostrate Roger, nearing delirium as the light dawns, thinks that he's surrounded by primroses and wild violets and hears skylarks singing like a choir in the sand dunes. He's back in Ireland again! He feels happier and more content than at any time during the dreadful past year in Germany.

A local farmer walking along the shore in the early morning light is unaware of violets or skylarks but does notice the strange little canvas dinghy that's washed ashore. He discovers a knife on the boat's bottom and also finds a hurriedly buried ammunition tin under the sand. He goes off to tell a neighbor, who in turn carries the news to the barracks of the Royal Irish Constabulary in the nearby village of Ardfert. Roger, meanwhile, his fever subsiding, realizes that Monteith and Beverley are long overdue and may well not be able to return. When he sees a police officer in the distance coming toward him, he quickly tries to bury the few papers, including the German communications code, that are still on his person. Constable Riley is too quick for him: he reaches Roger, points his loaded gun directly at him, and brusquely demands to know what he's doing there. Roger assures Riley that there's no cause for alarm; he's simply a nature lover and a writer who's wandered somewhat off course.

"Give me the name of a book you've written," Riley demands.

"The *Life of St. Brendan,*" Roger replies, without missing a beat. He's surprised at his own quick-wittedness in conjuring up the area's patron saint.

Riley remains suspicious. He yells across the road to his partner, a Sergeant Hearn, who's been searching the nearby area. Roger's still-wet clothes and sand-caked pants don't strike Hearn as standard gear for bird-watching, and he demands to see identifying papers. When Roger is unable to produce them, the two officers cart him off to the Ardfert police barracks, where he refuses to give his name. A search of his person turns up some sort of shorthand chronicle of events, plus a scrap of paper in German—enough to warrant his detention. Meanwhile, a search of the area around McKenna's Fort is made, and the kits—carrying maps, ammunition, and other incriminating items—are unearthed.

Roger is taken to the Tralee police barracks and locked up. A sympathetic officer tells him, "I think I know who you are, and I pray to God it won't end the way of Wolfe Tone" (the Irish revolutionary hanged by the British in 1798). Roger tells him that he's come to stop the uprising scheduled for two days hence, that it stands no chance of success. "If it did," the officer replies, "we'd be with you to a man." He asks Roger why he didn't simply shoot the two police officers who arrested him on the beach. "Because I didn't want to injure a fellow Irishman," he answers. "Plenty of them will be injured," the officer replies, "if it becomes known that Roger Casement is here in prison. The Volunteers will storm the barracks to try and rescue you, and not one of us will be left alive."

The next morning, thanks to the friendly officer, Roger is allowed to walk unmanacled to the railway station. Before leaving he distributes the few items he still has on his person to those who've crossed his path in Tralee—including his walking stick to Sergeant Hearn, the man who arrested him. By this time word has spread throughout the area, and people line the route to the station. Roger realizes that if he gives the signal, an attempt to rescue him—and a likely riot—will follow. He doesn't want the blood on his hands. Beverley is also apprehended; he manages to abscond but is quickly recaptured. Monteith has better luck; he's passed from hand to hand and eventually makes good his escape to the United States.

After a long trip by rail, they reach London early on Easter morning. Roger is taken directly to Scotland Yard, given breakfast, and put in a windowless room containing only a small table and five chairs, one of which is attached to a desk neatly stacked with writing materials. Within a short time, Basil Thomson, assistant commissioner of Metropolitan Police, enters the room, followed by two other uniformed men as well as a younger man in civilian clothes, who quietly slips into the desk chair.

Basil Thomson introduces the two men in uniform as Capt. Reginald Hall, chief of naval intelligence at the admiralty, and Superintendent Patrick Quinn, an officer in the Military Intelligence Unit of Scotland Yard. He doesn't introduce the young man. The three officials seat themselves at various spots at the small table opposite Roger.

His tone friendly, Thomson tells Roger that he looks "rather cadaverous" and asks if the breakfast was sufficient.

"Yes, thank you," Roger replies, aiming at a neutral tone.

"I hardly recognize you without your beard," Captain Hall says. "In every photo I've seen, you've been bearded."

"I shaved it off recently. A rather naive attempt at disguise."

Thomson, rather abruptly and sounding less friendly, turns to face Roger: "Tell us your name please."

"You know my name already," Roger quietly responds.

"Apparently some people are impersonating Sir Roger Casement."

Roger laughs. "I'm not one of them. You have my word."

Unamused, Thomson cautions him: "This is no light matter."

"I know that," Roger says briskly. "I'm accused of high treason. I don't care a rap about that. What I want now, what must be done now, is to stop a threatened uprising, to stop useless bloodshed."

"I'm surprised," Patrick Quinn throws in. "You've been a noisy advocate of Irish independence."

"And that's why I beg you to publish at once the fact that I've been taken prisoner. Perhaps that might stop preparations, do some good."

"It's better a festering sore like this should be cut out," Reginald Hall responds.

There's a stunned silence. Roger finally speaks, softly: "By 'festering sore,' I presume you refer to the call for Ireland's independence." He pauses. "*At this moment,* that call is premature."

"Which makes it the ideal time to put it down," Hall replies.

"You seem to be in favor of taking lives . . . so long as they're Irish ones."

"To call off a revolt," Hall coldly responds, "is merely to postpone it. Better to let the rebellion take place. It will be put down with force. Permanently."

"You say, Casement, that you want to stop an uprising," Thomson says, "but we're well aware that you yourself hatched the plot, and the Germans sent you to Ireland to get it started."

"You're quite wrong," Roger replies. "The German General Staff and I have long been at odds."

"They supplied you with money to seduce Irish prisoners to join your so-called brigade."

"Your sources are poorly informed," Roger calmly says. "I've never accepted a penny of German gold. I offered the Irish prisoners no money, and they asked for none. They joined the brigade because they believe that Ireland should be free."

Another considerable pause follows. Then Roger unexpectedly says, "May I ask what you charge me with?"

"You are not charged," Hall responds.

"When Sergeant Hearn arrested me, he charged me."

"What did he charge you with?" Thomson asks, looking vaguely bored at the necessary but repetitive exchange.

"With aiding the landing of arms on the coast of Kerry."

"You are not charged at present," Thomson responds. "But it is certain that you will be. You are not bound to answer any question put to you, but anything that you do say will be used as evidence against you."

"I understand," Roger quietly replies.

Hall places a piece of crumpled paper in front of Roger, who recognizes it at once as the German communications code he'd earlier tried to destroy.

"And this?" Hall belligerently asks. "What do you say to this?"

Roger studies the piece of paper, silently picking out culpable phrases: "await further instructions . . . more rifles are needed. . . ."

"Yes," Roger says in subdued acquiescence. "Yes, I have seen this before."

"And these?" Thomson asks, putting some additional fragments of paper in front of him. Roger sees at a glance that the torn pages are bits of the occasional diary he's been keeping.

"What, for example, does this entry mean?" Thomson continues. "Wed. 12. Left Wicklow in Willie's yacht."

"The places are not real places. Nor the names. They're substitutes, codes to jog my memory." On this score Roger's memory needs no jogging, though he isn't about to say so. "Willie's yacht" is the submarine U-19, which they boarded on April 12.

Thomson next produces an interview with Casement in a German-language newspaper in which he refers to Germany's "righteous" war against England.

"Yes," Roger acknowledges, "I said that, but that quote is only a small part of the interview."

"Political views are not political acts," Thomson replies. The remark startles Roger: is Thomson offering me a way out? he wonders. If so, he rejects it: "What I say, I must act on," he responds, in a gesture of gratuitous self-incrimination. Perhaps he simply wants done with it all. "None of my actions have been dishonourable," Roger continues, "which you will one day learn. I have done nothing treacherous to my country."

"Your country? And which country would that be?" Quinn asks, his sarcasm apparent.

"Ireland is my country, as you well know. I've perhaps committed many follies in trying to help my country according to what I thought was best. And in this last act of mine, in coming back to Ireland, I came with my eyes wide open ... knowing you were bound to catch me." Roger's voice has become more excitable—a combination of lingering fever and strong feeling. "Knowing all the circumstances," he continues, "I came from a sense of duty. I know more than you think I know, but I will not involve other men. . . ." Roger sinks back in exhaustion.

"No doubt you do know more," Thomson remarks with satisfaction.

"I don't care what happens to me," Roger says quietly, as if to himself. "I have long gone past that."

Though the interview continues for some time, the rest is redundant, mere drafts of wind caressing the bird of treason now circling the room in full sight.

Toward the end of the examination, a clerk enters the room and whispers something to Thomson, who then turns to Roger: "They've found some trunks of yours in your old lodgings on Ebury Street and brought them here. We'll need the key from you."

Roger's expression doesn't change. "Tell them to simply break open the locks. There's nothing inside of them except for some old clothes and a few other personal items."

After the interview is over, and Roger remanded to a cell, a clerk notifies Thomson in a conspiratorial whisper that he's found two large notebooks in one of the Roger's trunks from Ebury Street." He then beats a hasty retreat, as if fearful of being forced to say more.

The notebooks happen to be among the shorthand diaries that recount Roger's sexual adventures, and after glancing at a few pages Thomson recoils in horror. He later describes his feelings: "It is enough to say of the diaries that they could not be printed in any age or in any language"—which is tantamount to Thomson admitting that he is a student of neither history nor anthropology.

Two more sessions, more or less repetitive, follow, with much the same ground being covered again and again. But toward the end, Roger varies the unchanging rhythm of the exchange, jumping rather precipitously onto oratorical high ground: "I do not believe in the justice of your cause," he says with tight-lipped passion. "I do not think that you are justified in getting my people in Ireland to fight for you—to fight for British trade. The Home Rule Bill is a lie. The government never means for it to come off, and they put it on the statute book solely to trap Ireland into arms. I have always been an Irish separatist in heart and thought."

Taken aback, Thomson attributes Roger's intensity to exhaustion and patronizingly reminds him that he participated in the Boer War and has been invested with the CMG. "Feeling as you say you do, why did you not refuse the decoration?"

"I would have had to retire from the consular service—and that I could not afford to do."

"For a man who puts principle above all else," Thomson sarcastically remarks, "that should have been a small price to pay."

"No, not small. Others relied on me. For myself alone I would have left the service. I can live on very little."

That ends the exchange—and the interrogation. That same afternoon Thomson confers with the attorney general, Sir F. E. Smith, and they decide to forgo a summary military tribunal for high treason, opting instead for a civil trial—"lest in after years," as Thomson puts it, "we should be reproached with having killed him secretly." Casement is remanded to the Tower of London.

. . .

It is the afternoon of Easter Sunday. Months earlier, the Military Council of the IRB made the decision to lead an armed uprising against the Crown on the day of resurrection. For weeks the planning and preparations have been heating up. In issue after issue of the *Irish Worker,* the socialist James Connolly has been writing about past revolutions, characterizing those that failed as "defeats that are often more valuable to a cause than loudly trumpeted victories." In the so-called mosquito press—evanescent publications like the *Spark* and Arthur Griffith's *Scissors and Paste*—the drumbeat for independence builds.

Despite the rising agitation, the leading British officials in residence at Ireland's Dublin Castle—Augustine Birrell, the chief secretary, and Lord Wimbourne, the lord lieutenant—seem to have barely caught a whiff of the mounting fever, though Wimbourne is pugnacious by temperament. Birrell, oppositely, prefers evasion to confrontation. He recognizes that Dublin Castle is "switched off" to the main currents of Irish life, and he's long adopted a sensible policy of benign neglect; he makes no attempt to censor or squash the proliferating number of anti-English newspapers and pamphlets. He recognizes that only a small segment of the Irish public favors armed insurrection and, in an effort to keep it that way, makes no move to curtail freedom of expression. Birrell's official position is that what he currently sees and hears in Ireland is no more than the usual tiny number of blustering "fanatics" venting their familiar complaints, with perhaps a touch more vigor than usual. It's actually a *lot* more than usual—though Wimbourne doesn't hear it, and Birrell refuses to name it.

The old Fenian Tom Clarke is the senior figure in the Military Council, and his handpicked lieutenants include men who Roger has long known and variably admired: Patrick Pearse, Sean MacDermott, the poet Thomas MacDonagh, and, Roger's most recent acquaintance, Joseph Mary Plunkett, the young firebrand who visited him in Germany the year before. And then there's the militant Con Markievicz, who's taken to wearing a cartridge belt around her waist and carrying a Mauser rifle and who for months has been agitating for the Citizen Army to "storm" Dublin Castle.

There are firebrands aplenty, though no agreement about where the blaze should be ignited. As Robert Monteith, still in hiding at the time, would later say with only slight exaggeration, "It would appear that no one outside the Military Council was to be fully trusted, and that those within the Council did not trust one another." On one matter there is widespread agreement: the IRB, the Irish Volunteers, and the Citizen Army put together still amount to only a small minority in Ireland. The revolutionaries believe that to attract larger numbers to the cause, the first strike must be thunderously theatrical, assured in execution, and an undisputable success.

Eoin MacNeill, the putative head of the Irish Volunteers, has belatedly discovered that the IRB has been secretly in control of the organization for some time. When he learns that an armed rebellion is to commence on Easter Sunday, a furious MacNeill vows to stop it. He tells Patrick Pearse that "there'll be no waste of lives for which I am directly responsible. I will not allow a half-armed force to be called out. . . . I'll do everything I can to stop a Rising—everything, that is, short of ringing up Dublin Castle." Pearse is unmoved. "We don't need you anymore," he tells MacNeill. "It's no use you trying to stop us. Our plans are laid and will be carried out."

Bulmer Hobson agrees with MacNeill that the Rising is woefully misguided; in his view guerrilla warfare, not direct confrontation, is the only strategy that holds out any hope of success. Outmanned, outgunned, outtrained, the Irish rebels are, as Hobson and MacNeill—and Roger—see it, courting suicide in attempting directly to confront the superbly equipped British troops. But Hobson is still in disgrace for the role he played in getting Redmond's contingent of supporters on the Volunteers' Provisional Committee several years back, and MacNeill is a leader with no following.

MacNeill does what he can. When he learns that the *Aud,* with its shipment of arms for Ireland, lies at the bottom of Queenstown harbor, he issues an order canceling the Volunteer "parade" on Easter Sunday, and he places an ad in the nationalist *Independent* newspaper to the same effect. Both gestures sow chaos and disarray. Local units of the Volunteers don't know whether to assemble as planned or to stand down as MacNeill has ordered. Most of the Volunteer groups cancel their planned maneuvers, but some do assemble— only to disperse in chaotic confusion. Con Markievicz offers to shoot both Hobson and MacNeill but is talked out of it.

The Military Council of the IRB holds an emergency meeting on the morning of Easter Sunday and, amid tears of rage at the "moderates," votes to go ahead with the Rising—but to postpone it until noon of the following day. In some form, the council decides, the event must come off despite the awful odds against its success—"the soul of Ireland," as James Connolly puts it, "demands it." MacNeill, persuaded that the rebellion cannot be stopped, does an about-face and decides that out of duty he must join it; as another dissident puts it, "Well, I've helped to wind up the clock—I might as well hear it strike." It's an attitude that Roger fully shares, though at the moment he's impotent to act on his sympathy. Hobson still refuses to participate, and the IRB places him under arrest. Though soon released, he forever after carries the brand of "coward."

By the next day, Monday, April 17, a mood of exultation has taken hold among the leaders. At noon some 1,500 green-shirted—and greenhorn—Irish Volunteers assemble in ragtag formation in Dublin, complemented by some 150 members of the Citizen Army. Their orders are to occupy the iconic General Post Office, an impressive neoclassical building on O'Connell Street, and they succeed in doing so in short order without—for the moment—a shot being fired in opposition. Word that a rebellion has actually begun spreads quickly. Outside the GPO, onlookers gather to stare in amazement as the rebels joyously raise the green tricolor flag of the Irish Republic over the building, and Patrick Pearse, the gentle embodiment of Celtic idealism, appears outside the building and jubilantly reads his grandiloquent proclamation: "Irishmen and Irishwomen, in the name of God and of the dead generations from which she receives her old tradition of nationhood, Ireland, through us, summons her children to her flag and strikes for her freedom."

Following the high-flown rhetoric, Pearse adds a set of dubious remarks about how Ireland "having patiently perfected her discipline, having resolutely waited for the right moment to reveal itself . . . she now seizes the moment, and, supported by her exiled children in America and by gallant allies in Europe, but relying first on her own strength, she strikes in full confidence of victory."

The body of the manifesto gives wishful thinking a whole new dimension, encouraging an expectation of triumph that circumstances don't warrant and won't permit. MacNeill again tries to counsel caution, but the Military Council is in thrall to gallant bravado. It chooses not the "right moment" but—with German arms at the bottom of the sea—a misjudged one. In relying on "her own strength" the proclamation mistakes the enflamed enthusiasm of a few for the committed determination of the many actually needed for success.

Yet that's not the whole story. A number of the IRB leaders accept from the beginning that defeat is likely (while holding on to the slender hope of victory), and they offer their selfless sacrifice in the name not of immediate success but in the belief that the uprising will serve to resurrect the Irish spirit and lead ultimately to the creation of an Irish Republic. It's very much akin to the attitude Roger displayed when he told Thomson, "I don't care what happens to me. I have long gone past that."

Roger is being held incommunicado in the Tower—no visitors, no lawyers, no change of clothing from the sand-caked and filthy garments he was arrested in, not even permission to converse with the two soldiers who guard him in shifts. His shoelaces and suspenders are removed as a precaution against suicide. The lightbulb burns above his head day and night. He has no appetite for the food brought him and is threatened with force-feeding. One of his guards, a Welsh corporal, breaks protocol and, when the other guard is preoccupied, whispers to Roger that there's been an uprising in Dublin. He offers no details.

Roger is frantic with conflicted feelings. Between the time he learns that the *Aud* had been blown up and being taken to the Tower, he's sent word in every way possible that the Rising should be canceled, that without full German backing it's doomed to failure and will cause needless bloodletting. Even as early as the year before, when informed that German assistance would be limited to twenty thousand rifles, Roger had told Joseph Mary Plunkett that an armed uprising would be suicidal, an "act of idiocy." Yat he had also told Plunkett that though he strongly disapproved, should an uprising nonetheless go forward, he would "stand or fall beside you. I, who have always stood for action (but not this action and not in these circumstances) could not stay in safety while those living in Ireland who have cherished a manly soul were laying down their lives for an ideal."

The choice, in April 1916, is no longer Roger's to make: he's a prisoner of the British government. But his circumstances can't confine his yearning for a free Ireland, nor prevent his agonized sympathy from engulfing him as he lies sleepless at night, the light in his cell never turned off, the guards never absent, the cold never abating, the bed lice feeding freely on his flesh. He's told that his lack of visitors is due not to British policy but to the lack of requests to see him: his friends, he's led to believe, have abandoned him, appalled at his heedless actions.

Meanwhile, the occupation of the General Post Office is followed by the haphazard seizure of other buildings—Boland's Mill, Jacob's Biscuit Factory—in the center of Dublin. Patrick Pearse, transported by his own words, is in a state of blissful elation. At the other end of the emotional spectrum, the old revolutionary Tom Clarke is operating through a lens of tough-minded resignation: "We shall all be wiped out," he matter-of-factly tells one of the young rebels, adding that "at all periods in the history of Ireland the shedding of blood has always succeeded in raising the spirit and morale of the people."

In some of the narrow lanes surrounding Sackville Street, savage fighting erupts and the toll of dead and wounded begins to rise precipitously. Most of the rebels are young, inexperienced, and untrained. They're primarily armed with the unreliable Mausers seized during the Howth gunrunning episode two years before and notable for their powerful kick—often knocking over, and sometimes wounding, their owners. The rebels are no match for British artillery and machine guns—of which they themselves have none—nor do they have the manpower to close the ports and prevent the British from landing reinforcements.

England's first line of defense is the superbly trained and armed Royal Irish Constabulary, and in a stand-up fight the IRB and its supporters are at a woeful disadvantage. As direct combat heightens, so does the looting of stores and the gathering of excited onlookers who—shockingly close to the bullets ricocheting off adjacent walls—dress up and prance about in finery as if participating in an amateur theater production. The general confusion and improvisation that typifies the action around Sackville Street is characteristic of the haphazard skirmishing taking place elsewhere in the city, much of it dissolving into the kind of guerrilla warfare that Bulmer Hobson has long insisted is the only plausible form of armed insurrection.

Not that it's successful this time around: by Friday of Easter Week, looters have had better luck than insurgents. Any number of shops around Sackville Street have been wrecked, the oil depot on Abbey Street blown up, and buildings everywhere set ablaze. British artillery finally forces the central garrison holed up in the General Post Office to scatter to the side streets, where a number of fierce clashes take place. By Friday evening, nearly 500 people are dead, more than 2,500 wounded, buildings and shops destroyed over a wide area, and the toll on civilians shockingly high. Midday on Saturday, the Military Council—or what remains of it—makes the decision to surrender. The leaders know they face trial and probable execution but take comfort in the notion that the populace has been radicalized and that the rank and file will live to fight another day.

Ireland's mood is in fact difficult to read. So many have died in the European war and so many others are still fighting under the British Crown that when captured rebels are led through the streets of Dublin, crowds of onlookers in the mostly Protestant, working-class areas curse and hurl objects at the prisoners. There's limited sympathy in Protestant Ireland for an uprising that's widely seen as a predominantly Catholic affair. (At the GPO, the rosary has been said communally every night—including by such anticlerics as John MacBride and the Marxist James Connolly.) At the same time, the conviction rapidly grows that the Irish Party and its head, John Redmond, have seen their day; affection for Great Britain and a willingness to maintain affiliation with the empire has become associated with ruthless suppression—and, even more than before, with Protestantism. In the broadest terms, it's Catholic Ireland that wants independence.

By the end of Easter Week, Roger is still being held in the Tower of London and is still without counsel or visitors; the writing material he's been briefly allowed has on April 28 been removed without explanation, and he's told that henceforth, for an indefinite period, he'll be held incommunicado. Roger's devoted cousin Gee—now a teacher at Queen Anne's School in Caversham—and her sister Elizabeth Bannister immediately leave for London on hearing of Roger's arrest and move into a hotel. But for the next seven days, they're unable to find out where Roger is imprisoned and how they can get to see him. As if in a hall of mirrors, they're callously shuttled from one government office to the next, meeting with denials and rebuffs at every turn.

Desperate and out of options, Gee decides to seek the advice and help of Alice Green, recently alienated from Roger over what she considers the "madness" of his German venture but still retaining deep fondness and regard for him. Alice agrees to meet with Gee and, after briefly venting her exasperation at the foolishness of the Rising, puts that to one side and joins the Bannisters in actively seeking a way to find Roger, to judge his state of mind, and to get him proper representation. Alice comes up with the name of an Irish solicitor, George Gavan Duffy (son of one of the founders of the mid-nineteenth-century Young Ireland Movement), who at some earlier point had met Roger, and she asks Duffy to represent him. Duffy immediately agrees. He somehow manages to learn that Roger is being held in the Tower; on May 1 he writes to him directly to say "I shall be very glad if I can help you in preparing your defense."

Duffy sends a copy of his letter to the governor of the Tower, along with a covering note asking that—"if Roger wishes to see me"—he be allowed "an interview with him at a very early date." Day after day passes with no reply. The bureaucracy, it seems, is otherwise engaged. Gee and Alice Green hear rumors that Roger may be shot at any time, a rumor that seems frighteningly plausible. They go back and forth to the Tower seeking information, begging for some word of Roger's condition. They're rudely ignored, given stony stares, shunted aside. Only one officer, a Major Arbuthnot of the Life Guards, proves willing to give them a word: "Bring fresh clothing," he tells them. "He is badly in need of fresh clothing. I will write to the governor and try to get you an interview."

When news of the fate of the IRB leaders does emerge, it's terrifying. Though John Redmond, among others, works behind the scenes for commutation, the prisoners are tried under the wartime Defence of the Realm Act by summary, secret courts-martial; death sentences for the leaders are passed—and carried out with alarming speed. On May 3 Patrick Pearse, Tom Clarke, and Tom MacDonagh are taken to the prison courtyard and shot. It's announced that more executions will take place shortly. And they do. The following day, four more men, including Joseph Mary Plunkett, are executed. On May 5 only one man is shot—John MacBride, a member of the IRB Supreme Council who had *not* been involved in planning the Easter Rising. "Only *one* today," people whisper hopefully; "perhaps the worst is over, the killing will stop." And for two days it does. Then on May 8 four more men are executed. The death sentence of one person is commuted: Constance Markievicz. Of the seventy women arrested, she's the only one placed in solitary confinement, and she will remain in jail for several months. But "on account of her sex," the death penalty is deemed inappropriate.

Public opinion, initially hostile to the IRB for the widespread destruction and slaughter attendant on the Rising, rapidly shifts in the direction of pleading for greater leniency. Testimony from British soldiers spreads about how, during the fighting, most of the Irish insurgents treated their prisoners with gallant respect; "they were the cleanest and bravest lot of boys I ever met," is how one English officer puts it. Jailers and loved ones of the condemned report that the men spoke of their fate not in sorrow or anger but with exalted certainty that their deaths would ultimately bring about Ireland's freedom.

Through word of mouth, descriptions of the condemned spread through ever-widening channels: Patrick Pearse, it's learned, told his court-martial, "When I was a child of ten I went down on my bare knees by my bedside one night and promised God that I should devote my life to an effort to free my country. I have kept that promise. . . . We seem to have lost. We have not lost. To refuse to fight would have been to lose; to fight is to win. . . . You cannot conquer Ireland. You cannot extinguish the Irish passion for freedom. If our deed has not been sufficient to win freedom, then our children will win it by a better deed." Joseph Mary Plunkett and Grace Gifford marry in his cell shortly before his execution, his handcuffs briefly removed for the ceremony—then clamped back on immediately after it.

Word also spreads that none of the men executed dignified British vindictiveness by pleading for mercy; they insisted on entering pleas of not guilty, eloquently demanding to know how they can be guilty of treason to a country to which they do not pay allegiance. Prime Minister Asquith himself—and not solely for prudential reasons—rises in the House of Commons to speak eloquently of the "young men, often lads . . . misled, almost unconsciously, I believe, into this terrible business. They fought very bravely and did not resort to outrage."

Voices urging that retribution be leavened with mercy are increasingly heard. John Redmond warns Asquith that the executions are contributing mightily to the Irish Parliamentary Party's swift decline in plausibility and popularity. George Bernard Shaw writes the prime minister that in his view "the men who were shot in cold blood, after their capture or surrender, were prisoners of war, and that it was therefore entirely incorrect to slaughter them"; besides, Shaw adds, "an Irishman resorting to arms to achieve the independence of his country is doing only what Englishmen will do, if it be their misfortune to be invaded and conquered by the Germans in the course of the present war."

In the United States, John Devoy and the Clan furiously denounce British "barbarity," and there's concern in Westminster that Irish American anger will deter the Wilson administration from joining the struggle against Germany. John Quinn, Roger's host when he was in New York and no fan of what he calls the "horrible fiasco in Ireland," eloquently deplores the executions in a letter to Joseph Conrad: "If England had announced after the revolt had been quelled, as it was within three days, that technically the lives of the leaders were forfeited but that she did not propose to imitate Germany, that they would be imprisoned during the term of the war, that the rebels would be deprived of their arms, that would have made an impression in this country [the United States] that nothing could have effaced."

William Butler Yeats, in his famous poem "Easter 1916," sums up the conflicted feeling of many that the Rising's seemingly useless sacrifice of lives nonetheless carries the imaginative seeds of new possibilities:

> Was it needless death after all?
> For England may keep faith . . .
> MacDonagh and MacBride
> And Connolly and Pearse
> Now and in time to be,
> Wherever green is worn,
> Are changed, changed utterly:
> A terrible beauty is born.

In another sign of a shift in public opinion, George Gavan Duffy, having received no response to his request to meet with Roger and after cooling his heels for nine days, is finally told on May 9 that he will be allowed to see his client. When he's ushered into the damp, airless cell—the windows boarded up except for a single pane for the sentry to peer in at the prisoner—Duffy is appalled at Roger's appearance: cadaverous, ill kempt (he is *still* wearing the clothes he was arrested in at Banna Strand), his beard half-grown, his eyes bloodshot; he seems dazed, halting in his responses to Duffy's questions, unable to recall the most familiar names and dates.

Roger's sympathetic Welsh guard has kept him up-to-date on the series of executions taking place in Dublin, and Roger tells Duffy that as a matter of solidarity he too hopes for a military court. Reluctantly, Duffy has to inform him that the decision has already been made for a civil trial instead. Given Roger's fame, the government doesn't want to risk offending neutral nations with a secret trial and a summary execution. Two days after Duffy's visit, the Bannister sisters are also finally allowed to visit Roger; for the occasion, the guards quickly dress him up in the fresh clothing the sisters had sent days before. There are tears all around, and Roger finds some cheer in the news that Monteith is alive and being kept safe in serial hideaways throughout Ireland.

Alice Green, meanwhile, has been active on several fronts simultaneously. In a letter to Prime Minister Asquith, she threatens to reveal the awful conditions under which Roger is being kept unless they're at once improved. They are; Roger is transferred from the Tower to Brixton Prison. Alice also turns to some of Roger's old friends and admirers to raise money for a proper defense. John Devoy, neither much of a friend nor admirer, nonetheless comes through with £1,000. The next highest donation (£700) is from Sir Arthur Conan Doyle, followed at £200 by Alice herself, Gee (who can ill afford it), and William Cadbury, the chocolate magnate and Roger's old supporter during the Congo campaign. Cadbury makes it clear that he has "no sympathy whatever with his alleged actions in Germany" but does want Roger "to have every proper opportunity of stating his case. Until sufficiently proved otherwise," he tells Alice, "I shall believe that the unwisdom of recent months has been largely caused by his serious state of health"; in any case, Cadbury adds, "I cannot forget the past years of his noble and unselfish life."

Just before being transferred from the Tower to Brixton Prison, one of the guards—clearly a history buff (and probably as well a disciple of the Marquis de Sade)—tells Roger that no occupant of his cell at the Tower has ever escaped the hangman. Roger, smiling wanly, replies that he has no expectation of breaking the pattern.

PART 5

The Trial and Its Aftermath

GAVAN DUFFY IS HAVING DIFFICULTY FINDING senior members of the London bar willing to join the defense team. After several flatly turn him down, not even bothering to explain their refusals, he finally settles on his own brother-in-law, Alexander Martin Sullivan, known as "Serjeant" (an archaic term for the antique office he holds at the Irish bar). Cousin Gee considers Sullivan a "most unfortunate" choice—"a man entirely out of sympathy with Roger and his ideals." Unlike Duffy, Serjeant Sullivan isn't remotely sympathetic to the nationalist cause; to the contrary, he sits on a council formed to encourage young Irishmen to join the British armed forces and has been heard contemptuously referring to the men who took part in the Rising as "gangsters." Sullivan has been admitted to the English bar but never practiced there; he lacks any experience in English criminal law.

This is precisely what attracts him to the case: here is a chance to make his name in London. Even so, Sullivan accepts only after requiring "handsome payment"—and he gets it, to the tune of 500 guineas, painstakingly raised by the Bannister sisters and Alice Green. For junior counsel, Duffy turns to Artemus Jones, a Welsh barrister. J. H. Morgan, professor of constitutional law at London University offers, as an old acquaintance of Roger's, his expertise free of charge. Another adviser is the American Michael Francis Doyle, who had handled Roger's lawsuit against the *New York World* (for having claimed he was in the pay of the Germans) after John Quinn had refused to, and who is an ardent supporter of Irish independence. Gavan Duffy, at the demand of his law firm, is forced to dissolve his partnership in punishment for taking on the Casement case.

The defense team is no match for the prosecution. Its senior barrister is no less a personage than Sir F. E. Smith, currently the attorney general, as well as a staunch Ulster Unionist long among the most prominent of Edward Carson's allies. Smith has himself been widely charged, and recently, with treason to the Crown for encouraging Ulster's armed preparations to resist Home Rule and for approving the importation of guns from Germany. It seems obvious to Roger's champions that Smith should recuse himself from serving in the case. But for Smith, to stand down would be the equivalent of acknowledging that there are legitimate similarities between his case and Roger's.

Smith insists there's no comparison at all, that (as he puts it), "from the moment Germany made her tiger spring at the throat of Europe, I say from that moment the past was the past in the eyes of every man who wished well to England"—in other words, *sensible* Irish nationalists and Irish Unionists alike declared a truce for the duration of the war. Smith insists that Roger, on the other hand, has been bent on giving aid and comfort to the enemy *during* wartime (precisely *who* is the enemy is of course the very definition at issue). Smith refuses to recuse himself. Known as a man of pronounced ambition, he isn't likely to forgo a leading role in a trial that everyone assumes will be historic. Nor is he a man known for his generosity of spirit—though much admired for his confident self-regard, his shrewd interrogations, and, not least, his masterful talent for behind-the-scenes manipulation of politicians and journalists alike.

The trial is set to begin at the Old Bailey on June 26, 1916. Three judges will oversee the court: the lord chief justice, Sir Rufus Isaacs; Mr. Justice Avory, whose admirers call "tough-minded" and his critics "ruthless"; and Justice Horridge, elevated to the bench for his services to the Liberal Party and cursed with a distracting facial tic that allows for a variety of alarming misinterpretations.

Roger is determined to have a proactive defense and to play a forceful role during the four days of scheduled testimony; to that end he will stay in constant consultation with his attorneys. Thanks to far better treatment at Brixton than during his stay in the Tower—Roger is finally allowed blankets, his own clothing, visitors, counsel, and reading and writing materials—his health rapidly rebounds. His mind clear and his energy improved, he takes a passionate interest from the start in preparing his defense. Roger understands fully the trial's symbolic potential: the emphasis he prefers is on Casement the Irish rebel, along with its corollary, the immorality of British imperialism—the presumed right to invade and rule less powerful nations with distinctive histories and cultural patterns far different from England's own.

It's important to Roger—as he puts in a long note to Gavan Duffy before the trial begins—to emphasize "that the idea, the aim, the responsibility for the rebellion arose with Irishmen, in Ireland, and was carried to an issue by 'themselves alone.' . . . The *only* possible way to defend me is to let me hang myself and justify my 'treason' out of the pages of Irish history." He feels, in other words, that the best defense is for him to admit full responsibility for his actions and to accept in full the consequences. Roger is well aware that the world is watching, and he wants to be sure the right message is delivered: the Rising wasn't the work of the Germans or of a maverick individual like himself but rather of Ireland's rebellious spirit as embodied in its long history of resistance to English domination.

Serjeant Sullivan has a quite different take on the line of argument the defense should pursue. It's a narrow, legalistic one, designed to prove *his* mastery of the law rather than, as Roger wishes, to strike a blow for Ireland—for all those colonized for the profit and advance of their masters. Sullivan lays out his planned defense in detail two weeks before the trial is scheduled to begin. The other attorneys, as well as Gee Bannister and Alice Green, are present during the discussion.

"It's of crucial importance," Sullivan stresses to the others, "to challenge the meaning of Edward III's 1351 Treason Act, under which Roger is charged. Written in Norman-French, it's been uniformly interpreted to refer *only* to acts of treasonable adherence to the king's enemies committed *in his realm*." Sullivan turns to face Roger directly: "I do not feel, under the precise wording of this statute, that you have committed treason."

"You're going to base my *entire* defense on that?!" Roger is too nonplused to be diplomatic. "What about Irish *nationalism?!*"

"What about it?" Sullivan belligerently replies. "Concrete points of law are what matter in a case of this kind. Not airy sentiments."

"George Bernard Shaw doesn't happen to agree with you," Roger replies with some heat.

"Beg pardon?" Sullivan is thrown off stride. "What possible bearing, in heaven's name, can the opinions of Mr. Shaw—I presume your reference is to the playwright—

"It is—"

"Have on the outlines of this defense?"

Gavan Duffy steps in and tries to calm the waters. "Roger is referring to a letter from Mr. Shaw that the *Times* rejected but the *Manchester Guardian* has printed. It argues that—"

"If I may?" Alice Green interrupts.

"Yes, of course," Duffy replies. "You were there, after all."

"It's like this, Mr. Sullivan. At my request, Beatrice Webb, whom I know somewhat, arranged a lunch between the two of us and the Shaws so I could ask them to contribute to Roger's defense fund. Charlotte Shaw is deeply sympathetic and wants to contribute. She's quite wealthy, you know. But Shaw wants first to be sure that Roger will pursue what he calls a 'proper' defense."

"Rather presumptuous of him," Sullivan says with obvious annoyance.

Duffy laughs. "Mr. Shaw would never deny his presumption! He feeds on it!"

"Let the man write his plays," Sullivan continues. "Let the defense counsel attend to the niceties of the law."

"I must say," Gee gently adds, "that I found Mr. Shaw's proposed defense both logical and appealing."

"I see," Sullivan replies, his voice steely.

Roger takes up the argument: "Shaw basically agrees with me. He thinks I ought to deliver a thunderous oration of defiance. He's even written the speech he wants me to deliver! Very kind of him, I must say, though we differ somewhat in emphasis. Only somewhat."

Sullivan is barely able to control his anger. "Would someone care to explain what it is that Mr. Shaw proposes?"

"Well," Roger says amiably, "he's no fan of the Germans, that much he makes clear. 'Prussian Junkers,' he says, 'are far more sinister than English imperialists.'"

"A view I very much share," Alice Green throws in. "But Roger does not."

"What Roger does not agree with," Roger explains, "is Shaw's insistence that I plead 'not guilty.' My own impulse is to tell the court, 'You have no right to try an Irish rebel in an English court.' At the heart of Mr. Shaw's scenario is the insistence that I am a prisoner of war, the representative of another *nation,* and that in wartime it is contrary to international law to hang the soldiers of an opposing army."

"I rather liked Mr. Shaw's analogy to Garibaldi," Gee quietly offers.

"Well, I'm no Garibaldi," Roger responds, "since I failed, where he succeeded. But I suppose the analogy is accurate in one sense, only one—that in my awkward way I was trying to do for Ireland what Garibaldi did for Italy— and he did it, I might add, to great applause from England."

Sullivan has been impatiently pacing the confined space during much of this exchange. He now stops and says, "Let me understand this, if I may.

Mr. Shaw is advising you to dispense with counsel and to conduct your own defense in court?"

"That is true," Roger smilingly says. "He would feel that the technicalities of a medieval statute are not what this trial is or should be about. The real case is what constitutes nationhood. He points out that British opinion currently strongly supports the right of every Serbian to strike—by force—for independence from the Turks, though ruled by them for five centuries. Why do not Irishmen have the same right in regard to England? The answer is: they do! Shaw advises me to declare openly that 'I am neither an Englishman nor a traitor; I am an Irishman, captured in a fair attempt to achieve the independence of my country.'"

"Since my earlier question has not been answered," Sullivan stonily says to Roger, "I will repeat it: have you decided to defend yourself? If so, it would be good of you to notify counsel. I should be content to withdraw at once."

"For heaven's sake!" Alice Green says forcefully. "Roger cannot possibly defend himself! Not in his current condition. At the peak of his powers, perhaps. But worn down by calumny and imprisonment, he's in no shape to mount a defense."

"I'm feeling a good deal more like my old self," Roger protests, "than I did only two weeks ago."

"Which means?" Sullivan angrily persists. "Are you prepared to defend yourself in court or not?!"

"Roger, please—we beg of you!" Gee and Alice speak nearly in unison.

Roger looks somewhat mournful. "I must rely on my family and friends. They are all I have."

"Very well, then," Sullivan sternly replies. "*Until further notice,* I will sustain my efforts in the defendant's behalf."

"And I thank you for it," Roger replies, a trace of regret nonetheless apparent. "Hopefully we can together outline a defense that embodies both our approaches."

"By all means—if you feel up to the study of medieval statute."

Aiming to maintain some semblance of amicability, Gavan Duffy quickly changes the subject. He turns to Alice and playfully asks her if she ended up "getting any money out of old Shaw?"

"He said he doesn't give money to lost causes."

"I think it would be more accurate to say," Roger adds, "that he would not support a defense focused on the notion of 'treason.' He says I'm a prisoner of war and no more a traitor than any Serb captured by the Turks."

"He was adamant," Alice adds. "A defense that hinges on legal definitions of treason, he said, will end with the lord chief justice paying high compliments to Roger's learned counsel—and with Roger being sent to the gallows."

The phrase hangs in the air for a few seconds. Then Sullivan turns abruptly on his heels and bids the others a firm "Good afternoon."

After he's gone, Alice wrinkles her brow with displeasure: "To be more precise, what Mr. Shaw said was 'Serjeant Sullivan will get his compliments, and Casement will get his rope.'"

"I care less about the result," Roger replies, "than the course of the argument that precedes it. Sullivan's strategy seems to me dishonorable. It puts me in the false position of trying to weasel out through legal technicalities from defending the cause I care about: Ireland's right to be free. Shaw has the main point: the thing to fight for is not my life, probably lost already, but the cause of Ireland. . . ."

Gavan Duffy tries to dispel the gloom: "That's too dark a view, Roger. I mean, as to your own fate. Among other things, you omit completely the process of appeal. Do let's remember the recent case of Captain Lynch. The court proved without the shadow of a doubt that he was among the leaders of an Irish Brigade fighting on the side of the Boers and sentenced him to death. Yet on appeal his sentence was commuted. As yours will be, if it comes to that."

What no one wants to say, but what all are well aware of, is that Roger's case has an added complication that sets it apart from Captain Lynch's: his diaries. Two months earlier, during Roger's initial examination, the police had taken possession of several trunks he'd left at his lodgings—and in them were found the shorthand diaries recounting his sexual adventures. Basil Thomson had glanced at them and recoiled in disgust. But he held on to them, and their contents have been surreptitiously circulating.

As early as May 3—while Roger is still in the Tower of London—Capt. Reginald Hall, the chief of naval intelligence who assisted Thomson in Roger's initial interrogation, calls a select number of prominent English and American press representatives to his office and shows them photographic copies of certain revealing pages from the diaries. "As you will see," Hall pontificates, "Roger Casement is a moral offender unworthy of public sympathy." Ben S. Allen, a member of the London bureau of the Associated Press, speaks up. "Captain Hall," Allen announces, "has earlier shown me actual manuscript pages from the diaries—indeed, he offered them to the Associated

Press for its exclusive use. I told him, as I now tell you, that I cannot in conscience treat the diaries as genuine without directly asking Casement himself for authentification; nor would I feel comfortable using select pages out of context—one must see the entire diary—and even then, I would have to submit the pages to the AP's London bureau chief for approval."

In essence, Allen—who earlier met and admired Roger—is attempting to prevent Captain Hall's efforts to circularize the diary material, and he tells Hall to his face, "I do not believe the man I had met and grown to admire tremendously wrote that diary." Allen certainly means well, but in trying to "vindicate" Roger from charges of "degeneracy," he conflates—commonplace in that generation—homosexuality with immorality. Allen becomes the first in a long line of those who will insist, against the evidence, that Roger's diaries are forgeries designed to besmirch his reputation—the underlying assumption being that homosexual acts cannot coexist with an estimable character.

Despite Allen's resistance, Captain Hall does leak portions of the diary to the press, and it has the desired effect. Within days photographic facsimiles of diary pages are being circulated in London clubs, in the House of Commons, and in select corners of "polite" society. Gavan Duffy hears the gossip. So do Gee and Alice Green, who protest the skullduggery to leading members of the legal profession; that includes, among others, Sir John Simon, who'd refused to take on Casement's defense but now joins a minority who vigorously denounce the *perverted* attempt to smear Roger's character by leaking the contents of his private diary.

F. E. Smith, lead attorney for the prosecution, has few such scruples. He instructs the junior members of his team to offer defense counsels Serjeant Sullivan and Artemus Jones an envelope that contains diary pages describing "acts of sexual perversion" that Roger has committed with other men. Along with the envelope, F. E. Smith sends a message: the defense might want to consider entering a plea of "guilty but insane"—with the diary pages serving as "proof" of mental unbalance. Possibly Smith actually believes that homosexuality is a decisive marker of insanity and is therefore offering the material in a genuine effort to spare Roger from the gallows—it's what one of Smith's junior counsels means when he characterizes the gesture as an "act of Christian mercy."

Anyone who knows Smith well, however, recognizes that the quality of mercy is, with him, decidedly strained—mercy *not* being regarded as a prominent feature of his professional career. Ruthless chicanery has been far more central. In Roger's case, Smith *wants* the defense to take the bait and enter an insanity plea. The whole tenor of Roger's notable career, in Smith's calculation, would then argue against such a judgment, thereby forcing a debate that would require airing the content of his diaries in full.

In any case, Serjeant Sullivan does not rise to the bait. He refuses to receive the material, saying it has no bearing on the case and he has no wish to read it. Perhaps, some feel, he should have; a plea of insanity might be the only way Roger can escape the noose. "I knew it might save his life," Sullivan later says, "but I finally decided that death was better than besmirching and dishonour." Those sonorous words serve to conceal rather than elucidate Sullivan's motives: a plea of insanity would rob Sullivan of a unique opportunity to impress the London bar with his legal acumen. He continues to believe that the brilliance of his technical argument in regard to the Treason Act of 1351 will prove irrefutable and will lead to acquittal. *That* attitude might be called deranged—out of touch with reality—but in any case the point is moot: Roger would never sanction an insanity plea; it would be tantamount to acknowledging that anyone who engages in homosexual acts or champions the cause of Irish sovereignty is disordered, unhinged. Many would agree with the linkage, including Oscar Wilde's antagonist Edward Carson, though he might employ less inflammatory rhetoric.

Meantime, the Foreign Office is doing its part to stir the pot. It has long been compiling a file marked "Private, Confidential" on its troublesome one-time employee and on Roger's "supposed proclivities to unnatural vice" (to quote one of his detractors). As early as the second week in May, the Foreign Office sends the "Private" file to F. E. Smith, who, along with Sir Edward Grey, head of the Foreign Office, comes out against the dissemination of the material. But two members of the F.O.—Lord Hardinge, the permanent undersecretary, and Lord Newton, the assistant undersecretary—take it on themselves to circulate the file surreptitiously and zealously.

Lord Newton thinks his action beyond dispute: "It is perfectly obvious," he writes, "that we shall have to face a huge pro-Casement propaganda, and unless we are prepared to make some use of the material in our possession it will be almost impossible to combat it successfully. . . . Large numbers of influential persons in the States and elsewhere honestly believe Casement to be a misguided hero, and it seems only reasonable that they should be enlightened as to his real character."

Sir Cecil Spring-Rice, the British ambassador to the United States, is among those who receive the file, along with copies of pages from Roger's diary. He, in turn, dutifully passes on the material to a variety of Irish American and Catholic newspapers. The file includes evidence of Roger's relationship with his one-time Norwegian lover, Adler Christensen, and further reveals that Adler is on offer to travel to England from the States to give evidence against his former friend. Adler's readiness to betray Roger isn't taken up—thanks to Sir Edward Grey honorably stepping in and sending word to F. E. Smith that the offer should be ignored. John Devoy believes that Christensen might show up anyway, and he lets a confidant know that the Clan-na-Gael has interfered with any plan Adler may have in that regard: "*We kept him here*," Devoy writes, in a somewhat chilling condensation. Told of Adler's treachery, a chastened Roger thinks it "quite possible he has sold himself to the British Government," yet he rather poignantly holds on to a shaky hope: "I *don't* think he would injure me."

Roger's past seems suddenly upon him. A cablegram arrives from none other than Julio Arana, Roger's old antagonist in the Putumayo. Its contents are astonishing; he was "obliged to wire you asking you to be fully just confessing before the human tribunal your guilts only known by Divine Justice regarding your dealings in the Putumayo business. . . . Inventing deeds and influencing Barbadians to confirm unconsciously facts never happened. . . . Frightening them in the King's name with prison if refusing to sign your own work and statements. . . . You tried by all means to appear a humanizer in order to obtain titles, fortune, not caring for the consequences of your calumnies and defamation. . . . I pardon you, but it is necessary that you should be just and declare now fully and truly all the true facts that nobody knows better than yourself."

Judging by the aggrieved tone of the cablegram, one might deduce that Roger's Putumayo investigation has led to harsh punishment for Arana and his gang of cutthroats. In fact, nothing at all has been done. In May 1915 nine men had been indicted—but easily escaped and were never pursued, let alone recaptured and tried. (Arana himself will live to a ripe old age, surrounded by wealth and honors.) Roger seems to have derived a bit of grim humor from Arana's bizarre effrontery—"Think of it!" he writes his old friend, Richard Morten, "asking me to confess my 'crimes' against him!"—but the humor is subsumed under the sadness Roger feels for the unrelieved, ongoing plight of the "poor Indians."

By mid-June Roger's diaries have been dispersed still further, and the newspapers have become full of innuendo about his "depraved" character and "dissolute" morals. The whispering campaign has by now reached his close friends. When Richard Morten—their ties go back some twenty-five years—visits him in Brixton Prison, he asks Roger at one point, "What about the other thing, Roddie?" The allusion is obvious—as is the implication that material from the diary has been spread rather widely. "Dick, you've upset me," is all that Roger can manage in reply, but he later amplifies his concern in a letter: "I am sorry you came. It upset us both—me more than I can tell you. Please dismiss from your mind all that was said—rub it out for ever. . . . It has been one of the true joys of my life to have had you for a friend so many years—and one of the bitter griefs to lose you."

But of course Morten can't simply erase what he's learned about the diaries, no more than can any of the other friends and supporters who've heard the gossip. Roger himself becomes sleepless and fretful after Morten's visit and decides to talk the matter over with Gavan Duffy, who he rightly assumes is well aware of the circulating reports. As a result of their talk, Duffy writes directly to Morten: "my client begs me to impress upon you the great importance of talking to nobody under any circumstances about any of the matters you discussed yesterday."

The Bannisters, as well as the canny Alice Green, have long since deduced Roger's sexual attraction to men. As Gee writes to Roger's sister, Nina, who's living in America, "Now that Morten has blurted it out, we could discuss it more or less"—that is, within the limited context of courtroom considerations: Would the prosecution openly employ the information in the diaries? Would they be content to limit the charge to treason, or would they indict Roger as well for the same "crimes against nature" that had destroyed Oscar Wilde? Only the American lawyer Doyle—it *would* be the American—asks Roger directly if he's kept a "homosexual diary." Roger denies it.

Duffy tells Gee that he's decided to take no formal notice whatever of the allegations surrounding the diaries: they haven't "the remotest connection with the case on which I engaged and these rumours are simply spread about from the lowest and most malicious motives, a proceeding which is beneath contempt and which it would be preposterous to expect me to notice." When still in Germany Roger had predicted to a friend that "the English government will try now most to *humiliate* and *degrade* me." The process by mid-June is well advanced.

The day of the trial finally arrives. Roger's expectations vary as widely as his moods. When feeling optimistic—which is infrequent—he doesn't doubt that the vast majority of the English people want to see him hanged, but he feels the English *government* dare not comply, nor, in his view, do they "as individuals" *want* to see him hanged. Indeed, he believes that if they were able, they'd wish back to life the Patrick Pearses and James Connollys already killed—and certainly don't want to *add* to the rolls. Far more often, though, Roger thinks a guilty verdict is a foregone conclusion. He also feels, on balance, that his sentence will be commuted—not out of charity or remorse but because the British are keen to have the United States enter the war, and that could be jeopardized by a U.S. press now moving toward a version of the insanity defense: the view that years in the tropics affected Roger's mind, and you don't—or shouldn't—execute a man not responsible for his actions. Roger himself is ambivalent about the prospects of commutation—in most moods he feels that becoming "a British convict for life" is "far more dreadful to contemplate than death."

The four-day trial begins on June 26, 1916, and marks the first time in some three hundred years that a knight of the realm has faced a trial for treason. For the occasion a new dock has been erected, putting the accused in full view of the jury. Roger is dressed in one of his own dark suits—recovered from the trunks he left some years before with his friend Francis Bigger—dramatically offset by a white collar, shirt, and vest. The prisoner looks vigorous and self-contained—very much a knight of the realm, and his appearance draws admiring whispers from the packed courtroom.

The king's coroner reads out the indictment: "Sir Roger Casement, you stand indicted and charged on the presentment of the Grand Jury with the following offence—High Treason, by adhering to the King's enemies elsewhere than in the King's realm." The coroner further details the charge: attempting to seduce Irish prisoners of war in Germany from their allegiance to the king; setting out from Germany on a "warlike" expedition against England; landing arms and ammunition on the Irish coast in preparation for an assault on English sovereignty. "How say you?" the coroner asks in sonorous conclusion, "do you plead guilty or not guilty to the charge of high treason?"

Before Roger can answer, Serjeant Sullivan is on his feet: "There is not anywhere in the indictment an allegation of any act done anywhere *within the King's domains.* I am not speaking merely of within the realm, but within any territory in which His Majesty claims dominion of any kind." Sullivan has laid out his entire strategy in two sentences. Chief Justice Isaacs at once cuts the ground out from under it: "I would draw counsel's attention to a number of previous rulings to the effect that in 'cases of great magnitude'"—cases involving the charge of treason, for example—"such motions are properly made only after the prosecution has presented its case." Sullivan—whose main intention from the beginning has been to impress the court and secure entry to the English bar—sheepishly accepts the rebuke, along with a flourish of exquisite deference to the chief justice: "I am deeply and sincerely and gratefully cognisant from my experience in this Court of the kind of spirit of fair play that is accorded to any stranger who ventures within your precincts."

The coroner proceeds to repeat his question: "Do you plead guilty or not guilty?"

Roger's voice is firm: "Not guilty" (just as George Bernard Shaw advised).

The next hour is devoted to standard challenges to the jury from both defense and prosecution. That task completed, F. E. Smith rises to deliver his brief opening address: he speaks of the gravity of the charge—"the law knows no graver"—and then proceeds, with much learning, to quote from innumerable precedents over the past five hundred years to support the "common-sense view that treason committed overseas is still treason" (so much for Sullivan's belabored distinction between treason conducted within or without the realm).

Moving on, Smith characterizes Roger as an "able and cultivated man, versed in affairs and experienced in political matters." He is *not* a man, Smith stresses, who has been a "lifelong rebel against England"—to the contrary, his long career in the consular service culminated in 1911 in a knighthood. With just the hint of a smirk, Smith reads aloud from Roger's letter to Sir Edward Grey in 1911, thanking him for the honor in language ("I am much moved at the proof of confidence," etc.) Smith characterizes as "that almost of a courtier." (What he omits entirely, of course—he may not have known—is Roger's unhappy soul-searching and reluctance at the time.) The central mystery of Casement's life, Smith insists, is how a loyal courtier in 1911 became a defiant traitor in 1914, a man "blinded by hatred of this country."

Following his speech, Smith calls to the stand two witnesses who confirm that Roger received his pension from the Foreign Office as late as October 1914—which is to say, *after* he had ceased being a "loyal courtier." They're followed by seven of the Irish prisoners of war, who describe Casement's appeals to them at Limburg and testify as well to what they claim was the punishment and starvation that the German authorities—purportedly at Roger's behest—meted out to those who refused to join his brigade.

Serjeant Sullivan does little more than cursory cross-examinations. Nor does he—at this or at any other point in the trial—bring up the potentially devastating argument that F. E. Smith, as a bitter political opponent of Roger's, should have recused himself from appearing for the prosecution; nor why, on his failing to do so, the lord chief justice himself did not reject Smith's participation on the grounds of his having been a leader of the Ulster Volunteers, a man who had sanctioned smuggling arms and, like Edward Carson, had defiantly embraced the label of "traitor" that some assigned him. Just in case Sullivan is tempted, F. E. Smith has already scornfully preempted the accusations by claiming that Irish and English have put past quarrels behind them in a common struggle against German "aggression."

The first day of the trial confirms Roger's worst fears about Serjeant Sullivan, and at a conference with his legal team that same evening, he expresses his doubts with vehemence: "I don't want my so-called past achievements to be paraded in court as if they somehow compensate for my villainous behavior lately. *Please!*"

"I don't understand," Gavan Duffy says. "Your past record is notable and *should* be weighed in the scales. People have short memories. They need to be reminded of what you did in the Congo and the Putumayo."

"I won't have it," Roger adamantly replies. "I want the focus on *Ireland*. I'm as proud, or prouder, of trying to free the Irish as I am of working to improve the lot of Africans and Indians."

Duffy is feeling a bit passionate himself: "One isn't exclusive of the other. It's all of a piece: your sympathy for subservient people, your wish to end their suffering."

"Don't make me sound noble. . . . I was assigned a job and did it."

"Forgive me, Roger," Duffy responds, "but that's false modesty. Very few would have reacted to the 'job' the way you did. You have every right to feel proud of what you accomplished."

After a slight pause Roger quietly says, "I am, Duffy, I am. . . . You're quite right."

"Do you wish to protest the business about your pension?" Serjeant Sullivan interjects, his humdrum tone conveying his indifference to the answer.

"Don't bother," Roger coolly replies. "Not that Smith has it right. Until I decided to go to Germany, I was quite entitled to my pension. But I drew on it only until June 30. Never mind. That's trivial compared to what else is on the table. Like my letter to Grey about the knighthood."

"You *do* want me to bring that up?" Sullivan sounds surprised.

Roger finds the question incredulous. "Of course I do! Smith's misinterpretation of my letter should be challenged. He's venomous."

"Challenged how? He read out *your* words. I can't rewrite your letter." Sullivan smiles at his caustic rejoinder, which he considers unanswerable.

Roger ignores the hostile overtones: "What I'm suggesting," he evenly responds, "is that the letter's content be analyzed differently. I was somewhat surprised, frankly, that you chose not to analyze it at all. Have you no plans to defend my *character?*"

"Perhaps I insufficiently understand it," Sullivan sullenly replies.

Duffy, ever the peacemaker, jumps in: "What Roger may be suggesting—only he can say—is that we show how reluctant he was to accept the CMG in 1905—so reluctant, he thought, as to preclude any possibility of future honors. Is that not so, Roger?"

"Precisely so. I never even opened the package containing the CMG insignia. I told the Foreign Office that as a matter of policy no honor should be conferred without prior consultation and consent. They ignored me. The knighthood came out of the blue."

"The effusive language of your letter to Sir Edward Grey cannot be gainsaid," Sullivan acerbically remarks. "*You* may think it sounds begrudging and perfunctory, but I assure you others read it quite differently."

Sullivan does has a point, and Roger knows it. "Perhaps you're right," he acknowledges. "We should move on to a more central issue."

"Gladly." Sullivan feels gratified at the concession.

"The most important matter to me is Smith's attempt to portray me as a very late convert to Irish nationalism. It's true that I was a loyal servant of the Crown for a considerable period. It was my experience in the Boer War, then the Congo, and later in the Putumayo, that brought my nationalism—my sympathy for all colonized people—to the surface. But my love for Ireland has always been deeply embedded in my soul. Ask my cousin Gee—even as a youngster I covered the walls of my room with pictures of Irish heroes."

"Surely you acknowledge some evolution in your thought?" Sullivan sounds almost indignant.

"That's in the nature of being alive," Roger replies. "My only point is that I do not wish you to 'clear' me of the charge of being an Irish nationalist. I'm an Irish patriot, not an English traitor. Thus far you've been portraying a man who did not break the law—the law, that is, as defined in 1351. But I *have* broken the law. Several times over. As did Thomas Masaryk in breaking his pledge of allegiance to Emperor Franz Joseph by championing Czechoslovak independence. So must anyone who tries to cut the legal chains that bind them in servitude."

Roger could hardly have stated his wishes more explicitly, yet on the second and third days of the trial Serjeant Sullivan proceeds as if stone-deaf. Things go according to *his* plan, not Roger's: the 1351 statute is explored in minute detail, every word scrutinized, every parchment crease measured for intent.

The prosecution calls a large number of witnesses from the Banna Strand area to demonstrate that Roger had indeed landed there, as well as the police officers who arrested him. Though the accuracy of their accounts isn't in dispute, this time around Serjeant Sullivan, for some mysterious reason, does decide to cross-examine. But the only new bit he manages to elicit is the name of a holy well in the Tralee area—that, and a ripple of tut-tutting from the audience at the revelation of the early hour at which farming folk awaken. These weighty matters ascertained, Sullivan concludes his cross-examination—shocking some in its brevity—and the prosecution rests its case.

It's the predesignated, permissible moment at which Sullivan is permitted to air his argument about the technical merits of the case, and he does so at excruciating length. His contention is that Roger cannot be guilty of high treason for the simple—not to say, simplistic—reason that under the 1351 statute, a man must be "in the realm" to be found guilty.

Professor Morgan backs up Sullivan's contention with erudite reference to precedents established both prior and subsequent to the reign of Henry VIII, announcing his certainty that no medieval judge would have found Roger's actions treasonable. Medieval judges, alas, are not, at the moment, sitting on the bench. The lord chief justice, after consultation with his colleagues, comes to the conclusion everyone expects: "notwithstanding the learned and able arguments that have been addressed to us," the chief justice announces, Sullivan's motion to quash the indictment is denied.

There is one surprise. Sullivan calls no witnesses for the defense: no one to draw the parallels between Roger's case and that of those two English heroes Garibaldi and Masaryk; no one to attest to the profundity of Roger's commitment—his long-standing commitment—to independence for Ireland; no one to recall his profound efforts in the Congo and the Putumayo to relieve the suffering of enslaved peoples, humanitarian feats that have brought Britain great acclaim for its "generosity of spirit."

In the absence of defense witnesses, the chief justice announces that Roger will be allowed to make a statement before the jury retires to reach its verdict.

Roger draws the prepared speech on which he's worked for many days from his waistcoat pocket and in a low, somewhat hesitant voice addresses some of the many issues his counsel has failed to mention. The statement is unsworn, allowing for no cross-examination.

"I wish to respond," Roger begins, "to some of the prosecution's allegations." First, the pension he had drawn had been due to him for services rendered. As for the knighthood, he would have refused it if consulted in advance, but since Sir Edward Grey announced the distinction without asking for his agreement, he could not refuse it without discourtesy—and without resigning his consular position, which he could not afford to do, having no other source of income and with others reliant on him.

Roger turns next to more immediate matters: "I never asked an Irishman to fight for Germany," he insists. "I have always claimed that he has no right to fight for any land but Ireland." Nor, Roger continues, is he to any degree responsible for the rations of Irish prisoners of war being reduced to the point of starvation, purportedly, in reprisal for not joining the Irish brigade. "It is an abominable falsehood. As is the imputation that for German gold I sold myself to any man or to any Government. . . . I never asked for nor accepted a single penny of foreign money. It was offered to me in Germany more than once, and offered liberally and unconditionally, but I rejected every suggestion of the kind, and I have left Germany a poorer man than I entered it." Finally, as for F. E. Smith's "veiled allusion" associating him with the Easter Rising, "he has brought forward no evidence in this case from first to last." Since the Rising has been mentioned, however, Roger reiterates categorically that "the rebellion was not made in Germany and that not one penny of German gold went to finance it."

It is now Serjeant Sullivan's turn to address the jury, and for the first time he employs the argument Roger had wanted him to use throughout: "The prisoner is not a countryman of yours. He is a stranger within your gates. He comes from another country where people, though they use the same words, perhaps, speak differently; they think differently; they act differently." Sullivan proceeds to emphasize a point that not even Roger previously made explicit: the Irish brigade was recruited to augment the preexisting Irish Volunteers, itself formed to counter the Ulster Volunteers, whose activities had included the importation of arms, *with German assistance,* in threatened resistance to the Home Rule Bill. Sullivan then unexpectedly adds the still more powerful—and inflammatory—point that the Ulster Volunteers originated "with the avowed object of resisting the operation of an act of

Parliament which had the approval of the rest of the country. They armed and nothing was said to them; they drilled and nothing was said to them; they marched and countermarched; the authorities stood by and looked at them."

F. E. Smith rises quickly to his feet, his face contorted with anger. "I am most loathe to intervene," he says, directing his remarks to the chief justice, "but I have heard a great many statements as to the importation of rifles into the north of Ireland which are uncorroborated, and I deeply resent the—"

Like a shot, the chief justice interrupts Smith to plant his feet firmly on the prosecution's side: "We have allowed you great latitude," he sonorously, and sternly, admonishes Sullivan. "You are stating a matter which is not in evidence and which I have no recollection of being in evidence."

At just this point—when he's finally hit the mark—Sullivan falters. Will he press ahead—or backtrack? Does he dare underscore the obvious parallel of Carson and F. E. Smith boasting of their gunrunning and embracing the charge of "treason" to Casement's comparable activities? To do so will obviously outrage Smith—and thereby destroy any future prospects he might have at the English bar. And for what? For the defense of a degenerate who clearly stands no chance of acquittal and who implies that counsel is misrepresenting him?

An instant is all Sullivan needs to make his decision. He apologizes to the court—apologizes slavishly and repetitively: "I am exceedingly sorry your Lordship did not intervene sooner. . . . I am sorry if I transgressed, and regret that the rein was not applied. . . . If I have been carried away too far, I am exceedingly sorry."

When Sullivan first rose to address the jury he seemed a man transformed, willing and eager to take on the formidable F. E. Smith and confront him with the hypocrisy of his own history. But his courage proved as fragile as an eggshell, breaking apart at the touch. The chief justice's reprimand might have produced, in a stronger man, anger and resistance. In Sullivan it produces a pitiable debacle. He starts to retrace his steps, haltingly: "If it may please your Lordship . . . might please your Lord—" and then suddenly collapses into a chair. He's able, barely able, to say, "Pardon, m'lord . . . but I have . . . have broken down. . . ." The chief justice immediately clears the court.

When the fourth and final day of the trial begins the following morning, Artemus Ward, the junior counsel, rises to explain that Mr. Sullivan, on doctor's orders, is unable to proceed and that he, Mr. Ward, will conclude the address to the jury. Having no sympathy with Irish nationalism, Ward does so with dispatch, focusing on why Roger went to Germany and settling on an apocryphal, patently retrospective argument: "He went for the purpose of forming an Irish Brigade to strive for something they had a right to strive for, the protection of their countrymen if they were coerced or tyrannized by armed forces in Ireland which were not controlled by the Executive Government"—in other words, as a safeguard against the Ulster Volunteers.

When F. E. Smith's turn comes to summarize the prosecution's case, he makes short shrift of Ward's weakly formulated defense: "Why did he go to Germany? His case before you and through the lips of his counsel is that he went there to make sure there would be some men who would be strong enough to balance the Volunteers in the north of Ireland after the war. Where do you think would be the place in which his efforts might be most fruitful if that really was his object?" Smith, with a contemptuous nod, gives his own answer: "Ireland, of course!" He then demolishes the defense's case as nothing more than "after-thoughts and sophistries" that at the time bore no relation to Casement's real reason for going to Germany and forming the brigade—namely, "to assist in a rebellion against England."

When it comes time for the chief justice to instruct the jury, he adopts both the argument and in part the rhetoric of the prosecution: "If he knew or believed that the Irish Brigade was to be sent to Ireland during the war with a view to securing the national freedom of Ireland, that is, to engage in a civil war which would necessarily weaken and embarrass this country, then he was contriving and intending to assist the enemy."

Roger is removed from the dock and placed in an adjacent room to await the verdict. Within less than an hour, the jury files back into the courtroom. The unanimous verdict: "Guilty." Roger shows no visible reaction. The king's coroner steps forward and addresses Roger directly: "Sir Roger David Casement, you stand convicted of high treason. What have you to say for yourself why the Court should not pass sentence and judgment upon you to die according to law?"

The convicted, as all are aware, is entitled to make a speech from the dock, and Roger takes a number of pages of blue prison foolscap out of his pocket and, with a nod to the chief justice, proceeds to read the statement he's been working on for weeks. He begins by protesting the jurisdiction of the court; he asserts the fundamental right of an Englishman to be tried by his peers, which in his case should have meant an Irish court. "This Court, this jury, the public opinion of this country, England, cannot but be prejudiced in varying degree against me, most of all in time of war." Given these circumstances, Roger solemnly declares, "The argument that I am now going to read is addressed not to this Court but to my own countrymen."

Unlike his attorneys, Roger forswears excuses and rationalizations and embraces a single line of argument as his defense: his duty as an Irishman to fight for the independence of his country. He takes the high ground and occupies it eloquently, beginning with a rebuttal of his own counsel's words. In Artemus Ward's peroration—which could as well have been delivered by the prosecution—he'd spoken of the "many mistaken sons of that unfortunate country who have gone to the scaffold, as they think, for the sake of their native land." Roger gives voice to a quite different view of those in the past who have struggled in vain for Ireland's independence: "Ireland has seen her sons—aye, and her daughters too—suffer from generation to generation always from the same cause, meeting always the same fate, and always at the hands of the same power; and always a fresh generation has passed on to withstand the same oppression. . . . The cause that begets this indomitable persistency, the faculty of preserving through centuries of misery the remembrance of lost liberty, this surely is the noblest cause men ever strove for, ever lived for, ever died for. . . . I stand in a goodly company and a right noble succession." The packed courtroom greets his words with the absolute attention and silence that connotes respect.

Roger then goes on boldly to assert that in the current war being waged in Europe "small nationalities were to be the pawns in this game of embattled giants"; he can therefore see "no reason why Ireland should shed her blood in any cause but her own, and if that be treason beyond the seas I am not ashamed to avow it or to answer for it here with my life." Adroitly introducing the Ulster parallels that his attorneys have deferentially avoided, Roger speaks of the fact that "a constitutional movement in Ireland is never very far from a breach of the constitution, as the Loyalists of Ulster have been so eager to show us . . . [as in] the refusal of the English army of occupation at the Curragh to obey the orders of the Crown" in putting down potential Ulster resistance.

Then, toward the close of his speech, Roger takes on F. E. Smith and the prosecution with trenchant directness: "The difference between us was that the Unionist champions chose a path they felt would lead to the woolsack; while I went a road I knew must lead to the dock. And the event proves we were both right. The difference between us was that my 'treason' was based on a ruthless sincerity that forced me to attempt in time and action what I said in word, whereas their treason lay in verbal incitements that they knew need never be made good. And so, I am prouder to stand here today in the traitor's dock to answer this impeachment than to fill the place of my right honourable accusers."

At that powerful moment, the courtroom hushed in profound silence, F. E. Smith smiles sardonically and audibly whispers, "Change places with him? Nothing doing." He then rises from his seat and ostentatiously, with rude nonchalance, walks out of the courtroom with his hands in his pockets.

Roger ignores Smith's insolence and proceeds to his peroration: "Self-government is our right, a thing born in us at birth; a thing no more to be doled out to us or withheld from us by another people than the right to life itself. . . . If it be treason to fight against such an unnatural fate as this, then I am proud to be a rebel, and shall cling to my 'rebellion' with the last drop of my blood."

He turns to the chief justice: "My lord," he says, "I am done."

The law clerks move behind the three judges and place the traditional black caps—in a manner somewhat askew—on their heads, as Justice Horridge's facial tic works overtime, mimicking, so it appears, a broad grin.

What follows is ancient routine. Turning toward the dock, the lord chief justice mechanically intones the usual phrases: "the gravest crime . . . conclusive guilt . . . duty devolves upon me . . . that you be taken hence . . . and be hanged by the neck until you be dead . . . and may the Lord have mercy on your soul!"

Roger bows toward the bench, and smiles.

· · ·

Roger isn't remanded to Brixton but taken directly from the courthouse to Pentonville Prison, the huge fortresslike structure, completed in the mid-nineteenth century, that for a time in 1895 housed Oscar Wilde. He's stripped of his civilian clothes and given the convict's blue outfit and felon's cap (that "dreadful cap," Gee calls it) to wear. For the first few days he does little more than sleep, but it isn't long before Gavan Duffy presents him with a dilemma: whether or not to appeal the conviction. Roger is reluctant: in his view an appeal is bound to fail; why give his opponents another opportunity to humiliate him publicly? He's satisfied to let his final statement to the court stand as his permanent legacy. Duffy appeals to Gee to intercede, and she brings the matter up on her first visit.

"Public opinion," she tells him, "is beginning to shift—I wouldn't call it a groundswell exactly—in your favor. Plus there is the recent precedent from the Lynch case."

"My case is different."

"Quite right!" Gee is determined to persuade him. "Lynch not only advocated for the Boers but joined them on the battlefield against the British army!"

"That's not what I meant. I'm not simply a traitor. I'm a 'moral degenerate'—or haven't you heard?"

Startled at Roger's direct reference for the first time to the gossip in circulation, Gee is thrown off guard. "I expected . . . I mean, wasn't it surprising the prosecution didn't bring up those . . . those forged diaries? F. E. Smith must have known they'd be proven fake."

Roger realizes that Gee needs the protection of the "forgery" theory and deliberately passes over it. "Smith did make one veiled reference to the diaries. But why risk being tarred with scandal mongering when you've already got an airtight case for treason? The British aren't big on dirty stories—not delivered in public anyway."

"Well, they've done their best to spread the nonsense *outside* of court." Gee is tight-lipped and angry. "As if there's a word of truth in it!"

"Did I tell you what Bulmer Hobson reported?"

"Bulmer? No."

"Sir James O'Connor told Bulmer that—"

"James O'Connor?"

"You know, Ireland's attorney general, against independence. . . . Anyway, during a break in the trial one day, O'Connor reports that F. E. Smith comes running down the corridor after him, calling out, "O'Connor! O'Connor! I want to show you something!" Then he hands O'Connor copies of some diary pages. O'Connor refuses to look at them. First decent thing I've ever heard about the man."

There's a brief silence, which Gee quickly fills.

"Alice wanted me to tell you that she agrees with Duffy. She thinks you should go forward with the appeal. Even if it fails, it will open the way to take the case to the House of Lords, where the prospects do look brighter."

"Didn't I tell you? I've been stripped of my knighthood. Official word came yesterday. That should bring the Lords running—in the opposite direction."

"Oh, Roger, if there's even a chance. . . ." Gee mumbles mournfully.

"Gee, my dear, think of the contradiction. . . . I've denied the legitimate right of the court to try me. If I appeal their decision, I've acknowledged that they had the right, after all, to decide my fate. It's inconsistent."

"No, it's illogical. We Irish pride ourselves on illogic!" They both laugh.

"Surely, my good woman," Roger says playfully, "you aren't referring to the Virgin birth? They'll have you in the docket too, if you're not careful!"

He suddenly reaches down to the floor of the cell and retrieves a small piece of bread. "Aha!" he says triumphantly. "That's one morsel the rats won't get!"

"Rats?!" Gee is genuinely horrified.

"Of course, dear cousin. Prison and rats. Noise and stench. They go together like sugar and spice. Maybe an appeal," he chuckles, "might at least get me a transfer!"

Seizing on the narrow opening, Gee is quick to jump in. "Duffy says there are several good grounds for appeal, that first of all—"

"Oh my, I see I've opened the floodgates. Very well, let's have it out."

Gee exhales with relief. "Your acts don't constitute treason as defined by the statute of Edward III's that—"

"Oh no, dear cousin," Roger breaks in, "Not *that* again."

"They say Mr. Sullivan has quite recovered from his unfortunate—"

"His unfortunate *ambition?* Don't you believe it! Sullivan wants the chance to display once more his keen knowledge of mysterious medieval matters known only to initiates. But why should I give it to him? The man's *mis*represented me thoroughly. Made me into some sort of dreamer and fool. . . ."

Gee hurries him off the point: "And, second, there's the matter of the chief justice's prejudicial instructions to the jury, which left them scant choice but to convict."

"*That* argument does have merit," Roger acknowledges. "Not that merit will weigh a farthing. . . . Politics is what dictates court verdicts, not niceties of law—though barristers deny it. What is 'treason,' after all? It's all in the vantage point. The Austrian emperor calls Masaryk a traitor for declaring Czechoslovakia's independence; the Czechs call him a hero. So do I!"

Gee tries to capitalize on Roger's burst of energy: "Exactly—an excellent example, dear cousin!" Even to Gee, her enthusiasm sounds forced, but she ploughs determinedly on. "You see, there *are* grounds for appeal; there *is* a very good chance that—"

"All right, Gee, all right! But you'll see how pointless it all is. . . ."

And so it is that on July 17 a recovered Serjeant Sullivan once more presents his arcane discussion of the 1351 statute, this time before the court of criminal appeals—and bolstered with still more precedents unearthed by Professor Morgan's admirable scholarship. Once more the presentation leaves the justices unmoved; they again compliment Sullivan on his ingenious performance and again turn down the appeal unanimously. "The subjects of the King," they intone, "owe him allegiance, and the allegiance follows the person of the subject. He is the King's liege wherever he may be." So translucent do the justices view their hazy formulation that they don't even bother to call on Attorney General Smith for a rebuttal. Roger describes his own attitude in a letter to Alice Green: "I sat looking on at the actors with a quite detached and even cynical smile—especially the wigs."

To bring an appeal from the criminal court to the House of Lords requires a certificate of fiat from the attorney general stating that a point of law "of exceptional public importance" is at stake, making it in the public interest to proceed with a further appeal. In Roger's case, the attorney general happens to be the same F. E. Smith who has served as his principal prosecutor. Gavan Duffy believes that Smith is capable of impartiality and will rise to the occasion. He labors over the wording of his letter to Smith on the rose-colored assumption that a just argument is capable of moving an unjust man. To be sure, Duffy is shrewd enough to hint as well at the importance for Smith's own reputation of having "the Highest Tribunal" pronounce on the lower court's decision—on "the need of demonstrating to the prisoner's fellow countrymen and to the world that the prisoner has had the advantage of every possible recourse open to him at law." The decision is Smith's, and Smith's alone. Without a sideway glance, he moves directly into the breach: "appeal denied." The date for Roger's execution is set for August 3.

A furious Gavan Duffy issues a statement to the press, emphasizing that in this case the attorney general happens to be the lead prosecutor. Anyone else can see, Duffy argues, that if ever a case deserved consideration by the House of Lords, this is it: "If the determination of what is high treason is not of 'exceptional public importance' . . . what can be? And should it not be dealt with and settled by the highest Court in the land? . . . Yet Sir F. E. Smith, from whom there is no appeal, whose antecedents in Ulster are well remembered, has refused the certificate and shows no inclination to reconsider his determination."

The end game is rapidly approaching. Nothing is left now but the possibility of the king's clemency, which itself hinges on the recommendation of the cabinet as a whole. The cabinet, in turn, is likely to be responsive to public opinion, though not bound by it.

Public opinion is in this case difficult to read—not least because it's been deliberately manipulated. Excerpts from Roger's diaries have been shown early, and shown widely—even more widely than Roger's defenders have guessed. On June 29—while the trial was still in process—a telegram marked "Secret" had gone out from the British Foreign Office to a Capt. Guy Gaunt, naval attaché to the British legation in Washington. It read in part: "Photographic facsimile and transcript of Casement's diary ... is being sent to America by today's mail.... Could you arrange to get Editors of Newspapers and influential Catholic and Irish circles informed indirectly that facts have transpired which throw an appalling light on Casement's past life, and which when known will make it quite impossible for any self-respecting person to champion his cause.... [The diary] is a daily record of amazing unnatural vice ... and is the worst thing which has ever come into the hands of persons with the widest experience of cases of this sort."

The dutiful Captain Gaunt sees to it that typed excerpts from the diary are circulated widely. An official in the Foreign Office notes with satisfaction that "the disclosures [are having] the effect of completely alienating U.S. sympathy from Sir R. Casement." That may have been overstating it, though the revelations do undoubtedly injure him. Not everyone, however, not by any means, is alienated. John Quinn, Roger's host when he last visited New York—and in sharp disagreement with his radical nationalism—continues to view him as incorruptibly "honest and honorable ... a man of the utmost austerity and purity." He accepts what he calls Roger's "technical" guilt for attempting to pry Ireland loose from the empire but is nonetheless determined to save him from the hangman.

Quinn mounts a forceful campaign, writing letters to editors, cabling powerful people to lend their names to a plea for clemency, and personally arguing the case with British officials in New York and Washington—at one point sending a twenty-four-page memorandum to the Foreign Office, outlining the merits of reprieve on both humanitarian and prudential grounds. In late July—at almost the exact hour F. E. Smith is refusing to issue the certificate that would have allowed an appeal to the House of Lords—Quinn sends a cablegram to Sir Edward Grey, signed by twenty-five prominent Americans, "all of whom," as the cable states, are "pro-Ally in their sympathies" and ask "for clemency in the case of Roger Casement."

When naval attaché Gaunt, following his instructions, hands Quinn copies of certain pages from Roger's diary, Quinn at first dismisses them as forgeries. "Never by word or act," Quinn insists, "by tone of the voice, by a gesture or the slightest syllable or letter was there a shadow of a shade of anything of a degenerate about him." At that point Quinn's close friend, the British ambassador to Washington, Sir Cecil Spring-Rice (whose niece had participated in the notorious Howth gunrunning episode), manages to persuade Quinn that the diaries *are* genuine. He nonetheless continues to exert pressure for clemency and by cable asks Gavan Duffy "to give . . . [Roger] my love."

When Asquith asks Walter Page, the U.S. ambassador to England, if he's seen the diary, Page replies that he's been given photographed copies of portions of it. "Excellent," Asquith replies. "And you need not be particular about keeping it to yourself." He isn't. Among those Page notifies is Robert Lansing, the U.S. secretary of state, who he warns against becoming involved with a clemency plea because of the "unspeakably filthy character" of the diaries.

In New York John Devoy and the Clan-na-Gael—despite the mixed feelings Devoy has long harbored toward Roger and though in little doubt that he *is* (in Devoy's words) "an Oscar Wilde"—come out strongly on the side of a reprieve. Through Roger's American attorney, Michael Francis Doyle, Devoy sends $5,000—in today's money roughly $50,000—to help defray legal expenses. When Doyle hands Roger the check in his cell, he bursts into tears. Some twenty million people of Irish descent live in the United States in 1916, and a group of Irish American leaders, including Devoy and a number of congressmen, feel it ethically incumbent on them to present a petition directly to President Woodrow Wilson, asking him to intervene with the British government. With England eager, even desperate, for U.S. entry into the war, a plea from Wilson could quite possibly turn the tide. But on receiving the petition, the president's reply is curt: "It would be inexcusable for me to touch this." He gives the same brusque response to a personal plea from Roger's sister, Nina, who's currently living in the United States.

In the U.S. Senate a resolution is introduced calling for clemency in the treatment of Irish political prisoners—Casement is not mentioned by name—but though it passes easily (forty-six to nineteen) its transmission to London is "unaccountably" delayed. A furious Devoy points out that while many Irish Americans and former black slaves were fighting on the Union side during the Civil War, Woodrow Wilson's father, a Presbyterian minister, "was desecrating a Christian pulpit by railing in favor of human slavery."

There's also considerable sentiment in the African American community for Roger's reprieve. W. E. B. DuBois rejects the charge of treason and publicly refers to Roger as a "patriot" and a "martyr"—a characterization echoed by Marcus Garvey as well. But perhaps the most eloquent voice raised among African Americans is from the Negro Fellowship League, founded by the remarkable Ida B. Wells-Barnett in 1910 to aid newly arriving black migrants from the South. In asking for clemency, the NFL's petition reads, "We feel so deeply grateful to this man for the revelations he made while British Consul in Africa, touching the treatment of natives in the Congo. But for him, the world might not know of the barbarous cruelties practised upon the helpless natives. Because of this great service to humanity, as well as to the Congo natives, we feel impelled to beg for mercy on his behalf. There are so few heroic souls in the world who dare to lift their voices in defence of the oppressed who are born with black skins."

In Ireland radical nationalists are of one voice in denouncing the diaries as the English government's malignant forgery and declaring the allegation of homosexuality untrue: Roger Casement is *not* a homosexual. Bulmer Hobson calls the charge "the dirtiest bit of English propaganda. . . . All this talk about vice makes me want to assault the people who say it." Alice Green is among the very few of Roger's close friends who at the time regard the diaries as authentic. Francis Bigger is—to his own horror—another. When he opens several trunks Roger left with him years before, he discovers considerable additional material confirming Roger's homosexuality—and burns all of it. Bigger's nephew is heard telling people about the material his uncle's discovered; several IRA members let him know that if he values his life, he'll keep his mouth shut.

Among those who aren't radical nationalists, the rationalizing process takes some unpredictable turns. A long-standing antagonist like John Redmond experiences no psychic turmoil over the issue: as expected, he flatly refuses to associate himself with any plea for clemency. But another prominent Redmonite, Col. Maurice Moore, chief of staff of the National Volunteers, joins the Gaelic Leaguer Agnes O'Farrelly in getting up a petition declaring that while it has "no sympathy with the actions of Roger Casement in Germany," it nevertheless urges a reprieve. Even the Catholic primate cardinal Michael Logue, an implacable opponent of the nationalists, places himself prominently on the side of "mercy and charity."

Oppositely, some of Roger's oldest friends reject him utterly, or at most lend, belatedly, lukewarm support. E. D. Morel, Roger's comrade in arms during the Congo struggle, falls into the latter category, Herbert Ward into the former. Ward, whose close friendship with Roger goes back some thirty years to Congo days, not only refuses to sign a petition for reprieve but has his son's name—Roger Casement Ward—legally changed.

There are compensations, of a sort. William Cadbury gets up a petition of his own that avoids all mention of matters sexual and concentrates instead of Roger's estimable humanitarian work. Arthur Conan Doyle, too, gets up a petition; his is signed by a remarkable number of prominent figures, among them, Arnold Bennett; G. K. Chesterton; Sir James Frazer; John Galsworthy; John Masefield; Beatrice and Sydney Webb; Israel Zangwill; the editors of the *Nation,* the *Contemporary Review,* the *Daily News,* and the *Manchester Guardian;* and the presidents of such august institutions as the Royal College of Physicians, the National Free Church Council, and the Baptist Union. George Bernard Shaw refuses to sign—but only because he fears his name will put off others; instead, he writes up a statement of his own and sends it directly to Prime Minister Asquith.

The indefatigable Gee Bannister shrewdly concentrates her petition efforts on luminaries from the Bloomsbury set, known for the intricacy of their own nonconforming sexual partnerships: Dora Carrington, Duncan Grant, Leonard Woolf, and Lytton Strachey are among those who become signatories. Alice Green is also tirelessly active in Roger's behalf; in a letter to the *Guardian* she makes the telling point that the French president has recently hosted a state banquet in honor of four "traitors" who had raised troops among their German and Austrian countrymen to fight alongside the Allies.

The steady stream of petitions continues to mount—there's even one from "Ulster Liberals"—yet public opinion remains sharply divided. The personal appeal of the archbishop of Canterbury, Randall Davidson, embodies many of the divided feelings currently in play. On the one hand, the archbishop stresses the undoubted fact that for many years Roger "battled nobly on behalf of the oppressed native folk. . . . His name will rightly be held in honor for what he then did." On the other hand, the archbishop offers his opinion that the "perplexing contradictions" in Roger's sexual relations may not "technically" mark him as "out of his mind" but do clearly show him "to have been mentally and morally unhinged." The archbishop's verdict? "A reprieve would be wiser than an execution." Wiser—not more just. The recommended grounds? "Insanity."

With only two weeks remaining before the scheduled execution, the matter finally reaches the cabinet. Initially, it too is sharply split. Sir Edward Grey is the most prominent of the members opposed to execution, Attorney General Smith among the most vocal of those favoring it—vocal to the point of threatening to resign should the court's decision not be upheld. Smith impresses on the cabinet that by Casement's own account in his diaries, the nature and frequency of his sexual contacts is "incredible," and the diaries, Smith stresses, *are* a "faithful and accurate record." Sir Edward Grey, joined by Lord Lansdowne, his predecessor in the Foreign Office, uncomfortably respond that they are against executing Casement only because they do not wish to create a martyr. But they certainly do *not* advocate giving him his freedom. No, he should be permanently confined to a criminal lunatic asylum.

At this point in the cabinet debate, Sir Ernley Blackwell, the legal adviser to the Home Office, emerges as a key figure. In a July 15 memorandum, he sets out the central argument for execution: "It is difficult to imagine a worse case of high treason than Casement's. It is aggravated rather than mitigated by his previous career in the public service, and his private character—although it really has no relation to the actual offence with which he is charged—certainly cannot be pleaded in his favour. Casement's diary and his ledger entries, covering many pages of closely typed matter, show that he has for years been addicted to the grossest sodomitical practices. Of late years he seems to have completed the full cycle of sexual degeneracy and from a pervert has become an invert—a woman or pathic who derives his satisfaction from attracting men and inducing them to use him."

According to Blackwell's analysis, if a homosexual man becomes fully active sexually, he turns into a woman (or a "pathic"—the passive partner in anal intercourse)—and the definition of a woman offered is that of a masochistic seductress. High treason, it follows, can be recognized and defined as aberrant sexual behavior, not, as ordinary folk might have thought, giving comfort and aid to the country's enemies. Roger Casement deserves to die because he's queer—"pathic"—not because he tried to ship arms from Germany to Ireland. In this confused moral tangle, only William Butler Yeats seems to have put the matter squarely: "If Casement were homo-sexual, what matter?"

Throughout the cabinet debates, the overriding issue of the war remains, of necessity, foremost. The deadly conflict is currently bogged down in stalemate, and the corpses of millions saturate the ground. A month before Roger went on trial, the German Fleet and the Royal Navy engaged each other in the major Battle of Jutland without altering at all the balance of power at sea. On land a decisive moment seems to have arrived when the Russian army breaks through in Galicia and threatens to overrun Germany's ally, Austria-Hungary—yet six months later the Bolshevik seizure of power shakes all of Europe, leaving the ruling classes on both sides of the struggle fearful of contagion.

Compared to the immense upheaval and suffering of these months, the trial of a rebellious Irishman may not be a mere speck on the horizon, but nor is it sufficiently consequential to hold international attention for very long. It doesn't help Roger's case that the press carries story after story about the gallantry of Irish troops—their loyalty, in contrast to the traitor Casement, to the empire. As Alice Green writes to William Cadbury at the end of July 1916, "The war has formed all minds into a single groove."

When the cabinet meets on July 27, the ministers are nearly equally divided on the question of execution. The foreign secretary, Lord Crewe, circulates a letter from the poet Eva Gore-Booth, sister, confidante, and political ally to Constance Markievicz (who is herself still in prison). Eva and her life partner, Esther Roper, are longtime activists for women's rights, and in that very year of 1916 they establish the radical journal *Urania* (then a somewhat common term—invented by the pioneering figure Karl Heinrich Ulrichs—for homosexuality). Eva insists in her letter that Casement's defense attorneys failed to raise *the* most significant point—that Casement had arrived in Ireland "in a frantic attempt" (as she puts it) "to dissuade the Sinn Féin leaders from what he considered the fatal mistake of the Rising"; he willingly faced "almost certain death for the sake of preventing bloodshed and misery in Ireland on this matter." She does not add that Roger tried to halt the Rising primarily because Germany had failed to provide sufficient arms and officers to allow for success. Still, Gore-Booth's letter apparently has a significant effect on several wavering members of the cabinet—that is, until Ernley Blackwell circulates his own "gross sodomy" memo, which convinces most of the waverers. The virtue of trying to prevent a bloody uprising is no match for the heinous crime of committing sodomy.

Blackwell also introduces a new piece of evidence that serves further to dampen dissent. He dissects—for the first time thoroughly—Roger's agreement of December 1914 with the Germans, and in particular the proviso that if the Germans, due to English naval superiority, prove unable to transport the Irish brigade to Ireland, consideration might be given to using the men in Egypt to strike a kindred blow for national freedom against British forces. Hammering in the final nail, Blackwell circulates as well an undated note in Roger's hand that's attached to the 1914 agreement: "There is enough in these papers to hang me ten times over. If I had been thirty-three instead of fifty-three, the arms would have been landed . . . and I should have freed Ireland, or died fighting at the head of my men."

Ernley Blackwell's documents and arguments have the desired effect: the cabinet, in the end, votes unanimously to proceed with the execution. On August 2 the governor of Pentonville is told officially that there will be no reprieve.

Throughout the furious contentions of the preceding months, Roger seems to have grown calmer by the day. "I have a happier mind than I had for a long time," he writes Alice Green. When she pays her last visit to him, he is—so she reports to William Cadbury—"calm, serene, saying that he has now no nerves and is perfect master of himself." He repeats three times over that "all is good now." Another prisoner in Pentonville catches sight of Roger one day and leaves behind this description: "his face was wonderfully calm. . . . He seemed already to be living in another world; there was not a trace of anxiety or fear in his features."

On July 29 Artemus Jones and Professor Morgan make a last-ditch effort to persuade F. E. Smith to grant a certificate of appeal to the House of Lords. They pointedly raise the issue of the diaries, arguing that the government, by disseminating the material, has unfairly biased the press and the public against clemency. Smith remains unmoved. "There is not a word of truth in these complaints," he tells Jones and Morgan—in the apparent belief that public opinion cannot be swayed or need not be heeded.

As the day of execution approaches, Roger asks Father Carey, the prison chaplain at Pentonville, to receive him into the Catholic faith. The decision shocks some of his friends; they've known Roger in the past to have mocked the church's self-importance and retrograde conservatism, once going so far as to assert that the Catholic Church "has done more to injure Ireland than the foreign Church [Anglicanism] could ever accomplish." Nor is he himself free of doubt about conversion: "The trouble is: *am I convinced?*" he writes Gavan Duffy, "or do I only *think* I am? Am I moved by love? Or fear? . . . Part of the appeal *seems* at times to be my fear."

The decision has been coming on for some time; when in Germany, Monteith noted that Roger always kept Thomas à Kempis on the table next to his bed. Yet as recently as his stay in the Tower, Roger has continued to express reservations: "I don't want to jump, or rush or do anything hastily," he writes on a notepad, "just because my time is short. It must be my deliberate act, unwavering and confirmed by all my intelligence." By his own account, he does reach such a state of certainty, yet even then the rebel in

Roger remains alive and well. When Father Carey's superior stipulates that Roger must express sorrow "for any scandal he might have caused by his acts, public or private," before he can be received into the church, Roger flatly refuses. "They are trying," he tells Gee, "to make me betray my soul." A way out is found when Father Carey learns that Roger's mother had him baptized as a young child. That means he can be regarded as already a Catholic, one simply in need of reconciliation with the church.

Roger now sets himself to writing his last letters to close friends. To William Cadbury, he asks that he "please help the school children at Carraroe for my poor sake. . . . Love and affection to you dear, honest, faithful and affectionate friend." To his old friend Richard Morten he strikes a different note: "God deliver me," he writes in reference to the trial, "from antiquaries as these to hang a man's life upon a comma, and throttle him with a semi-colon." Further, he retroactively indicts Serjeant Sullivan to Morten for never having entered the substantial body of evidence showing that he'd been intent on trying to *stop* the Rising and expresses regret that he hadn't followed his instinct and served as his own counsel. Then he turns his thoughts back to Africa: "The Civilizers are now busy developing it with blood and slaying each other, and burning with hatred against me because I think their work is organized murder."

For all his newfound tranquility, Roger is not a man transfigured. He remains very much a human being, subject to sharp swings in mood. Gee is the last person allowed to see him, and she finds him "for the first time broken and sorrowful." He tells her that the day before he'd tried to send a final message to Herbert Ward—his old friend from Africa days, a man who'd once told E. D. Morel that "no man walks the earth at this moment who is more absolutely good and honest" than Roger—yet Ward has refused even to accept the letter, a grievous rejection that Roger feels deeply.

"What will you do, Gee," he asks her, "when it is all over?"

"Roger, dear Roger, let us not talk of that. . . . I will . . . I don't know what I will do. . . ."

"Go back to Ireland, Gee. Leave England. Leave it for good. And one more thing, dear Gee . . . one more—" Roger voice chokes up with emotion.

Gee tenderly takes his hands in hers. "What Roger? What, my dearest boy? . . ."

"Don't let me lie here in this dreadful place," Roger sobs. "Take my body back to Ireland with you. Promise me, Gee. Let my body lie in the old church-yard in Murlough Bay."

Between her own tears, Gee gives her word, though she knows the decision will not be hers to make.

"I don't want to die and leave you and the rest of you dear ones, but I must."

"Now, now, Roddie . . . even as we speak, the petitions to the cabinet continue to—"

"No, no, Gee. Don't delude yourself, my love. I don't. They want my death; nothing else will do, it seems. . . . And, after all, it's a glorious death, to die for Ireland. . . . I could not stand long years in a place like this—it would destroy my soul."

The warders interrupt. Time's up. Gee must go. She stretches out her hands to Roger in a last farewell, as they both sob uncontrollably.

In the corridor, awash in grief, barely able to stand, Gee begs one of the warders to call her a taxi. He refuses. "Pull yourself together," he angrily tells her, then shoves her out the gate, locking it behind her.

On August 2, the final evening before the execution, a tiny group of five, including Gee and Alice Green, go to Buckingham Palace, hoping to make a personal plea to the king for commutation. They're turned away, told that the "prerogative of mercy" constitutionally rests with the home secretary—who refuses to receive them.

Roger writes a last message: "My good will to those who have taken my life, equally to all those who tried to save it. All are my brothers now. . . . Now as I stand face-to-face with death I feel just as if they were going to kill a boy. For I feel like a boy. . . . I cannot comprehend how anyone wants to hang me."

On the morning of August 3, Roger makes his confession to Father Carey, who reports that he "sobbed like a child." At the stroke of 9:00 A.M., Roger's hands are tied behind his back, and he walks to the scaffold with (in Father Carey's words) "the dignity of a prince and towered straight over all of us." The executioner later calls him "the bravest man it fell to my unhappy lot to execute." A crowd has gathered outside the prison walls. At a few minutes past nine, the bell sounds, signaling that the execution is completed.

Gavan Duffy, on behalf of Roger's family, requests that the body be given to his relatives for burial in consecrated ground outside the prison, with the promise that the funeral will be kept private. Ernley Blackwell, vindictive to the last, denies the request on behalf of the home secretary, writing that "the law requires that the body shall be buried within the walls of the prison." Duffy protests the "grievous wrong," but the authorities are adamant. That same day Roger's body is thrown into quicklime in the yard of Pentonville

Prison. "It is a cruel thing to die," he'd written in his last letter to Nina, "with all men misunderstanding."

For fifty years a consistent effort is made to reclaim Roger's remains, but to no avail. Finally, in 1965 the government allows his bones to be dug up and returned to Dublin. A huge throng turns out in the pouring rain to welcome home their Irish hero. Civil servants are given the day off, and many schools and businesses are closed. He lies in state for five days as half a million people file past his coffin and is then buried with full honors in the Republican plot in Dublin's Glasnevin Cemetery.

AUTHOR'S NOTE

Every work of history is a construct. It is also an inquiry (the very meaning of the Greek term *historia*). Inquiry in turn implies, even requires, imagination—an adjunct of objectivity, not its enemy.

Professional historians base their versions of the past on the limited evidence that has survived; that evidence is always partial, never complete. Additionally, historians bring to bear, on the accidental fragment that has come down to us of the whole story, their own idiosyncratic experiences and values (often unconsciously held). The inevitable result is a somewhat skewed, subjective product that at best approximates objectivity but can never achieve it—which is why each generation finds the need to rewrite history in response to the pressures of an ever-shifting climate in values and perspective. Maya Jasanoff has recently pointed out that "if postmodernism has taught historians anything, it's that subjectivity can't ever be avoided." Yet, as Jasanoff laments, "historians writing for a general audience still more or less follow the forms set by the Victorians."

In her view, and mine, there remains room in historical writing for informed speculation that moves beyond traditional constrictions. Pressed for a capsule term, I've called this book a *biographical novel*. I stick to the known historical "facts," imagining only what is absent from the record and doing so by letting whatever shards of evidence that do exist point me to presumptively likely feelings and opinions for the personalities involved (though the actual historical record doesn't definitively say so). Unlike many historical novelists I do not invent past events out of whole cloth; I fill in the gaps based on what is already found in the record. Except in the dialogue sections, all material placed within quotation marks comes from primary sources—above all, from the printed versions of Casement's diaries.

In a recent interview about her process, Hilary Mantel has said, "For me, it is about using everything that is there and using as well the gaps [in the evidence].... I try to make it up based on what is on the record. So even my wildest speculations will have a root somewhere." Exactly. *Luminous Traitor: The Just and Daring Life of Roger Casement* is reliably based on the "latest word" in historical scholarship—though I'd also like to believe that it profitably moves through and beyond it. As someone once said, "History cannot teach us, but historians might."

The literature on Casement and the worlds he traversed is large. The material on which I've relied most heavily is Casement's own diaries, all of which have finally been published: Jeffrey Dudgeon, ed., *The Black Diaries;* Angus Mitchell, ed., *The Amazon Journal;* Roger Sawyer, ed., *Roger Casement's Diaries* (the 1910 diaries); Seamas O. Siochain and Michael O. Sullivan, eds., *The Eyes of Another Race* (the 1903 diary and Casement's Congo Report).

Other kinds of primary sources have been of central importance, in particular the transcripts of Casement's trial for treason and the contemporary accounts written by his compatriots and co-conspirators—especially Walter Hardenburg, *The Putumayo;* H. Montgomery Hyde, *Famous Trials 9: Roger Casement;* Mary Kingsley, *Travels in West Africa;* Robert Monteith, *Casement's Last Adventure;* and E. D. Morel, *Red Rubber.*

Until quite recently biographical studies of Casement have variously underplayed, denied, censured, or deplored his homosexuality. Two of those studies, by B. L. Reid and Brian Inglis—though some forty years old—remain of considerable value for the nonsexual aspects of Casement's career. Of other historians whose work I've consulted, I'm particularly indebted to John Campbell, Tim Pat Coogan, Matt Cook, Mary E. Daly, Reinhard R. Doerries, Jeffrey Dudgeon, R. F. Foster, Katherine Frank, John Hope Franklin, Terry Golway, Jordan Goodman, Kevin Grant, Anne Haverty, Marnie Hay, Adam Hochschild, H. Montgomery Hyde, Alvin Jackson, Tim Jeal, Robert Kee, Stephen Koss, Brian Lacey, Geoffrey Lewis, Mary S. Lovell, Daniel Melready, Angus Mitchell, Bruce Nelson, Emmet O'Connor, Thomas Pakenham, William E. Phipps, Seamus O. Siochain, Sonja Tieman, David Van Reybrouck, and Margaret Ward. Of special value has been the new source material turned up by Casement's two most recent biographers: Jeffrey

Dudgeon and Seamus O. Siochain. Their accounts do discuss Casement's homosexuality, and their tone is not censorious. Yet both do seem uncomfortable with the extent of his promiscuity, minimizing or gently disparaging it, as well as (to a lesser extent) his rejection of monogamy and coupledom— thereby skirting certain essential ingredients in Casement's startling contemporary posture.

ACKNOWLEDGMENTS

I'm once again greatly in debt to the talented group of people at the University of California Press who have done so much, in so many different ways to bring this book to fruition. My splendid editor, Niels Hooper, was a huge asset in helping me to convert a first draft manuscript to a finished product; I learned to trust his instincts even when I sometimes balked initially. I'm also much indebted to Alex Dahne (Publicity Manager), Bradley Depew (Editorial Assistant), Peter Perez (Public Relations and Communications Director), Aaron Smith (Cover Artist), Emilia Thiuri (Production Editor), Lia Tjandra (Art Director), and Jolene Torr (Marketing Manager). I thank, too, the anonymous reviewers who made invaluable suggestions at an early stage, as did my partner—still my best critic—Eli Zal.